D1715987

BLOODSPORT AT HIRAM BOG

A Maine Mystery

Page Erwin

To Charlie Todd those other co-authors. Best Wishes

Page Erwin

HILLIARD HARRIS

HILLIARD HARRIS

P.O. Box 275
Boonsboro, Maryland 21713-0275

This novel is a work of fiction. Names, characters, places and incidents
either are the product of the author's imagination or are used
fictitiously. Any resemblance to actual persons, living or dead, events,
or locales is entirely coincidental.

BLOODSPORT AT HIRAM BOG Copyright © 2007
by Page Erwin

First Edition-August 2007
ISBN 1-59133-217-6
978-1-59133-217-6

Book Design: S. A. Reilly
Cover Illustration © S. A. Reilly
Manufactured/Printed in the United States of America
2007

—for Wesley McNair

Acknowledgements

With gratitude to our old writers' group (now defunct), the Rabbit Brush Writers of Santa Fe, NM: Sonny Cooper, Bob Parmalee, Sharon "Bluebird" Ross and Albert and Jenn Noyer for their relentless and occasionally trying efforts to keep us on-track. Thanks to our readers and experts: Public Information Officer Trish Hoffman of the Albuquerque PD, Karen and George Crislip, MD, John Ford Sr., Carolina Lozano, Butch Parenteau, John Carroll, MSWC, Diane and Wes McNair, and Ruth and Ted Bookey; and to our providers of local insight, Dave Clements and our friends, the Ladies of the Comfort Inn: Penny, Joyce, Ruth, Rose, Eleanor, Romaine, Maddie, and Blanche.

Thanks, too, for the encouragement of our loyal friends and family: David and Barbara Page, Cyrena Zarucchi, Bob and Betsy Norris, Robert Cooperman, Marta Terlecki, MD, Bob Gregory, Sande Ferguson, Bill Hershey and Sarah Schwartz, Rob Kresge, Pari Noskin Taichert and all the members of Croak & Dagger, the Albuquerque chapter of Sisters in Crime.

...Would it matter if I told you people live here—the old man from the coast who built the lobster shack in a hayfield; the couple with the sign that says Cosmetics and Landfill; the woman so shy about her enlarged leg she hangs her clothes outdoors at night? Walk down this road awhile. What you see here in daytime—a kind of darkness that comes.

—from "Seeing Mercer, Maine"
12 Journeys in Maine by Wesley McNair

CHAPTER 1

The battered, black, '83 Chevy pickup inched its way onto the edge of the ice and rolled slowly toward the middle of the bog. Earl Bagley tapped the brakes and came to a dead stop on what he hoped was thick ice. He rolled down the window and listened. No cracking.

On this early January morning in Venice, Maine, Earl thought life was pretty damn good. He wore an L.L.Bean plaid parka, navy balaclava, fur-lined mittens, some extra heavy flannel-lined pants, and a fine pair of gumshoe rubber boots that came up to his knees. The mercury stood in the mid-teens on this Sunday morning, and, after only a minute or two, Earl's nose began to drip and freeze on his upper lip, and his teeth verged on pain. But the peace and quiet of Hiram Bog made it worth fighting the elements. He might catch a pickerel; better yet, tempt a granddaddy bass loitering on the frigid bottom. Two-dozen shiners from Jake's General Store swirled in the minnow bucket. Then, too, there was a six-pack of Coors Lite to fend off thirst and a flask of Yukon Jack to insure warmth. Best of all, he'd escaped the Sunday morning service at the Venice Union Church.

This morning's sky was covered by a high, thin layer of cream-colored clouds. The sun burned through, a silver disk with a lurid, urine yellow halo around it. This was the kind of day that the locals called a "weathermaker," promising snow by nightfall. Around evening, it would start coming down in soft white sheets, draping the trees and slithering across the roads.

Earl took a handful of Cheez-Its from his jacket pocket, ground them up in his mittened hand, and scattered the crumbs onto the ice to feed the chickadees. "Come chick chick. Come get your snack." Their gleeful small talk pleased him as he fished. Sometimes he'd have them eating out of his hand.

Earl walked duck-footed around to the back of the truck, lowered the tailgate then scooped some icy snow onto it to reduce the friction. After all these years, he understood the little hut, how to lever it down and scoot it into place. As for getting it back into the truck, well, other ice fishermen were bound to show up in the afternoon.

Although he risked another hernia, Earl pulled and tugged and finally got the shack down with a resounding thud that echoed back off of Whiskey Hill. He listened to hear if he'd cracked the ice. Nothing but silence. Then, with a stout length of rope, he dragged the shed a few yards to the deepest channel of the bog, where he remembered seeing bass jump at flies last summer. *Let's see. Prob'ly straight off from that duck box over there.*

The duck box stuck up on a post along the shoreline as did dozens of others. Lester Moulton and some Wildlife students from nearby Amnesty College set the boxes every year. Some folks considered the tree-huggers to be a pain in the ass, with all their talk of environmental stewardship and endangered species. Earl reckoned the worst thing they'd done so far was to lead a recycling drive. As a result, all eight hundred residents of Venice had to sort their garbage. They'd even set out recycling bins beside the General Store. *By God, a man's garbage is his own damn business!*

Earl walked over and retrieved a ragged broom from the back of the truck. A thin skin of snow from last night's Alberta Clipper covered the ice, and he wanted more visibility. The sweeping would warm him some before he sat down to do some serious fishing. Swinging the broom back and forth in a wide arc, Earl dusted a path from the truck to about where the fishing shack would stand, then cleared a large circle around the magic spot where he would drill.

Tossing the broom back into the truck bed, he grabbed up the gasoline engine-operated auger to bore his hole. Each year, the auger proved more awkward and difficult to handle. Earl remembered when he could heft it with one hand, but he now dragged it using both hands, the tip of the auger scratching a snaky trail across the ice.

After six ferocious yanks on its starter pulley, the stubborn tool coughed and caught on, chugging and sputtering its way through the thick ice, flinging little white chips and flakes up onto the lattice of his bootlaces. When he'd completed the hole to his satisfaction, he locked the auger inside the truck cab.

"No sense askin' for trouble," he muttered, knowing that the Gossam boys often made the rounds of the parking places where fishermen kept their trucks, while the old fishermen were dozing in their shacks. "You never know when a fellow will forget to lock his truck, but them Gossams ain't ever gettin' my beer again!" Earl groused. He'd told Olive it was only one six-pack. Next time it might be the whole truck.

He didn't tell Olive that he'd also lost a plastic case containing ten CDs, raising the estimated loss to over one-hundred-and-fifty dollars. He'd sure miss those Willy Nelson, Dolly Parton, and Chet Atkins songs.

As he coaxed the shack over the uneven surface toward the watery opening, he had an odd feeling. Something wasn't right. He often had these premonitions, but he usually ignored them. He stopped and listened. The chickadees twittered and buzzed in a tree not far off. A murder of shiny crows flapped off toward the east, cawing as they went. But the sharpest distraction from wintry silence was the angry buzz of a chain saw beyond the northwest tip of Hiram Bog. That's where the drowned town of *Old Venice* slept beneath the lily pads. As a boy, Earl had steered clear of Old Venice. His school buddies swore they'd seen "things" beneath the surface in the cellar holes near the shoreline.

The chainsaw droned like an angry hornet. All winter long the poor folk of Venice cut wood for their stoves, especially old deadfalls and white ash that didn't need to be seasoned and gave off plenty of heat. It was the only fuel they could afford what with oil prices on the rise.

Earl smelled the sweet aroma of wood smoke from nearby houses. *I'll bet they're burnin' maple. Yup! That's sugar maple all right.*

What was he trying to prove, a man nearly seventy, out alone, dragging gear all over a frozen pond? *Never mind frettin' over old age. Won't change nothin'.* Earl lined up the shack above the hole. Position was crucial so as to allow him to sit comfortably on the little padded bench that swung down on hinges from the wall.

Earl took pride in his little shack. He'd built it himself, mostly of old aluminum doors and panels framed up with two-bys he'd gotten at a bulk flood and fire sale. A third-hand window gave him a view of the road. *Don't need no Gossams sneakin' up on me.*

Earl hung the bait bucket on one nail and, on the other, his ditty bag with the beer, whiskey, two tubes of Tom's beef jerky and a box of Cheez-Its. Then he stuck his head out and took one last look around. Not a soul stirring. The saw had stopped, and the crows had set down somewhere on Whiskey Hill. The black and green lace of the forest that fringed the bog held its silence.

Earl examined the ice where he'd swept and noticed a dark shadow beneath. Often the silhouetted shapes of water lilies waved like Japanese fans, rubbing soundlessly against the bottom of the ice, hibernating until spring when they would come alive, yellow tubes erupting into rubbery green leaves and fleshy buds. By mid-summer, the lilies would half-cover the bog, turning it into an old fashioned oil cloth, and providing plenty of snags for his lure and tangles for the motor. But this shadow stood apart, less delicate and more compact.

"It ain't my problem," he grumbled. "Prob'ly somebody's pup-tent or maybe an old tarp that sank after the last thaw." He closed the shed door and exchanged his mittens for a pair of Army surplus woolen gloves with the fingertips cut off. To amuse himself, he dipped the end of his forefinger into the water, knowing that if he plunged his entire hand in, the pain would be bone-chilling. Of course, if he fell through the ice, he'd be dead in minutes.

Carefully he baited the treble hooks, making sure that the wiggling, silvery bait was on to stay. The little shiners were slippery and, with his arthritis, he had trouble positioning them, but finally arrived at that satisfying moment when he dropped his line into the dark, swirling water. It might be hours before he got a nibble, but that was part of the excitement.

3

He pictured a huge pickerel, bathed in shimmering speckles of purple, gray and black. Pickerel might be bony, but, once Olive had filleted and fried it, what a fine fish. If he caught a big one, he'd go home early. That'd please Olive, and he liked to please his sweet-faced, gray-haired wife. Earl settled onto the bench and took a swig of Yukon Jack.

He found himself feeding more and more line into the water. He didn't remember the bottom being this deep, but the line kept disappearing into the greenish-black void, then, abruptly, it went taut. *How could somethin' be bitin' this soon? By Jesus, this could be the granddaddy of all bass. Wouldn't that beat all!* Earl pulled the line in, hand-over-hand as the excitement rose. "What the hell—?" He stared at what the treble hook held. "Jesus, this ain't no bass!"

He didn't know if the words had actually left his mouth, but he did know that his mouth was as dry as burnt toast.

The sharp barbs of the hook had pierced something reddish. *What the hell?* He gave the line a hard yank, and suddenly a pink sleeve appeared. He couldn't take his eyes off the thing. Then a puffy bluish hand emerged. *Jesus!* The nails of the hand were a curious purple, a color he'd seen his teenage granddaughter Susie wear. This female hand, with two fancy gold rings on it, had to be connected to something. *Oh Lord! What the hell—? It's an arm, that's what it is!* What was he going to see next?

The horror of his situation struck Earl numb, as numb as if he'd fallen into the water. He gave another tug and more of the sleeve emerged, a sopping, pink tube. "What the hell do I do now?" Earl was shaking, and not from the cold. He held his working hand with his left to steady it. *What if it gets away?*

He was forgetting to breathe, but a loud nervous laugh suddenly exploded from his throat, rippling out across the ice as he saw himself in the scene. "The one that got away!" He laughed again, then he began to cry, standing there in the little fishing shack, his feet firmly planted on either side of the hole, the fishing line stretched taut.

Regaining his wits, Earl secured the line to a nail inside the shack until he was satisfied that the body wouldn't drift off. He managed to unstraddle himself from above the hole and get the door open, but his knees were ratchety. Once out on the ice, he fell back against the outside of the shack like a sack of feed. On his second attempt, Earl managed to stand and realized that he'd banged his funny bone and lost the feeling in his left hand. Using the window ledge for support, he rose to his full five feet, eight inches and gulped in cold air that made his teeth ache.

Clear your head, old man! Think!

Earl's eyes darted from truck to shack, to Bog Pond, each image jerking as if he were in a home movie. He felt as if he'd done something wrong, but what? A free floating sense of overriding guilt enveloped him. Would the next of kin come looking for her, Miss Pink Sleeve?

"I'm looking for my daughter. She was last seen wearing a pink jacket." He laughed again, knowing full well the inappropriateness of his thoughts.

"Sorry, Miss," he said to the hand in the shadowy water. His nervous giggling subsided, and he rubbed his hands together. They felt anesthetized. He pulled his mittens back on. The bell of the Venice Union Church tolled from the other side of the township, punctuating the unreality of his situation.

Earl realized his quandary. Couldn't the line snag and snap? Could the hooks somehow come loose? Hurrying to the truck, he stepped into a little mound of snow left over from sweeping, slipped and fell smack-dab on his tail bone, but felt no pain. *Gotta tell somebody.* Seizing a mitten in his teeth, he rummaged through his pockets until he found the keys, fumbled at the lock and got the door open, pulled himself into the driver's seat and sighed with relief. The Chevy started right up, rolled across the bog, then crunched its way onto the ice-encrusted road.

Earl stared down the Bog Road at the shabby wooden houses with their add-on shacks and sheds. They wouldn't pass code, but then Venice didn't have any codes. That was why so many poor people could afford to live there.

Finding a body wasn't something he'd tell the Gossams. If this was murder, were they the culprits? *No telling what they were capable of, come to think of it.*

Gotta get the law. Let 'em know everything, which ain't much, he thought, as the old Chevy S-10 skittered and rattled over the rutted, icy road toward Jake's General Store.

5

CHAPTER 2

Since Earl was a regular, no one in the General Store took any particular notice when he pulled right up to the front door, tumbled out and walked in, still breathless.

The usual crowd was gathered around the cappuccino machine. When it was first installed, folks had laughed at Jake's newfangled, big city ideas, but they soon changed their tune. In no time, customers could be seen sipping "Yuppie" coffees from dainty brown paper cups as they gingerly leaned near the lobster tank, another of Jake's fancy ideas that had paid off, especially with the tourists.

Jake looked at him and asked, "Earl, how're ya doin'? You don't look so good." He then glided over to the tired-looking woman cashier and winked. "Ain't Earl lookin' a bit green around the gills to you?"

She glanced at Earl and shrugged, then busied herself, refusing to commit to any opinion that might mean she was playing favorites.

"Listen, Jake, I gotta call the game warden or the sheriff," Earl huffed.

"Phone's right there, where it's always been," Jake snapped, but he couldn't help noticing Earl's ashen face. Jake was curious. Nothing happened in Venice that he didn't know about, and minor crime was his bailiwick. Citizens of Venice swarmed to the store in times of news worthiness like bees to the hive. And there were other attractions. If you wanted to buy some imported weed, provided Jake knew you and was in a good mood, he might accommodate your needs. If you wanted booze after hours or on Sundays, you went to the semi-trailer out back. *So why,* Jake thought, *does a quiet, law-abiding man like Earl need the law?*

Earl fumbled with the phone and, still in shock, punched in 911 like he'd seen on TV, but got a loud squeal. "You know the number, Jake?" Venetians repeatedly voted down 911 service, suspecting that it was a government ploy to invade a person's privacy and maybe, eventually, take away a man's guns. Some said that satellites were photographing all the houses and outbuildings in Venice. He turned to Jake.

Jake walked over. "Who'dya wanna call? Game Warden?"

Earl caught his breath and mumbled, "Guess so."

Jake dialed, listened, spoke a few words, then turned the phone over to Earl. "I talked with the Missus. Says he's comin' to the phone."

Jake hovered nearby, so as not to miss anything. He wore the usual flannel shirt with rolled-up sleeves, tight, faded jeans, Timberlake work boots, and a stained white storekeeper's apron. His thin, brown hair was slicked back. For a man who often sampled the deli food, he remained wiry. With practically no eyebrows, his face had a shiny, peeled onion quality, and his eyes bulged out a bit.

Earl looked at Jake, sighed, then spoke into the sticky black telephone receiver. Alice Varney was still on the other end. "Alice, could you put your hubby on? I know it's Sunday and all, but I gotta' tell him somethin' right away! It's urgent!"

Earl shifted from one cold foot to another. His wool socks were itching. He shook off a chill as he waited for the Game Warden to come on the line.

"Bud, this is Earl Bagley down ta' the Venice General Store. I got me a big problem."

As the Game Warden asked more questions, Earl hemmed and hawed. Finally he explained, almost at a whisper. "Well, uh, I was ice fishin' down to Hiram Bog, and I caught a...I hooked a..." He glanced at Jake who was actually leaning in to hear better. A bunch of snowmobile tourists huddled nearby, discussing which trail to take.

"I hooked a human HAND!" Earl blurted out.

The tourists turned and stared at Earl. Jake sidled over.

"What you sayin', Earl?" Jake leaned in and whispered. His off-center, beaky nose twitched as he smelled the Yukon Jack on Earl's breath. "Earl, you been drinking?"

Earl covered the receiver with his hand. "Yeah, I been drinkin'," he muttered, his face flushed, "but I ain't drunk."

Earl turned away from Jake and talked into the phone in a stronger voice. "It looks like a woman, wearing somethin' pink. She's all swolled up, and she sure is dead. I think you'd better hurry. What do I do now?"

He listened to the warden's advice, then replied, "Sure, she could get loose, but I tied the line." After a pause Earl resumed speaking. "But you know that current—it's always pullin' stuff down toward the channel that runs down to Lake Mallacook." Earl started to hang up the phone then jerked it back up, accidentally giving his ear a whack. He winced. "Oh, better bring ice saws," he shouted, "'cuz you can't get her out through the hole I drilled."

Jake whispered under his breath, "Jesus! Who could it be?" Then, as his audience grew, Jake grinned and added, "Geeze, Earl, how'd you manage to catch a dead body?" There was excitement in Jake's eyes.

"I'd sure druther caught a bass."

7

The shrill cry of the ambulance siren cut through the twenty-degree air as the vehicle rolled as fast as it dared over the icy spines of Venice's back roads. The curving, twisty roads could be bladed off better, but the plow crew didn't like going out in inclement weather. "Too risky."

The game warden, Bud Varney, had already arrived, as had the sheriff's local deputy, Hal Hines, who lived only a mile away. Bud looked fine in his clean-as-a-whistle, carefully-pressed, green uniform and his shiny green parka with the brown fake-fur collar. Bud took great pride in his job and did it well, aside from favoritism and minor, judicious bribe-taking. He'd also called in his deputy in Amnesty, Walt Smith. The men laid out yellow police tape, spiking it down around the perimeter of the shack and the general area where the body seemed to be lolling beneath the ice.

Warden Varney announced that, in his view, "She was no doubt killed somewhere else, maybe on the opposite shore, as the underwater currents would have moved her body to this side." The others nodded in agreement.

"Bud, shouldn't we drape some tape over around the bridge?"

"Don't bother, Walt. The snow plow woulda' scraped off any clues, and, besides, the snow's damn near two feet deep over there."

Little gusts of wind skimmed across the frozen bog's surface, whipping up cyclonic snow-spirits that scooted across the ice and vanished into the tree-line. Above it hung a milky sky. The yellow tape chattered in the wind, threatening to come loose.

Earl's hut had been tipped back and scooted away from the hole. Kneeling over the opening, the Game Warden examined the pink sleeve.

"No telling how long she's been here. Nice rings. If we put a rope around her wrist, her hand could come off. That skin ain't stable. It's sorta' floating on the bones."

More sirens announced the arrival of the paramedics, followed by the new sheriff of Thoreau County, Sam Barrows.

"Damn, he musta' picked it up on the scanner," Bud muttered.

Impressive at six-feet-four, Sam tramped across the ice toward Bud and the others and announced in his best John Wayne voice, "Okay, what do we have here? Brief me." As he waited for an answer, Sam cast a sweeping glance across the scene. "You haven't touched the body, have you, Bud?"

"First of all, Sam," Bud asserted, standing as tall as he could, "technically speakin', this is a catch in an environmentally protected, government designated wetland." He poked his chin up toward the hulking sheriff. "So, if it's a criminal thing, then it goes to the State Police and not to the County," he snapped, rising up and down on his toes, attempting to gain some height. Bud Varney only stood about five-feet-seven in his boots.

Sheriff Barrows took a deep breath and seemed to grow another inch. "Here's the deal, Bud. I'm on the scene, and the State Police aren't. So I'm taking possession of the body. The way I see it, it's clearly under my jurisdiction. It happened in my county, damn it!"

8

"Okay! Okay! She's all yours, but let's get the body out of there," he answered, kicking the snow.

Bud sidled up to Walt. "Barrows is from away. Besides, 'til he took office, we always got to handle the big crimes directly with the state." Bud's ears had turned red and purple.

Volunteer firemen arrived in the 1962 tank truck. Twelve men were now on the scene, including Donald Wells, the crime photographer from the *Midcoast Sentinel.*

Four men in parkas cut a rectangle in the ice using long-handled ice saws, then attached grappling hooks to it.

"Like liftin' a giant whale and just as slippery," Bud jibed.

They managed the task with some difficulty, setting and resetting the hooks and chains, always mindful that they were dealing with a human corpse, not a whale. The winch from a Wagoneer whined as it drew the chain up taut. Sheriff Barrows pronounced it secure, and the huge blue-gray block of frozen bog water rose up and flopped down onto the thick crust with a thud that echoed to the depths of the pond. Sam leaned over the hole and shook his head. He wanted zero screw-ups. This might turn into a big case.

"No tellin' how long she's been under. Careful of the hands and feet. Need plenty of points of contact. Place those grappling hooks on her clothing and give it equal distribution. Okay, take it nice and easy, and don't tear any flesh! We gotta preserve whatever evidence is left."

Five men hauled and hefted until the body was landed on the ice near Earl's fishing shack, but things were not as they had seemed. The pants and underwear were gone, and the pickerel had obviously been nibbling at appendages.

The first one to state the obvious was Deputy Hal Hines. "I'll be damned! It ain't a miss, it's a mister!" He rubbed his hands together.

"Yup! The apple had a stem on it," Bud Varney chimed in, eliciting a frown from the sheriff.

Earl came forward hesitantly, tapping the Game Warden on the sleeve. "I think I know who it is, Sheriff." Earl didn't feel too comfortable with Sam, this person from away. He'd rather deal with Bud, who'd played high school football with his sons. Until six months ago, it'd been Bud Varney whom the Venetians had always depended upon for law enforcement.

Sam hadn't been born in Thoreau County, let alone Venice. So what if his great aunt was from Galway. Although he'd been duly elected sheriff by a slim margin, many still eyed him suspiciously. His only claim to fame was that he'd played quarterback at the University of Maine at Orono for two winning seasons. He'd worked on the Portland Police Department for years, rising to the rank of detective. Then, when his aunt died and left him her old Victorian house and a substantial sum of money, he quit the force and moved to Galway.

"Well, let me in on it! Who is it?" Sam snapped.

"By God, it's Lester Moulton. Who else would wear fancy gold rings?" Bud was peering down at the body.

"You positive?"

"Yeah, I'd know him anywhere, even if he wasn't all swolled up." The game warden was pleased to be taken seriously. "Look at that watch and his gold rings."

Sam leaned down and poked at the hand. "These aren't cheap rings, that's for sure! Wait a minute. Look here, in the inside breast pocket." He pulled out a limp, waterlogged leather wallet and extracted a laminated Maine driver's license and a wad of soaked bills. "'Lester Moulton, Lake Road, Loonport,' it says here. Guess that eliminates doubt."

Earl and the Game Warden nodded their heads in agreement.

Hal Hines bagged the wallet, license, and seventy-two dollars. The sheriff directed them to turn the body over, then raised his hand. "Hold it. Donald, better take your detail photographs first. I think I see an exit wound but with the puffy skin it's hard to tell. Been in the water a long time."

After the body was turned back face-up, the sheriff leaned over it and pointed to a hole at the waist. "Large caliber entry wound. We might never find out for sure, but my bet's on a deer rifle. That'd be the weapon of opportunity. It's a through-and-through. Men, we're looking at murder, plain and simple! And, look! His calendar watch stopped at 4:30, either a.m. or p.m. on November 29th. That puts the murder on the day after Thanksgiving." The minute Sam announced the estimated time of death, he wished he hadn't. *Now the whole town'll know.*

The Game Warden piped up. "That's the last couple days of deer season when everybody's got buck fever. Well, we can rule out robbery as a motive, Sam. Nobody'd pass up those rings. Coulda' been a hunting accident, couldn't it, Sam?"

Earl decided to interject an opinion, to which he thought he was entitled. "Seems to me that Lester mighta' been out here puttin' up duck boxes. Never hunted in his life, so 'twasn't that. More likely he'd be at a cocktail party or a flower show." Earl sucked on a cold tooth. "Besides, around Thanksgivin' was wicked cold that week, remember? Look what he's wearin', that fleece-lined, pink jacket and a sleeveless sweater underneath it and a flannel shirt under that. Then, first week of December, everything froze up tighter'n a fish's ass."

Hal piped up. "So the question is: who hated the queer enough to shoot him and dump him here? One of his fancy gay friends, that's who." Hal was holding a long handled saw and jammed the end of it into the ice for emphasis. "They're always jealous of each other."

Sam felt cold and wished he were home with Darla. "That's enough speculation, Hal," he barked. "Put that saw in the vehicle. And, Donald, we need some more close-ups. Who's next of kin?"

"Betty Moulton, Route Ten near the Amnesty town line," Hal answered in a subdued voice. "Want me to tell her?"

"No, I'll take care of it on my way out of town." Sam didn't trust Hal to deliver the news with anything resembling sensitivity.

Sam turned toward the medics and pointed at the pink, bloated body. "Bag him up and get him to Augusta, pronto."

Just then Jake pulled up in his panel delivery truck and brought down a cardboard tray with a dozen coffees and some day-old donuts. Jake was mighty disappointed that the body had been removed and said so.

"Who's the guy they're loadin' into the meat wagon?"

The reference to the victim being male didn't escape either the sheriff or the game warden. Earl had thought it was a female. Both law enforcement officials began jotting in their notebooks.

After the ambulance drove off toward Augusta, the men lingered at the bog, huddling in clots, discussing their theories about the crime. The wind was now gusting better than twenty knots and last night's snowfall was blowing across the bog in powdery billows, stinging their reddened faces. Gradually they drifted toward their vehicles, their legs tired from the flow of adrenalin.

Sam didn't think for a second that Earl was a killer, although he'd discovered the body. However, one thing was for sure: this was no accidental shooting. Sam needed a written statement from Earl, but since the Sheriff's Department was located in Galway, over twenty miles toward the sea, he couldn't ask Earl to travel that far. The old man didn't look well, and it would be asking too much. Instead, he decided to meet Earl at his farmstead on the Bangor Road. He'd stopped there once on a routine stolen car theft. He stomped his feet to get the circulation going, dismissed everyone, and set off to notify the victim's next of kin, Lester's sister, Betty Moulton. Her house was more or less on the way to Earl's place.

CHAPTER 3

Monday morning, before first light, Sam awoke from a shallow night's sleep. He made coffee, and then took out his shaving mug, one of the few mementoes of his dad who had died when Sam was only ten. Sam whipped up a lather with the boar bristle brush, then put a hot towel over his face. The warmth helped him relax. He'd been tense all night, waking several times, the image of Lester's disfigured corpse filling his head.

Why was he chasing cold corpses when soft, sexy Darla was in the next room? And what did she see in him anyway? Could he make a woman ten years younger truly happy? Darla was daddy's girl, and her dad, Captain Jack McClellan, had offered to make him a partner in the fishing business. Sam had turned down the offer, having seen plenty of cases where mixing family and business led to bad blood and worse.

Sam plucked the straightedge razor out of its velvet-lined case, snapped it open, and then slapped it back and forth over the leather strop. He daubed the thick suds on his cheeks and jaw and began drawing down the stubble with the finely honed Wilkinson steel edge. Though old-fashioned and time consuming, it was a way of honoring the memory of his ancestors and how they had lived. As he maneuvered the razor's edge around the cleft in his chin, he thought of how his obligations—to the body in the bog, and to the body in the bed, Darla—clashed. This time around, he had to do the balancing act. He stopped shaving as he looked in the mirror and imagined a second failed marriage. No, he wasn't gonna let that happen.

Sam hated failure, and Belle brought it all back. His first marriage to Wanda Drapeau had collapsed beneath the weight of his absence. There had been no children to fight over. After the divorce, he stayed on the Portland force as a detective, and during the months that followed, Detective Belle Whittaker entered his life. Belle had impressed Sam with her skill and savvy, Sam didn't have a clue about her growing affection for him. Soon they fell into an easy affair, having good times whenever schedules permitted: Boston Red Sox games, the Frontenac Hotel in Quebec City, the pink sands of Prince Edward Island. But that was long ago. At least he'd gotten a friend out of the deal, Duchess, the Shepherd-Retriever mix that

Belle had given him.

Belle had crept into his dreams last night, dark and stunning with steely blue eyes and high Native American cheekbones. Uninvited, but there she was, beckoning to him. He knew that her unit had been called in on the Moulton case, and that he'd see her within a day. Would the look in her eyes be triumph or sadness? Either way, he'd be lost.

This morning he let Darla sleep. She had a part-time job as a high school guidance counselor with a specialty in grief counseling but didn't have to go in today. As he dressed, Duchess brought him his rolled-up socks. He patted her on the head, then put on his holster and gun, swilled down the last of his coffee, and left the house. *Damn! I should have left her a note. I don't deserve that girl! I'm hopeless!*

Barb Palmer, his secretary, greeted him with an affectionate "Howdy!" He grinned and headed for his office. Barb was a pleasant looking woman in her fifties with short, brown permed hair, intelligent brown eyes, and a sprinkling of freckles. After the loss of her husband, she'd learned to be single and content.

She handed him a printout list of addresses and phone numbers of people he needed to interview. "Good list for starters," he said, handing it back to her. "Might as well set up some interviews, Barb. I want to talk to Betty Moulton first thing, before I check out Lester's lake house. I got the key yesterday when I notified her of Lester's death, but I just couldn't interview her then."

"I don't think Betty and Lester were close, if you catch my drift." Barb was so thorough and knew the territory so well that sometimes Sam thought she ought to be a deputy. Her late husband had been one and loved it. Sadly, Deputy Fred Downing died in the line of duty attempting saving a child from the icy waters of Galway Harbor.

On the computer Sam typed up a full-text report based on yesterday's notes. Through the open blinds in the window he watched Barb setting up interviews in Amnesty and Venice, twenty-five miles to the north. Through the single outer window, he could look down on the town of Galway, like an old-fashioned Currier & Ives card. Most of those Victorian homes and shops were over a hundred years old. Beyond lay the ice-edged bay. January was the best month of the year for lobsters. He wished he could chuck work and spend the day lobstering with Darla's dad, but duty and Lester Moulton called.

Barb leaned into the doorway. "Sam, you *did* want me to set up these appointments for today, right?"

"Sure, I gotta get a move on." Sam picked up his sidearm, his jacket and his hat. "This case is already cold enough." He gave Barb a wink and a smile.

"You got your crime kit, digital camera, and your Thermos?"

"Ten-four. Thanks, Ma!"

Smiling, Barb returned to the stack of paper work with its lake cabin

13

break-ins, domestic disputes and assaults.

Sam had just cleared the Galway town line and entered Deering when his cell phone began playing "Turkey in the Straw," which meant an incoming call, as opposed to Brahms's "Lullaby" which would mean voicemail, or "Ghost Riders in the Sky," his pager tune.

"This Sam Barrows?" A husky female voice batted against his ear like an unwelcome insect.

"Go ahead. Who's this?"

"Bet...on"

"What? You're breaking up," he shouted. In some parts of Thoreau County, cell phones were useless.

"This....ty Moo..ta...out...house."

"Just a minute." He laid the phone down and waited until the cruiser reached the top of Barker Hill where there'd be line-of-sight with the Mount Dix antenna. Soon Betty Moulton's voice rasped through the cell phone.

"This is Betty Moulton. I wanna go over to my brother's house with you."

"Hell, Betty, I'm not even to *your* house yet. Didn't my secretary call and set up an appointment for noon?"

"Yeah, but that's durin' my lunch break. I only got so much time, ya' know."

Sometimes Sam wondered why he'd run for election in the boondocks where his constituents were apt to be so ill mannered. Days like today, he wondered why he hadn't stayed in Portland and tried for the Chief of Detective's slot. Belle's striking face popped into his mind and he remembered why. "Why do you need to get in over there?"

"I wanna make sure nothin's missin'. Take inventory. You police are gonna be traipsin' through that place. How do I know somebody like Hal Hines ain't gonna pick up somethin' and walk off with it?"

That did it. Sam barely managed to control his temper. "Miss Moulton, in all my years of police work, nothing's ever gone missing from my crime scenes. Besides, I won't allow anyone, not even kin, to contaminate the area."

"Humph," Betty grunted into the telephone. She started to speak, but Sam cut her off.

"I'm sittin' here on top of Barker Hill so I can get better reception, but I gotta get moving. Your house, five past noon." He snapped the phone shut without waiting for any more bullshit from Betty, and took off on State Road 6 North toward Venice.

He pulled into Betty's black-topped driveway at 12:05 pm. No cars were visible, but there was an Excel travel trailer parked around the side of a

14

buttoned-up, three-car garage with padlocked steel roll-down doors. The single-storey ranch-style house had white vinyl siding and gray trim and would've looked more at home in the Bangor suburbs. Sam didn't have to wait long.

A beefy, green Dodge Ram three-quarter ton pickup roared into the driveway, stopping within inches of the cruiser. Betty Moulton descended from the truck cab in her Mackinaw jacket and brown slacks, slammed the cab door and motioned the sheriff to follow her. A mop of loose red curly hair topped off her face. She had a squarish jaw with an under bite, thin lips, pale complexion, brown eyes set a bit too close together, five-feet-three, maybe four at the most. She unlocked the back door, and they passed through a mud room. As they entered the kitchen, he smelled Pine-Sol. The no-frills kitchen had enough white paint and metal surfaces to qualify as an autopsy room. She offered coffee.

"Black, thanks," he said, hoping that it would stave off his hunger.

"Got some banana bread I just made. Want some?"

He couldn't imagine any cooking taking place here, but he was willing to risk it. "Sure, thanks."

"I'll serve it in the living room," she announced as he walked through an archway into a neat but sparsely furnished living room. Beige drapes half-covered a picture window. Furnishings included a blue couch, matching upholstered chairs, a neat maple desk, and a tower filled with CDs that he went over and inspected. All the CDs seemed to be Country and Western or Bluegrass.

Sam's eyes wandered over to a large velvet painting of a stag standing by a lake in front of a violent sky. Sam also noted a large screen TV and a rack packed tightly with gun magazines: *Field & Stream* and *Outdoor Life*. No family photographs anywhere.

Betty set a paper plate with two slices of moist looking banana bread on the coffee table. He devoured both pieces. Sam hated paper plates.

"Delicious! So you shoot? I noticed the gun rack."

"Yup! Some were my pa's. Others I picked up at gun shows. Got receipts or permits for everything. S'pose that makes me a prime suspect." She bit into a piece of banana bread, then took a gulp of coffee.

"I won't kid you, ma'am. Next of kin are always under suspicion. I have a few questions, and I'm going to take notes."

"Shoot!" Then she realized she'd made a joke and laughed loudly, sort of a honking sound.

"I need to know where you were the day after Thanksgiving."

"I don't put up with all this holiday crap. Just an excuse for greetin' card companies to move product. Anyway, I worked, handlin' all those late Thanksgivin' cards."

"Where did you take your lunch break?"

"Back room of the PO. Got me a microwave, hot plate, and a little refrigerator. That day I had a tuna, lettuce and pickle sandwich and a diet

15

Pepsi."

Sam folded up his paper napkin but couldn't find a waste basket. Perhaps Betty didn't generate any waste. Maybe it wasn't allowed. He shoved the napkin into his pants pocket.

"How are you able to recall so clearly?"

"Cuz that's what I have *every* Friday, and it ain't for religious reasons, let me tell you."

"Describe your relationship with your brother."

"It was okay. We was civil. He had his life, I had mine. We sorta grew apart when he went off to New York, and we were never close after that."

"Do you know if your brother had any enemies?"

"It'd be easier to count his friends. He was a nice guy, too nice to his buddies. They didn't always act proper, you might say. They got stupid sometimes, rowdy, and raised a little hell over at the lake house. That turned a lot of the neighbors against him. Not that it mattered, most neighbors bein' summer people from away. I told him more'n once to control those Nancy-boys, but I guess he needed 'em to feel important."

"How'd you mean 'important'?"

"Like a big shot, like a guy who has a following. If you want to know more, you'll have to ask them."

"Where would I find them?" Sam was still hungry. He'd stop at the Maude's Country Diner when this interview was done.

"I never liked a damned one of 'em, and all I know's first names: Bruce, Chuck, Alan and Clair, of course. You'd find this stuff out if you'd get a hold of my brother's address book."

"What enemies did he have among the locals? Can you be more specific?"

"Nobody liked him much except those he helped. The Zuchettis, those new people, liked him, and their neighbor Chuck Shaw did. They had that *culture* crap in common. Of course, Chuck's wife Rhubarb didn't. Hell, she don't like anybody."

Sam was growing impatient. "What about enemies?"

"The Ridleys, that bitch mother and her spoiled son Jake, had no use for my brother. Oh, and Angus up to the dairy farm didn't have no use for him neither. Mooseman, that nut case up beyond Angus's place, had a bone to pick ever since Lester tried talking to him one day. Moose was out on the road screamin', half-naked. It was around the start of deer season, Les said. Moose was apt to get shot, so Les pulled up beside him and told him how much danger he was in. Moose said, 'Mind your own damned business!' That's all I know. Check out his neighbors over at the lake. They might know somethin'."

"Let's backtrack. About the petition—"

"Didn't get off the ground. Moose ain't the only crazy in town. Jane Ridley, the Jesus freak, she's not all there. She mighta' gotten some names, but knew folks around here don't hold with gangin' up. I coulda' told her it was stupid, but she don't come into the PO, *ever!* Gets her camp mail about six or seven months of the year by rural delivery: RR3, Box 224. My route girl can tell you where it is over on the Lake Road, way in behind a red pine plantation. All I know is she gets a lot of religious crap from down south."

"When your brother didn't make an appearance after Thanksgiving, weren't you worried?"

"I ain't my brother's keeper. He kept his own counsel and I kept mine. Did I tell him when *I* was going out of town? Hell no! But I do know he wasn't gonna do anything special for Thanksgiving, and he mentioned he might drive to New York City. Said he needed to get away. If his friends couldn't come to see him, he'd go there. When I didn't see his Caddie around, and the route girl said his mail was pilin' up in the box, I figured he'd gone to the Big Apple, so I held his mail. Thought a postcard would show up for me at the PO with a picture of the Lincoln Center Christmas tree on it." A look approaching regret crossed her face, the first sign of possible grief that Sam had detected.

"Lester's mail comes through Venice? I thought his place was over in Loonport."

"It is, but it's on the south side. His mailing address is Venice, but he pays taxes and votes in Loonport. That's what the politicians'll do for ya."

"You didn't happen to notice anything peculiar in his mail, did you?" Sam asked. Betty was noted for harvesting information from peoples' correspondence.

"Naw. Just the usual stuff. Phone and utility bills, bank statements...a few...Christmas cards." Sam detected a little hitch in her voice at the word 'Christmas.' Maybe she wasn't as hard as she seemed.

"Well, that's about it for now," he said, rising from the chair. "I'll return the house keys when we're done."

"Hope you can get it all done pretty quick. I gotta' pick out his best suit, tie, all that stuff, for the funeral director, and it oughta' be done tomorrow. Why don't you just make duplicates of the keys?"

"Ma'am, sorry, but you won't be able to have an open casket."

"Oh God, I didn't think—" Betty's face paled and Sam noticed moisture collect in her eyes, but she quickly recovered. "I'm his executor. I gotta see his will."

"I'm sure his attorney'll have a copy."

"Stammer," she snorted, "that conceited nincompoop's prob'ly lost the thing."

"Either I or one of my deputies will turn the keys over to you as soon as we can. I'll let myself out. Thanks for the banana bread." He turned and looked back at the sterile kitchen where she was wiping up invisible crumbs. "Oh, by the way, do you know if he had any life insurance?"

"Loaded, far as I know, and I'm chief beneficiary." She let out a horsy laugh. "S'pose that puts another nail in my coffin."

Sam let himself out. Betty had hemmed him in a bit when she'd pulled up earlier, and it took three moves to squeeze past the over-developed Dodge Ram. He stopped for gas at Jake's General Store then headed up Route Ten toward Amnesty, a double chili cheese burger and fries in his sights. On the way, he picked up the phone and checked in. "Barb, yes, hi!"

"Glad you called. The CIU team chief called from Augusta–a Lt. Belle Whittaker. Says she knows you and they'll rendezvous with you at the scene between one-thirty and two, as long as nothing 'more important' comes up." Sam heard her chuckle. Upon hearing Belle's name, he'd felt a little boyish excitement.

"Ten-four, Barb. Check in with you later," he said, closing the cell phone. He had the radio but didn't like using it. It seemed like every other house in this part of Thoreau County had a snoopy whacko in it listening to his scanner.

As he pulled into the lot at Maude's Country Diner, he realized how busy it still was, even at twelve-fifty. The snowy parking lot, plowed down to gravel in places, was filled with trucks, cars caked with salt-sand, and SUV gas guzzlers.

Upon entering, Sam could smell the combination of fish frying and hamburgers grilling. He headed for his favorite spot by the corner window so that he could look outside as well as have a good view of everyone that came and went. He knew one thing that'd be good: the coffee, since a new pot was made about every hour. Jake Ridley's girlfriend, Susan, wasn't working, but Sam's favorite, Charlotte Leighton, was, and she set a steaming cup of hot coffee in front of him as he sat down against the wall in the corner.

Keeping his back to the wall was a habit left over from his detective years. He'd learned his lesson one night in a Portland bar. A guy he'd previously arrested got roaring drunk and came at him from behind with a broken beer bottle. A quick thinking waitress warned him, and when Sam spun around on his bar stool, he nailed the guy in the groin with his size thirteen shoe, and the beer bottle went flying. From then on, he headed for the wall and had a soft spot for waitresses.

Charlotte grinned and asked, "Hey, good lookin', gonna have the usual? Say, we got some tasty homemade onion soup today, big gobs o' cheese floatin' on top, the way you like it."

"Hi! I'll pass on the soup. How's it going? You still giving Bill a hard time?"

"Nah! Kicked him out right after Christmas. I'm fancy free now." She gave his shoulder a gentle nudge. "Why, you interested?"

Charlotte was about thirty-five, two-hundred fifty pounds, with a pretty face and flawless complexion. With three kids to support, she worked two jobs, here and cleaning rooms at the local B & B.

"I'll have my regular: double chili cheeseburger, fries, and keep the coffee coming. Maybe apple pie later, if it's fresh."

"Course it's fresh, and you got it. No ice cream on top 'cause you're watchin' your weight. Right? Me too." She gave him a wink.

"Right." He realized that Betty's banana bread had only whetted his appetite. He looked around at the inescapable holiday decorations. It could have been a Hallmark showcase with its leftover Christmas decorations: strings of tiny red felt stockings trimmed in gold ric-rac, cellophane wrapped candy canes, and cut-out silver bells. Next would be Valentine's Day with its naked cherubs firing arrows at red hearts, followed by green shamrock mobiles and leprechaun cutouts for St. Paddy's Day. Compared to the yuppie fakeness of Portland, Sam rather liked the hominess of Maude's.

Lunch appeared with an extra helping of fries courtesy of Charlotte. The cheeseburger was greasy but loaded with flavor. He accidentally overdosed the fries with ketchup, but ate them anyway. Charlotte refilled his cup and sat opposite him, her face growing serious.

"Any breaks in the Moulton case, Sam?"

"Nothing to speak of. Say, did you know Lester?"

"Sure did. Nice guy and good tipper. Good luck finding his killer. I mean that!"

"Thanks, Charlotte. By the way, who'd he usually come in with?"

"Alone, always alone, and he'd order lemon meringue pie, if we had it." A customer rang the bell at the register, ready to cash out. "Sam, I gotta go," she said, "but I'll let you know if I see or hear anything. And…good luck."

I'm gonna need a lot of luck on this case.

19

CHAPTER 4

Box 224 on the Lake Road marked Mrs. Ridley's camp, and Sam finally caught sight of it, but no tracks in or out. It was only a half mile from Lester's. He slowed the cruiser to a crawl. Off to Sam's right, several seasonal cottages snuggled up to the water's edge. No tire tracks leading to any cabins or garages, no signs of activity, no smoke from chimneys or melted patches on roofs indicating heat escape. To the right of Lester's stood a two-storey monstrosity with a glassed-in porch facing the lake. A poor imitation of Victorian architecture, the ungainly house wore a layer of dented gray aluminum siding with yellow trim. The mailbox read *Borghese*. A foot of ice on the roof indicated a vacant house. Beyond was a small boat launch pulled onto the shore.

Sam crept past Lester's to a single-storey cottage covered in puke-green T-111, buttoned up tight, windows shuttered. No garage, but, off to the left, a tipsy aluminum shed. Nearby, a large doghouse lay on its side, locked in crusty snow. After Memorial Day, the scene would come alive, complete with barking mongrel, burning burgers and barefoot, squealing kids. But for now, nobody was home.

He backed up and turned into Lester's place, pulling up close to the garage, leaving room for Belle and her CIU van.

Compared to its neighbors, Lester's house was ostentatious, painted creamy beige with pink trim. Sam could see the ghost of the original cottage, before Lester added dormers and a rambling porch, two stained glass windows and frills. As he crunched through the snow, he observed no other human tracks. Coyote and dog tracks ringed the house and tiny v-shaped indentations indicated frequent visits by scurrying mice to the crawlspace.

Sam began his search at the garage, stopping to admire the wide expanse of frozen lake with its occasional open area where a spring bubbled up. A small floating dock was locked into the ice at the lake's edge, indicating the absence of its owner since before the freeze. Massive boulders loomed along the edge of the lake, slabs of ice leaning against them. A pair of mergansers sat atop one of the boulders, their black, prehistoric looking wings outstretched. Sam suspected that Lester had often fed the wild fowl and they missed their generous host.

He put on disposable gloves, found the correct key and let himself in. Lester had carefully placed aluminum foil on all the garage windows, so Sam had to switch on the overhead bulb. The time was one thirty, so he had a half hour of privacy before the team arrived.

There was Lester's '73 Cadillac Coupe Deville, faded robin's egg blue with a new Landau top. It looked to be in excellent condition, although one front tire slumped a bit. The front license plate spelled out *BLU-BIRD*. The vehicle was unlocked, and Sam found the driver's seat set within one notch of the full-forward position. *Who was the last person to drive this baby? Not Lester. He was six-foot tall. This seat was set for someone less than five-foot six. Betty stood about five-three or four. That wouldn't rule her out as the last driver. Not about to leap to any premature conclusions.* The glove box revealed nothing unusual except for uncluttered neatness and maintenance records going back thirty years to 1972. The one previous owner, a male, had lived in East Hampton, Long Island, New York. *An old boyfriend of Lester's?*

The garage had been methodically arranged. On one side a rusty wheelbarrow huddled next to garden tools, an upside-down, wooden rowboat on saw horses, an oil-stained stand that might've housed an outboard motor, a set of oars, fishing gear, and a family of life preservers hanging on pegs. A long workbench dominated the other side with tools hanging from pegboards, grouped according to type and size. A pine bureau, *sans* drawers, rested atop the workbench, next to it, a set of white porcelain knobs, shellac, denatured alcohol, stacks of sandpaper and an electric sander. The furniture refinisher had left in the middle of his project and obviously planned to return.

A Craftsman jigsaw was attached to the end of the workbench, and behind it were stacks of cutout rectangles of wood. Sam picked up a piece and sniffed. *Hemlock.* He examined plans tacked to the wall, instructions from Ducks Unlimited on how to build a duck box.

Obviously, this workshop had served as Lester Moulton's safe haven. Sam could imagine Betty piling up the goods and hauling them off to the Holcomb-Deering Auction house to be sold to strangers. Sometimes Sam had trouble maintaining professional objectivity. Suddenly, he was filled with rage at the murderer. The garage roof creaked under the shifting weight of winter.

The sound of the CIU van's pinging diesel and anticipation over seeing Belle quashed his anger. *What'dya know, they did come, and on time!* Tightness gripped his jaw and he noticed his heart thumping against his rib cage. He took a deep breath, letting it out slowly as he exited the garage. Sam snapped off his disposable gloves, walked over to the van, and shook hands with Belle Whittaker. "Long time no see, Belle, how ya' been?"

"Fine, and how's life in the sticks treatin' you?" She smiled with those gorgeous teeth. Her beauty exceeded everything promised by his vision of her the night before. And here she was, in the Maine State Police and leader of this CIU team. Happy with her life, she had a small condo in the outskirts of Augusta.

Belle turned to her teammates. "This is the Sam I've been fillin' you in about. He's a straight shooter and a good guy. Jack Coolidge and John Watson, Sam Barrows."

"Good to meet you both. Welcome to Loonport and Thoreau County." They were wearing disposable gloves, so they didn't shake hands. John Watson was a tall, handsome newcomer in his early thirties, and the first black officer assigned to the crime unit. His area of expertise was latent prints, blood pattern analysis and body fluids. "King of Blood Spatter" Belle said. Sam felt confident that the team was first class.

"I doubt that we'll find much of value here," Sam stated. "I'm guessing Lester was shot out in the woods. The interior of the home seems to me an unlikely murder scene. Let's do the garage first."

Sam filled them in on what he'd found in the garage as they followed him in. Belle could be a wise-ass, but no one was more thorough, and she agreed with his opinion concerning the height of the Caddy's last driver.

Belle noticed the gas gauge. "Hey, it shows less than a quarter of a tank. Wouldn't he have kept the tank at least half full in winter? That's what rural Mainers do, right?"

Damn, I missed that! "Good point, Belle. You're sharp as ever." He looked at her, at that old smile that spelled 'sex.' "And this guy was really careful about details. Look in the glove compartment. I'm surprised he doesn't have a copy of the birth certificate of every mechanic that ever touched this Caddy. But the position of the seat bothers me. My initial assessment is that someone, a short person, could have driven this vehicle into this garage, then made a getaway. It sure as hell wasn't Lester Moulton. He was over six feet."

"Could've gone down like that, or, since he was a neatnick, maybe he slid the seat forward to vacuum the floor of the back seat." She pointed at the garage wall. "There's a Dirt Devil hand-vac hangin' right there."

Watson grabbed the Dirt Devil and inspected the bag. "Empty."

Belle turned to him, "Be sure to check for prints on the door handle, gear shift, rearview mirror...hell, you know your job better than I do. Sorry." She tugged on her hat.

"No, ma'am, feel free to remind me of anything. We can't be too careful. And the dash might give us something." He smiled.

"What's that?" Belle pointed toward the oil-stained wooden rack.

"Yeah, I noticed that too." Sam ran a gloved finger across the stains. "Looks like an outboard motor rack—clamp marks and oil stains. Haven't spotted any motor so far. Better keep our eyes open."

As they finished up, Sam handed the house key to Jack Coolidge, who walked over to the house with John Watson. They undid the yellow caution tape and seal from the side door.

Belle snapped off the garage light and then held Sam back inside the doorway with one hand. She'd removed her ball cap. Her face was only a few inches from his, and he could smell minty toothpaste and a trace of perfume. "By the way, Sam, do you ever think about Portland, the Harbor City? Or our toes in the sand on P. E. I.?" Belle's hair was pulled back into a French twist and, he had to admit, she looked better than ever with her eyes like blue lakes, her aquiline nose and full lips. The dark complexion inherited from her Maliseet Indian mother added to her exotic appearance. She wore only lipstick and eye liner. Belle wrapped her hand tenderly around his forearm, giving it a little tug. "Sam, it's a real kick working with you again. Remember those great nights you and I shared? The good times at Gritty McDuff's Tavern? But you had to go and take that damned boat ride!" She gave his arm a gentle squeeze that bespoke yearning. "Yeah, I heard about it."

Sam blushed, and she let go of his arm and changed the subject. "So, Buddy, how's Duchess?"

"About the best friend I ever had. Brings me my socks, sticks, the newspaper, anything she thinks I need. And, yeah, sometimes I do miss...Portland. But, on the whole, I like it out here on the frontier of regress." He gently removed her hand from his arm then held it briefly before releasing it. He wasn't going to admit it, but, at this moment in a dead man's garage, he was near the melting point. He recovered and poked her roughly on the shoulder.

"C'mon, let's go. The barn over there is Lester's, too. I haven't checked it yet." He closed and locked the door, and they crunched across the snow. "Has the case gotten much press in Portland and Augusta? Any chatter in the Hallowell watering holes?" Sam needed to know how much pressure he might get from the governor's office.

"Yeah, big time! The gay community's stirred up, saying you rednecks don't give a shit about another dead gay. They still haven't gotten over the kid being thrown off the bridge in Bangor, and the blonde kid that wound up frozen in a snow bank over in Bethel. You people in 'Throw-up' County might not care, but the folks in the outside world do!" Her smile still had the power to captivate.

"I'll thank you not to demean our little paradise of *Thoreau County*," he countered as they entered the barn. It was so full of antiques that they could barely squeeze between stacks of chairs, tables, hutches, and fainting couches. Much of the nineteenth century had been crammed into the barn and wore a coating of fine dust. On the far side, an old Chevy truck, its fenders laced with rust, sat up on blocks, its hood raised in salute.

"Nothing useful here," Belle stated flatly. "Let's join the rest of the guys in the house. Can't waste time with nostalgia."

"Yeah, that was then, as they say," Sam mumbled, sliding the barn door shut and locking the hasp.

Once inside, Sam looked around. "Barn's full of junk, hasn't been touched for a while, so let's concentrate on the house. This is a cold case, so we need to look for what's here *and* for what's not here. The killer's had six

23

weeks to return and cover up evidence. As for outside, we've had a dozen snows with lots of melting and icing up. All the more reason to look hard. Apparently the vic was here the day before Thanksgiving, because there's some mail on his coffee table. The latest postmark's Portland, Nov. 26th, two days before Thanksgiving. So he brought in the mail on Wednesday the 27th or later. No postal delivery on Thanksgiving. The delivery gal does the Lake Road around one o'clock every day. I saw her today on her way in. That puts time of death any time *after* 1:00 p.m. on the 27th."

"Second that," Belle asserted, "unless person or persons unknown brought in that stack of mail, but it's not likely. We're looking for any indication of foul play, guys, like bunched up scatter rug, scarred doorway, disturbed dust patterns, heel dragging, anything! Lucky for us, he was a neatness freak, so anything out of the ordinary should stand out. See something disturbing, Sammy?"

She knows I hate that nickname. Sam was staring at a painting on the wall near the fireplace. "Sorry, I was admiring this self-portrait of Clair, one of Lester's closest friends."

"You sure? Doesn't look like a Clair to me," Jack observed.

"Well, this was before Clair became Clair. It's done in oil paint. Clair's a pretty decent artist. Looks like he was in his early twenties."

"You interviewed this Clair yet?" Belle was now all business.

"Not yet. She's been out of town, in Boston. Due back tomorrow, my secretary learned. She lives in downtown Loonport."

"Ha! Isn't that an oxymoron, 'downtown Loonport?' Is that where the National Loon Convention is held?" Belle was checking out Lester's magazines, mostly *Architectural Digest,* the *New Yorker,* and *Atlantic Monthly.*

"Yeah, and they dance to 'Looney Tunes.'" He looked over at her, squatting down by the magazine rack. "Another thing—Lester and Clair were extremely close. That makes Clair a possible suspect. Jealousy maybe. And Lester's sister, Betty, assuming she inherits everything. Now there's a person with motive *and* means. Did I mention she's a crack shot, with racks of rifles? But she's got an alibi. She's the Venice Postmaster, says she was at the PO all day, including her lunch hour. Easy enough to check."

They moved around the living room, scrutinizing the matching rose colored velvet Queen Anne's couch and chair, the polished spinet, the Chippendale desk and chair, a coffee table with antique postcards under glass. On the floor lay handsome Oriental rugs bathed in the warm glow of stained-glass windows.

A four-poster dominated the master bedroom, with a six-over-six dresser holding neat piles of underwear and clothes along with boxes of condoms and fancy-wrapped guest soaps. A maple hope chest lay at the foot of the bed, filled with fancy linens. He thought they might have belonged to Lester's mother, or perhaps grandmother, as some were yellow with age. The closet held high-priced suits, shirts still plastic-wrapped from the cleaner's, designer ties, silk dressing gowns, sweaters, and cord and chino slacks. Nothing seemed amiss. His mahogany jewelry box was filled with men's jewelry that no self-respecting thief would leave behind. They looked at one another.

"Nothing here," Belle admitted, "except that he sure as hell wasn't robbed. Let's check the other rooms. Sam, you take the kitchen and you two check out the bathroom, especially the medicine cabinet."

The well appointed kitchen was spotless: a stainless steel Wolf range with hood, a fancy French press coffee maker, and a Cuisinart. When Sam opened the refrigerator he found it half full of rotten food and sour milk. "Nothing's exploded. Here's a moldy tomato, liquefied salad greens, and a furry cucumber. Looks like a man who expected to make a salad when he got home."

"Stop! You're makin' my mouth water," Belle hollered from the spare bedroom. All three came into the kitchen to see the spectacle of food gone bad. Watson held his nose. "I won't eat salad for a week!"

Then Jack referred them to the bathroom. "Hey, guys, you gotta see this." Belle was used to being one of the guys.

Sam and Belle looked around in amazement. The Roman-style tub was enclosed in pink marble, and decorated with two naked cherubs of white marble with gilded wings. Their arms were upraised, hung with many strings of beads. An assortment of body oils and salts lined the tub surround. On the wall hung a huge, framed young male nude, a Picasso reproduction. *During Picasso's blue period,* Sam thought, but he wasn't about to say this aloud. Against the wall, a French provincial occasional table held an assortment of fifty or more tiny bottles of cologne, mostly men's. Pink towels, monogrammed LM, hung from the racks. *Much more Soho than Loonport.*

Watson pointed to the medicine cabinet. "Wanna do the honors, boss?"

"My pleasure," Belle announced, peering in. "All the standard remedies: Dristan for the nose, Visine for the eyes, ear wax remover, Preparation H, K-Y Jelly, tube of toothpaste. That pretty well takes care of the orifices. Now for the innards: Tums, Alka-Seltzer and Pepto Bismol. Here's Aspirin, Advil and Tylenol." She popped off the tops of the pill bottles and checked the lettering stamped into the tablets. "All the markings appear to be correct," she announced, returning the bottles to the shelves. Prescriptions: Three Codeine tabs left over from last August. Dr. Preston, DDS, Bangor. Must've had a toothache that went away early. And no sleeping pills. Not one damn thing out of the ordinary here. He certainly wasn't a prescription drug abuser."

She handed Sam two paper evidence bags. One was a calendar featuring a different dog every month, the other a slim brown leather address book. "The calendar's significant because it reveals appointments he expected to keep during the missing weeks. The address book should locate all his friends. But you know all that, Sam." He felt relieved at her more playful mood.

Belle pointed out the window toward the lake. "Hey, we'd better look out by the beach in case someone took Lester away by boat."

"Yeah, let's go." They walked out into the still, chilling air. "And my deputy shoulda' strung tape out there." Sam was doing a slow burn at himself and at Hines. He'd tape off the area before he left.

As they combed the snow, Belle asked, "Tell me, was the lake free of ice the day after Thanksgiving, and what about the bog?"

Hal had checked these two factors the day before with Bud Varney. "The lake was only partially frozen and the bog, too, with ice just around the edges." Watson was finding and bagging some frozen cigarette butts and an empty Wicked Brew beer bottle wedged in the ice.

It suddenly occurred to Belle and Sam simultaneously. Sam was the first to speak. "Did Lester have another boat, an old John boat, maybe? The way it's coated with dust, I bet the sharpie in the garage hasn't been used since summer."

Belle looked at Sam. "The killer could've shot Lester here in the yard, hefted him into his own boat, then put-putted across the lake to the bog, using the motor that's missing from the garage. Right? Or are the lake and bog even connected? Am I way off base, Sam?"

"You're almost never off base. Coulda' happened that way. The bog *does* connect to the lake, but you gotta know your way around out there—submerged logs and the ruins of old Venice, not to mention dead ends in the floating fields of lily pads—according to the game warden."

"*Old* Venice?"

"Yeah. Bud tells me the original village was torched back in the mid-nineteen hundreds. Firebug. Folks gave up and rebuilt elsewhere. Most moved to Loonport and Amnesty, then voted to build a dam."

"Damned expensive way to put out a fire!" Belle commented.

"Anyway, if that's the way it went down, then our killer's someone who knows both the lake and bog. The question I have to check on is: On the day after Thanksgiving, did anyone see a person or persons in the boat or hear anything like a gunshot? No. Stupid question. Of course they heard gunshots; there were still two more days of hunting after Thanksgiving. But, maybe somebody saw something. I'll have my men canvas every year-round cottage. There aren't many at this end of the lake."

Belle piped up. "Yeah, maybe one of your bright citizens noticed a guy hefting a dead body into a boat but forgot to mention it to anyone."

Sam shot her a look. "Or did a *woman* take Lester to the bog? She'd have to be rugged, not your normal specimen of 'the fairer sex,' because a dead body is heavy as hell to lift in and out of a boat. It's clunky and awkward to handle."

"Lots o' luck, pal," she said, giving Sam a narrow-eyed stare and a business-like handshake. "I have the feeling you're gonna need it."

Sam waved goodbye as they backed out of the driveway, then took the roll of yellow tape to cordon off the beach area before twilight faded.

It was four-thirty, and he still had a good two hours of work waiting for him in Galway. Seeing Belle hadn't been nearly as bad as he'd thought it would be, but those minutes in the garage and barn hadn't been easy. He considered the two women. Belle radiated sexual power and independence. Her strength made him feel secure. He didn't have to worry about her as if she were a peach that might bruise.

On the other hand, Darla was sweet and pliable, and she cared about what he wanted and needed. Besides, he'd passed the point-of-no-return when he married Darla. He posted the trees by the little frozen dock. *Poor Darla. I've moved her into my aunt's old house and haven't the good sense to help her make it her own. Oughta go to the bank and get the money so she can shop for new rugs or curtains maybe.*

CHAPTER 5

Monday morning Sandy Zucchetti drove her Saturn down to the General Store to buy a few supplies. Normally she'd have driven the Red Rocket, a 1985 Chevy pickup, but it was stuck behind a ridge of frozen snow left by the plowman. Sandy was a tall woman in her late fifties, hair swept up in a ponytail, bangs, and large hazel eyes hidden behind bifocals. Walking miles in the Maine woods helped her stay trim.

The parking lot was packed with vehicles. When she entered the store, wearing faded jeans and a green parka, she noticed a crowd gathered around the counter where a little sign would be taped to the cookie jar asking for donations for victims of house fires or accidents. The previous week Kenny Marble had stove up his snowmobile on a stump. He was recovering but had no insurance on himself or the snowmobile.

After living in Venice for six years, Sandy and Frank were catching on to how the law "worked." There were plenty on the books, some going back to when Maine was a colony of Massachusetts. When Sam Barrows won the sheriff's election, he announced that he and his deputies would be enforcing the law in the entire county, not just the south end around Galway, but Thoreau County was a lot of territory to cover. *It must be six hundred square miles,* she thought, *and Bud Varney's a lot handier.*

Slow response time was one reason why Sandy and Frank kept a shotgun leaning next to their bed and a thirty-eight special handy in the bed stand drawer. Frank had a law enforcement background. Over the years, they'd often heard shots near Whiskey Road Corner, and isolation made them vulnerable.

Sandy spied a friend, Nin Forrester, over by the breakfast cereals and headed for her. Nin was a slightly plump, blonde grad student in her late twenties with a disarming smile. She'd been deep in conversation with Cleona Burgess, the frisky spinster who lived in the oldest house in Venice, way up Whiskey Hill Road near the bog. Cleona walked everywhere in the early mornings in search of birds. Sandy thought it odd that Nin would be chatting with Cleona, a retired school teacher. Cleona's thirty years in the classroom had given her strong opinions far different from those that Nin espoused as a modern University grad student. Still, Cleona, a gal of seventy-five, was a sage old woman and the best 'birder' in Venice. As a member of the Friends of Fowl Society, Cleona had worked closely with Lester to preserve ducks in Venice.

"What's all the buzz about?" Sandy inquired. Cleona looked dumb-struck and said nothing, not at all like her.

"Oh, Sandy, you'll never guess who Earl Bagley fished out of the bog yesterday," Nin exclaimed. "Lester Moulton!"

Sandy blanched. "What are you saying? You can't be serious!"

"My God, he's your cousin, isn't he? Sorry!"

Sandy stared at her neighbors.

"It's such a shame!" Cleona added, shaking her head.

"But how'd it happen? Did he drown?"

"I don't really know. They say Earl cut a hole in the ice to go fishing and there he was." Nin shifted the shoulder strap on her purse. "It's awful."

Feeling as if she were choking, Sandy unwound the scarf from around her neck as tears pooled in her eyes. "I can't believe it! He's such a nice man. How did he drown?"

Nin was talking unusually loud. "I don't know, but they think it's a homicide. We haven't had a murder since Linda Dixon was shot on purpose by deer hunters, using the excuse that it was her fault because she was wearing white mittens."

"And mother of twins, she was," Cleona murmured.

"I wonder how Cousin Betty's taking it." Betty was Lester's only sister.

Nin continued to speculate, not so much about the victim but about the crime itself. "Jeeze! The bog's not that far from us, especially your place, Cleona!"

"Ayuh. Only a quarter-mile. Walk down there most every mornin'."

"Doesn't it make you nervous?" Nin asked. "Ned'll be worried sick."

Ned, a high school teacher, was a sweet guy, but Sandy worried that he'd taken to drinking on weekends, reverting to his former life as a country boy. Then her thoughts returned to Lester, and she said, "I thought he'd gone off to New York to see his pals when there he was—" She raised her hand to her cheek. "Oh, my God!"

Nin changed the subject. "They say Earl was plenty shook up, so the sheriff took his statement at the farm rather than dragging him all the way to Galway."

"Good. At least Barrows has a heart, unlike old Sheriff Belcher." *I'll call Betty*, she told herself. "Gotta go." Sandy left the two women standing there then hurriedly finished shopping, buying the last copy of the *Midcoast Sentinel* so that she and Frank could learn the details.

On the way home Sandy considered who might have done her

29

cousin in. *How many enemies did Lester have?* She knew that he'd created controversy when he'd returned to Thoreau County from New York. Was he killed because he was gay? Sandy recalled that a gay college student had been thrown off a bridge in Bangor, and another had been beaten up in Waterville and nearly died. She felt in her heart that Lester wouldn't hurt a fly. Sure, he had a few raucous house parties with his New York friends, but that was no reason to kill him.

People like Jake Ridley's mother, Jane, had stirred folks up. Jane Ridley was a strange woman, both in appearance and behavior. Although over sixty-five, she dyed her hair bright red. She owned considerable property on the lake and ran a summer camp for evangelically-minded parents and their children. Folks were puzzled as to why Mrs. Ridley kept the camp's activities so secret and allowed no visitors. She didn't publicize or advertise; apparently she didn't have to.

Sandy pulled into the ice-crusted driveway. *Family is family and Betty's a cousin, so I should call and see how she's doing.* Betty was a loud, rather surly woman, totally lacking in tact. The thing that griped townsfolk most was Betty's lack of ethics as post mistress. Nothing was secret. Locals heard who was dunned by creditors, who might be audited, who had tax liens. Although Betty could have lost her job for breach of regulations, no one reported her because she was otherwise extremely efficient at her job, and besides, they enjoyed the gossip.

She thought back to the last time she'd seen Lester. It was when she'd wanted to repair an antique trunk and sought his expert advice on hinges. They'd ended up discussing books.

As she went up the cellar stairs and stepped into the warmth of the living room, she hollered, "Frank!" She set the groceries down on the kitchen table. "Frank!" His jacket was missing from the front hall. Then Sandy heard the familiar clucking and honking. He was out back giving food scraps to the chickens and geese and making sure their water hadn't frozen. She called from the back stoop, "Honey, leave that. I've gotta talk to you!"

"What's wrong?" he asked, hanging up his jacket by the wood stove.

Seated together at the kitchen table, Sandy told Frank all she'd heard. "You know, Frank, the way law enforcement is here, they'll probably never find the culprit."

"Or culprits." Frank rubbed his forehead. "It's just awful."

They read the paper together. Lester's picture, an old one, was on the front page. When it was taken, he'd had a lot more hair, and he was wearing a perky bow tie, white shirt, and a suit. His face was free of the worry lines he'd acquired since coming back to Maine, and before his sporadic drinking sprees had caused his skin to become somewhat doughy. Also shown was the photo of the body bag being lifted into the ambulance.

"Sam Barrows is handling the case," Sandy commented.

"Yeah, under the new setup, Bud Varney wouldn't be involved unless it was a hunting accident." Frank snickered at the thought of Barrows and Varney trying to get along.

Sandy fixed a pot of coffee and then put away the rest of the groceries. She thought of calling Betty but put it off, remembering that she'd be at work at the post office.

Frank rose from his chair in the computer nook to get some coffee. He'd retired from twenty-one years in the Air Force. After flying for seven years, he'd become an agent in the Office of Special Investigations, the OSI. He'd investigated numerous homicides and hate crime cases, and also taken FBI courses at Quantico. That, plus Frank's six years in a Roman Catholic seminary as a teen, had made him into a somewhat warrior-like and cynical agnostic.

Sandy poured the coffee. "Honey, I have an odd question. Why don't I feel sorry for Cousin Betty?"

"Uh...let's see. Because she's a relative? Or because she can't keep her mouth shut at the post office about other people's business? Hell, I don't know." Frank smiled.

"I suppose that's it—she's obnoxious. Complete opposite of Lester. Now *she*'s the closest kin I have in Venice."

"His murder is a damned shame. I'm sure Barrows will do his best."

Frank had a neatly-trimmed gray beard, mustache, and an incipient bald spot. His physique was amazing for a man of sixty, because he worked at it. The locals tended to like Frank well enough, up to a point, but some folks looked upon Sandy as rather brittle and stand-offish. She'd never be accepted because she was "from away"—New Hampshire—and had too much education for a woman. Frank, being "Eye-talian," was way beyond the pale.

"I know the sheriff's trying, but what does a guy from Portland know about what goes on up here in the hills of Venice?" Sandy scowled. "He only came up here to campaign once, and that was at Maude's Diner in Amnesty."

"You have to give law enforcement a chance. It all depends on the hard evidence. Besides, we don't know that much. We might think we belong, but we don't. Fact is, we're 'from away.' You know how hard it is to pry information out of a Venetian? The sheriff's gonna have the same problem."

"I don't care how stubborn and close-mouthed the natives are, we have to stand up for Lester," Sandy insisted. "Let's start by making a list of suspects."

"Okay. Fine. Put Betty at the top of the list."

"Why? Because she's kin?"

"Exactly! Kin are always prime suspects. And unless there's something that says otherwise in his will, she gets everything: the lake house, paintings, a barn-load of antiques, the Cadillac, the old truck. She could sell the whole lot and make a bundle! Not to mention life insurance. If that isn't motive, what is?"

31

"Have a heart. Lester was Betty's only close family. They may not have spent holidays together, but that doesn't mean they hated each other. Imagine! I'm her only other kin."

"Then maybe *you're* a suspect. What if Lester changed his will and left everything to *you*? Ever think of that?" He patted his knee, hoping for a cat to sit in his lap, but being obstinate, none came.

Sandy looked at Frank with a sad expression on her tired, pretty face. "Hey, come to think of it, I'm *not* the only relative. Remember those obnoxious distant cousins who showed up at the auction house last year? Lester was selling some paintings done by his transvestite pal, Clair, to raise money for AIDS research. Anyway, those religious whackos tried to halt the auction. Claimed the paintings were indecent. I thought they were rather well done nudes myself. The auctioneer had to make them leave, remember? It was ugly."

"Oh yes, those so-called 'Christian' followers of Jane Ridley. Betty let 'em have it, on the spot. Probably Lester wouldn't have cut her off. So let Betty's name stay."

"And Jane Ridley, certainly. Remember that dumb petition she started against Lester?"

"Yeah, to prevent Lester from playing the pump organ at the Venice Church. How could I forget that? She only got nine or ten signatures, so she gave up."

"But how could a woman her age shoot a grown man and then dump his body into the bog?" Sandy walked over to the window and looked out at the snowflakes from a passing flurry; they seemed to wander and never land. "She's ten years older than I am, and she's got bad arthritis."

"Maybe she got one of her followers to do it, claiming it was God's work. Think of the heinous crimes committed in God's name, like the Spanish Inquisition, the Crusades, the Conquistadores, Catholic enslavement of the California Indians, the Serbs in Kosovo—I could go on." Frank gleefully amended the list to read 'Jane Ridley and/or followers,' then rose to feed the fire in the old Glenwood stove.

"Who else? We ought be able to come up with at least half a dozen," Sandy offered.

"Don't worry. That won't be hard."

CHAPTER 6

Almost everyone in Venice knew about the Gossam clan, and no one expected to see them at Lester's funeral. They never attended funerals and weren't about to set foot in a church. Gossams preferred to bury their dead in their own yard, which was permitted under the Maine Pine Box Law.

On this cold Maine day, the Gossams were holding a family meeting at the patriarch's home. Forty-three-year-old Gus was built like a wrestler, except that his beer belly belied years of letting himself go. His four-day-old grizzled beard contrasted with his shaved head. Gus had the largest Gossam abode, although he hadn't gotten around to finishing the second floor of the tarpaper covered house. Once spring arrived he'd steal some asphalt shingles for siding. For now, one floor was all he and his family needed.

The living room/dining room held an assortment of chairs, piles of newspapers, and orange crates that served as tables. The ragged orange and brown plaid sofa was covered with dog fur, beer stains, and clutter. Two overstuffed chairs, relics of the Seventies, dominated the corners. Two mottled brown pit bulls, eager to play, circled the sofa where their master sat. Chained up out front, a Doberman, unhappy with his shabby dog house and bowl of frozen water, lunged and snarled. An old sleeping bag spewed chicken feathers from inside the dog house onto the tired brown ice and snow where the feathers stuck like leaves.

Inside, the family spent a lot of time watching Gus's prize possession, the thirty-six inch color television. Sometimes the whole clan gathered for big events like *Survivor*. Currently cartoons blared, filling the stale air with sounds of chaos. The set received jacked satellite signals funneled through a stolen dish and a jury-rigged black box. Torn green plastic shades hung from curtainless windows. Worn scatter rugs and a braided rug, its edges curling, helped keep the cold out, as the house squatted on sills above the frozen ground. An ancient wood stove, the only heat source, hissed and sputtered in the corner.

Gus struggled up from the soft belly of the couch and looked around. "Mute that damn TV. I'm callin' this meetin' to order. How many we got, Sarah?"

33

His wife Sarah counted heads. "Eight." She didn't include the two toddlers in a playpen off in the corner. The official census of the Bog Road Gossams had never been documented, but it included numerous children by various sons and daughters, a veritable Gordian's Knot of Gossams. Some children weren't exactly sure who their mothers, aunts and uncles were, but family was family. The Gossams of Venice had never been counted, not since the township tax census takers had been threatened off the property in the 1850s, when the earliest Gossams from Northwest Scotland via Scully Square, Boston, had arrived and taken possession of the land.

Anthony and Booth, Gus's favored sons, had been ordered to be there. Sarah Gossam, in her early forties, looked much older, bent, with gray hair. She took little pride in her appearance. Her face had gotten in the way of Gus's fist a few times too many, and she had several missing teeth and her nose had been broken. Once she'd been a real beauty, back when she was fifteen and dropped out of school to have Gus's baby. He'd eventually married her, so he could train a son the right way. Anthony, Gus's pride and joy, was the chosen son, and now others had to survive Anthony's violence.

Gus stood up, stuck his thumbs in the front belt loops of his jeans, and announced, "I've called us together for a reason! I been down to the General Store and learnt that queer, Moulton, who dealt antiques over to the north shore of the lake...he's been murdered less than a mile from here. Got caught up in Earl Bagley's fishin' hooks." Gus chortled loudly. "His fancy jewelry and watch wasn't stole, so they ain't come round here askin' questions. However, they ain't got the guy who did it yet, so now they'll 'widen the search,' as they say on TV. Us Gossams always get blamed for everything, cuz they got it in for us. Somethin' gets stole, they question us, some girl gets raped, they come lookin' fer Gossams. We sure as hell don't live in no free society!"

"Well, whadda' we s'posed to do about this dead guy, Pa?" Anthony had earned a dishonorable discharge from the Marines during the first month of basic training. "Do we need alibis?" He still wore his hair in a Marine cut and had ramrod-straight posture. Tall and trim, he was physically so strong that his father had ceased to threaten him. On an upper arm he wore the *Semper Fidelis* tattoo. On the other shoulder a skull and dagger. His 'uniform' was now camouflage pants, a khaki T-shirt, and a faded flannel shirt.

Gus grinned, revealing several missing teeth. "The cops think the deed was done day after Thanksgiving, so that clears you, Sonny Boy, cuz you was in the Thoreau County slammer on that drunk and disorderly charge."

Anthony smiled with pride. "Damn straight, Pa! I'm off the hook."

The group got the joke, recalling that Lester Moulton was "caught" on a hook. A few Gossams snorted with laughter.

"How about you, Booth?" Booth was named after Lincoln's assassin, John Wilkes Booth, a hero of the elder Gossam.

Booth, twenty years old, red haired, and raw boned, had quit school when he was sixteen, although he was smart enough to finish. He worked odd jobs such as stealing logs from cutting sites, and sometimes he served as a substitute school bus driver who got a kick out of going too fast and scaring the kids. He was lot heavier than his brother Anthony and resembled his dad. His latest theft was a set of skidder tire chains from Slug Willard's cutting site, a dangerous game.

"Don't worry, Pop. I was huntin' all that day. Didn't kill nobody." He was slumped in an overstuffed chair, lighting a cigarette.

Gus became slightly rattled, rubbing his four-day growth of stubble, thinking that Booth's alibi would be hard to prove. Gus turned to Sarah. "Fetch me another Bud Lite." At his age he was watching his weight, though much of his two hundred and fifty pounds was muscle. He grabbed the can from Sarah and turned to Booth. "Listen, lame brain, talk like that'll put you back in the slammer. They think Lester mighta' been shot by a deer hunter. Duh!"

Booth's mother wasn't Sarah, but Rosie, one of Gus's girlfriends, a handsome redhead who'd waitressed in Maude's Country Diner. When Rosie died of a miscarriage, Sarah had accepted Booth, age two, without hesitation. Nowadays, Booth did just enough wood gathering and garbage dumping to make her life easier.

Gus's son-in-law and his wife from up the road sat toward the back.

The second youngest daughter, Dori, was plump and quietly pretty, and she helped her mother whenever she could. Sometimes Sarah didn't know what she'd do without her little angel. Dori was beginning to show breasts, and that worried Sarah more than anything. Too many men and boys around, and that could only lead to trouble. Dori was smart and loved to read, but this morning she'd been watching cartoons.

The Gossams' youngest child, Lois, crouched awkwardly in a corner. A scrawny, dark-haired child of about eight, she rarely spoke because of a stutter. When there were family disputes she blended into the woodwork in fear of her father. At the moment, she was picking at her faded blue sweater, worn over a flowered skirt. She was a bit slow and hadn't learned to read until this year.

Her father teased her. "You g-g-got anything to add, Lolo?" He tossed a flimsy magazine at her.

"No, Pa. Why you c-c-callin' on me?" She pushed the magazine away.

"Just checkin'." He smiled warmly. "Want you to be p-p-payin' attention is all." He crushed his empty Bud can and tossed it toward the corner. Lolo gave him a wan little smile. At the darkened edge of the room, she appeared almost feral with her stringy hair and dark, peg-shaped teeth.

Looking around, Bill timidly asked, "What was the caliber of the shell? This faggot got himself shot, right?"

"Haven't released that information yet. Those cops are smarter than they used to be. And don't underestimate Sheriff Barrows. He's big and ugly, but he's smart." Gus smiled paternally at his brood. In his own way he loved all of them, and he would protect them with his life if necessary.

"So, Bill and Anthony, get with it. See if you can't find someone to say Booth was huntin' with you, far away." Gus paused and ran the back of his hand across his stubble. "You didn't bump that guy off, did you, Booth?" Some family members laughed nervously, and they all stared at Booth.

"Well, if I did, I wouldn't tell the world about it, would I?" His father looked disgusted, so Booth quickly added, "Hell, you taught me better'n that, Pop." Anthony snorted, and, Louie, one of the grandkids in the playpen, began squalling, snot from his nose running down his chin.

"Shut that punky kid up, Lois. Give Louie a pacifier." He reached into the couch cushions, found one and tossed it to Lois who dropped it, then stuffed it between Louie's puckered lips. Louie bit down hard on the pacifier and continued to wail around it, his bald little head turning even redder.

Unable to think of anything more to say and not wanting to compete with little Louie, Gus rose from the couch. "Well, you all better get your stories straight. This here meetin's over."

The Gossam's youngest son, Andy, hadn't been at the meeting, since he was working at Jake's General Store as a stock boy as many hours as he could. During the school year he sang in chorus, and ran with the track team, taking the last bus home. Although he was only fifteen, he'd skipped two grades and was now a junior. Far and away the most intelligent Gossam ever, his teachers made it their mission to "save" him, and why not? He was bright, quiet and attentive. With his dark hair and sharp features, he was a handsome teen. He felt ashamed when people gossiped about his dad or brothers, and when he saw the name "Gossam" in the "court docket" section of the *Galway Republican Journal*.

Avoiding home seemed the easiest solution, though he hated leaving his mother unprotected. The previous summer he'd built a hut by the edge of the woods where he could be by himself, far enough away from the house so that he could escape the sound of his father's voice. He'd installed one old window and a dented aluminum door. He couldn't find shingles, so he draped a length of tar paper over the roof and tacked it down with furring strips he'd salvaged from pallets at the store. The hut was unbearable in summer, so he read outdoors under a spruce tree, going inside only when it rained. In winter he wore mittens, fur hat, second-hand ski parka, and sat on a deer skin of his father's. Sometimes he'd rest against hay bales for extra warmth, breathing in the sour-sweet smell.

A few weeks earlier he'd approached Gus about making the hut more comfortable. "Pop, can I run electricity out there? I learned how in Shop Class. I could hang out there and maybe run a heater in winter or a fan in summer. I'd do all the work myself. I know how."

"Why in hell should I waste electricity just so's you can run away from your chores? Use your pea brain, why don'tcha? Sometimes, Andy, I wonder who your father is!"

Gus wasn't a big listener. Occasionally he'd take a suggestion from Booth or Anthony, but never from Andy. Once Sarah held up the newspaper to show Gus Andy's name on the Honor Roll. He promptly rolled the paper up and tossed it in the wood stove. Sarah had to go to the store and buy another copy. No point in Andy's asking his mother about the cabin. Sarah'd back her man every time, except when he was threatening one of the kids. Then she'd tearfully beg Gus to stop, only to be struck. The personnel at the Waterville Hospital ER knew her well. "I took a bad fall down the stairs" or "This boy of mine, clumsy as a new-born calf. Fell off the porch."

Andy's big dream was to run away and never come back. But who would bring his mother bouquets of wild flowers or A-plus test scores? He was determined to hang in there for another year and a half until graduation. If only he could test out of some courses it might be earlier. Then he'd try for scholarships, go to college, graduate, and move away, maybe even to Portland or Boston. Finally he could get his mom and little sisters out of the house. For now, he'd dream about Anna, the awesome Finnish girl who worked at the deli counter.

CHAPTER 7

Sam Barrows sat at the oak table in their cheery yellow kitchen, sipping his second cup of coffee. He was wearing his uniform, minus the Smokey Bear hat. He walked over to the window and looked down on the little seacoast village of Galway. *My God, it's a beautiful town. Except for the phone lines, this scene could be 1850.* Living in his aunt's home had given him some kind of direct line to the past and a steady stream of memories.

He tried to recall his aunt more clearly, comments she'd made, reminiscences she'd shared about Galway. He felt that he'd never fully appreciated her, and now he was living among her things, preserving her possessions. Why hadn't he asked her more questions when he was growing up? Well, kids never did because they had different priorities as youths. Wasn't her grandfather a sea captain? When Sam found the time, he'd dig around at the Historical Society, see if he could locate a Captain Adamson. He certainly enjoyed living this close to the sea. He watched the boats until Duchess brought in a tennis ball and dropped it in his lap. He tossed it into the living room. She brought it back, tail wagging, demanding more. She'd play with him until she was worn out if he let her.

Galway was still a quiet village, although the Atlantis National Bank, with its four-acre telemarketing center building under construction, was bringing in droves of new people. With a major real estate boom underway, he'd never have been able to buy this stately old Victorian on his own, and he worried about the inevitable rise in taxes that building growth brought with it. Fancy homes and condos were popping up all over town, and some historic old residences had been sacrificed. *Can't fight progress, but Aunt Nina would turn over in her grave at all these changes.* She'd been born in 1903 up in the southeast bedroom, facing the sea. Progress was anathema to her. She'd always resented the automobile, beginning with the first one in town back in 1911.

He could remember his aunt sitting in a rocker in her neat little kitchen, then painted gray, watching the boats leave the harbor at dawn. She was a small, wiry woman with her gray hair pulled severely into a bun. A network of wrinkles covered her face, including laugh lines at the corners of her faded blue eyes. Sam always wondered why she'd never married and wished he'd asked. If he had, she'd have given him a sharp, sassy retort.

The house required a lot of work. The foundation needed shoring up, the roof demanded new shingles, and the house could use a new paint job. He'd already taken care of the plumbing and wiring. He wasn't about to ask Darla to live in an unsafe house.

As a kid, he'd always visited in summer, counting the days until his trip with his folks from Portland to "Downeast." This was his first winter in Galway. Powdery snow now trimmed roofs of Victorian houses and dusted branches. Far to the right, the Congregational Church steeple pointed toward heaven. Doves perched on the telephone wires, and above them seagulls circled in great arcs of expectation. He yearned to see trawlers loaded with haddock and sea bass, but now it was mostly lobster boats. The Gulf of Maine had been nearly fished out. Herring and sardines were but a vague memory.

Galway Bay was still clear of ice, and a few fishermen, including Darla's dad, headed out toward Matinicus for a harvest. Fishing was a rugged life and could be particularly dangerous during winter. His aunt had told him stories of lost fishermen and their vessels. She spoke of how the bay used to freeze up so tight every winter that they drove oxen teams across it, never losing a one.

Sam returned to reality and the gulf of discouragement about the Moulton case, as dark and murky as the waters of Hiram Bog. A seemingly innocent man had been murdered, his body dumped, and, so far, the killer had gotten away with it. *What am I missing? Maybe it's staring me in the face. I know one thing: those Venice people know more than they're telling.*

And there was another problem: the press. The *Portland Press Herald* wanted an interview and the *Midcoast Sentinel* was planning a series on gay-related killings in order to crank up the anxiety. They hadn't gotten this excited about a crime since the heinous knifing of three nuns in the convent in Waterville a few years earlier. Two of the nuns had died and another barely survived, remaining in semi-seclusion in the convent. The emotionally disturbed young man, Michael McGuire, who wielded the knife, was locked up in the state hospital. Sam hoped he'd be there for the rest of his life, while Darla, ever the counselor, felt sorry for the overweight, wild-eyed boy. They often debated whether the criminally insane should be imprisoned or hospitalized. Sam thought Darla was too soft hearted.

He wanted to minimize the gory details of the Moulton case and had stressed to the news hounds that there were several suspects under investigation. So far he'd suppressed the facts about mutilation of Lester's privates. If the press got hold of that tidbit, they'd turn it into two-inch headlines, and it wouldn't stop there. The Galway newspaper had already hinted at the "unhappiness of citizens" over the lack of action. To make matters worse, Sam had no suspects for the string of break-ins at the lake. Maybe alert pawn shop clerks would report attempts to fence goods—or not.

Galway was twenty-five miles from Venice and thirty from Loonport, so he wanted to organize as many interviews with suspects in one trip as possible. What he really wanted to do was to stay home and go back to bed with Darla, who'd wandered into the kitchen and was reaching up into the upper cabinet, stacking clean dishes, an activity that showed off her curves to their best advantage.

Back in the Portland days, the long hours and emergency phone calls had severely strained the marriage until it broke. He and Wanda had thought about children, but it didn't happen, part of the reason why, after four years, they'd divorced amicably. He'd heard that Wanda's real estate career had taken off. *Good for her. Besides, I have Darla and Duchess and a new career now.*

Then in between Wanda and Darla, there'd been those unsettling good times with Belle Whittaker. What was that all about? Now it seemed like a melancholy memory, except for Duchess, his faithful shepherd. Belle was like a hurricane that blows in, rearranges the landscape, and then you're left to pick up the pieces. No way of knowing what damage it did until long after it passed. Sam didn't have a clue about how to characterize his affair with Belle. In some ways she was more of a pal than a lover. He could discuss any case with her, and, with her deep understanding of male motivation, she'd been instrumental in helping him solve a number of cases.

With Belle, sex had been rough and wild, a way to get relief from the pressures of the job. He'd been naive and never expected the relationship to escalate to something serious. Not once had they discussed marriage. He'd wanted her in his life full-time, but, after Wanda, he wasn't going to tip his hand or beg for hers. His happiness wasn't going to depend on a woman. Then once he'd met Darla, sweet, soft, pliable Darla, he'd let the good times with Belle die out like an untended fire. But had he forgotten Belle? No one who'd met her could forget Belle.

Summer before last, he'd come down to Galway for some much needed R and R. His Aunt Nina was still living but she was not well. He stayed with her that June, and she suggested that he go deep sea fishing. "You're gettin' in my hair, Sammy. Why don'tcha go off with Jack McClellan and catch us some cod, if there's any left in our part of the sea." She'd known Captain McClellan since he was a boy. Had auntie set him up?

Anyway, that was the day he met Darla. He'd never forget that moment on the boat, seeing her fetching face, her blonde curls edging an old bandana, and her overalls covered with chum and fish blood. He was besotted. They'd often laughed about meeting on her dad's boat while she helped chum the waters. She said that their special bird should be the seagull. His aunt had died that September, as the color began to turn.

Darla, the antithesis of Belle, made him feel twenty years younger. He liked sitting around watching her and talking with her about the future. So far Darla had proven to be an extremely understanding and loyal wife, and he wished he could spend more time with her. She had a degree in Counseling from Bates College over in Lewiston, and he'd encouraged her to put it to use as a part-time crisis and guidance counselor at Galway High. He didn't always agree with Darla's theories of human behavior, too client-centered, and he thought her too understanding, almost a bleeding heart, but she'd certainly make a great and loving mom if they ever had children.

Can't sit around here all day. "C'mon Duchess, girl. We gotta go to work."

Duchess's tail wagged and her brown eyes followed Sam's every move.

Batting her long lashes, Darla asked, "Sam, don't you want more coffee? Have to leave already? You got in so late last night, I feel as if I've hardly seen you." She kneaded his shoulder. "We're like ships passing in the fog."

"I know what you mean, hon. Okay, pour me a warm up. You know, my schedule won't always be this hectic. We're in the middle of a crime spurt. I don't like being away from you either, but today I've gotta do interviews in Amnesty, Venice and Loonport. Then I gotta plow through paperwork when I get back." A little chill ran up his back as he rested his hand on the comfortable curve of her hip then gave it a squeeze. "You married a cop, Darla. I'm sorry." Sometimes he wished he were a carpenter or a plumber.

"I realize that, and I knew it going in, but why not do the paperwork at home?" She bent over and kissed the back of his neck. "I'll help you. I could transcribe everything to computer disk."

"Unfortunately, I've gotta have access to other reports. Think about it this way, sweetie. Could your dad pull up all those lobsters if he weren't out to sea?"

Darla padded over to the sink in her matching bunny slippers. Her pink chenille bathrobe clung to her long, trim legs.

"Listen, let me set up this interview." He began punching numbers into his mobile phone. "The sooner I start the day, the sooner I come home, and we can fool around." He hugged her around the waist and kissed her as he waited for Barb to pick up. Darla returned the kiss deeply. "Just a minute, Barb." He pushed the mute button. Feeling excitement surge through him, he kissed her back and felt the round warmth of a breast fill his hand. But Barb's sobering voice was coming through the cell phone. "Sam, Sam!
You there?"

"Sorry, babe," he said, letting Darla slip away. She kissed him on the forehead. "Later, big boy," she teased.

Barb told him Mrs. Ridley would like him to call her, which he did. Jane Ridley answered on the second ring, hemming and hawing nervously.

"Mrs. Ridley, you don't have a choice." Sam set his coffee cup down a little too hard.

"Well, I could meet you at my son's house, I guess."

Darla lifted Sam's cup and wiped up the spill, then smiled. It was hard to be all business with Darla standing there pressing her breast against his shoulder. He spoke into the phone. "Now why would you want to drive over to your son's house in Venice when you're right in town there in

41

Amnesty?"

"You see it's just that my place is so...central..."

Sam glanced at his notepad. "Jane Ridley, 910 Main Street, Amnesty, Maine." She wouldn't want her neighbors observing a visit from the law.

"All right, Mrs. Ridley, but I want to talk with you alone, understood?" He thought that maybe he was getting too soft hearted, but he did seek some kind of cooperation from her.

"My son's home is right next to his store."

"I know where it is. Okay, I'll meet you at ten."

Jane Ridley said a curt goodbye, and Sam snapped his cell phone closed. He turned to Darla. "You know the game warden mentioned something about a guy named Frank Zucchetti. He's married to Moulton's cousin, and he's an old pro at investigations, used to be Air Force Office of Special Investigations. Thought I might get some tips on the Moulton murder. Maybe I'll give him a call. Can't hurt, and I don't have any good leads yet."

"Sure. The sooner you put somebody away for that murder, the sooner you can take a week off to spend with me. I'm not naggin', darlin'. I just miss you so much when you put in these long days, and I worry, too." She stood on her tiptoes, and gave him a long, passionate kiss.

"Hey, where's your hat? Oh, here it is." She placed it on his head. They kissed again, and then he walked out to his cruiser, Duchess trotting at his side. He opened the door and she leaped into the passenger seat, giving him that "What're you waitin' for?" look.

No telling how many phone calls Barb would want him to return. It was going to be a long day. He'd inherited a skilled secretary who never missed a beat, who'd been on the job for a dozen years, and he hoped she'd stay on another dozen. He enjoyed seeing her smiling face and her bright blouses that never matched anything. She wore very little make-up on the pleasant face that greeted him every morning. Sam had once told Darla, "Barb's a real Maine woman, tough but kind."

Darla was pleased that Barb was part of Sam's support system but was even happier that Barb wasn't young and beautiful. *Never mind*, she told herself. Sam was head-over-heels in love with her.

CHAPTER 8

After dropping off Duchess at the office where she could get all the attention she demanded, Sam headed north on Route Six for a series of interviews.

He knocked on the dented steel door to Jake's bungalow. On the second knock, it swung open, revealing Jake and his mama. A thick haze of cigarette smoke hung in the room. Their looks said they'd been in a strategy huddle getting their stories straight prior to the interview. Jake began by making excuses. "I gotta get over to the store. Things been disappearin' lately. Maybe I should have you investigate shopliftin' instead of botherin' my mother over nothin'."

"Hold on, Mr. Ridley. I'll be questioning *you* when I'm through with your mother, so stick around the area."

"Yeah, okay." Jake went through the door, closing it hard behind him. Sam watched him through the cloudy window as he did a cavalier strut around his new Porsche. When he reached the store, Jake mumbled through clenched teeth, "Fascist son-of-a-bitch!" He had to check on inventory. He'd been truthful about losing items through shoplifting or employee theft, and he knew he'd have to keep a better check on merchandise, but he was worried more about his mother's state of mind and what she might reveal. A slip of the tongue might set the cops to nosing around where they didn't belong. He didn't need that.

Jane Ridley's fingers tapped her worn Gucci handbag. Perspiration darkened her hairline, revealing dark roots among the red. She looked around the room, everywhere but into Sheriff Barrows' icy blue eyes. Her cotton skirt and lightweight, cardigan sweater seemed inappropriate for a windy January day. She made motions to light up.

"I'd prefer it if you didn't," Sam replied, fanning off some of the lingering stale smoke with his hat.

"Well, it *is* my son's house, and you're making me nervous." Her lips quivered. "I've never been questioned by a sheriff. I was well acquainted with the last sheriff; he attended my church." She stuffed the Marlboro Lights back into her purse.

Ignoring her comments, Sam took in the room. It was worn and ordinary with an old leather couch and chair and retro-seventies furnishings.

A huge sound system and liquid screen television covered one wall. He looked through the doorway into the kitchen. Dishes were piled high in the sink and a grungy tee shirt hung off the back of a chair. Sam felt grateful that the smoke was covering up the smell of sweat, corn chips, pork rinds, and God knew what else might be hanging in the air.

"How well did you know the deceased?"

"If you must know, I couldn't stand the man. His kind, they're a danger to society."

"And what *kind* is that?"

"You know what I mean. You must've arrested some of those perverts. That man was a sodomite!" She spit out the words, then licked her lips, craving a cigarette or a drink.

Sam took copious notes. "Ever talk with Mr. Moulton?"

"I had nothing to say to him. I don't *associate* with those people. They aren't my kind."

"Did you ever threaten him in any way, Mrs. Ridley? Think before you answer."

"Of course I didn't!" She hesitated, then continued. "I got a petition going, that's all." Her mouth was locked in a grim smile of satisfaction.

"And what was that about, exactly?"

"I didn't want him playing the organ in my church, that's what." She opened her purse, removed a pink tissue, then snapped it shut.

"And did the petition succeed?" The sheriff was becoming irritated with Mrs. Ridley, now bending forward in her chair noisily blowing her nose.

"No, we could only get eight signatures. I prayed over it but failed. Then Mr. Moulton changed churches, went over to Loonport where they don't have high standards, so I guess we did win after all." She made two little barks, smoker's cough.

"And did anyone other than those signatories help you get rid of Mr. Moulton?" He couldn't help but notice the maple gun rack filled with hunting rifles and the two skinning knives mounted next to it.

"Nobody else," she murmured meekly.

"But you used the pronoun 'we' a minute so. Who is 'we'?"

"Well, I might have asked friends who work with me at my summer Bible camp. They've always come to my aid. They're good people." She looked up at the ceiling, fidgeting with the tissue in her sleeve.

"Okay, let's try again, Mrs. Ridley. Who do you mean by 'we'?" Sam was quite uncomfortable in the sagging chair and wished he could get up and walk awhile. He felt a hitch in his left hip. *This damned chair's gonna set my back off.*

Mrs. Ridley straightened her sleeves. "Don't I have pastor-parishioner privilege?"

"Ma'am, are you an ordained minister?"

"I took some courses at the Moody Bible Institute."

Sam was losing his patience. He set his pen down on the coffee table, rubbed his chin, and then picked up the pen and continued note-taking.

"Do you know what 'obstruction of justice' is, ma'am?"

"Well, I *do* watch television."

He couldn't conceal a slight smile. "Good! Now answer truthfully. Are you or are you *not* an ordained minister?"

"No—technically speaking."

"Thank you! In that case, I'll need the names of your helpers."

She nodded, pulling a pencil and notebook out of the beat-up Gucci bag. *Must be a knock-off* Sam thought as he waited for her to jot down and hand him a list of helpers.

"And where were you on the morning of the day after Thanksgiving?"

"I drove from home right to my son's store about 8:00 AM. You know it used to be my husband's store. Albert made it what it is. He died of a heart attack...only thirty-seven." Sam could see how premature death might seem a viable option.

"And how long did you remain at the store?"

"All morning. My son can vouch for me." She flicked her tongue across her upper lip to overcome the dryness.

"And what did you do there all morning? Isn't that unusual for you to hang around your son's place of business like that?"

"I neatened up shelves. I've done that ever since my husband's death." She fidgeted with the buttons of her sweater. "Jake needs me."

"Can any customers vouch for you?"

"Isn't my son's word good enough for you?" she whimpered.

"What did you do about lunch that day?"

"I took an Eye-talian sandwich from the deli and ate it in my car on the way home. Pepperoni, tomato, onion, lettuce and oil."

It's funny how people remember the little things.

"Who waited on you at the deli counter?"

"For pity's sake! How should I remember that? I might've just gotten it myself, or maybe it was that foreign girl, Anna something-or-other. Why do you need to know every little detail? And before you ask, I drove straight to Amnesty. No stops."

"That's nice, Mrs. Ridley. Now, you need to recall everything you did for the rest of the day after Thanksgiving. What did you do when you got home?"

"I stayed in all afternoon, doing Bible study and some crocheting."

"Can anyone vouch for your whereabouts all afternoon? Make any calls?"

The tears began to swell at the corners of her eyes, liquefying her mascara. "I don't know. This is police harassment, and I'm tellin' my son. You haven't read me my rights or told me that I could have a lawyer present."

These people watch too much television.

45

He'd heard enough for one day, and stood up abruptly. "Ma'am, you're not under arrest. This is only a preliminary inquiry, and we can wrap it up now. If you should think of anything else, here's my card."

Jane took the card without looking at it, folded it and stuffed it into her Gucci knock-off. She then removed her cigarettes and lighter, snapped the purse shut, and spat out, "I doubt that anything will occur to me."

Sam doubted it as well. "If you're going to the store, tell your son that our interview has concluded. He's next."

Jane Ridley stepped lively as she left her son's little house and headed over to report everything to Jake as quickly as possible, but the sheriff decided to beat her to it. With his long legs, Sam did a quarterback end-run to the side entrance of the store that went through the bottle recycling room directly to the deli counter, where he found Jake sampling cheddar cheese. Before Mama Jane could open her mouth, the sheriff demanded, "Jake, I'll see you now. Follow me. We can do the interview in my patrol car."

The interview provided nothing new. The sheriff started out by asking if Jake could account for his whereabouts on the day after Thanksgiving. Anything Jake told him would be viewed with skepticism.

"Sure, I was here all day. I ain't rich. Can't miss out on business when the Little Missus forgets the canned cranberry sauce."

Jake's left eye was twitching, a nervous tic. The sheriff leaned in for closer observation. "But you're talking about *Thanksgiving Day*. All right, we'll start there. So where did you eat Thanksgiving dinner? And please track the time that various events occurred."

"I hung out at my girlfriend's in Amnesty for an evenin' meal, around, I don't know, six maybe, and stayed over. Her name's Susan, Susan Johnson." Jake smirked. "We had a sleep-over." He started to take out his cigarettes, but the sheriff stopped him by raising his hand.

"She'll verify that, I'm sure. I need her name, address and phone number." Sam took his notebook out and began writing.

Jake provided the information too eagerly, Sam thought, knowing Susan Johnson would back him up.

"Mr. Ridley, do you own a hunting rifle, and, if so, what caliber?"

"Hell, I own a gun rack full. This is *Maine*, man, not *Portland!*"

Sam disliked Jake on principle, but now he had specifics. He'd interviewed "Jakes" throughout his career. They were often unattractive, cocky, and felt that the world owed them a living. A percentage had been abused, but, unlike Darla, he hated to medicalize deviance. Sam knew one thing: Jake couldn't be trusted. He took a closer look. Jake was lanky, his brown hair thin, and his eyes a pale, lifeless blue. He had poor posture and a hollow chest. His nostrils were red, belying a possible coke habit. Like his mother, Jake had trouble looking people in the eye and seemed always to be sliding away, his movements sort of snake-like. Deputy Hines had told Sam about Jake's string of girlfriends.

"So let me understand this. You worked at your store all

Thanksgiving day. That's admirable, helping the community like that. But what about the day *after* Thanksgiving."

"Just finished tellin' ya, I was with Susan."

"How long were you with this girlfriend of yours?"

"Uhh, we slept late 'cuz she didn't have to go to work, and then I splurged and took her down to Maude's Country Diner, where she works, for lunch, then I dumped her off at her mom's trailer over towards Deering."

"And then?" The sheriff was growing weary of Jake's evasiveness.

"And then I come back here to my house and caught some z's, awright? I was feelin' a little spaced because I hadn't gotten much sleep the previous night. Got the picture?"

Sam had had it with this jerk. "Who can vouch for your being asleep in your house all afternoon?"

"I was in bed alone for Christ's sake. Who'd ya' think can vouch for me? I don't have a personal maid, ya know." Jake stabbed at the car door handle.

"Okay, that's all for now, but don't leave the county." Sam tucked away his notebook, gave Jake a slight wave and added a cursory "Thanks." Then he started up the Crown Victoria, and turned on the defroster. The conversation had steamed up the windshield. A feeling of disappointment crowded his thoughts, like the thick gray clouds moving in over the hills to the south. Sam felt he hadn't done well at all with the interrogations. *I'm not done with Mr. Jake Ridley, or mommy dearest. They seem close, maybe a little too close.*

Before leaving the parking lot, he called Barb. She'd done her homework and arranged for the interview with the Johnson girl.

It was early afternoon when he stopped at Maude's Country Diner and had a greasy double-chili-cheeseburger, fries and some tasty apple pie. Then he spoke with Susan, who happened to be his waitress. She seemed uncomfortable out in the dining room, so Sam interviewed her in the storage room. She was a thin girl who'd worked too many hours, smoked too many cigarettes, and looked old before her time. Her bleached hair and excess make-up didn't help. He noticed her eyes flinch at the mention of Jake's name. But, as expected, she backed up Jake's alibi and told him nothing that advanced the case.

Sam wanted to head back to Galway to catch up on paperwork, but duty called. Since he wasn't too far from Loonport, he checked his list of contacts and called to see if Clair LeBlanc, Lester's transvestite best friend, was back in town. And she said she'd be "happy to receive him."

Clair lived at the end of a quiet dead end street, a small middle class house with tired aluminum siding, turquoise shutters missing a few slats, and a front-porch roof that sagged dangerously due to a rotten column. Apparently she couldn't afford house repairs. Clair's slightly beaten-up Volvo was parked out front, with a lace garter, a crystal and a feathery Indian sun-catcher hanging from the rearview mirror. A plastic Virgin Mary stood atop the dash board. She'd covered all bases.

Before Sam could ring the bell, Clair stood in the doorway looking rather melancholy. She had on a pink velour leisure suit with pearls and large pearl earrings. Her limp, faded red hair hung loose to her shoulders, and she wore heavy make-up, including bright red lipstick. Once inside, Sam found himself standing in a very neat Early American style living room looking around at the many landscapes on the wall. An expansive oil of Lake Mallacook rested on an easel near a bay window. "This is really exceptional! Your work?"

"Yes, but that one's not finished. Won't you sit down, Sheriff?"

"First, I'd like to offer my sincere condolences, Miss LeBlanc."

"Please call me Clair. And yes, it's terrible! I'm just devastated." She plucked a tissue from a needlepoint-covered box. "Lester was a saint, and I was blessed to have known him, but if we talk about him I'll just weep. I've been crying off and on ever since I got the phone call in Boston." Her eyes looked red and puffy.

"Oh. Who called you?" Sam chose a pink, velvet wing chair with Queen Anne legs.

"Why, Betty, of course. She didn't want me to hear it from somebody else."

"You drove to Boston when? Sorry, but I have to ask this."

"The day before Thanksgiving to spend the holiday with my eighty-year-old mum. She still lives in Jamaica Plain, in an apartment house. I see her every month or when she needs something done. But how I wish I'd stayed here in Loonport. Les invited me to Thanksgiving dinner, but I turned him down. If I'd stayed, he'd still be alive." With this admission she openly wept and grabbed more tissues.

Or maybe you'd be dead, too, Sam thought, noting the gold rings on her long, tapered fingers. A claw-set ruby matched one that Lester had been wearing.

Sam didn't doubt that this was a genuine display of affection over her loss. Still, he had questions. "I've heard a lot of very positive comments about your friend. I'm sure that he'll be missed. Now I have to ask some questions which might make you uncomfortable."

Clair looked shocked. "What do you mean, Sheriff?"

"I mean that you may be able to help with the investigation—and call me Sam. You knew him very well. Can you think of anyone who would benefit from his death? Who hated him enough to kill him? Even someone from your circle of friends?"

Clair looked out the window, then down at her polished nails. Sam thought her remarkably good looking for a transvestite, and convincing as well, although her hands and jaw were a bit large.

"How impolite of me. Sam, would you like some tea? Tea always makes me think more clearly. Doesn't it you? Please say you'll have a cup. I have a great many varieties from which to choose."

Sam wasn't a big tea drinker, but, in this case… "Sure, something with caffeine, please."

Soon Clair returned, carrying a tea set on a silver tray. "I chose for you Stout English Lifeboat Tea, and shortbread cookies I made myself."

Sam helped himself to several, even though he was watching his weight.

Clair became intense. "Now, about Les's enemies. I'm sure I'm not the first to mention the Ridleys. They tried to make Les's life miserable, manufacturing lies, forcing him to give up his organ playing at the Venice Church. And what had he ever done to them? Nothing!"

"Was there anyone else? Think outside the box, Clair, folks whose animosity wasn't so obvious." He ate another cookie, savoring the overdose of eggs and sugar.

"Well, the Italian family in the house to the right of Les's…they occasionally complain." Sam noticed the use of the present tense and chalked it up to denial.

"We had some great parties, especially when Les's pals from New York visited, and I'm the first to admit we might've been too obstreperous. The Borgheses are a big, traditional family, and, while they might complain, I can't imagine any of them resorting to violence. They also claimed we swam in the nude, but all the men had on g-strings. Maybe it was wishful thinking—or poor lighting." Clair laughed softly, her face reflecting the memory of good times.

"The Italian cottage is closed up tight. Anyone else? And how many boats did Les have?"

"Two, the one in his garage and the john boat. Why?"

"Just part of the investigation, ma'am. And the john boat had a small motor on it? These cookies are good, and fattening I'll wager." Sam smiled, wiping the crumbs from his lips.

"Sure it did. Lester had a bad shoulder, arthritis, and couldn't row very well. By the way, Sam, I can tell you're a man who doesn't have to worry about his weight. Why, I'll bet you work out regularly." She poured them both a second cup of tea and used silver tongs to drop another lump of sugar in Sam's cup.

"Well, I should. But what about Les's enemies? Can you think of anyone else? Maybe someone in Venice or Amnesty?"

"Let me think. There was a flap a few years back about the drama group Les directed. Some parents thought theater wasn't good for their sons. You know, if they keep taking art, music and drama out of the schools we're going to have a generation of hooligans, thugs, and techno-gang members in long black coats. Don't you agree, Sam?"

"Actually, I do. I've spoken at school board meetings, defending the arts. But try to remember more specifically, Clair. *Which* parents?"

"I can't recall offhand. It was years ago. And then there was that tiff about duck boxes. I think Gus Gossam, that old thug, called Les and said, 'Get those fucking duck boxes out of the bog. Don'tcha know it's practically in my front yard?' Mr. Gossam said that the next thing you knew, Hiram Bog would be a wildlife refuge."

"Well, isn't it a wildlife refuge?" Sam stirred his tea.

"Yes, that's how unbelievably ignorant Mr. Gossam is. The Amnesty College students have been instrumental in making it so. They're wonderful young people. They clean up the waterway every year, and they really appreciate Les's building the duck boxes and setting them out. You know they have an Avian Studies program at the college. They also teach Silviculture and Wildlife Management. Les was a real supporter of the program. He gave not only money, but his time as well."

"You're being most helpful, Clair. So...does anyone else come to mind?"

"Well, it just occurred to me that one time something terrible happened. A young girl got dumped in Lester's front yard. She'd been hurt, beaten up, and she named Booth Gossam as the perpetrator. Her mouth and wrists were taped. It was terrible. I was there that night. Lester was so gentle with her, removing the tape. The poor thing was so embarrassed. Oh, I haven't told you the worst...she was naked. I think it was meant to embarrass Lester, but, of course, it was the poor girl who was mortified."

"Why haven't I ever heard about this? When was it?"

"Summer before last. And you wouldn't have heard about it, not officially, anyway, because the girl refused to go to the hospital or press charges. She was so frightened, she left town. Her name was Alicia Montez, a migrant Mexican girl up here working in egg production barns."

As Sam took notes, Clair picked up the tea things. When she returned from the kitchen Sam asked one last question. "Clair, Les's friends from New York. None of then were here around Thanksgiving?"

"No, exactly the opposite. They thought they'd see him in New York perhaps, because Les was thinking about driving to the city the day after Thanksgiving. It wasn't definite, but why would they come here if he was going there? It makes no sense. Besides, I'll tell you, Sam. Those boys loved Les. They'd do anything for him. He'd been sort of a Guru to them when they lived in Soho. I'd like to think that they love me as well." She looked down shyly, and then walked to the door with him, her hand on his sleeve.

He handed her his card, and she tucked it into a pocket of her pink leisure suit. "You've been a big help, Clair. And I enjoyed the shortbread cookies and tea. I may need to talk with you again." He started down the steps. "Oh, by the way, your artwork is terrific. I saw some of it over at Lester's place."

"Oh! Did you used to visit Lester?" She placed her spread hand across her collar bone.

"No. Just when the Crime Investigation Unit and I went over the place," Sam said, flushing slightly.

"Let me know when you want to model for me." Her wide grin made Sam wonder if she was making fun of him. On second thought, she was probably always looking for nude models. Sam shook his head, his face pink with embarrassment, and climbed into the cruiser. He noticed curtains move in the bay window across the street. Good old Maine, where no visitor to a neighborhood goes unnoticed. Now if only someone had seen a john boat crossing Hiram Bog.

Meanwhile, back at the General Store, Jake had taken the afternoon off to watch a football game on his wide-screen TV. He nursed a six-pack and a bag of pork rinds, stretching his legs out on a beanbag chair in his drab living room.

Two clerks were on duty, the older one, a battered Vietnam War vet, and Sharon, a middle aged woman. Young Andy Gossam was busy restocking the shelves, and fellow teenager Anna Eloranto was making pizza dough. Earlier, she'd handled six pizza orders, but now it was fairly quiet at the deli counter.

As the hardest working employee, Andy was always on the job except when he was in school. No chip off the old block, he'd come to work early and hung his jacket on a nail in the back room. A brown paper bag held his peanut butter and jelly sandwich and a bag of chips. He stood in the doorway of the deli counter and watched Anna scrub the cutting board. Her dad had dropped her off early. To Andy she looked older than her years and very rad. He sauntered over to the meat and cheese prep area trying to act cool.

She looked up, smiling shyly. "Hi!"

Nearly melting, Andy watched her wipe down the cutting board where she proceeded to trim several Vidalia onions. Then she placed the first one in the machine and began slicing. The whirling stainless steel blades looked so dangerous that Andy felt a shiver of fear for her as she continued stuffing in the onions. The onion vapors were so strong that tears rolled down Anna's cheeks. She glanced over at him and gave him a weak smile. Andy shot one back.

He thought about how Anna never noticed him in the halls of Mountain Top High. She was always surrounded by giddy girls, none as pretty as she. *And why would a cool girl like her notice me? I'm a total geek, a dweeb, and my clothes are totally crappy. Sure, mom keeps them clean, but anyone can tell they're hand-me-downs from the Salvation Army.*

Look at her. Her skin's awesome and her face is prettier than Gwyneth Paltrow's. If she ever smiles at me again, I'm gonna die. Shoot, she'll never give me a second look.

He'd once overheard her tell their math teacher that she'd been born in Finland. Andy didn't know where his great grandparents had come from...Maine, he guessed. Some were buried up in the old graveyard.

Anna was so beautiful. He'd overheard Jake say that business had increased at the deli, and Anna was the reason. Who wouldn't want to look at her? And, besides, it was really decent pizza for the price.

Andy wasn't in her league. He was a Gossam, part of that no-good tribe of lowlifes over by the bog, in the far north end of Venice. He'd turned to leave when Anna asked, her nose sniffling, "Hey, would you hand me a tissue before you go?"

"Sure." He held out the box. "Want *me* to slice that stuff? They've started a waterworks, huh?" His heart skipped a beat or two.

"No thanks." Anna wiped her eyes. "You're in my trig class, you know, but, like, you never speak. Stuck up?" She giggled, and he knew she wasn't being sarcastic, just cute.

Andy smiled and shook his head negatively. "No way!"

"Well, you're so quiet nobody knows you're, like, even there. Is trig tough for you?"

"Nope." He fiddled with a stack of paper plates stacked beside him, and some fell on the floor. "Oh, shit! Guess you can't use these." He took on a sheepish look.

"Don't worry. Toss 'em. Who's gonna miss a few paper plates?"

"I sorta' hide out in the back of the class. Trig, it's kinda' easy for me. Why? Is it, like, creepin' you out?"

"Sometimes, but Papa helps me." She displayed a dazzling smile. He looked behind him to be sure it was for him.

"I always come in early 'cuz I'm trying to save money for college. I get in as many hours as I can. You?" He studied her figure, alluring beneath her tight, white cotton blouse, jeans, and the required red and white plaid plastic apron. Her long brown hair was caught up under a white cook's cap revealing soft, curly wisps at the base of her neck.

"I was saving up for a car, but papa found me an old junker Saab. He says he'll have it ready for me when I turn sixteen. I can hardly wait. My papa's pretty cool!"

"And when's that? Your birthday, I mean?"

"March tenth. I'm a Pisces. When's yours?"

"April fourteenth. I guess I'm an Aries but I don't know what that means really." He thought to himself, *How true is that! I don't know what anything means.* He picked up a crate of cabbages and placed it on the counter. "Gonna make slaw any time soon? I love that stuff!"

"Nah! Got plenty in the fridge. Hey, I'll look up your sign for you and tell you how neat it is to be an Aries. But I need your ascendant sign. That means the exact time and location of your birth. Get that stuff for me and I'll give you a full report. Okay? I don't necessarily believe all that stuff, but it's way fun. Mama's really into it, big time!"

Will my mom know any of that? I doubt it. "Sure. That'd be neat." He put the box of cabbages away. "Thanks! I gotta get back to restocking the shelves. Jake's been a real butthead lately." He looked around to be sure Jake wasn't there, then walked closer. He didn't trust Jake and he was sure Anna didn't either.

"Clue me in. I know he suspects we're eating some of his *prosciutto,* when it's him that nibbles at the cheese like a rat."

She smiled and looked down at her apron. "He's talking about mounting a video camera in here. Like he's gonna trap us with a home video. Yeah, right. Picture us with ham hanging out of our mouths."

"You're puttin' me on!" He looked up at the rust-spotted tin ceiling.

"Nope. He's been bummed out all day. Might have something to do with that body they found in the bog. That was awful, the drowning and all. I saw the sheriff's car at his house earlier. And his mom came in here all freaked out."

Wanting to change the subject so that he wouldn't have to explain where he lived, Andy walked closer and whispered, "Well, he'll never put a camera back there in the recycling room." He could smell her perfume which reminded him of lemons. He realized he was way too close to her and suddenly backed away, bumping into the counter.

"Why not? It's his store; he can do just about anything he wants."

Andy looked around to be sure they were alone. Then he whispered, "Well, 'cuz that's where he sells booze after hours, and...Jeeze...I've said too much all ready." He remained only a foot from her.

"Andy, don't worry! I won't tell anyone."

"I know, but I gotta learn to keep my trap shut. Besides, I need to get back to work."

She paused and straightened the neck strap on her apron. Andy thought her white, tapered fingers were awesome, even covered with onion juice.

"Okay. Listen, Andy, get me those facts and I'll write up your horoscope. By the way, did they ever find out why the man was in the bog?"

"No. I live near there, but I don't know anything." In a softer tone he added, "Poor guy. That kind of crime really sucks!" He wished he hadn't mentioned living near the bog. *I'm always saying dumb things! Now she'll put two and two together and know that I'm one of them.* Then he remembered that she lived way over on the other side of Venice, two ridges over, maybe seven miles. Unless her dad took her fishing at the bog, she wouldn't have seen his house or the mess surrounding it. Besides, everybody knew Mr. Eloranto had five trout ponds. Why go to the bog?

"Well, gotta rearrange all those bungee cords. Somebody messed 'em up." He didn't want to leave, to break this unreal spell, but this job was too good to lose. Although Andy was underage, Jake let him work extra hours and paid him under the table.

As Andy attacked the bungee cords, he felt as if he could fly. A cup of cappuccino would taste great, but he didn't want to spend the dollar and a half. *Does Anna drink coffee?* Probably yes; her family was laid back. They let their kids drink, go naked in the sauna, and no curfews. How cool is that!

If I bought Anna a cup of anything, she'd think I was a dork. Maybe when I know her better. Am I way stupid or what?

53

CHAPTER 9

The Zucchettis parked their car down the road from the church and walked through the slush. Another Alberta Clipper had come through the previous night, but now the afternoon sun shone brilliantly in an azure sky, melting the top inch of powdery stuff. Little wisps of steam rose from the ice along the edges of the road where the salt-sand had worked its way down to the asphalt.

Quite a crowd was there to see old Lester off, including his sister, Betty, friends, and the just plain curious. Jake was there, with a smirk on his face—but not his Mama Jane. Some of the "mourners" wanted to see if Clair, the transvestite, would make an appearance, and there she was in the back row, sitting next to two of Lester's New York pals. She wore a black feathered hat, a long string of pearls, and an embroidered, black wool serape over a shocking pink bouclé suit. An odd mixture, but Clair was famous for flamboyant fashion statements.

"I'm glad so many showed up. There are the Stammers, the Swensons, the Finnish couple, the Wells's, Hal Hines without his wife, the Bagleys, wow, even Frenchie's here!" Sandy hugged her husband's arm as they entered the church.

"Yeah, a lot of the morbidly curious, but they won't have an open casket to gawk at. Too much decomp, I'm afraid."

Sandy smiled. "Dear Les. If they did have an open casket, they'd never get his make-up right. He told me once he wore only Esteé Lauder."

In the foyer of the small wooden church, they were greeted with perfunctory hugs from Betty. Sandy asked herself why she didn't get on with her cousin. *Perhaps it's because Betty's a blabbermouth about the post office. Not her fault...she's the result of a little mix-up in the gene pool. I'll try to be nicer to Betty in the future.* Sandy was always making resolutions, but few lasted more than weeks or, at the most, months.

"What's he looking at me for?" Sandy asked Frank as they settled in a rear row. She was referring to the regular circuit minister, Reverend Brand. He took his turn at this church once a month, but Sandy hadn't heard him preach because she didn't attend Sunday services. Venice had only one church and the congregation was shrinking. Now the regulars numbered about a dozen on a good day. On alternate Sundays the group went to Amnesty Methodist Church, Loonport Unitarian Methodist, and Dixville Congregational. The only other time the church was used was for weddings and funerals.

"Probably hopes you'll get up later and say a few words."

"No way!" she whispered, squirming a bit in the pew.

Sandy recognized most of the faces, including her closest neighbors Rhu and Chuck Shaw, Nin and Ned from down the hill, the spinster Cleona Burgess, and other near neighbors including Loraine and Guy Swenson, the boat builder. Then there was the town clerk, Jean Cowling and her husband Mike. All the selectmen and former selectmen attended, including Angus MacTeague and his sweet wife Mabel, minus their six children.

The Stammers and the Swensons had arrived in Venice in the early Seventies in answer to a call from an organic farmer. Old Wiley French had placed an ad in the *New York Times* for carrot thinners, and he'd gotten marijuana smokers. It all went hand in hand. What he was really looking for was a way to spice up his sex life. They had lived communally in a large, creaky barn up near the east town line. On Frenchie's fields everything grew well from good weed to parsnips, potatoes, squash and, of course, carrots. The crops were sold at roadside and delivered to fancy restaurants in Portland and Boston that wanted immature, fetal vegetables for their Yuppie clientele. But for his penchant for alcohol and loose women, Frenchie could have made some money. This Bohemian back-to-the-land commune had attracted lots of Flower Children from the boroughs of New York. Ironically, many went on to graduate to the middle class, becoming what they'd despised: lawyers, business people, nurses and doctors in Central Maine. Most had stayed in the Thoreau county area. Some were here today in support of Lester's lifestyle and his right to maintain it. After all, hadn't they come to Venice in search of an alternative lifestyle?

Chuck Shaw was in attendance because he just plain liked Lester. His wife Rhu came as an unwilling participant for the sake of appearances, sitting stone-faced in a black suit so old it looked rusty. Chuck had always enjoyed picking up a bargain piece of furniture at the auction and then refinishing it, sometimes letting Lester sell it at his barn, then they'd split the commission. They'd also shared stories about New York, because Chuck had grown up in New Jersey, only fifty miles from The City. After Chuck earned his Masters, he and Rhu brought their three children to Venice and moved into a dilapidated farmhouse that had once been a stagecoach stop and later, a doctor's home and office. He served as a science teacher and track coach at Mountain Top High, but his real love was fixing and refinishing furniture. Chuck'd turned the house into a fine looking place.

"Chuck's gonna miss Lester something awful," Sandy whispered to Frank. "Who's he gonna argue with about antiques?"

The church was a plain, utilitarian, clapboard building without frills. Built in the mid-nineteenth century, it replicated the Dixville Union Church, the Amnesty Union Methodist Church, and maybe a hundred other

Union Churches throughout central Maine, each serving a seven-by-seven mile township. Up front, near the organ, stood a wooden library table laden with four massive flower arrangements. More stood in white wicker baskets at the side of the altar. An elaborate cross made up of pink carnations edged in yellow chrysanthemums and baby's breath leaned slightly askew against the front of the casket. Sandy guessed that it was from Clair.

The pastor's podium resembled a Rotary club prop, except for the rough-hewn cross fastened to its overly varnished plywood front. A linen cloth edged in gold was draped over it. Behind the altar hung a large home-sewn quilt with crudely embroidered bible scenes. 'Pre-Primitive' Frank had exclaimed when he first saw it. The only other wall decoration was a painting of a sweet-faced Jesus who looked like Charlton Heston knocking at a cottage door.

Frank whispered, "Jesus, it's like something on the Independent Film Channel." Sandy shushed him and smiled at the nearby MacTeagues, who nodded their heads solemnly like the little doggies in the rear windows of cars.

As people took their places, the reed organ up front began to huff and wheeze under the puffy hands of Helen Champagne. Once, Lester had been the primary organist, but after the petition business, he'd given up coming to Venice. Instead, he played a better organ, one that was in tune, and for more money, at the Loonport Unitarian Church where they had welcomed him.

As Frank had suspected, the coffin was closed. A large photo in a gilded, rococo frame atop the casket revealed Lester as he'd looked a decade earlier. His cheeks were rosy, lips full, eyebrows carefully arched and the bulk of his hair, always nicely combed, swept across his bald spot. He was good looking for a man in his fifties who'd lived a slightly dissipated life. In the photo he wore an immaculate, gray Pierre Cardin suit that Sandy had seen before, with a yellow and black silk tie with an Escher-like design. *He was a classy guy.*

Reverend Brand began benignly enough by thanking all those in attendance for coming to pay their respects. "It is at times like these that we thank our Father in Heaven for all the days that He grants us to live on His earth and to do His work. And when one is suddenly, brutally, taken from our midst, it is to the Lord that we must turn to for forgiveness and understanding, for the Lord giveth and the Lord taketh away."

Frank tried to pay attention, but his mind drifted off to the disparate congregation. A career in criminal investigation had taught him that often the killer returned to one of two places: the scene of the crime or to the graveside funeral. But since it was January and the frost line went down seven feet or more, there would be no burial. Lester would be stored for the winter in the below-freezing crypt at Webster Hill Cemetery. Then, after mud season, the ground would be free of frost and could be excavated. Only then would he be interred. Not wanting to wait for the thaw, the killer or killers might be sitting here in this overheated church. Frank wondered why

56

the sheriff wasn't there, quietly observing. *Probably too much crime today.* His mind slipped back to the past, how farmers used to cut the pond ice into giant blocks, skid them into the barn and literally keep the body on ice till the spring thaw. *Well, Les will be a neighbor for a while. That crypt is right next door.*

Even the thought of such frigid conditions didn't keep Frank from sweating. The building had now become stifling, because Earl had fired up the wood stove. It was belching heat up through the cellar vents in the old, pine wood flooring, and the aroma of beeswax, sweat, and fetid lily pollen swam in the heavy atmosphere of the little church.

Frank turned toward Sandy. "I see Hal Hines is here, standing in the back, checking out the crowd for strange behavior."

Sandy glanced around. The only likely suspect she could spot was Jake. Would he have killed Lester simply out of hatred for gays, or maybe to please his mother? Was he that much of a momma's boy, and could Mama Jane exercise that kind of power over him? She didn't really know them well enough to guess.

Meanwhile Reverend Brand arrived at his summation, then turned to Reverend Palmer. Sandy bumped Frank's elbow and whispered, "Look! That jerk from the auction debacle is going to sermonize!" She squirmed in the extremely uncomfortable maple pew. Venice's founding fathers hadn't designed them with the human species in mind.

Now one of Betty and Lester's distant Palmer cousins, a preacher and close friend of Jane Ridley, would run the show. *Glad he's from the Palmer side of the family and no kin to me,* Sandy thought as an uncomfortable feeling crept over her.

Reverend Palmer studied the audience, then smiled. His thick reddish hair lay flat against his skull and his heavyset face glowed with a clean just-scrubbed look. He was well dressed and sported a yellow carnation in the buttonhole of his pale blue suit. He looked harmless enough, but his smarmy voice irritated Sandy and Frank.

"...and it is only right and proper that we should gather together on the sad occasion of the death of one of our brethren and pray for his soul. Oh, and pardon me. Let me introduce myself. I'm Reverend Palmer from Alton. And we thank the one true, living God who watches over us for His compassion. And I say 'compassion,' brethren, because there are those among us who knew Lester Moulton and who passed judgment upon the lifestyle in which he chose to live. There are those among us here today who participated in a lifestyle which is abhorrent and despicable in the sight of God." His volume rose. "Our heavenly Father calls upon us to forgive, but never to approve of the licentious. The immoral and corrupted sin must not be condoned. But the question we must ask ourselves today is, 'Would the Lord Jesus Christ have forgiven the sins of this mere mortal, Lester Moulton? Would the Lord have turned the other cheek to the lust and prurient choices of Brother Moulton's life?' For Brother Moulton was taken from this earth without benefit of spiritual guidance and therefore unrepentant, thereby placing his soul in jeopardy. Will our brother burn in the fiery depths of Hell?"

Sandy noticed that a few of the older folks, like Angus and Mable MacTeague, were moving their lips and nodding in agreement.

Preacher Palmer rambled on, "...for the Bible says, in Leviticus XX: 13, 'If a man also lie with mankind, as he lieth with a woman, both of them have committed an *abomination*: they shall surely be put to death; their blood *shall be* upon them. For He is the Lord your God, which brought you out of the land of Egypt, to give you the land of Canaan, and to be your God'."

Sandy noticed out of the corner of her eye that several people were standing up and leaving the church. She wished that she and Frank could leave.

Reverend Brand had begun fidgeting with his buttoned shirt cuffs as his guest carried on. Reverend Palmer could say what needed to be said, while Reverend Brand wouldn't lose any of his Venice congregation. "The Lord Jesus Christ would have forgiven this sinner had our brother Lester confessed his shame and sought salvation. The Lord looks kindly upon the lowliest sinner, even the worst predator that roams the earth, if that sinner will renounce his sins, repent, and take Jesus Christ as his personal savior. As Christians, let us try to understand his transgressions, his disregard for the sanctity of marriage, and his ignorance of God's divine plan. Let us pray for our lost brother, that his soul will not burn for eternity in Hell, but that he will find redemption. We ask this in Jesus' name. Amen. And now, brothers and sisters, let us bow our heads and say 'Praise the Lord'!"

Only a few subdued voices repeated Reverend Palmer's command. Then the church was still as an attic.

Preacher Palmer looked around and stepped away from the podium, as Reverend Brand nervously regained control of the proceedings.

"And now please join me in the Twenty-Third Psalm, followed by one of Lester's favorite hymns, *'Abide with Me.'*"

Sandy felt the heat rise from her neck up to her forehead. She rummaged in her large purse for a tissue and mopped her brow. "Is my face red?" she whispered.

"Sure is, honey, but don't feel bad. My left leg is numb. I must be suffering from funeral-leg. Anyway, it's all bullshit."

Sandy was far from alone in her indignation. Many of the congregation turned and looked at one another with varying degrees of chagrin. The person they felt badly for was Betty. It was too late to feel sorry for Lester, but Sandy also felt mortified for Lester's gay friends. She wanted to rise, stride to the front and say, "Friends of Lester Moulton, we are not gathered here to cast stones, for let those without sin cast the first stone. We're here to pay our respects. RESPECTS, you bigoted, holier-than-thou asshole!"

As usual, Sandy *thought* a good speech but lacked the nerve to deliver it. Frank would say, "It won't do any good. Let it go."

Frank turned to Sandy as if he could read her mind and said,

"Wonder if Betty'll have the last word."

"Well, somebody needs to defend Lester."

As if on cue, Betty rose and walked heavily to the podium. Three elderly ladies from The Grange stared at her in anticipation, looking as if they were going to faint from the heat. Candle flames flickered as Betty passed them by. Sandy stared at the great gobs of brownish-yellow wax that hung on the edges of the candlesticks, then at the huge religious quilt thumbtacked to the wall.

Now the entire congregation focused on Betty Moulton. Here was one smart woman, but she wasn't the son that her father had wanted after the first born, Lester, had turned out to be something of a sissy. Betty was broad shouldered, heavy jawed, with a deep voice. This morning she looked unusually fine in a black pinstriped men's suit and yellow tie. As an act of respect for her brother, she'd obviously been to the hairdresser's, and her shaggy, thick mop of auburn hair had been fashionably cut and styled. Sandy pondered, *Her brother's dead and suddenly Betty's decided to look good? Strange.*

Betty slowly looked around then began in a deep and dignified voice. "We're here today to pay our final respects to my dear brother, Lester Moulton. We're here because many of us loved and respected him. This is not the time to preach morals or cast aspersions. It's a time to thank God for the privilege of knowin' my brother. God has dealt each of us a different hand.

"Who among you hasn't been helped by Lester, hasn't profited from his generosity or wisdom? And what charity hasn't benefitted from his kindness? Some of you aren't even aware of Lester's many good deeds. He read books for the blind, he volunteered at the library, he organized benefits for AIDS research, he carried old folks to church on Sundays and to the polls to vote and to town meetin's. I could go on."

Her voice had broken on the last sentence, and she was forced to pause. Reverend Brand dashed over to her with a Dixie cup filled with water. A few drops dribbled onto the lapel of her black suit.

Betty continued. "Whenever there was a need, Lester was always among the first to respond. He stepped up to the plate and done what needed to be done." Her voice broke again. "My brother was a gentle spirit, with a kind and understandin' soul, and above all, a generous heart. Maybe he dressed flamboyant sometimes, and maybe he had colorful friends from his Columbia days. I see some of them here today. Above all, he was *loyal.* Some folks in town thought his English too fancy, or his manners too fussy, and that ticked 'em off, but he was a friend to all. If anyone's gonna go to Hell, it ain't gonna be Lester!"

With her words lapsing into country parlance, she stared at her Palmer cousin, her eyes brimming with angry tears, and then at Reverend Brand who had allowed the visiting preacher to insult her brother's memory.

Not one soul had gotten up to stop Palmer, although Chuck Shaw said later that he was preparing, in his head, a grand and eloquent defense of his friend Lester. Sandy understood well, as she had done the same thing. And so, with no more eulogists stepping forward, Reverend Brand called for a final hymn, the ubiquitous *Amazing Grace*, and the people present walked by Lester's casket with quiet respect. Then all but Jake Ridley adjourned to the Six Star Grange hall up the road for refreshments.

CHAPTER 10

Curling up on the cushy couch near the woodstove, Sandy read the front page of the Saturday *Midcoast Sentinel*, then turned to Frank. "They're blaming Sam Barrows for not solving the case. How about giving him time? He may not be able to find the killer 'til the spring thaw. It's a cold case."

"Not his fault it's cold, and that's a silly pun." Frank picked up another log and added it to the glowing embers in the wood stove, then read over her shoulder: "'GOVERNOR VOWS BOG KILLER WILL BE CAUGHT.' Humph. He's worried about the gays raising hell. If the state and county gave Barrows the funds he needs, it'd be a different story. This state should get its priorities straight. Hey, does the paper cover the funeral? Maybe it's on the dead folks' page."

"Frank, think of the stats. Our fair hamlet is seven miles long by seven miles wide and contains eight hundred and ten inhabitants, not counting pit bulls, Holsteins, and coy dogs."

"So?" Frank folded the paper over into quarters.

"So, that means we have only sixteen point five inhabitants per square mile."

"Hell! No wonder we have no one to talk to. Now that Lester's gone, there's only Chuck, and maybe Guy Swenson—on a good day."

"Let's face it. Some people are glad Lester's gone. He never fit in, no matter how much good he did. Now his neighbors on the lake can breathe a sigh of relief."

"Hey, here's a reference to that imbecile, Reverend Palmer." Frank pointed to the paper. "He's got an ad on the 'Attend the Church of Your Choice' page. Wanna write him a fan letter?"

Sandy was sitting at the computer writing a letter to her older daughter in LA. "No thanks! But I've been thinking, it's funny—our nearest neighbors—Chuck's a really neat guy, but he's married to his exact opposite."

"In my opinion, Rhu and Chuck are mortal combatants in a failed marriage, each so angry with the other that they won't loosen their grip," Frank sighed. "Nothing we can do about that, and it's none of our business anyway."

61

Page Erwin

"Then there's our neighbor, Slug Willard. He's rotten to his family, his pets. And he makes other people's lives rotten by dealing." Sandy stopped typing.

"So what's your point?" Frank sounded defensive.

"Point: Venice is not a happy place, and sometimes I wonder if *you're* happy here. We haven't made many friends, that's for sure. Venice is drowning in its own xenophobia, and it's never gonna change."

Frank's face reflected sudden grief, as if it were his fault that they'd moved there. "I guess no place is perfect. Maybe Venice *was* a bad choice. I'm sorry."

Sandy read his face. "Get it through your thick head, Frank. I'm happy wherever you are, because I love you, you idiot! But one thing's clear, we're happiest when we mind our own business and leave town affairs alone." Sandy mashed the "print" button, and the machine buzzed like an angry hornet.

"Yeah! We're always gonna be outsiders. Remember what Angus MacTeague told us a while back?"

Angus, like Earl Bagley, was a retired dairy farmer, a man without a herd. His son-in-law, Lennie Beaudoin, Bonnie's ex, was a tall, good-looking farmer who kept a breeder herd pastured and barned on Angus's acreage. About sixty head of Holsteins and a black Angus bull, and Sandy enjoyed watching them. Lennie lived in a mobile home in Amnesty but came up every day to check on the herd. It provided Angus with cows to watch and no milking chores.

Living near the top of Whiskey Hill, Angus owned the finest view in the county, all the way to New Hampshire's White Mountains. Rumor had it that he was threatening to sell part of his property to a land developer. Angus had triple chins and a choleric complexion that suggested high blood pressure. In his youth he'd been a rugged, handsome descendant of the Scots and had a kilt made with the MacTeague tartan to prove it. It wouldn't fit him now, of course.

Back in the Eighties, Angus had invested in the latest carousel automatic milking setup, thinking that someday sons would take over the dairy, but they didn't share his love of milking big, bony Holsteins, or the heavy, sweet aroma of wet hay and manure. He'd sold some equipment, but the processing room, all those shiny milk tanks and sinks, remained. Now the herd was limited to his son-in-law's replacement heifers—no milk production.

"Why didn't Angus keep a few cows?" Sandy asked, hitting the 'print' key.

"Milk prices in Maine always did get his dander up, so I guess it was all or nothing." Frank shook his head.

"Do you know that he talks to the barn cats? I overheard him one day from the porch. He was sort of cooing to them, saying, 'Do you miss the big girls, kitties?'"

On their walks up Whiskey Hill, Sandy and Frank often stopped in

62

at the MacTeague's. Mabel seemed to enjoy their visits, and Angus liked having a sparring partner, although lately he'd been quick to take offense.

"It's like waiting for a bomb to drop. If it weren't for Mabel, I wouldn't visit at all," Sandy commented.

Only two weeks before, Frank had chided Angus about selling out to any hot looking real estate gal who might show up. Angus had puffed up, but Sandy managed to defuse the situation by saying that everyone knew Angus wouldn't do such a thing. Instead of accepting the compliment, Angus faced Sandy with flashing anger and barked, "You're from New Hampshire, what do you care? You people always sell out."

Frank tried to figure out the *non sequitur*. Taken aback by the angry tone in Angus's voice, Sandy, who factored in rudeness as local custom, replied, "What's New Hampshire got to do with anything? Besides, my grandmother was born in North Berwick, *Maine!* Or don't you consider the Berwicks to be in Maine?"

"Well, that don't count!" Angus mumbled and walked off to the milk room saying he was going to feed the barn cats. Mabel was upset and tried to distract them by offering them some cookies to take home. They'd left without the cookies.

"Come to think of it, we haven't been back since," Frank remarked.

Frank tried to avoid trouble with the neighbors. He'd seen enough ugly behavior as an Air Force OSI agent and just wanted to be left alone with Sandy, his retirement check and his pottery studio. "Well, Angus can't help it that he doesn't know any better. He doesn't get along with anybody. Terminal xenophobia."

"No, it's deeper than that," Sandy said.

"What's eating him about our neighboring state?"

"Mabel let it slip one day. Seems Angus flunked Freshman Algebra—"

"Let me guess. The prof was from New Hampshire?"

"Precisely. The prof had come up here from UNH." Sandy had attended the University of New Hampshire. "See how it all fits?"

"Guess we'd better avoid the subject of education altogether from now on so he won't go nutty. When it comes to schools and teachers, he's off his rocker. Surprised he even lets us into his kitchen."

"Furthermore," Sandy switched to a serious tone," that's precisely why he hates Chuck's wife, because Rhu's still teaching. Angus thinks senior teachers should quit, so the school board can hire teachers right out of college, two for the price of one."

Frank walked over to the small-paned front windows and gazed out at the hills that separated them from Galway and the sea. Today the trees were lightly coated with snow and the sky was silvery with herringbone patterns of pink clouds against a light blue wash. Silvery birches punctuated the green, dusted with white. Myrick Hill Road snaked up toward the summit, probably the second best view in the county.

Several families lived up there including the Hines' attorney Stu

Stammer and the Elorantos. Beyond them were the Wells, the news photographer, his Greek wife Olympia and their two beautiful daughters.

"You know what? We oughta' don our winter gear and trudge up to the MacTeague's. The exercise'll do us good, kid, and I need to learn what Angus has to say about Lester's murder."

Sandy got up from the computer and put her hands on his shoulders. "If I recall, *you're* the one who vowed to stay out of town affairs."

"Town affairs, yes, I'm not getting wrapped around the axle about them. But Lester's murder—that's another story. He's your cousin, for one thing, and you're right: people don't give a damn about his getting shot and dumped into the bog to feed the fish." Frank headed for the coat rack. "Get your duds on, babe. We're goin' for a hike."

The temperature had been dropping since the wee hours of the morning, and a draft whistled around the old front windows. Snow draped the trees, but it was tired snow, with brittle ice edges, and when the wind gusted, chunks fell off and clattered onto the steel roof. The driveway was rutted with frozen brown mud and black ice.

As they walked up the hill into a North wind, they checked animal tracks. Sandy discovered a fawn's bloody leg that a coyote had dragged through the woods. "Beneath all this fantastic beauty, what a violent place the Maine woods are," Frank observed.

Just as they climbed to where the dirt road swung off to the east, Sandy spied a black plastic bag on the lower side of the road. "Damn! Some bastard's dropped off another bag of innards and legs. Jacked deer! Think it's part of the fawn?"

"Naw!" Frank grunted, pushing it with his boot. "An adult carcass by the weight of it. When we get back home, I'll call Bud Varney. He won't be able to tell anything, but at least he'll take it away. The rest of it's probably in Slug's freezer."

This kind of scene made Sandy ripping mad, but she wouldn't bring it up at the MacTeagues'. She had nothing against hunting in season, but both she and Frank were outraged. Warden Varney would try to track down the culprit, but there was usually too little evidence to go by and never a witness.

Frank changed the subject. "Hey, I thought of another reason to talk with Angus. We're running short of wood. Don't have enough to last through spring."

"Prob'ly' not." Sandy listened to what she'd just said. Was she getting stingy with words? *God, I'm starting to talk just like an old Mainer. Well, as long as I don't start sounding like Angus.*

"We could order another cord from him. His son Sonnie's been cutting up logs for months, and look at that big pile of maple and birch curing in the lower pasture."

They arrived at the slippery MacTeague driveway. Hilly pastures, white with snow and divided by the dark stitching of stone walls, led up toward the Rockwell place, a long-since deserted farmstead. The crest of the hill was punctuated by tall spruces. Closer to the farm were the leavings of agricultural life: several dead tractors, a rusty cultivator, three rolls of reddish barbed wire in coils like giant hair curlers, skeletons of motorcycles and snow blowers half buried in snow, and beyond all this, the calf shed. Come spring, there'd be three or four milk-fed calves penned up, dumb little beasts awaiting their destiny as *osso bucco* and veal medallions in a Boston restaurant. Sandy said it gave her the shivers, but Frank just shrugged, saying, "That's life and death in Vacationland."

Before they could knock, Mabel opened the red wooden door, delighted to see them. She turned back to the kitchen from the little entry way. "Angus, look who's here!" She was a pudgy woman with thinning hair, tortoise shell glasses, and a once-pretty face. Her teeth were bad because Angus refused to pay a dentist. "Teeth ain't necessary," he'd mumbled. Mabel was dressed in her usual farmer's wife uniform: polyester slacks, long-sleeved flannel shirt, white socks and comfortable old leather shoes.

Sandy and Frank sat at the sticky chrome and red plastic table in the heavy atmosphere of wood smoke and creosote backing up from the wood stove. Angus habitually over-choked the damper in the stove pipe to make the fire last longer.

Even though most of the MacTeague family had moved away, the leaves of the table were always in place, making it almost eight feet long. On it were hen-shaped salt and peppers, a plastic basket of paper napkins, and a week's worth of newspapers.

"Well, how's the quiltin' goin'?" Mabel asked. It was one thing they had in common, and it was a safe, no-risk subject.

"I've been working on one in reds, tans, and browns, just a patchwork design. Drop by and see it, Mabel."

"The Schwann's man come by just yeste'day. Had a nice visit. You two want some ice cream?" Mabel asked.

"Thanks, Mabel, but no, we're both watching our waistlines." Frank wondered how many Maine farm women bought food they didn't really need from those men who drove the big yellow box trucks.

They chitchatted for a while about the weather. Mabel heated water in the microwave and made instant coffee. Angus agreed to sell them a cord of wood at ninety-dollars, a fair price. Although he didn't seem too cheerful, the sale and the check lifted his spirits some.

"Well," Angus spoke up. "What's up with our local murder case?"

"It's hard to solve a crime that happened over six weeks ago and has damned few clues," Frank commented. "It gives new meaning to 'cold case'."

Angus nodded, then excused himself. He grabbed his coffee cup and ducked into the dairy processing room. All was idle out there except for Angus's passel of black and white barn cats. Frank had an inkling that

Angus kept his hard liquor out there. Mabel's face took on a dark look, and they all fell silent as they sipped their coffee and nibbled on cookies until Angus returned. He still held his coffee cup in a tight grip.

"Well, I damned sure wish that high falutin' sheriff'd get to the bottom of it. Makes you wonder who among us is capable of killin' someone," Angus blustered. He flopped down heavily, "Worthless sheriff! And that Lester—he's the one got my son int'rested in actin'?"

Mabel stirred her coffee nervously, looking over at Sandy.

Frank said, "If Sam Barrows wants to find his killer, he's got lots of suspects to check out." He wondered how far to push the subject.

The wood stove was now sloughing off waves of warmth, and Sandy felt uncomfortably hot. It reminded her of the funeral. She'd taken off her outer gear, and now she wished she could peel off another layer. She dragged her chair farther away from the heat, making a screeching sound on the old gray and white linoleum.

"Give Sam Barrows a break. He's got a lot of miles to cover, and there's been a rash of crimes in Galway ever since Atlantis National Bank money came to town. They're buying up land right-and-left, including coastline." Frank's tone was more strident than he'd intended. He knew it was useless to try to defend law enforcement, but did it anyway.

Angus wasn't through venting, so he continued, raising his volume. "Lonnie was home for Thanksgivin' and we was havin' a nice visit. In fact, all our kids was home 'ceptin' for Connie."

"You'd have liked to meet her," Sandy teased Frank. "She was the beauty queen runner-up for Miss Maine, right, Mabel?"

"Ayuh! Got herself a career singin' in a New York night club, so she don't get a chance to come home much anymore. Her picture's right on the top of the 'frigerator there."

Sandy thought to herself, *I know why Connie doesn't come home. She can't stand her old man.*

Frank rose to look out Angus's back kitchen window. He saw hundreds of rolling acres of woods. Up the road and to the left, toward the bog, was Mooseman's hut. Frank had never had a conversation with the man folks called crazy, but he'd seen him waving his arms about and yelling into the air. He was wild and unwashed. How could anyone survive in a hut that small with no running water? Mooseman was strange to be sure. Frank wanted to change the subject, but maybe Mooseman wasn't the topic to choose.

"Sure is beautiful up toward those pastures and along the woods. Seen many deer lately?" Wild game was a safe subject. Angus knew a great deal about the Maine wilds.

"Ayuh! A few come nosin' under them old apple trees. Most of 'em are yarded up now, a' course, up under the branches in the spruce grove." Angus sounded calmer.

Frank sat back down after declining another cup of coffee.

Angus went out to the barn to bring in an armload of wood. While he was gone, Mabel walked over to Sandy and whispered that Angus and Lonnie had gotten into a big row. "Please, folks, don't bring it up again," she whispered.

Suddenly Angus returned, all flushed and puffy. "If you ask me, the U.S. Navy's sinkin'. You know, my proudest years was spent on a destroyer in the Pacific durin' World War Two. Back then the Navy stood for somethin'!"

Frank smiled. "Yeah, I know. You're always in a good mood when you return from the ship's reunion!"

Sandy wondered why Mabel had brought up the day-after-Thanksgiving argument.

"Well, ain't hardly nobody left ta go ta reunions. They're all a'dyin'," Angus snorted. "Lonnie should never've enlisted. He was a good boy and plenty smart in high school, 'cept for wantin' to be an actor." Angus shifted in his chair.

Sandy took over. "Oh, I remember when we first arrived Frank asked if I wanted to get back into amateur theater. Loonport had a little theater group back then headed by Lester and his partner. Can't recall his name, but he died of AIDS. That's when the group disbanded."

"AIDS is ruinin' this country." Angus was out of his chair, standing, hulk-like, by the stove. He loomed, threatening with his large, arthritic hand gripping an eighteen-inch-long round of maple that he'd plucked from the woodbox.

Sandy said, "Chuck told us Lonnie starred in lots of Mountain Top High School productions and was *really* good."

Angus turned away to stuff the maple round into the stove. The door of the firebox clanged shut. Angus faced Sandy, but said nothing.

Feeling uneasy, Sandy stood up, donned her winter apparel, and smiled. "Gee, honey, it's getting' late. We've gotta go to the post office. Didn't realize how late it was getting. Thanks for the goodies, Mabel."

Frank got up and added, "Angus, you can dump that wood by the upper side of the house where I've cleared a space. Anytime in the next couple of weeks would be fine."

Angus nodded; Mabel showed them out.

On the walk home, Frank went over the conversation. "So, what the hell was Angus on such a tear about? And Mabel was trying to censor us. So, big deal, Lonnie joined the Navy. Seems logical to me."

"It bugs me that Angus is so touchy about the Navy."

"Lonnie most likely joined up because his father served proudly during the war. Wanted to follow in his footsteps." Frank was now half-shouting to be heard above the gusting wind and crunching of boots on snow. The temperature was still dropping, freezing his nose and sinuses, and he rearranged his scarf to cover his numb chin. "Lonnie's about thirty, good-looking and smart enough to know that his gorgeous older sister pissed off her dad by going to New York. Now Angus has lost two kids to the outside world. Still, Lonnie's joining the Navy should have pleased Angus." Frank went on, "I don't know why we keep trying to make sense of Angus anyway, the way he lurches from one thought into the next."

Now, just in sight of their house, they stopped to watch some chickadees that had been following them. "Chick-chick-chick," Frank called as they hopped around the bare branches. Sandy pointed at the fawn's rib cage. They hadn't noticed it before. A dozen chickadees perched on the ribs, pecking away at pink fatty tissue stuck to the bone. "Birds gotta eat."

Frank stomped his feet as they entered the front door. Once inside, he hung up his gear and fed maple rounds into the stove.

She shrugged, kicking off her boots. "Good to be home where it's peaceful."

"I'm curious about the MacTeague clan," Frank ruminated. "The whole family, minus Connie the torch singer, was home for Thanksgiving: the oldest, Bonnie, and her two kids, maybe the son-in-law, Lennie, Donnie with his three, Sonnie, the lumberman, and slow Johnnie."

Sandy became thoughtful. "What a shame Johnnie hit that pine tree with his head in the motorcycle accident over to Pride's Corner. He'll never be right. You know, Angus has a lot to deal with."

"Don't be too upset about it, Sandy. I talked with Mabel. She intimated that Johnnie used to have a wicked bad temper before the accident. Then, whammo, into that pine tree. He comes out of the coma a month later meek as a lamb. Been kind and helpful ever since."

Sandy took out her quilting. "I suppose that's some sort of silver lining."

Frank stood up and stretched. "Well, it's almost lunchtime. I'm going down to the store. Need anything?" He piled on jacket, scarf, hat and mittens.

As he headed down Route Ten, Frank looked in the rearview mirror and noticed a sheriff's cruiser turning onto Whiskey Hill Road.

A few minutes after Frank left, the phone rang, but when Sandy answered, no one was there. She wished Venice had Caller ID. Carefully she logged time and date on her computer. They almost always called when Frank was out. *Is it Rhu or Slug, or maybe even Nin for some perverse reason?*

She sat down on the couch and let her mind wander. *Poor Mabel. I should visit her more often. She's got a lot bottled up.*

Frank had warned her earlier, "You can feel sorry for Mabel, but don't get all wrapped around the axle, sweet thing."

When Frank returned he brought her a treat, Humpty Dumpty potato chips fresh from the plant in Waterville.

"You know what I like, Frank?" Sandy popped the bag open. "The total lack of quality control. These are really salty. Every new bag is a surprise."

"Hey, did you see the sheriff's car go by while I was gone?"

"No. Missed it. Probably the Gossams again." Sandy didn't bother to tell him about the hang-up. "So how's the list coming? Are we putting Angus and Lonnie down as suspects?"

"I'm not sure. Wish I could see Sam Barrow's list. Meanwhile, it's mid-day, the sun is practically invisible, and it sure feels like more snow. Wind's blowin' like fury. Hey, what's for lunch? I'm starving."

"Well, if you'll put on your jacket, cap and mittens back on and trudge out to the hen house and get us some eggs from our biddies, then I'll make your favorite, salmon loaf. And be sure their light is on. It's not gonna warm up today at all."

"Yeah," Frank answered on his way out the door, "it's gonna be even colder than the Moulton case." He closed the door and stepped out into a frigid blast of wind.

CHAPTER 11

"Hey, Hal, wanna go on an interview with me? I'll be in your neck of the woods." It was late Saturday morning. The next day would mark one week since Lester's body had been fished out of Hiram Bog, and Sam had no solid leads.

"Venice, you mean? Hell, yes! Wanna come over to my place for lunch? Laura's a great cook. When we headin' over there and who we doin'?"

"Goin' right now to interview Mr. Angus MacTeague and wife. Hope you don't mind the smell of cow paddies."

"And what do you want to do about lunch, my place?"

"If your wife doesn't mind. Thought she was working full-time over at the insurance office in Amnesty."

"Naw! Quit that when they kicked Warren, my youngest, out of day care. She decided these are crucial years and opted to stay home with him 'til the first grade."

"Well let's do it, then we'll see how the time fits. You can call Laura, but I don't want to put her out. Make sure the cruiser's got a full tank, and I'll get us a thermos of coffee."

"Ten-four."

By eleven-fifteen they were turning onto Whiskey Hill Road. "Damned nice scenery along here. You ever hunt in these woods, Hal?"

"Naw! My side of Venice has all the deer you could ask for, and an occasional moose or bear. I never luck out on the moose lottery though. Did you know that a lot of this land was covered with sheep a century ago?"

"Don't you mean cows?"

"Nope, sheep! Would I kid my boss?"

Sam preferred to let that question slide.

Hal continued, "That's the Zucchetti place back on the right."

"Never met 'em."

"Retired Air Force. Sometimes I think Venice is becomin' a retirement village."

"Not likely," Sam commented. "What a view!"

"See all the way to the White Mountains. There's Mount Katahdin off to the north. Back in the early days all these woods were cleared: sheep pastures, apple trees, bean and potato fields. More sheep than people back then, but the bottom dropped outa' the wool market after the Great Depression. Now the sheep are gone, but the trees are back."

"Okay, Mr. Expert. Tell me why this road is called 'Whiskey Hill'?"

"Can do, boss. Venice doesn't have many secrets I don't know about..."

Yeah, and you tell everyone within earshot, Sam thought.

"The name comes from a still that was up in the woods beyond the Zucchetti place. Prob'ly some rusty scraps 'n tank parts layin' around. Old timers say that during Prohibition this road was busier'n a cat coverin' shit." Hal smirked. "Angus wanted to change the name to MacTeague Road in the worst way, brought it up at Town Meetin' a couple years back, but the town turned the motion down. "Listen, Sam, you don't really think Angus is a viable suspect?"

"Hell, I'm looking at anyone who had an axe to grind with the victim. Regardless of how unlikely it seems that an old half-crippled farmer would kill, I gotta' cover the bases. *Capisce?*"

"Well old Angus might be a stubborn prick, but he doesn't have the stones to kill anybody. Besides, last time I saw the old fart at the general store, he was walkin' with a cane. He's got a lot of things wrong with him, includin' wicked bad arthritis."

Sam shook his head. "So I've heard, but I had one case where a paraplegic killed a guy by strangling him."

"So how you want to play it? Good cop, bad cop?"

"Good cop, quiet deputy, unless I give you a signal," he grinned.

"What signal is that, boss, and what do I do if I see the signal?"

"Tell you what, Hal. If you see me twist my ear, you start askin' some hard questions. Got it?"

"Right!" Hal puffed up with pride. He checked his collar and tie in the side view mirror, admiring his light tan.

"Can I ask you a personal question, Hal?"

"Hell yes! Fire away." He looked and acted more youthful than his thirty-five years.

"What I'm gettin' at is that it's the dead of winter and you got yourself a helluva tan. You been visiting that tanning salon over by the college?"

"C'mon, boss. I ski, snowboard, even ice skate. Outdoors every chance I get. Four kids can drive you outside. Three boys'n a girl. Say, you and Darla plannin' a family?"

"Who knows? We're just playing it by ear."

"You'll never make a baby that way." Suddenly Hal thought he might have overstepped his boundaries. In a softer tone he added, "Just kiddin', boss."

Sam smiled to reassure him as they pulled into the icy MacTeague driveway. "Whew! Mighty ripe manure in these parts. Let's get this over with."

Mabel met them at the side-porch door, rearranging her apron. Barb had let her know they were on their way, and Angus was reigning at the kitchen table. After asking if they wanted coffee, she headed for the microwave with two mugs of water. She and Angus were already drinking theirs. A pot of what smelled like venison stew bubbled on the stove.

Angus motioned for them to sit. As Mabel plunked down the two mugs, she tried to excuse herself, but Angus countermanded her. "Stay right here, dearie. Ain't nothin' but a coupla' nosey cops." He gave a twisted little smile and rolled his eyes.

"Actually I'd prefer to talk with both of you together. Won't take long. I know it's nearly lunch time. Sure smells good."

"Well, we're here, ain't we?" Angus wheezed a bit and reached for some saltine crackers that were ingloriously stacked on a paper plate.

"As you know, we're investigating a homicide, so we're interviewing everyone who might've had contact with the victim. How well did you know Lester, Mrs. MacTeague?"

"Oh, call me Mabel."

"Sorry...Mabel. And thanks for the coffee."

"Yeah, thanks. I needed another cup." Hal repositioned himself in the hard chrome and plastic chair.

"Forgive my bad manners. You do know Hal, right?"

"Oh yeah, we know him. He votes against damn near everything I bring up at Town Meetin'. Ain't that right, Hal?" Angus was smiling, but his eyes narrowed. "You still fixin' up that old place of yours, Hal? Sinkin' good money after bad? Never gonna get your money back on that place, and you know, don'tcha, the more you fix it up, the higher your taxes gonna go."

"Mabel? About Lester..." Sam was trying to get the conversation back on track, and Hal wasn't helping.

Hal looked irritated and wouldn't let it go. "I'm curious, Angus. What makes you think I wanna sell?"

"Well, everybody sells, push come to shove." Angus was fiddling with little sugar packets. One tore open and sugar ran down the crack where the table leaves joined.

"Can we get back to the question at hand, Mabel?" Sam said pleasantly.

Mabel lolled her head for a moment. "Well, I thought Lester was a very nice man. Never did a bit o' harm. Too bad you just missed meetin' his cousin."

"Really, who?" Sam asked, playing dumb.

"Sandy Zucchetti," Angus grumbled, tapping the salt shaker on the tabletop.

Sam took out his notebook, shielding what he was jotting down. "So, Angus, what about you?"

"Lester Moulton, humph. Whoever done him in, well—maybe they did the town a favor." Angus unwrinkled his lips into a puckerish smile.

"Angus, what a thing to say! Sheriff, he don't mean it."

"Hell I don't! Ain't up to you to explain what I mean. I don't need no interputter. Get me another cup of coffee." He picked up a pink packet of sweetener and turned to Hal and said, "I gotta' use this goddamned saccharine 'stead of sugar. Damned diet!"

"When was the last time you saw Lester, Angus?"

"Damned if I know. Don't keep no diary." He grunted and then looked at Sam, who had a decidedly stern look on his face. "Mabel, we seen Lester at the Auction when we was lookin' for a big platter for Thanksgivin', didn't we?"

Mabel assumed a thoughtful expression. "May-be."

Sam rubbed his ear, waiting to see if Hal would pick up on the signal.

Suddenly Hal shot a question at Angus that was both pertinent and valid. "Sir, word is that your son Lonnie was home on leave from the Navy over Thanksgiving. That you two had an altercation. He reportedly took your red pickup truck without authorization, drove it to Waterville, and left it at the bus depot before leaving for Norfolk, Virginia. Is that true?"

"Lonnie and me had a private conversation, then I lent him my truck. So what?" Angus sipped the instant coffee and curled his lips. "My younger son Johnnie and me went over and picked it up the next day."

"You allowed your truck to sit overnight in a bus depot in Waterville?" Hal leaned toward Angus. "Gimme a break."

"I don't give a flyin' fig what you believe. That's what happened." He turned to Mabel with glassy eyes. "Ain't that right, Mabel?"

"Ayuh! Sure thing, Hal, Sheriff." She stared out the window at the top of the woods line.

There was a lull, and Sam sensed that nothing more of value might be gained by staying longer. Besides, Angus didn't look well. His color was off. However, Hal was warming to the task. *Better not accidentally scratch my ear again.*

Sam stood up and grabbed his hat. "Anything else you wanna ask, Hal?"

"One more question. Angus, you got a thirty-thirty?"

"Does a cow eat hay? 'Course I got me a thirty-thirty, three or four of 'em. Got a thirty-aught-six and a twenty-two Hornet an' a Savage, got axes an' knives an' plenty more handguns. Why? You workin' fer the Fed'ral Guv'm'nt all of a sudden?" Angus let go of a big, phlegmy laugh.

Sam frowned. "Would you be willing to submit your weapon to a ballistics test?"

"Guess so. Take yer pick. Think I let my son-in-law borrow one of 'em to kill coydogs that's been jumpin' his newborn calves."

The room fell silent except for a hiss and a snap from a log in the wood-burner at the end of the stove.

"I think that'll be all for now. Thanks, Mabel, for your hospitality." Sam put away his notebook, but Hal was still writing. Finally, Sam opened

73

the door, forcing Hal to disengage.

The wind was howling as they climbed into the cruiser. Inside the car, the frigid air made their breath visible. Sam noticed that it was sticking to the windshield in fern-leaf patterns. Hal turned eagerly to Sam. "How'd you think it went, boss?"

"You did fine, but we didn't pick up a single lead. That's just a cranky, pissed-off old man. Did he attend the funeral?"

"Sure enough. I watched him—nothin' unusual. Wanna head up to my place now, boss?"

"Yeah, right now lunch sounds good."

After lunch, on the drive back to Galway, Sam said, "You've got a nice family there, Hal. Laura seems like a fine woman. Good looking house, too." *Wonder where he gets the money to do all that.*

Hal beamed with satisfaction.

"You handled Angus real well."

Sam turned down the blower on the defroster. "Who looks good for the Moulton murder so far?"

"Well, I went over your case notes in the computer, interviews, autopsy and so-on. If you want my opinion, I wouldn't go much further than Slug Willard."

As they topped the hill south of Deering, a horizontal flurry of snow nearly put them in a white-out condition. Sam slowed the cruiser to thirty-five. "What about one of the Gossams?"

Hal sucked a tooth and looked out the window at the blowing snow. "They're a wild bunch, but after all these years, why start killin' people now? What would be the motive?"

Sam tapped a gloved finger on the steering wheel. "There's always a first time. What about Jake? He's as slippery a snake as I've ever met. Tell me about him. You must've gone to school about the same time."

"Mountain Top Class of Eighty-eight. His old man died when Jake was a junior. Had a younger sister that died of leukemia a few years before. After that, his mother Jane went the born-again route while Jake went sort of ape-shit. He could get all the booze he needed out of the store for wild parties in the woods down by the lake. Sometimes by the bog, on the west end. The whole gang, boys and girls, would go down there, build a bonfire, then fade off into the bushes to make out."

"Sowing wild oats," Sam remarked, playing devil's advocate.

"Actually, got more serious than that. Story goes that one night Jake got pretty crazy with about a dozen of 'em down there all drunk and stoned. They went skinny-dippin', and Jake dared Minnie Hopkins to dive down into one of the old cellar holes underwater there where Old Venice got sunk. She didn't come up."

"What do you mean, Venice got sunk?"

"Town fathers dammed up the west end of Hiram Bog. Plenty of

74

pissed-off people had to relocate."

"So, what happened with the Hopkins girl?"

"Divers went down and found her next mornin' trapped inside what used to be an old brick furnace. Got herself stuck in there, panicked and drowned. Pretty gruesome."

Sam glanced over at Hal. His face was blanched white and he was staring out into the blowing snow. "How'd you remember all those details?" Sam asked.

"Becuz I was there that night—" Hal gave a little shudder. "Hey, boss, ya' mind turnin' up the heat? It's gettin' cold over here on the passenger side."

"Well, I can see how all that death and dying could change a young fella." The two men fell silent. Pellets of snow swirled and slapped against the windshield as the wipers squeaked back and forth. They cleared the final hill and dropped down into the city limits of Galway.

"That bog's a damned spooky place," Hal half whispered.

"Let's get a handle on this case. The personal history about Jake presents an interesting scenario. Now: motive, means, and opportunity. He's known as more or less of a mama's boy, right?"

"Sort of..."

"And Mama hates gays. Calls 'em 'sodomites' and 'unnatural perverts', that sort thing. Jake's alibi for Thanksgiving and the day after isn't worth the powder to blow it to hell. All he's got is Mama Jane and Susan Johnson covering his ass, and neither one of 'em's reliable. Mama's a religious control freak and Susan's scared shitless of him."

"Could be." Hal shrugged.

A good DA could break either one of 'em. No question about the means. He's got a wall covered with guns and knives. So, Hal, where's the weakness in the case I just made?"

"Well, boss, when I build a three-legged stool, I try to make each leg the same length, so's you're sittin' level. Right now, you're slidin' off to one side because the motive leg is too short, in my opinion. According to my detective study manual, it helps to find out the precipitating cause of the crime."

"Right. If we knew that, we could nail the culprit. So, you're always hangin' around inside the General Store, but now I think you oughta' spend some time outside."

Hal's blue eyes lit up. "Like a stake-out?"

"Exactly. I'd like you to surveil the back of the store, especially those trailers. And behind the house, too. If we can catch him dealing in contraband or underage alcohol sales, maybe we can get a search warrant."

"Okay, but what about my regular shift? Or do I put in for overtime? And what car do I use?"

Sam shook his head. "No car. Put on your bunny fur-lined hat and long johns and sneak up on the place through the woods on the backside. For three nights, starting tomorrow night. Just skip your afternoon shift. If

75

you haven't spotted anything after three nights, we'll go to Plan B. Take along a large thermos of coffee with you so you can stay awake."

"Plan B? What's that?"

"I'll let you know when I know," Sam said as they pulled into the parking slot behind the sheriff's office.

CHAPTER 12

It was a typical cold, snowy Maine day, with the trees half-hidden by a new glazing of sticky snow under a brilliant blue sky. After letting the chickens out, Frank walked up the woods path to a clearing where he'd cut back the brush and saplings to allow the woodcocks to conduct the nocturnal diving and dancing necessary for creating more woodcocks. He saw snowy lumps. *Ah ha! The grouse have been diving into the snow to hide from the coyotes.* The predators were handsome critters, with wolf-like coats and heavy tails like German shepherds, but they did a number on farm animals.

Frank always checked on hen fencing for loose sections or freshly dug spots. He and Sandy liked their flock of Columbian Wyandottes almost as much as they liked their five geese. They prided themselves on not wasting food by giving them vegetable scraps.

Frank came in, bringing the cold with him.

"Everything okay, hon? You were gone a long time."

"Yup! I walked way up the path, saw grouse tracks, but I spotted coy sign. I can't tell coy from coyote."

"Well, I'd rather have coy sign than fox."

"New subject. You're keeping track of the suspect list? While I was out, I was thinking about it. Four names so far—Betty, Jane, Jake, and Slug. Think we should add Angus and Lonnie?"

"Absolutely!"

Frank glanced around the kitchen. "Hey, breakfast's almost ready. I wonder if the sheriff's talked with the Gossams yet."

"I heard at the store that Anthony's got an air tight alibi; he was in jail. That leaves Gus and Booth. Maybe we should add them both. If Sam Barrows comes up to see them, he might drop by here. Probably will since I'm related to the victim."

"He hasn't shown up to question Slug either, unless he interviewed him at a logging site, stealing trees. I wonder why he hasn't. Every day the clues fade and the case gets colder. He's undermanned, underpaid, and crime's on the rise. I'd like to help him if I could." Frank occasionally got bored with retirement. "He'll have trouble getting anything out of Slug. You know how Willard flaunts the law, and his freezer's full of illegal venison."

"Yeah, I think he's dangerous. Slug might come out firing."

"Hey, Bertha Willard was left the family cottage when her dad died. I wonder if Sam knows how close it is to Lester's. Maybe Bertha and Slug can see Lester's place from there."

"That's why summers are so pleasant around here," Sandy added. "No Slug. Did Lester have trouble with Slug, I wonder, or maybe buy weed from him?"

"Whoa! Let's eat breakfast first! And, by the way, that's a stretch. I know Slug hates gays, but—"

"How would Lester know about Slug's dealing?" Sandy interrupted.

"He *wouldn't,* unless *you* told Lester about it. You're the only common denominator that I know of. You can get into *real trouble* telling tales on that guy." Frank looked concerned. "By the way, who more than Slug would know every time I go out? Maybe he's tied to the mysterious phone hang-ups you've been getting."

"There's Rhu. She can see us right out her kitchen window."

Frank gently took Sandy by the arms. "Listen, don't *ever* let yourself be seen with binoculars looking out the front window. I *mean* it! Slug's a lowlife. We don't know what he's capable of, but any man who shoots his dog because it barks, well, *res ipse loquitur.* He was whining down to the store the other day about someone stealing his skidder chains. I heard him say, 'That sorry-ass thief'll be sorry when I get a hold of him. I'll ram those chains up his...'" Frank let go of her.

"Okay, I'll be careful, Frank." She sat on the couch. "But help me with the big picture of Thoreau County crime. I've been racking my brain to remember any violent crimes here in Venice, other than deer-jacking."

"Speaking of deer-jackings, I doubt Slug's a likely suspect—much as I despise the guy. He lacks motive and opportunity, so that leaves only means. Hey! I just remembered a really brutal crime right after we got here. It concerned Gus Gossam's son, Booth." Sandy's face looked blank. "He had a young girlfriend from Amnesty. They'd had a wicked fight. Maybe they got hold of some bad drugs. Anyway, one morning at the post office, your cousin Betty and I got to talking about it."

"Why haven't I heard this one?" Sandy asked.

"I never told you because I knew it would upset you," he said with his best expression of little boy innocence.

Sandy frowned. "I want to know everything. You forget that I typed up Rick's reports about crimes that would shock even you." Rick was Sandy's late husband, a former chief of police in Florida.

"Well, believe me, I dealt with some violent scenes when I was working OSI that I've never shared with you. Anyway, this personification-of-evil story was part of Betty Moulton's continuing series of 'Godawful Happenings around Venice'."

"So, what did she tell you?"

"Seems like Booth Gossam decides that Amnesty Girl, a Mexican migrant worker, had been disobedient. So he beat her up, duct-taped her mouth and hands, and dumped her out, buck-naked, over in Lester's yard. Lester and Clair saw her out there and called it in. There's a motive for you: kill the witness."

"Wow. That's horrific!"

"Yeah! It's about as low as anyone can get." Frank shrugged. "Sorry. Trying to spare you some grief."

"Spare me the spare-mes. It's not OSI classified."

"Well, if you want to know all this, *you* go get the mail from now on. Here's the kicker. Apparently she was so afraid of the Gossam Clan that she refused to press charges. It drove old Sheriff Belcher nuts. It was probably cases like that that led to his heart attack. All they could do was surveillance, but they got squat. It's only a matter of time before one of the Gossams gets nailed for a major crime. I wonder if Sam knows about the Mexican girl."

"Maybe Hal Hines filled him in, or he read it in the files. Lester's murder might put away some Gossams," Sandy said hopefully.

"I doubt it. That bunch always covers for one another. The only Gossam worth his salt is Andy. Hard to believe he's a Gossam. Say, you know who he's got a crush on?"

"No, who?"

All three cats were now sitting with Sandy on the couch, waiting for the answer. "That Finnish girl at the deli counter. She sure is pretty. Anyway, let's get back to the unsavory reality of Gossams and Willards. What if the Gossams are feuding with the Willards? Hatfields and McCoys..."

"Actually, I don't think they have anything to do with one another. I think it's a territory thing. Gossams have squatted around Hiram Bog for over a hundred years, and some of them even lived in the old town before it was flooded, but Willards have only been around the new Venice town center for a century."

"Well, I don't know what the solution is, but they're rotten apples for the most part."

"Hey, you know what?" Sandy suggested. "You should have coffee with Bud Varney and pick his brain."

"Sure," Frank agreed. "That shouldn't take long."

CHAPTER 13

The rolling hills of Venice are reminiscent of Wisconsin, with their pastures separated by vast stands of pine, spruce, cedar, birch and hardwoods broken occasionally by barn roofs. These aren't the true and straight barns of the new agricultural industry to the south, but barns that lean and bend from the frost heaves of a hundred or more winters. White plumes of smoke rise from the Skowhegan paper mill on the northwest horizon. To the north, far past the vanishing point of Whiskey Hill Road, rests the two-breasted loaf of rock called Katahdin, Maine's highest mountain. Between her bare breasts stretches a ridge of rock called Knife's Edge, where recently a Boy Scout was struck and killed by lightning.

On extremely clear days, Sandy loved to trudge up the hill and gaze at *her* beautiful Mount Washington, over in New Hampshire, nearly two hundred miles away. Whiskey Hill dominated Venice, but Myrick Hill, to the south, toward Galway and the sea, came in a close second. At the bottom of the hill, where Myrick Hill Road intersected Route Ten, lived the Forresters, friends of the Zuccchettis. Nin and Ned's place sat diagonally across Myrick Hill Road from Slug Willard's house. Because so much fill had been brought in to build up Route Ten, the Forrester house sat down in a depression on the south side of the highway. Frank always referred to it as "the house in the hole."

The Willard home on the opposite corner was in a state of gradual decay, but the Forrester place had been spruced up. Venice natives took a measure of pride in the young couple, even though they were "from away," for doing the work themselves and not hiring it out to city-people contractors from Bangor.

The Forresters had lively parties and created lots of gossip. One of the reasons was Nin's popularity, and why not? She was cute, funny and loved to tell long, off-color jokes. Today she wore tight, faded jeans and a pale blue sweater that matched her eyes. She played up her Dutch-Swedish heritage by enhancing her naturally blonde hair with a stylish pixie cut. Her best feature was her complexion, creamy and smooth.

Ned's inappropriate remarks gave her frequent occasion to blush. Nin had been a popular cheerleader in high school. Later, at the University, studying for her high school teaching credential, she'd waitressed at "Studs and Leather," a bikers' club on the outskirts of Bangor, making good money and loyal friends among the riders.

Nin and Ned sat at the dining room table working on a guest list. Ned was heavy set, with a reddish crew cut and ruddy complexion—a rugged man of twenty-nine.

"Here's who might show up at our next salsa extravaganza." She handed him the list. "Think they'll all come?"

Ned nodded and handed it back to her.

As a grad student at Orono, she placed great importance on giving successful parties. Maybe it wasn't exactly a town and gown situation, but it was a test of whether her university friends could mix with her Venice friends, not that she had many.

She laid out everything as carefully as if it were a lesson plan—food, drinks, chemistry of the guests. "By the way, where's Whiffenpoof? I haven't seen him in a couple of days." Whiff was part Maine coon cat and part wildcat.

Ned grabbed the list and pretended to be reading a report. "He was last seen wearing a pith helmet, sharpening his claws and gathering his gear for a major rat hunt. He's out hunting. Don't worry, babe. He always comes back. Tell you what. I'll put extra dry food out in the barn."

"Please do. I love Whiffie. So back to the list. Let's go over the food—nachos, tacos, tamales, a big batch of chili—I've already started it in the crock pot. And don't forget to buy limes on Friday and sea salt to coat the rims of the glasses."

"Done!" he grunted, lifting his heavy body out of the chair. He knew that he was getting a little beer belly. Ned walked over to the counter, took the lid off the pot, and inhaled deeply. "That's why I married you, Chili Doll!"

Ned didn't have a clue about what went on in Orono, so the tension between Nin and her thesis advisor, Gordon Wright, slipped past him. Whenever Professor Wright had a married, female teaching assistant, he'd advise her to postpone having children, since it would disrupt progress toward a post-graduate degree. He'd say something like, "A TA has to keep her priorities straight. Are you certain that you can put academic excellence before family?" At first, Nin had interpreted this as some kind of code. Was Professor Wright looking for a little extracurricular sex? But, when nothing further occurred, she had dismissed her suspicions.

Nin rose and grabbed her former college football player husband by the love-handles, giving him a little shake. "I love you, Neddy Teddy, but I've gotta get back to the party plan. Isn't it gonna to cost a lot? Couldn't we cut back on booze? You still planning to buy a keg at Jake's? Maybe we don't *need* a keg, honey. How about a half-keg?"

Like Nin, Ned prided himself on his bartending skills. "Yeah! We do need a whole one!"

"Remember my Orono crowd?" Nin reminisced. "They got pickled early and had to stay over. Not to mention your Mountain Top High gang. One of 'em upchucked off the back stoop. Okay, what else do we need?"

"That's it. I'll settle for one keg, but we'll have plenty of Dos Equis in the barn, stayin' cool. Guess you included that drip Wright. I can't stand the prissy SOB."

"Go easy, Ned. You know he can make me or break me when it comes to my thesis."

Ned rose from the table. "Well, I invited all my teachin' buds from my department. They'll rule. But who else from this dinky two-bit village is coming?" He laughed as he began to put on his outerwear.

She went down the list. "Chuck and Rhu, but they haven't RSVP'd, Guy and Loraine Swenson. Loraine's a tea-totaler, but Guy's a kick in the ass. The Stammers, we gotta stay on their good side in case we ever need a lawyer. The Smiths, but they can't come. That's about it."

"Why not the Finnish couple up the road?"

"Duh...maybe because we don't even know 'em?"

Ned wrapped a scarf around his neck and put on his rabbit fur-lined hat. "Ever hear of ulterior motives? The Finns really know how to party. Comes from all those long, dark nights on the Arctic Circle. They have a real nice sauna, and they come out of there, all sweaty, hot and naked, then whip each other with birch boughs."

Nin looked up. "What?"

"They whip each other with birch boughs and then leap into one of the Finn's trout ponds."

"In winter? That sounds wild!"

"Guy Swenson visits up there quite a bit. Says they're really cool, and that the Finn is a fantastic carpenter, and Guy oughta' know. He's a skilled boat builder."

"Okay. Invite 'em."

"Already did. Just forgot to put their names on the list." Ned grinned.

She found herself yelling at the back of Ned's jacket as he disappeared into the woodshed, "Who else did you invite without telling me?"

Ned shouted back, "Mooseman." Then he chuckled and closed the door.

Nin knew that her husband was kidding, but he was capable of pulling some pretty bone-headed practical jokes. Mooseman was the eccentric recluse who lived up on Whiskey Hill, beyond the MacTeague's. If he acted crazy when he was sober, how would he act when he'd had a few drinks? According to gossip, George Felker had been a successful junk bond trader on Wall Street back in the Eighties. Suddenly he'd lost tons of money and went nuts. He retired to Venice and built a primitive, one-room hut. It had electricity for his computer but no running water. Folks said he bathed in the brook.

Moose's worst offense was walking around outdoors half-clothed, usually wearing nothing from the waist down. In deer season, he'd leap and lunge through the woods in camouflage overalls, yelling at hunters, "Shoot me, shoot me!" while waving his hands in the air or making like deer antlers over his head. Nin thought a kinder, sweeter nickname would have been Deerman.

As Mooseman's neighbor, Mabel MacTeague had befriended the strange hermit, but others in Venice were suspicious of him and thought him capable of going off at any time. Some said that he was another Unabomber and had an arsenal stored in a bunker behind his hut.

Ned hadn't brought in any wood. Instead, he'd buzzed off toward the General Store on his Honda.

An hour later Ned returned. Nin had been studying a textbook on developmental disabilities. She closed the book. "Where've you been, oh wandering one?"

"Just out and about."

Nin smiled, detecting a slight scent of marijuana.

Ned had come in with an armful of wood. "I need hot chocolate. How about makin' me a cup with a splash of brandy in it, lovey? I'm in for a while." He tossed his hat and jacket onto a wall hook then rubbed his hands together and blew into them. "It's Goddamned cold out there this afternoon. Temperature's still dropping. Oh, by the way, I saw Whiff. He's fine, eatin' a mouse." He rearranged the logs in the woodbox. "An' I saw the sheriff's car go by, then turn off toward the Bog Road. No lights or siren."

"Maybe he's going to interview the Gossams. Probably Hal Hines. As far as I'm concerned, there's a good chance one of the Gossams killed Sandy's cousin, Lester. The sheriff oughta' just arrest all adult male Gossams and not release them until they prove they didn't do it."

"Or castrate 'em," Ned asserted. "That'd slow 'em down at least."

Nin made hot chocolate with generous shots of brandy.

"Jeeze, give the sheriff a break, Nin. I heard down at the store that there's been a series of break-ins. Someone's been driving ATVs out to those shut-up cabins on Lake Mallacook and robbing 'em blind. They especially like TVs, microwaves, stereos, you know, stuff that's easy to fence. Nobody sees 'em 'cuz they're in and out fast, usually in the dark." Ned dropped marshmallows into his brandied chocolate, splashing some onto the counter.

"All the more reason to round up the Gossams. Their yard is full of ATV's. They have access. You know, Chuck was telling me yesterday, while I was shoveling the edge of the driveway, that they steal everything. Even stole some of his best cabbages out of his garden last summer. Nothing's safe around the Gossams, and nobody's teenage daughter is either, especially not with Anthony and Booth around. God, they give me the Willeys!" Nin's voice rose to a shrill, angry pitch.

"Well, I'm glad we're not inviting them to the party then." Ned looked at Nin and laughed. "Let's build a humongous snowman, want to?"

The young couple eagerly donned their winter gear and headed out to the steep back yard where, twenty feet above them, cars and pulp lumber

83

trucks rumbled toward Bangor and beyond to New Brunswick, Canada. When they looked up, they could see only the bent guardrail. Drivers passing by couldn't see them, rolling up handfuls of snow.

"Nah, not here! No one'll see our masterpiece," Ned complained, shaking the snow off his mittens. "Let's build it out front and annoy the hell out of the Willards. They hate it when we have fun."

With that he threw a soft snowball at Nin's head and she got him back good, right on the chin. Then they fell into a snowy embrace.

"Just kiddin' about Mooseman," he said.

CHAPTER 14

Gus Gossam was sick and tired of winter, of sitting around feeling the cold. He longed for warm weather when he could go over to the bog, fish, drink beer and sun himself like a big ol' bullfrog. This pleasant daydream was interrupted by the sound of a car pulling into the driveway.

Sam sat in his cruiser, watching the old Doberman the color of cooked liver start toward him, a rope of saliva emerging from its curled lip and a deep growl from its throat. Sam had had run-ins with Dobermans, one resulting in his partner, Belle Whittaker, wearing the dog on her pant leg. This mutt was pulling the chain to its limits, but would the chain hold? Sam wished he had a Taser. "Down!" he commanded in his most vicious bark. The chain went slack as the Doberman dropped on its belly.

Wiping the grimy window with his hand to get a better view, Gus yelled, "Aw crap! It's that damned sheriff. He sure is big! Sarah, grab me a shirt, and take that apron off. You look like a cook, for God's sake."

"Well, I *am* cookin'! What'm I S'pose ta be wearin'?" She could afford to be bold, considering that the law was knocking on the front door.

Gus stomped heavily across the living room and yelled, "State your business."

Sarah turned the television down, then went to the door. Sam announced himself and asked to speak with Gus. Sarah timidly opened the door and Gus told him to come in. Two mud-colored pit bull pups over near the couch began to growl and threaten, but Gus yelled at them to shut up. They both whimpered and laid their slobbery jowls on the floor.

Sam stamped his feet on the small rug to remove excess snow and glanced around. Everywhere he looked he saw depression, including worn furniture and unfinished walls. Sam wondered about their level of poverty until he saw the thirty-six inch TV, the VCR, and the huge Bose speakers.

Gus invited him to "sit a spell." Sam began to adjust to the dim light and sour smells. He observed a small child in a corner playpen, a young teen watching it from the shadows, and Sarah hovering near the kitchen, clutching the door jamb. Gus flopped down in a tattered, overstuffed chair opposite the sheriff who settled onto the lumpy sofa. The place smelled like wood smoke, kerosene, stale beer and mouse urine. Sam hoped the interview wouldn't take too long.

"Thought you'd be around one o' these days. So cut to the chase. S'pose you wanna know where me and the boys were on the day after Thanksgivin'. Well, you was keepin' Anthony in a cell in Galway." He laughed. "Booth was huntin' all day and has buddies to back him up. My youngest son's a fuckin' sissy and don't hold with huntin'. Wife don't either, though I don't hear her complain when we bring home venison." The pups put back their ears and whimpered.

"And where were you on the day following Thanksgiving?"

"Right here with my honey pot, wasn't I, Sarah?"

"Oh yeah," Sarah mumbled, eager to return to the kitchen.

"I'm surprised. Thought you'd have been hunting with your son."

"Nope. That's where you're wrong. I'm on disability. Back acts up in cold weather and it was damned cold that day. But I s'pose you know that, don'tcha?" Gus stretched his arms in an effort to appear at ease.

Sam had heard rumors about Gus's abuse of family, and he wanted to observe Sarah's body language. He took out his notepad and pen. "Mr. Gossam, would you be so kind as to go outside while I speak with your wife?"

Gus rose from his chair "Listen! Anything she says she can say in front of me. Got that?" His posture was threatening, but then he looked into the sheriff's eyes. This was not a man to mess with.

In the makeshift house, Sam looked imposing. He gestured toward Sarah and then replied bluntly, "I can interview your wife at the sheriff's department or I can do it here. Your choice!"

Gus trudged into the kitchen, caught Sarah roughly by the arm, and none too gently shoved her in the sheriff's direction. Then Gus grabbed his red and black plaid hunting jacket and slammed out the front door, still wearing his cracked leather slippers.

"Sit down, Mrs. Gossam." No other adults seemed to be in the house, but the teen in the corner scooped up the toddler and took him into another room. Sarah slumped into the chair Gus had been using. "It's vital that you tell me the truth. Your husband's out of earshot, and anything you say will be held in strictest confidence. You know that, don't you?"

"Guess so." She refused to look the sheriff in the eyes, and her hand picked away at her apron.

"Where was your youngest son on the day after Thanksgiving, ma'am?"

Sarah looked around and then spoke quietly. "Andy was workin' down ta the store. He's always workin'. Booth was huntin' just like Gus says, and Anthony was in jail." For the first time she looked straight at him with a flicker of defiance. "You oughta know that, Sheriff."

Sam smiled. "You're right, ma'am. As a matter of fact, I do know that. Where was your husband that day? Think hard now."

Again, her eyes averted his, and she cleared her throat. "Don'tcha' believe him? He said he was here. We was low on firewood so he cut up a mess out there in the yard." She rose, walked to the window, and stared at a pile of slash wood and some old logs. "Booth helped bring it in." Suddenly her face betrayed both fear and confusion. "I mean...Booth woulda' helped if he'd been here. He helped bring some in the next day. He's a good boy, despite his record. He's good to me."

"Did you see your husband with a chainsaw or an axe?"

"Both, but he don't use 'em both at the same time." She looked a little dazed. "If you ask me, these are pretty foolish questions for a lawman to be askin'."

"But if your husband is on disability, how did he do either?" He wanted to crank up her anxiety level. Maybe she'd let something slip. "How long has your husband been on disability, Mrs. Gossam, and what was the cause of his initial injury?"

Fear flooded her face, and she squirmed in the chair. Then a kind of rage came over her, and she turned on him like a cornered animal.

"What would *you* know? You ever been without food and waitin' on a disability check and it don't come on time? My husband can't find work. Sometimes his back acts up so bad he has to lay flat on the floor. He has his good days and his bad." She was snapping at him like a mother coyote defending her pups. "We can't afford to buy fuel so he collects it from the woods roundabout. Day after Thanksgiving was one a' his good days." Her eyes filled with tears, and Sam felt a tinge of guilt that maybe he'd pushed her too hard.

His face softened. "That's what I needed to find out, Mrs. Gossam." He reached in his wallet and took out a card. "I think that'll do it for now, but keep my card, and, ma'am, any time you want to talk just call that number. Anything, okay?"

"Ain't nothin' *to* tell, but I'll keep your card. Now, could my husband come in out of the cold 'fore he catches new-monia?"

"Of course."

The sheriff passed Gus in silence and trudged to his cruiser. To rattle Gus he sat there for five minutes, looking around the yard, completing his notes, and calling the Zucchetti residence. Since it was on his way home, he'd decided to pay them a call. After all, the wife was kin to the victim and the husband was former law enforcement. W*orth a try.*

Sam rang the doorbell, and Sandy answered with flour on her apron. She was glad to see him. In his line of work, few people greeted him with, "Oh, come in! We've been looking forward to talking with you!" Hers was a welcome contrast from Sarah Gossam's face.

After he'd been invited to sit down, Sam consented to a cup of coffee. He smelled bread baking and couldn't help but contrast the Gossam interior with that of the Zucchettis. Braided rugs decorated the floor and a quilt hung on one wall. On the wide south windowsills squatted huge clay pots of coleus, geranium, and jade plants. Another wall was filled with books.

"Sheriff, I've been baking all morning. The bread isn't quite ready, but I've got cinnamon buns cooling and orange raisin muffins. Which would you like with your coffee, or maybe both?"

"One of each, please. And call me Sam."

"Frank's out splitting wood, but I'll give him a holler. He'll be delighted for an excuse to stop. I'm Sandy. Sorry, I should have introduced myself earlier."

"No problem. You're both pretty famous in these parts."

"Or *in*famous, more likely," Sandy laughed. Before he could say more, Sandy yelled out the back door. "Frank, the sheriff's here!"

After Frank took off his winter things, he shook hands and sat down opposite Sam. "Been looking forward to meeting you."

"Well, it's long overdue, but I been drowning in work. The department's not fully manned." A coal black cat with yellow eyes peered at him from the end of the couch, then sauntered over and sniffed at the traces of Duchess on Sam's boots.

"Yeah, I heard. They oughta give you more men," Frank said, settling into the Canadian rocker. "This is a heck of a big county to cover."

"I never knew how big. There'll be a heist over in Swanzey, then a boat theft in Ulster, a stolen car in Deering, a moose on a porch, and that's just one day."

"Hey," Sandy exclaimed, "Panther really likes you!" The cat had given Sam's shin a rubdown. He returned the favor by scratching the top of Panther's head.

"Yeah. I think she caught the scent of my best friend, Duchess, a German Shepherd-Lab mix. Anyway, I'll never be re-elected because the crime stats are going up, not down. I think the new boom in Galway has a lot to do with it. More money, more crime, more drugs. I think cocaine's coming in through the harbor."

"Listen, Sam, I wonder if I could be of any help. I mean, I have a detective's background with the Air Force OSI, and our perspective's a little different from most townsfolk because we're 'from *away'*." Frank grinned. "Only lived here six-and-a-half years."

"You beat me on that score. I've been here less than a year. But, hey, I can use all the help I can get." Sam smiled. "Besides, they think *I'm* from away because I was born and raised in Portland, even though I spent summers in Galway and went to the university. We'll never belong, and maybe that's just as well. Of course Darla *belongs* because her family's never left Galway since 1847."

They continued making small talk, and Sandy came in with a tray of goodies. Sam pronounced the coffee excellent, served in handsome stoneware mugs that Frank had made. Pottery was one of his many hobbies, although lately he seldom found time. The other two cats, Wolf and Tiger, hopped up and perched on the back of the couch, observing Sam with cautious interest.

"You made these? I flunked clay in kindergarten."

"There's a knack to it. Sandy can throw, too. But I just don't have time anymore what with farm work and the organic gardens, and, to be honest, I can't stand peddling my wares to shops. But if I get back to pottery this summer, I'll make you a duck mug."

Sam decided to take a chance. "Listen, I can't divulge details concerning an ongoing investigation, particularly interviews I've conducted, but I'd sure like your take on one aspect of the case. Any hunches about who might want to do in Lester Moulton? By the way, I sympathize, Sandy, I understand he was your cousin."

"Second cousin, and I liked him. What a horrible way to die. Folks around here are pretty skittish, but I'll let Frank fill you in on our hunches." She smiled and refilled his coffee cup.

"Sandy, tell Sam about the weird phone calls," Frank prompted.

"Probably not connected, but they come always after Frank leaves the house. When I answer, there's a lull and then a hang-up. It's a bit irritating!"

The sheriff took his notebook out and began writing. "How many have you received, Sandy?"

"Six or seven. I started documenting them two days ago."

"Honey, tell him what came in the mail today." Frank got up and stretched his legs, looking down the road toward the Willards'. He wondered if he should mention Sandy's unofficial stake-out. *What the hell! Might as well.*

"Here, I got this," Sandy said, shaking a note and envelope out of a paper bag. "It looks to me like a fake, printed scrawl."

The note was printed on ordinary blue-lined foolscap and read: "But out of what ain't your bisness." It was signed "Your good nabor."

Sam read it, careful to touch only the corners. "I'd say whoever wrote this obviously wants us to think they're uneducated."

Sandy agreed.

"You might get some prints off that," Frank suggested. "Sandy bagged it with a pair of tweezers."

"If you knew how slow our investigative services work around here, you'd laugh. I'll treat it as evidence, but don't hold your breath. Belle Whittaker, in charge of the CIU working this case, is top notch, but they give her more than she can handle, and they want everything done yesterday. Things were different in Portland. Nevertheless, if you should get any more of these, repeat the procedure. Frank, you've taught her well."

"To be honest, she's taught me a thing or two. Sandy was married to Rick Long, a police chief in Florida, long before she got together with me. She helped him study for everything from the Bureau's fingerprint course to forensic evidence gathering. She's good!"

Sandy blushed as she gathered up the coffee things. "Seriously, Sam, these phone calls didn't bug me til this note arrived. Obviously someone's trying to rattle my cage. Three families can see when Frank leaves. The Forresters down there—" she pointed toward the house-in-the-hole. "But they're good friends. In fact Nin has a little crush on Frank. Then there's the Shaws across the road, but Chuck Shaw's practically family. I'd trust Chuck with my life."

"What about Mrs. Shaw, if there is one?" Sam rose and looked down the hill at their century-and-a-half old white colonial.

"Oh yeah, there's Rhubarb, that's her nickname, and she loathes me, but she wouldn't harm anyone."

"Sandy, I've come across hundreds of people in my miserable career who wouldn't *hurt* anyone, yet left a hideous trail of blood and death. Let me ask you this: Would she, perhaps, enjoy making you feel nervous?"

Frank interrupted. "That's a yes, but she's a school teacher, and I don't think she could bring herself to misspell so many words in the note." Their hearty laughter broke the tension.

"That leaves the Willard house, right? I've had several complaints about them threatening and causing trouble. The oldest boy has a jacket, too. Bud Varney told me Slug's been reported for animal abuse, but by the time Animal Rescue arrives, there's no dog. What can you tell me, off the record?" He began jotting down more notes in a fine slanted hand.

"Well, Slug shoots 'em, an interesting way of destroying evidence, then goes and gets another. It's deviant behavior. And we think Slug's selling drugs out of his truck cab. Even on the coldest nights he'll be sitting out in that cab, smoking. He drives the semi periodically as an independent hauler—on disability, of course. Cheating on disability or Workman's Comp is a science around here. Guess it beats working for a living. Anyway, back to my report...then a car or pick-up will pull up near that old garage. It's always a guy, right, Sandy?"

"I've yet to see a female. It seems to be younger men, always wearing ball caps, jeans and jackets, country people. Anyway, they climb up into the cab, something is exchanged, and then after a few minutes they leave. Slug goes back into the house a bit richer, I'm sure."

"Sandy has been standing in front of those windows—I don't know. Anyway, she's been keeping tabs for what it's worth."

"That's great info, Sandy, but don't put yourself in danger. Frank must've warned you. If Slug were to see you, especially back-lit at night, he could get mighty edgy. There's nothing more dangerous than a nervous drug dealer, if, in fact, he's dealing." In a much lower voice, he added, "And it sure looks like it, doesn't it? Either that or he's handing out candy to good little boys."

Sam asked Frank about his years with the OSI, and Frank explained that his primary function was busting up fraud rings, but that he'd been pulled into all sorts of nefarious crimes.

"Look, this is great, but I've gotta get moving." Sam stood up and headed for the front door. "Listen, Frank, I can use all the help I can get. Let's talk again soon."

"Sure, by then we'll have the suspect list completed," Sandy said.

"We're computerizing it and adding to it from time to time,"
"What suspect list?"
"We've jotted down seven or eight names, and we've been doing some checking. Most people are cooperative because they know Sandy's nosey and the vic was her cousin. Want to get our take on it, Sam?"
"Sure, when you're ready, but don't keep me waiting too long on that list, and thanks again."

Two sets of curtains quickly closed as the sheriff turned out of the ice-caked driveway and headed down the hill. He wondered if he should have revealed so much to the Zucchettis about the case. He shrugged. *Guess it can't hurt.*

On the way back to Galway, Sam arranged by phone to see Stu Stammer about Lester's will. He'd seen Stu tap dancing in court a number of times and knew he was a bright and clever man, perhaps too clever. *That's not fair. I hardly know the man, but so far I don't much like him. I know one thing, his closing arguments are way too long. Guess that's a lawyer's prerogative. At least he's honest, maybe.*

Stu's secretary, a violet-haired woman in her sixties named Violet, was making motions to leave for the day. She grudgingly showed Sam in.

"He's been waiting for you, Sheriff," she said, pointing toward the inner office.

Stammer's office was small but handsomely furnished. One wall was lined with leather bound volumes of *West's*; the other had a picture window. Stu rose from behind his cluttered oak desk and greeted Sam with a wide smile.

"Good to see you, Sheriff! Please, sit down."
"Call me Sam. I see you have a fine view of the bay."
"Sure, wouldn't have an office in this town if I didn't. Beautiful, isn't it? Got me a little sailing yacht down there. You sail?"
"Afraid not. My wife's dad owns a fishing boat."
"Oh, yeah! Jack McClellan, that old salt. What a crusty old character!"
"Yes, he's a good man, but actually I'm here about Lester's will."
"Sure thing. My secretary pulled it for you. Want me to sum it up?"
"That'll do. By the way, did you know Lester very well?"
"Just as a client and by reputation. He wasn't litigious by any means. Kind of a sweetheart, really. What happened to him is a shame. You know, you can tell a lot about a man from his will."
"And it reveals...what?" Sam didn't have all day, and Stu was a talker. Stu walked around his desk and put a thumb in his suspender.
"You know, I came to Maine as a carrot thinner. Lived in Frenchie's barn right on the Venice-Dixville line for a year. We had a blast! Guy Swenson, Don Wells, a whole bunch of guys and gals, and we loved it here so much that a lot of us stayed. I met my wife, Lulu, at Frenchie's.

She'd run away from her wealthy parents and never looked back. It was part of the Seventies back-to-the-land movement. We smoked a lot of weed, but it didn't do us any harm. Hell, most of us became very successful."

"That so?"

"And you know the funny thing? Frenchie was on to something with his organic immature vegetables. Used to run whole truckloads to Boston once a week during the summer and fall. Way ahead of his time. Even had a herd of swine, which made it even more biblical, and we'd take turns slopping the pigs. He could've been hugely successful if he hadn't been more interested in sex, grass, and contra dancing than business."

"Yeah, Guy Swenson filled me in a bit when I met with him about a stolen boat. Every time I drive by that sagging barn, I imagine what it must've been like in its heyday, but let's get back to the will." He removed it from a folder. "Here's a copy. Basically a straightforward document."

Sam took the folder and said, "Could you sum it up for me? I need to get back to my office."

"Sure thing. It may surprise you but Sister Betty doesn't get everything. You interviewed her yet?"

Sam kept his peace.

"Anyway, Betty's the executrix, bound by the terms to sell the entire contents of house, garage and barn. After all debts are paid, the value of those assets will be divided five ways: Clair Monroe, the Friends of Fowl Society, AIDS Research Foundation of Maine, Pine Run Women's Shelter, and Betty. The house, property and Caddy go to Betty. Nothing to contest. Anything go to motive, Sam?"

"Sorry, can't discuss it, Counselor." Sam stood up and walked to the door. "Appreciate your time."

"Nice to see you," Stammer said, but the door had already closed.

After Sam finished up his reports, he headed home where Darla had a late supper waiting. He told her about his visit to the Zucchettis and his brief chat with Stu Stammer. He'd thought, uncomfortably, about Belle Whittaker off and on all day, and he decided to talk about it, well, part of it, with Darla. After a dessert of caramel flan, he stretched out in the Lazy-Boy lounge chair. Darla was knitting a baby bonnet for a pregnant teacher-friend at school and watching a "Law and Order" re-run with the mute button on.

"Darla, guess who I've been working with on the case?" He paused. Silence. "My old friend Belle Whittaker. She's as hard working and abrasive as ever."

"Is she as pretty as ever?" Darla raised her eyes from her knitting and bored them into Sam. For once he read her mind.

"I wouldn't say pretty, more like striking or...maybe handsome, like a well bred hunting dog."

"Cut me some slack, Sammy. She's no dog. Think I'm an idiot? I've seen her on the TV news. She's gorgeous and you know damn well she is."

Darla slammed down her knitting gear on the old trunk that served as a coffee table.

"Well, I guess she's sort of pretty, but not my type, Darla, and I'm not..."

Again she said nothing but glared at him. This passive aggressive, non-directive counseling stuff was getting under his skin.

"Listen, honey, I don't want an adversary when I come home from work. I want *you*."

Unconvinced, Darla looked dismayed and sank into the sofa.

He looked at her. "What? Am I saying this all wrong?"

She shook her head.

"I guess I'm lousy at expressing my feelings, aren't I?"

She softened. "Not really. I might've overreacted. Sorry." She straightened up the knitting and stowed it in her ditty bag. "You can make it up to me—and if we can turn in now, I'll let you try." She walked over and clicked off the television.

He followed her upstairs to the bedroom where she switched on the corner lamp. He leaned in the doorway and watched her slip off her clothes. Usually she'd put on a flannel granny gown off the closet hook, but tonight she went over to the bureau and pulled out a peachy satin baby doll trimmed with creamy lace. He caught a whiff of sandalwood as she closed the drawer.

"I bought this last week when I went to the Bangor Mall with the girls," she said, still turned away from him. Then she slipped it on and did a slow model's turn, stepping toward him. "They liked it. What do *you* think?" Her body was now against his, transferring warmth.

"I think...I think it's very pretty, sweetheart, but..."

"But what?" she said, tugging at his belt and kissing his neck.

"I'd like it better off." He slipped the baby doll from her shoulders, pulling it gently over her voluptuous curves until fell to the floor where it lay like a puddle of peach juice on the wide, pumpkin pine boards.

CHAPTER 15

By nine-thirty Saturday night, the fully-lit Forrester farmhouse was jumping. Across the porch, Nin had strung miniature red hot pepper lights that reflected on the snow and the icicles dangling from the soffits. Inside, poinsettias brightened up the old farmhouse. The sounds of Credence Clearwater Revival blared from the windows, opened a crack to let the hot air out. Cars filled the sloping expanse of front yard. From across the road, the Willards peered out their frosty windows, wondering why this college crowd was having so much fun.

"Well, damn! I've been nothin' but nice to that bitch," Bertha hissed. "She thinks she's better'n us, that's what. See if we help next time he gets stuck in the snow and needs a couple of rugged boys to help. She just acts like hot shit 'cuz she teaches at that college."

"It's a university, Ma! She teaches at the University of Maine at Orono." Billy said defensively.

"University nawthin'. That Ned, he just teaches English, Billy. Just 'cuz they got education, they don't need to be so high and mighty!" She snorted aggressively.

"I think she's pretty. Don't you, Pop?" Billy looked to his father for support as Bertha gave him a wilting look.

"I think they're nothin' but a bunch of faggots, just like that Moulton queer that got plugged over to the bog. Somebody musta' mistaken him for a wild turkey." Slug guffawed and shifted in his lounge chair.

Slug was a big man with a booming voice. Even when he was calm, his comments resounded. He was over six feet tall, had a muscular build, no neck to speak of and thinning reddish hair. He'd driven a truck, off and on, for most of his life. When business as an independent hauler slacked off, he headed for the woods, not always with a cutting permit, and skidded logs then hauled them to a Pittstown or Bangor lumber yard where the price varied from week to week. He was not a patient man, as his older sons learned early on. If the price was low, he'd be in a rip-roarin' funk all the way home.

Slug began to sell marijuana when, in exploring for a new wood lot to cut on, he'd discovered someone's field of dreams. Those dreams were

high quality, six feet tall, and ready to harvest. After that, he'd developed a
seed bank, and every spring he'd go into the remote areas of his neighbors'
woods to plant his eight-by-eight foot patches of grass. He and oldest son
Bobby even lugged in sacks of cow manure to make the weed grow faster
and bigger. As for merchandising, the cab of his truck seemed an ideal place
to sit and chat, make the exchange, and then scoot on into the house.
"Hell," he'd said to Mabel once, "ain't been caught. Don't fix it if it ain't
broke!" Everyone in the family knew about his new "hobby," but no one
ever brought it up in conversation. They knew better.

Younger son Billy was looking for affirmation, just this once. He'd
watched Nin plenty of times, and he liked everything about her except her
husband. He'd even dreamed about her. Once he helped her change a tire.

"Hell, I'm stayin' out of this argument," Slug finally boomed.
"Change the friggin' channel. I'm sick of the Simpsons. I wanna' see a cop
show. Find me an old *NYPD*, Billy."

Billy surfed until he found a rerun. "Wonder why Rhu didn't go to
the party. The Zookies walked Chuck home about ten. He must've been
drunk 'cuz he almost fell crossin' the road. Then the Zookies went back to
the party."

Bertha Willard rose with difficulty from her vinyl lounge chair. The
carpet was beige and the drapes tan with red roses. Her doll collection
adorned the bookshelves. Plant stands were heavy with geraniums and
begonias, and racks full of women's magazines filled in the corners.
Altogether, the room had a rather homey feel to it.

She, like Sarah Gossam, had been a fine looking girl back when
Slug had courted her, but with each of the three children, she'd put on
pounds, and now she weighed nearly two hundred. For years, she'd worked
behind the meat counter at Jake's where one morning she slipped on a stray
piece of fat and injured her back. She'd been collecting Workmen's Comp
ever since. Once Bertha left, Jake had hired "that baby-faced foreign girl" to
take her place.

"Well, Rhubarb don't go to parties. When she ain't teachin', she sits
home readin' them Book of the Month Club books." Bertha opened a can of
Coors Light and drank some. "A wonder she lets Chuck out of her sight."

"You the only beer drinker in this house? Goddamn, woman, you
don't need to be so spleeny. Open me up a cold one, but don't give me none
of that horse piss. I want a Bud."

Two of their three children lived with them. The oldest, Bobby
John, age 23, only stayed at the home-place off-and-on, depending on the
state of his love life. Presently, he was staying with a girlfriend and their two
children in a mobile home down in Deering. They regularly showed up for
Sunday dinner and dropped in when they were low on food.

Bobby John, usually called BJ, was the handsomest of the boys.
He'd been a star quarterback at Mountain Top, but due to his barely passing
grades he couldn't get into college, so he took to the woods on a cutting
crew. He'd wrecked two or three of Slug's cars, but Slug always managed to

locate another one for him. His repeated brushes with the law over drug use had turned his father even more strongly against the former sheriff, Belcher. He didn't have much faith in the new sheriff either. The fact that Bobby John looked remarkably like Chuck Shaw hadn't escaped Slug Willard's notice, but the matter was never spoken of. What happened over twenty years earlier was water over the damn. Strangely enough, Slug took perverse pride in how good looking his oldest son was, perhaps to irritate Bertha.

Nearly everyone in town noticed BJ's strong resemblance to Chuck. They knew that Chuck and Rhu and their four kids had come to Venice about twenty-five years earlier and used newlywed Bertha Willard as a baby-sitter. No wonder Chuck never said a word against Bobby John, or even Slug, for that matter. They wondered how Rhu could look at BJ's face every day in her classroom and be reminded.

The Willard that Chuck disliked was Billy, whose hobby seemed to be cruelty to animals. Another annoying habit was his joy in riding an old, noisy ATV around and around and around their back lot until it ran out of gas. When Billy was near driving age, Slug gave him an old junker that the boy finally rolled into a muddy ditch bank. He spun and spun the wheels, but it wouldn't come unstuck, and he'd crawled out with only a few scratches and a lump on his forehead. Some time later, Slug covered up the mangled hulk with the front-end loader, one of many pieces of heavy equipment that he'd come by. An array of other damaged ATV's and vehicles had collected in the back.

Little sister Becky longed for a pet, but every time they got a dog, it didn't live long. When her father was in a dark mood, any dog's life was at risk, especially if he dared bark at night, which, it seemed to Becky, was one good reason to own a dog.

The child was afraid of lots of things, especially her father's temper. She did nearly everything she was told and tried to anticipate Slug's next demand. Slug resented Becky's love of reading. "Seems like every time I need you, you got your head in a goddamned book. What good's that gonna do ya?" And it wasn't even a comic book, but serious reading like *Treasure Island, Little Women* and *National Velvet*. It drove Slug wild, and he began to pick on the child more than usual. Whenever Bertha saw things coming to a head, she'd send Becky on errands to other areas of the house. Whenever Slug stoked up, she tried to appease him.

Bertha's father had been a notorious cattle thief whose antics were known throughout downeast Maine. Her mother had died of lung cancer. The only time that Bertha had felt safe as a child was when her father was doing time at Thomaston Prison. When he finally died years later, she hadn't shed a tear.

When work slacked off, Slug's anger rose, and he'd rev up the drug selling out of his truck and take more chances. Bobby John helped his dad out when needed but had his own supplier in Amnesty.

Becky had the same sweet features as her mother at that age. Chubby little Becky, age thirteen, had the habit of wandering over to

Rhubarb's, especially in summer when Rhu wasn't teaching. As if to make up for bitter memories, Rhu often gave Becky pretties. In the past year she'd awarded the child an old Barbie doll, a plastic hand mirror, ribbons for her silky blonde hair and a hand-made child's apron. Rather than pique the ire of her mother, Becky carefully hid the presents under a loose floorboard in her room. Sometimes, when her parents were fighting or on a rampage about something, Becky would escape upstairs and lift the board. One by one she'd take out the gifts. Somehow they made her feel loved.

Rhu wanted a dozen grandchildren, but so far she had only one. She hinted and cajoled, and sent her daughters articles cut from women's magazines about ways to conceive. Rhu was ready to make baby clothes and knit booties. In the meantime, she'd borrow neighborhood children. How she envied Bertha who had two and Mabel who had five or six. Rhu had lost track. She also made friends with the paperboy and the lawnmower kid they hired every summer. Cleona had once mentioned to Sandy, "What a pity. Rhu is such a lonely soul."

Rhu proved to be a woman who asked too many questions. One time Becky knocked on Rhu's kitchen door because she smelled cookies baking. Rhu invited her in, sat her down, and let her have as many Toll House cookies as she could eat.

"Want some Coke or milk with that, honey?"

"Nope—I mean, no thank you."

"Is your mother's back better? Will she be going back to work soon?"

Becky thought it might be a trap. She hesitated, then volunteered. "Mama's back hurts a lot. She can't work." Becky smiled, her teeth caked with chocolate.

Sometimes, when she felt like being wicked, Becky answered truthfully. At other times family loyalty kicked in, and she claimed that she didn't know. Becky sensed that Rhu might be trying to get something on her mom and wondered why these two ladies disliked one another so much. Rhu also questioned Becky as to where her father and brothers had been the day after Thanksgiving. Becky thought and thought and finally came up with the correct answer, one that Slug had pounded into all their heads. "They all went hunting up near Monson, by the slate quarry." She was pleased that she'd gotten every word correct.

CHAPTER 16

By eleven o'clock, the party had taken on a life of its own. Although a few guests had left, many still congregated under the hanging copper pots in Nin's kitchen. A couple of guys were out back smoking weed. Meanwhile, several of Ned's teaching buddies hung out in the den admiring his colorful collection of Harley Hog posters. They'd also admired his workbench piled high with Harley parts that he planned to use rebuilding two machines. It was the only reason Ned ever went to the Sunday morning auctions, and Nin threatened that if he brought any more cycle junk into their small attached barn, she'd start scrapbooking or beading, two hobbies she'd always disdained. "There's hardly room for our cars in there anymore."

In the kitchen, Dave and Lena, two young archaeology instructors, were holding forth about the Red Paint People. "The dig begins in June," Lena said, "and it'll go on all summer. We can hardly wait!"

"She's trolling for volunteers," Dave offered, scraping up the last of the guacamole. "She's totally gung-ho about this."

Ann laughed, twisting her long auburn braid between two slender fingers. "All good archaeology is conducted on the backs and bodies of volunteers."

"Yeah, mainly on their backs," someone in the crowd cracked, creating an uproar of laughter.

"I've heard of the Red Paint People," Sandy interjected. "They're fascinating. No one really knows where they came from, right?"

"Not for sure," Dave answered. "Some think they're leftovers from early Viking explorers, Eric the Red and that crowd. Others say they're Danish-Indian creoles, and so forth and so on."

Sandy looked through the arched doorway at Frank, nursing the last of his second Sam Adams beer, staring out the window towards Slug's back field where all the old cars were buried.

"Hey, Mister Z, what'cha thinkin'?" Sandy asked, coming over to him and leading him by the hand back into the kitchen. "Get in here, Frank. The archaeology couple's talking about digging up the Red Paint People's bones."

"The dig is down at the coast, in Hancock County, only forty miles from Venice," Dave was explaining.

"And we just got grant money to further the work," Lena added with satisfaction, looking around for volunteer hands to go up. None did.

"Red Paint people?" came a voice from the woodshed. It was Ned. "Bog People!"

Dave asked, "What Bog People? They're in Northern Europe, not the New World. Not that I know of anyway."

"Yeah, right here in Venice," Ned said. "The Bog People of Venice, Maine, and you don't need a grant to dig 'em up." Ned giggled. "They rise up from beneath the ice!"

"Oh, we read about that in the Bangor paper," chimed in Lena, a long-legged biology instructor from Orono. "Boy, it's going to take some tricky science to figure that one out."

"No lie," her husband Mark commented. "As I understand it, he was in the water for well over three weeks. That's about how long it takes for a body to pop to the surface in near-freezing water temperatures...well, in this case, float up to the underside of the ice sheet. Bet he had plenty of nibbled places."

"Yuck!" Nin exclaimed. She had been standing at the sink rinsing glasses.

"He can't help it," Lena shouted across the room to her above the animated chatter. "His thesis was on 'Life Forms in Small Ponds'." Laughter reigned. Lena was a striking and intelligent looking woman of about thirty, wearing long dangly earrings, a tight red long-sleeved jersey and tight, well-worn jeans. Her raven black hair hung in a heavy braid.

Frank turned to Sandy, now standing next to him. "Well, 'Small Ponds.' That brings us right back to Venice, doesn't it?" He downed the last of his beer. He liked the bright irreverence of Dave and Lena.

Sandy smiled. "Yeah, Venice is a small pond, isn't it? Ever wonder why we're here? I'd rather be digging up *ancient* dead bodies than dealing with my cousin's remains."

"We heard about that poor man who was drowned in the bog. He was a relative?" Lena remarked. "Horrible! Who could have done such a thing? Sheriff have any leads yet?"

"He was my cousin. Sheriff's working on it, but he's got his hands full with all the crime in Galway. That new company, Atlantis National Bank, has brought prosperity, and prosperity has stimulated thievery. Now there're more BMWs, Porches and Caddies to steal. Come summer the gangs'll be stealing fancy iron yard ornaments."

"And boats," Guy Swenson added with a grin. "Listen! If they steal boats, they'll need me to build more. Free enterprise all the way around." After Guy had a couple of drinks, he took on the accent of an old sea captain, and he couldn't seem to help himself. Guy had a popular music show on Maine Public Radio, and lots of folks thought he was funnier than the famous Tim Sample. He played world-wide music, but it was his running narrative that folks tuned in for. Everybody but his wife, Loraine, thought he was funny.

Although Guy built wooden boats, the closest his house ever got to water was when the cellar flooded during mud season. In the Seventies he'd been one of Frenchie's boys, but then he'd left farm life and moved temporarily to Galway to learn boat building from a master. When he returned to Venice he'd fallen for Loraine Smith, store clerk at the Co-op, a thin, plain girl with a gentle spirit and sad brown eyes. When Guy inherited from his parents, he'd suggested they move to Galway or Winterport, but Loraine said no. So here was a boat builder, driving sixty miles round trip to ply his trade and teach at the world famous Boat Carpentry School.

You could spot Guy any time with his faded blue denim shirt and high-water jeans, sea captain's cap, beard and a jaunty step. He might've just climbed down from one of the tall ships.

Lena and her husband wandered off, and Frank drifted over to where Eric Eloranto was sitting, now talking with Guy. Eric was short, with a crew cut, a stocky rugged build, small nose, and a perpetually open expression on his face. He wore a Finnish hand-knit sweater and faded jeans. His gray-blue eyes were his most impressive feature.

"I hear you got ducks up at your place. Yah?"

Frank liked the gentle Finnish accent. "No ducks, but we've got five geese, two African and three Toulouse. They're real characters, but we have to keep 'em pretty close to the house so the foxes won't get 'em."

"Yah! I got me some ducks and I gotta keep de ice out of one of my ponds for 'em. I got de same problem, too, dose varmints. I shoot 'em when I sees dem." Eric nodded and took a swig of Wicked Ale. "You and de wife, you oughta' come up and visit. My wife, she's around here somewheres. She's a nurse at Townsend Hospital, so she ain't home much, but if you call first, we could fix up a time."

Frank extended the same invitation. He liked the Finn with his open, honest face. Maybe Frank could get him to do some work on their partially remodeled kitchen. With three daughters in school, Eric could probably use the extra cash, and Frank admired the workmanship of true craftsmen.

Stu Stammer, the attorney, and organizer of the upcoming town meeting, walked over to Frank. "Anything new on the bog murder, Frank?"

"Not that I know of," Frank answered off-handedly, keeping a distance in his tone.

Sandy couldn't decide if she liked Stu, but felt certain about her dislike for his wife, Lulu. Every time Lulu rode her Morgan horse past the Zucchetti place, Sandy would wave, but Lulu would usually ignore her. Sandy couldn't imagine why, unless it was because the Zucchettis weren't horse people, not that Sandy wouldn't like to be.

From her kitchen window, Nin noticed two grad students urinating outside, "making yellow snow" they'd said, not wanting to wait for the single upstairs bathroom. At least they'd walked far enough towards the woods that they were beyond the full illumination of the backyard flood light. After all, in Maine it wasn't against the law. They were noisy and obnoxious, and Nin wished they'd sleep it off in one of the guest rooms. "Hey, idiots, cool it!" she'd hollered out the window, but to no avail.

Having achieved a Margarita buzz, Nin vowed not to have another. She felt protective toward her career, and she wanted Ned to stay away from Dr. Gordon Wright, because, around him, Ned's directness had a way of setting Wright off. She loved the little boy in her husband, but recognized the need, on occasion, to control him.

Nin went into the pantry to get another box of crackers. Of course, Ned had forgotten to replace the light bulb, but she managed to make out the yellow lettering. On tiptoes in order to get the box off the top shelf, she sensed someone behind her and whirled around.

"Hey, girl! How's my gorgeous assistant tonight? Feeling no pain?" He moved up against her.

Think of the devil! "Hi, Dr. Wright. Uh, isn't this a tight squeeze?" Nin found herself crammed up against the shelves, still holding the box of Ritz crackers above her head.

"Yeah, I'm just bursting at the seams. You give an awesome party, kid."

"Thanks. Where's your lovely wife?"

"Mary's upstairs, taking a little nap," he whispered, kneading her thigh. "Two drinks and she's off to lala land. I notice you handle your booze well." He moved his hand to her chin, tilted her head, and kissed her as he placed his other hand at the small of her back and pulled her firmly against him. Nin allowed the kiss to linger for a moment, tasting the lime and salt on his soft lips, then immediately regretted it.

"You know what you do to me!" He tried kissing her again, this time on her neck. She moved. Then he tried working his way down the partially unbuttoned opening of her cashmere sweater, pressing himself against her soft body. Crackers spilled out of the box.

"Jesus, stop it!" she exclaimed in a loud whisper. "Do you know what Ned would do if he caught you?" Another dozen or so crackers clattered onto the pantry floor.

The good doctor was conspicuously drunk and slurring his words. "Don't worry, preddy lady. I can take care of myshelf, but right now I wanna take care of you."

In a deft move, Nin ducked under his arm and escaped the pantry, cracker box in hand, and headed toward the island in the middle of the kitchen.

As Sandy was getting ready to say good-bye, she glanced over at a flustered Nin. "Are you okay?"

Before Nin could reply, Dr. Wright exited the pantry, his chinos sporting an obvious bulge. He turned to face the sink and pretended to pour himself a glass of tap water. Nin walked over to him, too embarrassed to answer Sandy, and said, "What you need, Doctor, is strong coffee. I'll put the kettle on."

The professor didn't reply.

Raucous sounds drifted in from the side yard, the one facing the Willards, then something slammed into the window, cracking it. Nin looked at the fractured pane, then out into the frozen yard with its human-like forms flailing and hurling things. She saw a plume of snow swirling upward toward the street light at the corner of Myrick Hill Road and the Bangor highway. The chaotic scene reminded her of a Bruegel painting. Apparently, Ned had been out in the ten-degree weather having a snowball fight with his teaching buddies.

Nin's rage at Wright demanded immediate release. She leaned out the door into the blowing snow, her short blonde hair now porcupined into little spikes by static electricity. "Get in here, you friggin' idiots!" she shouted into the near blizzard, clenching a damp dishtowel with both hands. "I hope you jerk-offs get pneumonia!" She popped back into the kitchen and slammed the door shut. *All I need is trouble with Slug Willard and company!*

They did as they were told, trooping in like naughty school boys, the snow falling from them and turning to small puddles on the kitchen floor. Ned looked out of it and began to apologize. "Jeeze, I'm sorry, honey! I'll fix that window tomorrow, I promise. It was my fault." His face took on a sheepish expression. His eyes were red and his voice reedy. Meanwhile, his unruly teacher friends chortled with glee, as they smacked the powdery snow off of each others' butts and shoulders.

What if Ned observed Dr. Wright through the window, standing at the sink; did Ned throw the snowball deliberately? In order to divert her husband's attention, Nin tried hard to focus him on changing the music. "Honey! How about some lively salsa? Please change the record."

Dominating the living room was a Sixties-style six-foot-long maple console with a 45 record player. Ned was a connoisseur of oldies, and owned a valuable collection. Off Ned went, humming salsa, trying to please his lovely wife, followed by most of the crowd from the kitchen.

Nin then turned to her professor, smoothing down her damp, spiky hair. "As for you, Doc, you've been very naughty, too, so go upstairs, wake little Mary, and have her drive you home. If she's sobered up by now, that is."

"No. Tha's alright, Nin," he said in a soft, slurry voice. He leaned toward her and winked. "We could sleep over. I could be in your bed and Ned could sleep in Mary's." He laughed and reached for her arm, despite the fact that Sandy was still over at the round table.

Nin spun round, shot a fierce look at Wright, then gave Sandy an embarrassed 'help me' look, and headed upstairs to rouse Mary. Meanwhile the tea kettle was screaming, so Sandy took the initiative and decided to make real coffee in the French press. The professor seemed to have no clue as to who Sandy was, although earlier in the evening they'd entered into a debate about the imminent collapse of the public school system. Frank joined them, and asked where Nin was, as he wanted to thank her for a great party.

"She's gone to retrieve my little wifey, who can't hold her liquor."
Frank smiled at the irony then thought about the professor driving forty-miles back to Orono.

Suddenly Ned burst into the kitchen. "Howdy neighbors! Having a blast? Can I get you anything?"

Frank changed the subject. "Listen, Ned. Be careful that none of your buds drives tonight. Some of them are pretty hammered and the roads are bad and getting worse."

"Always the cop, huh Frank!" Ned rearranged his blocky shoulders and set his jaw. "Listen, folks can stay over if they want, but I'm not their babysitter." He instantly regretted his tone, realizing he wanted to stay on the good side of his lawman neighbor. "Hey, thanks for caring. I mean it, buddy," he said, putting his arm around Frank's shoulder.

Elsa and Eric Eloranto approached Nin, shook hands and thanked her for a good time. Although she was a nurse and dealt with people every day, Elsa seemed shy. "The food was great, especially the chili. Could I have your recipe sometime?"

"Sure, I'll have Ned run it up to your house one of these days on his motorcycle."

Eric interrupted. "Lucky guy. Elsa don't want me to get one, says I'm dangerous enough in a Volvo. Besides, if I had one, our girls would want to use it. Hey, wanna learn a Finnish word? I'm gonna say what a good time we had and goodbye now. *Minulla oli mukavaa. Nääkemiin!* If you just want to say hi or bye, it's *moi!*

Nin giggled. "That's neat. *Moi,* and drive safely!"

Soon the archeologists, Dave and Lena, said their farewells, then two of Ned's well-tanked high school buddies approached. Frank whispered to Ned, "You got enough room to let these guys stay over?"

Ned shook his head. "Nah, they'll sober up as soon as they hit the cold. Frank, my friend, you're just a worrier. Besides, they ain't goin' far."

Frank suggested coffee to Ned's pals and they agreed. That was all he could do.

In came a beaming Mary, the professor at her side. She was dark-haired and classy looking, and about ten years older than her husband. Contrary to her husband's pronouncements, she seemed sober enough. After some strong coffee, they put on their wraps. Then Dr. Wright spoke to Nin, his speech suddenly unslurred. "Monday I want to do the final edit with you on Chapter Ten. It might mean staying late, but we need to send it off to the publisher."

"I enjoy editing," Nin answered eagerly, "but I can't stay too late."

"You don't mind, do you, old man?" Wright rested his hand on Ned's shoulder and lapsed into a fake British accent. "That book will be quite the feather in her cap."

Ned seemed to miss Nin's sudden blush. "You all drive careful, now."

Sandy and Frank took it all in, then thanked their hosts and departed into the increasingly cold night. Across the road, Bertha Willard quickly closed the flowered drapes.

A thick blanket of sparkling new snow covered the ground, and Sandy and Frank had trouble climbing the hill due to the black ice crusted onto the road surface. By morning, the West wind would sculpt the snow into giant snakes that slithered across the low spots in the highway and drape every branch and telephone line. Sandy slipped once and Frank made a good save. He held her face in his snowy mittens and kissed her. "You were the prettiest girl there, Sandy Z."

"Well, I was the soberest, next to Loraine Swenson. What was her problem tonight?" She seized his hand and got herself upright. "Did you see her staring at Guy all evening?"

"Her problem *was* Guy. She hates parties and didn't want to come, Guy admitted it. He's a party animal and was having a blast telling stories. Everyone else loved it."

"Well, *I* had a great time. I'll reward you for being so sweet, Inspector. You wait." They laughed and threw small snowballs at each other, then continued up the hill toward the lights of their snug, cedar-shingled farm house.

"Oh, I forgot to tell you," Frank said. "Stu Stammer was asking lots of questions about the case."

"I know. I overheard. Think he's up to something?"

"Whaddya think? He's a lawyer," Frank said.

"So how'd you like Nin's professor?" Sandy asked.

"That blow-dried phony. We dared share our opinions on education, and he got defensive. What an asshole! I finally got fed up and told him about when I was an instructor at OSI School and my success with fear of failure as a motivational tool." Frank was busy banking the fire in the wood stove.

"He hardly let us get a word in edgewise," Sandy sighed. "How does Nin put up with him?"

"Put up? Come on, Sandy. He wants her to put *out*! That's the way grad school works. Don't you remember? Only from observation, of course?" Frank jiggered the last log into place, closed the lid of the wood stove and checked the damper setting. "You had to notice the chemistry. Sex and power pheromones oozed out of his every pore."

"Yeah, big-time. I've suspected it just from what Nin *hasn't* said over coffee. Did you know that Nin's helping him write a book about motivating disadvantaged students?" Sandy removed her sweater and started for the stairs. "Poor Nin, having to work with him."

"Translation: She does all the work and he gets all the credit." Frank checked the stove, switched off the light, and followed Sandy upstairs where the cats were waiting.

Once in their dormered bedroom, they quickly changed into flannel pajamas and washed up. The three cats, Panther, Tiger, and Wolf, were all vying for attention, rolling over, begging to sleep in the bedroom.

"They need quality time," Sandy **announced**, scratching Tiger under the chin. Meanwhile, Frank gave Panther and Wolf plenty of strokes.

"Can't blame them for wanting to stay with us tonight," Frank said. "Listen to that wind." A thunderous gust had burst onto Whiskey Hill, blown up from the Kennebec Valley several miles to the west, and now it was moaning through the trees on its journey Downeast. Frank gently deposited the cats, one by one, outside the bedroom door, gave them words of encouragement to see them through the blustery night, and latched the door. After a flurry of pitiful meows and a few feeble scratches at the door, there was silence.

Frank switched on the bedside radio, pre-set for Maine Public Radio late night jazz, where Miles Davis was pushing a tortured note through his trumpet. Under the covers, Frank cuddled Sandy.

"Now for some pheromones of our own," Frank suggested, pulling her close. Sandy wrapped herself around him, and gave him a long, lingering kiss.

Several minutes later, the phone rang, but when Frank answered, he heard only a hum on the line. "Damn! They don't even wait until I'm out of the house." He hung up and turned off the ringer. "Now, little lady, where were we?"

CHAPTER 17

Booth Gossam had downed eight or nine Budweisers and a couple of boilermakers at Amnesty's only bar and pool hall, Burt's Burps. Before that, he'd had a few hits off a bong belonging to his buddy, Louie, but he couldn't really feel its effects. *Lousy weed*, he thought as he pulled out of the parking lot.

Because Amnesty's only cop could be hiding out behind the barber shop, Booth kept the speedometer under thirty. Once he reached the town line, he sped up to fifty, although the road wasn't as clear as in town. Sometimes the salt-sand man didn't do as good a job as the Amnesty town plowman, and black ice always lurked where the plow blade had skipped, especially around Jake's General Store, where the road dipped between there and Little Pond.

Foremost on Booth's mind was getting laid. Back at Burps, he'd called Norma over in Dixville. Off and on, they'd get it on. Tonight she said she might still be up if he got there fast enough. By the time he hit the Venice town line all he had in his head were visions of Norma.

As he approached the intersection of Whiskey Hill Road, Booth thought he spotted a patch of black ice and tapped the brake a bit. Abruptly, the beat-up '78 Dodge truck stuttered and slewed across the icy spine of Route Ten. Suddenly Rhu and Chuck Shaw's house passed from right to left across the windshield, then back from left to right. He saw the rivets of the guardrail, gleaming silvery in the light of the quarter moon, heard metal grind against metal followed by the liberating sensation of flight.

"Wheeee," he sang out. He felt strangely free, and not for a moment did he worry about where the truck might end its long plunge through the cold night air. Suddenly, with a whoosh and a plop, it landed on all-fours.

When he awoke, he wondered what the hell a yellow submarine was doing in the middle of winter. But sure enough, the words, "We all live in a yellow submarine," were coming from those windows just a few feet away. *Yellow submarine, yellow lights, mellow yellow*, he thought, as he wiped something sticky out of his eyes. His temples throbbed and did he imagine the smell of gasoline? This was like in the movies when the car crashed and the fuel spilled and everything went up in an orange ball. *Gotta get out. Gotta get outa this friggin' truck!* The cab door wouldn't budge. Booth stuck his head out of the window and saw that the snow bank came halfway up the door. After much grunting and cursing, he managed to force the door open with his feet and wiggle his way out. He ended up sitting in the snow, dazed, wiping the sticky stuff out of his eyes. *Jeeze, it's blood. Musta' hit my head.* Booth crawled toward the light, leaving a red trail.

Sandy awoke from a strange dream in which she'd been wandering around in a huge Victorian mansion, going through bolt after bolt of calico cloth. As usual, she had trouble making up her mind. From the far end of the mansion came the insistent ringing of a bell. Someone was at the door, but she couldn't find the door. Suddenly she wasn't in a mansion but in her own bed. She sat up, confused. It was the downstairs phone. *Frank must've turned off the damn upstairs ringer!*

She reached for the phone, rubbed her eyes, and answered. "Hello." She expected a hang-up. The alarm clock read 5:15 AM.

"Hi, did I wake you?" Nin's voice sounded excited, nervous.

"Yeah, but that's okay." *Sure, I love being woken up before six.* "But how come you're not sawin' off logs, kid?"

"Can I please talk to Frank a minute?"

"Sure," she sighed and handed the phone off to Frank with no introduction, a habit of hers that Frank detested. "It's Nin. She sounds scared."

"Frank? Thank goodness you're awake. You know about the truck going off the road? Didn't ya' hear all the commotion?"

"Uh, what commotion?"

"Well, can I please come up there? I gotta talk to somebody. Ned's still out of it."

"Sandy, Nin needs to talk to us, okay? I'll make the coffee."

"Sure, why not? We're awake anyway." Sometimes Sandy was disappointed in Nin, in her occasional neediness, but, at other times, she could love her like a daughter. This wasn't one of them.

Nin looked a little wasted as she took off her gear and tossed it into the wooden rocker. She was having trouble catching her breath. Her hair was all swirls and spiky tufts, her eyes red and puffy, her complexion blotchy.

"You're not gonna believe this! A truck slid right off Route Ten into our back yard, right through the railing, about two this morning. We were still up, sort of, and then somebody was pounding on our back kitchen door. It was Booth, blood streaming, his bloody face pressed against the storm door glass." Nin was running all her words together. "Booth Gossam, the village rapist, of all people!"

Frank held up his hand. "Whoa, girl. Take a deep breath." He guided her into the rocker while Sandy headed for the kitchen and returned with a tray of steaming cups of coffee, milk and sugar.

"Anyway, Ned asked him what happened, and he freaked, then pointed toward the back yard. I looked out the window, and there was his crappy old truck! Ned handed him a towel, and I called the sheriff in Galway, then the ambulance.

"So then Booth says, 'What the fuck d'ya call the cops for?' Then he stumbles back out onto the porch, to the end of the house, and heads up the hill past your place. We saw him in the street light at the crossroads. A half hour later, the sheriff's deputy got here. We pointed him up the hill, but I guess he couldn't find him. Jeez, didn't you guys hear anything or see the lights flashing?"

Frank tried to digest what Nin was telling him.

"You slept through it?" Nin asked, sounding annoyed.

"Yeah," Sandy answered from the kitchen, "We actually can't hear much on the second floor, except the wind. So, did they ever pick Booth up? Gonna find a bloody trail when we go for our walk?"

"I don't know, but the wrecker'll be here soon to pull Booth's truck out...if they work on Sunday."

"Don't count on it," Frank said. "Nobody works on Sunday."

"Dear Chuck heard Booth go over the embankment and called to ask if we were okay. Wasn't that sweet of him? He's a really caring man. He couldn't see over the edge of the highway to where it landed."

"Think Booth's in the hospital? Head wound maybe?" Sandy inquired.

"Booth, honey. Booth!" Frank exclaimed, almost spilling his coffee. "He was probably drunk or high and feeling no pain. Maybe hit his head on the roof of the truck cab. Head wounds can cause a lot of blood loss. My guess is he's trying to avoid another DWI. Guys like Booth live forever and rarely go to jail." Frank looked over at Nin who now seemed more composed.

"Bad things only happen to good people. So we slept through it, but I'll bet Rhu didn't, unless she'd taken sleeping pills."

Nin smiled. "Yes, that's what Chuck said. If you ask me, Rhu self-medicates. I suppose it doesn't hurt that her son's a doctor."

"So, Nin, on the phone you said you had a question for me?"

"Yeah, now the guardrail isn't just bent! There's a ten-foot gap in it. Another car could go flying through, and with nothing to slow it down it could land right in the middle of our house!"

"And your question?" Frank was edging on irritability. He hated to be awakened before he was ready, and the living room was cold. He tried to decide whether to stoke up the wood stove or head back to bed. *If only Nin would leave. Sometimes she can be a pain.*

"I want to know if you'll get the sheriff to put in a good word about replacing the guardrail."

"Nin, I hardly *know* Sam Barrows. He dropped in once. And

besides, that's Highway Department business, not the Sheriff's Department. Don't worry, someone will put up caution signs, but the odds of another vehicle leaving the road at that exact location are practically nil, zip."

Nin wasn't convinced. "Honest to God, I hate this corner. I wish we lived in Bangor!" Then, being exhausted, she said she had to get back home.

They watched her trudge down toward her House-in-the-Hole. It wasn't yet light enough to see the accident scene except as the lights of passing vehicles caught the flutter of yellow caution tape where the railing was missing.

"How'd we manage to sleep through the first accident of the year?" Frank asked.

"I don't know, but I'm glad we did. I'm getting to an age where I need seven straight hours of sleep, or else I get grumpy. How about you?"

"Yeah, well, I am grumpy. Nin wears me out."

At eight-fifteen there was a heavy knock at the door. Frank went to answer, thinking irrationally that a bloodied Booth might be standing there. Instead it was the looming figure of Sam Barrows. "Looks like someone's had a good night's sleep."

"Sorry to bother you, but I was in the neighborhood investigating the accident down below."

"No bother. Come on in. Have some hot coffee. Say, they ever find Booth Gossam?"

"Yup. Fell into a snow bank up beyond the MacTeague place. He fought the EMT's, but they got him into the ambulance before he froze to death. Got a blood alcohol sample." Sam removed his heavy jacket and sat in the Canadian rocker. "Sure, I'll have some of that coffee."

"Say, the girl that lives down there, Nin Forrester, asked me to ask you when the guardrail will be replaced." Frank pointed down the hill. "She's worried about somebody else landing right on top of them."

"Beats me. I have no sway over those guys in Augusta. She oughta try calling the Highway Department." He smiled, envisioning the piles of paperwork over at the DOT office. "See where that gets her. She'll be lucky to get a guardrail by next winter."

The doorbell rang, interrupting their conversation. Sandy answered, and there stood Chuck: no hat, no mittens, holding a bag of donuts from the General Store, a wide grin on his face.

"C'mon in and meet Sheriff Sam," Sandy said, smiling.

After introductions, the four of them sat around the wood stove where Frank had a good fire going. They made quick work of the donuts. Chuck told the sheriff what he saw after the accident, which wasn't much, and they chatted about neighborhood crime.

Chuck brought up the subject of deer-jacking. "Some of these folks can't afford hunting licenses and can't make it on the measly amount of food stamps they get. They live off what they can jack, but that doesn't give 'em the right to dump that crap by the side of the road. You're lucky you don't have to pick up those plastic sacks of guts."

"Yuk!" Sandy exclaimed. "I hate those things!"

Chuck went on, "They stink to high heaven and draw the coyotes. But that falls in Bud Varney's domain. Lucky Bud!" Chuck also filled Sam in on the criminal past of Booth Gossam. Sandy asked how Rhu was dealing with the accident.

"She's pretty agitated about the truck. Says there've been two people killed on this corner since we moved here twenty some odd years ago. She's fit to be tied about the guardrail. Oh, and Sam, she wants Booth Gossam arrested if he isn't already." Chuck chuckled.

"Tell her I can't just go around putting people in jail." He smiled ruefully.

"She doesn't want you to arrest him for the accident, Sam. For Lester's murder! She's sure he did it, even if he does have an alibi. If you knew my wife, you'd understand." Chuck shook his head.

"How do you know if he's got an alibi?"

"Hey, sorry, Sheriff, but I'm afraid it's from your mouth to Hal Hines's ear. You might as well broadcast it on Public Radio. Hal hangs out at the General Store every morning and blabs everything."

Sam wasn't surprised, but it was another issue that he'd have to raise with Hal. One thing he didn't need was a loose cannon in the department, and he was already two men short. Sam knew that he'd been slow to clean house after taking office, but Darla had said, "Honey, give them time to get used to you."

Sandy changed the subject. "Hey, how'd you two like to see our subject list? Chuck, you might have some insight, seeing that you've lived here forever."

Sam's interest was piqued. "About time. I believe I asked for it last time I was here." He turned to Chuck. "Speaking of crime, what's your take on Lester's murder? Frank tells me you knew him pretty well."

Chuck rearranged himself in the chair. "Damned shame! Lester was one of my few friends. Nobody to grouse about antiques with now, but as far as who-done-it, I don't have the foggiest. Of course his being 'different' might've pissed somebody off enough to kill him."

Sandy interjected, "Well, Lester *was* and Betty *is* my cousin, and they're both 'different,' but in opposite directions. Actually, differences aren't that unusual in the Moulton family line." She smiled mischievously.

Frank rose, produced a list from the printer, and handed it to Sam. "Maybe you can help us with it, Chuck, but please don't mention it to Rhu." He knew he could trust Chuck, but nobody trusted Rhu.

"First and foremost is Betty. She's a gun-lover and probably stands to inherit big-time. That's means and motive—two out of three."

"Yeah, but she was working the day after Thanksgiving," Chuck said. "I know, because I went down there that afternoon to mail a package and she was bitching about having to work. So you can probably forget opportunity, unless she shot him in the dark."

Sam interrupted, "Frank, let me study the list so I can keep track of the names. In fact, mind if I keep this so I can make notes?"

"No sweat. I can just punch up a copy from the computer. Okay, next, we like Jane Ridley, maybe because she's whacko."

Sam smiled at Frank's reasoning. "Insanity's a common plea." He stared at the eight names on the list: Betty Moulton, Jake Ridley, Jane Ridley, Gus and Booth Gossam, Angus and Lonnie Mac Teague, and Slug Willard. "Eight suspects? Plenty to choose from."

Chuck frowned a little. "Naw, Jane Ridley's mouth goes a mile a minute, but she's not your shooter. She just sics God on you. Besides, she couldn't handle the guilt or the gun. You're way off, Frank."

"Really?" Sandy countered. "Religious people can be the worst kind of fanatics. What about Waco?"

"Well, the jury's still out on who the real fanatics were," Chuck chuckled.

"Okay, Chuck. Maybe I'll cross out Jane. But she's got the bucks to hire a killer. I don't hear you objecting, Sam."

Sam made a note next to her name. "No objection. She's a keeper. But how about her crafty, entrepreneurial son?"

"All bets are off with that guy." Chuck's face became animated. "Word's out that Jake's parties include nose candy and...whatever. S'pose you've heard that, Sam. I'll tell you, anything that would piss off Mama Jane, sonny-boy Jake will do."

"Praise the lord!" Frank exclaimed.

Sam had relaxed into the easy chair, finding high entertainment value in all of this Whiskey Hill banter.

Knowing he had an eager audience, Chuck continued, "Wouldn't be surprised if Jake did it. He's got so much on so many people, it'd be easy for him to blackmail someone into giving him an alibi. Never was honest, even when I had him in high school, always a sly little bastard. Cheated regularly. Who else's on the list?"

Frank wondered if maybe Jake had something on Chuck. Could it be the connection with Slug and his oldest son BJ? Chuck'd tell him when the time came.

Getting tuned-in to these small town relationships was tiresome, but Sam continued, "So, here's your mutual good neighbor, Slug. What's the motive? How do you link a macho tree-cutter and a gay guy? Did they even know each other?"

"Yeah. We couldn't get that one to track, hard as we tried," Sandy said with regret. Not one to sit idle, she'd taken out her new quilt to work on.

"Listen friends, be careful about Slug. I sure as hell wouldn't broadcast suspicions about him if I were you." Chuck tapped his eye tooth and looked thoughtfully at Frank, then Sandy. "He's vindictive. He'll shoot

III

anything in sight. Now would he shoot Lester? That's another question entirely, and, like you said, why? No apparent motive. What's your view, Sam?"

"I'd leave him on the list since you say he's gun-happy." He underlined Slug's name. "What about Angus and Lonnie here?"

"Angus? Why in the world would Angus make the list?" Chuck seemed flummoxed and turned to Frank, "Boy, you're reaching."

"Because, Chuck," Sandy said, "you told me that the day after Thanksgiving, Lonnie packed up and drove to the bus depot in Waterville and that Lonnie was all upset. Even left Angus' red pickup in the bus parking lot. Apparently he and his dad had some kind of run-in. Remember what time that was?"

"I don't know. Early afternoon, I guess." Chuck scratched his stubbled chin.

"So couldn't Lonnie have done it?"

"Naw, if Lonnie had wanted to kill anybody, it'd be his father. They've been at each other for years."

"Suspicious behavior around the time of the crime. Both MacTeagues stay." Sam jotted furiously. "Okay, let's talk Gossams."

"Den of thieves going way back to the founding of Venice. Violent. Lots of rapes and incest. Hell, they're so bad they've been omitted from the town history."

"And the bog's right in their back yard," Sandy added, rummaging around for her thread that Panther had rolled under her chair.

"The males in that family all have jackets a yard long, except for the lad, Andy, of course. I interviewed some of them. They stay on the list."

Sam finished his coffee. "Well, folks, I'm afraid duty calls. This has been mighty informative. If you think of anything else, let me know. And thanks for the refreshments."

Frank saw him to the door. "Look, Sam, I'd sure like to talk with you in more detail about Lester's murder, but obviously it can't be this morning."

"Sure, I'd like that. I'll be back in the area tomorrow. I could give you a call. Thanks again." Sam was so tall that his head almost touched a thick, two foot icicle hanging from the front door cornice. "Hell, that could kill somebody." He reached up, broke it off and tossed it in the snow. "Be seein' you. Good meeting you, Chuck," he hollered back into the living room.

Sandy came back in and sat beside Chuck. "Well, old man, how you been keeping?" Sandy gave him a gentle poke on the shoulder. He was her favorite neighbor and their best friend.

"Fine, except Rhu's been on my case about my smoking. Hell, she sneaks cigs out the back door often enough. I don't know what her problem is. She's either as nervous as a cat on a hot stove or half-dead in bed."

"What you need is a mug of mulled cider with a shot of whiskey or brandy. Which will it be?"

"I'll take cider with whiskey, a big splash, if you please! Still cold down to my toes, despite your good fire."

"Sure thing." Frank requested plain old mulled cider without booze. Over the years, he'd developed a sort of kid-brother relationship with Chuck. Frank didn't have any older brothers, so he could use a stand-in.

"So, what else is new, kids?" Chuck took his mug and settled back down in his favorite rocker. He had a habit of looking like he belonged there. "You two weren't at the auction Sunday."

"No, Nin came over all upset about the new Gossam ornament in her backyard. She can be a pest. Get anything good at the auction?"

"There was a huge crowd, seein' as it's winter, but I managed to get a couple of pretty little chairs, a Mickey Mouse lunch box and some books."

"So, tell me, don't you miss Lester when you're at the auction?"

Chuck's face took on a pained expression. "You know it! Sometimes I see the back of some guy's neck and think, 'There's Lester,' and then the fact of his murder hits me like a fist in the gut."

Sandy became more truthful than tactful. "What's Rhu's problem lately? Why's she keeping such a close rein on you?"

"How the hell should I know?" he asked, bristling slightly. "Doesn't let me out of her sight except to go to the store or the auction. Keeps her nose buried in a romance novel most of the time. That is when she isn't trying to run our kids' lives. I'm gonna have to build more bookshelves if she joins another book club."

"What's the matter, Chuck, doesn't she trust an old dog like you?" Frank was curious to know what'd gone wrong. He cared about Chuck and didn't give a damn about Rhu. After all, she'd never made the slightest effort to be friendly.

"Rhu hasn't trusted me since mid-August Seventy-nine, but that's a long story, and I'd have to have a hell of a lot more whiskey to tell it. Ever since Seth got hitched, she's been asking if Lucille is pregnant. Lucille's a hot ticket, and Seth's got more than he can handle with that one."

"Hate to be intrusive, but is Lucille pregnant?"

"No, not yet. But did I tell you that number one daughter Sally's pregnant? Her lawyer husband's over the moon! I wish they lived closer than Miami so I could see her more often. Susie's still single and singing in Philly. She's living with my sister and her actor-husband. Seems happy enough. Just think, old Angus and I both have daughters who sing for a living. They were both singing stars in high school, you know. But Seth's the one I worry about. He's kinda' naive and Lucille's a spender. My God, she wants a bigger house and a pool. You know the type."

Frank thought about it. "Yeah, I do. It's a good thing Seth earns big bucks. By the way, how do you like Sam? We think he's a straight-ahead guy."

"I agree, but anyone'd be an improvement over Carleton Belcher. That old crook had a hand in every deal in Thoreau County, including the 'Case of the Disappearing Marijuana'."

"Yeah, to which we made our minor contribution, remember?" Frank raised an eyebrow.

"That went on for years before you got here. Accusations involving bribery of witnesses, destruction of evidence, etcetera." Chuck leaned back in the Canadian rocker, coughed, and swilled down the rest of his cider. Sandy retrieved his mug and refilled it.

"A little drug pirating isn't all that unusual, unfortunately. We had plenty of that in the Air Force, though there the consequences were a lot worse than dying or losing an election. More like a trip to Leavenworth," Frank pointed out. "Sure, Belcher pulled that same stunt when he came and harvested that crap that somebody planted on our place a couple years back."

"Oh, sure. But your grass was small potatoes; excuse the mixed metaphor. We're talkin' semi-truckloads. This happened way before your time and never made the papers. Got the inside scoop from Charlie Bickford over in Amnesty. In Maine, it's a staple of the economy. By god, that's some dandy cider. Just what the doctor ordered."

"Thanks," Sandy said. "By the way, Chuck, has Rhu been calling me lately and not getting an answer?"

"Doubt it. Try not to pay any attention to her."

"No big deal. I've just been getting some wrong numbers and hang-ups lately. Please don't mention it to her, okay?"

As if on signal, the phone rang, and it was Rhu. She wanted Chuck to come home because she'd messed up the damper on their kitchen stove. "Rhu says the kitchen's filling up with smoke, Chuck. You need to go right home. I gather it's an emergency."

Chuck shook his head in a gesture somewhere between hopelessness and resignation. Obviously he didn't want to leave, so he lingered an extra minute while putting on his jacket, then hurried out across the snow-filled yard.

Sandy kissed her husband on the cheek. "Aren't you glad you're not married to Rhu?"

"Aren't *you* glad you're married to *me?*" Frank swept her up and planted a kiss on her lips.

CHAPTER 18

Thump...kathump...drip, drip...swissshhh...thump.

"Ugh," Frank groaned, opening his eyes and staring into the darkness of the bedroom. *Too many blankets! Feel buried alive!* He pushed the bedcovers off. Warmish, wet air had worked its way around the chinks in the old window casings and sleetish rain peppered the panes. He reached over and pulled back the curtain.

In the stingy light from the crossroads at the bottom of the hill he could barely see the outline of objects. Chunks of snow and ice were sliding off the steel roof and falling like great white cow paddies, two stories to the ground below. *Wait a minute. Too much light.* Half-asleep, he noticed the reflection from a dim pair of headlights pointed up the hill. The phosphorous hands of the alarm clock read four-thirty. *What the heck!!??*

"What is it, Frank?" Sandy half-whispered. She hated surprises.

"I don't know. Something going on down there." He pointed toward the bottom of the hill. "A car or pickup half off the road. From the way the headlights are tilted, I'd say there's a wheel in the drainage ditch. God, it's only four-thirty."

"Is that rain I hear?" Sandy sighed.

"Rain, sleet and fat, wet snowflakes. The January thaw has arrived."

"Great!" Sandy exclaimed, jumping up out of bed. "I'll get the coffee on if you'll stir up the fire. Why don't you go down the hill and see if they need help?"

"Probably another drunk Gossam," Frank muttered, cursing all ancestors and future descendants of the House of Gossam. Frank dressed, stumbled down the stairs, put on his gear and hurried down the hill, only to return within a few minutes. He rushed into the kitchen where Sandy was grinding coffee beans.

"Jeeze, Sandy, it's Angus down there, standing by his truck. Doesn't seem to know where he is. Holding his left arm in a weird way. Call Mable. Damned fool doesn't want an ambulance." Frank grabbed a dishtowel and wiped the snow and water off his face.

"I'll have her come down."

"Tell her to go straight down to the corner." Frank took off his jacket, hung it up, and put on a warmer one.

Her voice held steady. "No Mabel, he can't drive his truck. There's something wrong with him. He's kind of leaning against the hood. Any of your sons home?" She paused. "Someone should take him to the hospital. He doesn't want an ambulance." Mabel was asking a lot of questions. "Well, you can decide when you get down here, but he's gotta be checked at the hospital."

Sandy hung up and turned to Frank. "Here's a blanket we can take down. I'll call Chuck, too, unless he saw you down there."

"Naw! They sleep on the other side of the house. Yeah, call him. I'm going back down. Angus could be dead by now, stubborn cuss!"

"Okay. I'll be right behind you, soon as I call Chuck."

Soon four people hovered around Angus, who was still in a daze, leaning against the hood of his truck and resisting any efforts to move him. Sandy thought he'd had a stroke, maybe a serious one, from overexerting himself.

Chuck said "I'll go call the ambulance!"

Mabel pleaded, "No, don't! Angus'll be furious!" speaking as if Angus weren't there, and, in truth, he wasn't.

Sandy and Frank agreed with Chuck. Then suddenly Angus grumbled, "Dammit, I'm all right! Jus' gotta' get my arm movin'. Why don't you busybodies go back to bed and leave me alone?"

The red Ford pickup was slightly off the road, with the right front wheel stuck in the soft melting mud of the shoulder.

"He's been out checkin' the roads for excess runoff," Mabel offered in a shaky voice.

Years ago, before he'd become a Selectman, Angus had served as Road Commissioner, and he still felt a responsibility for controlling the water drainage on Whiskey Hill. Erosion could lead to higher taxes.

Frank took Mabel firmly by the arm and steered her off to one side. "As his closest kin, Mabel, you should make the decision. This is the 'Golden Hour' when what the docs do can make a difference. Who knows how long he's been standing here?" He held her gently by her rounded shoulders. "Listen, Mabel, he needs to go to the ER, *now!*"

Angus had no monopoly on stubbornness, and Mabel won out. She called her son Donnie on Frank's cell phone, and, within minutes, he was there, helping his raging, cursing father into the car. Then the MacTeagues started to head home.

Chuck turned to Frank and Sandy. "Listen, kids, if Angus doesn't make it to high noon, it's not your fault or mine either. Stubborn jackass! We did all we could."

"You know as well as I do he has no intention of going to the ER. He'd rather die in his armchair," Frank said, disgusted.

Once full daylight broke, Donnie returned to the corner, pulled the truck out of the ditch and had his slow brother, Johnnie, drive it home. By now snow-melt water was rushing down the gully alongside the road, and the sleet had turned to a dismal drizzle. The culvert carried the brown water into the dented storm drain. It was partially caved in from when Slug's son BJ had once lost control of his truck and nosed down into the drain works, knocking over the road sign and crushing the culvert pipe and concrete footing. The highway department had replaced the sign but never bothered to repair the culvert.

Later that day Sandy tried calling Mabel, praying for a report from Townsend Hospital. No one answered.

"He's probably gone to Amnesty to see old Doc Dow. You know Angus doesn't have insurance. He told me once that Doc Dow treats him for free as long as Angus delivers loads of cow manure for the doc's big garden."

"Sandy, Angus is one of those Depression guys, like our parents. They can squeeze the shit out of a buffalo nickel."

At ten Nin called, practically hysterical. This time she didn't ask for Frank but blurted out to Sandy, "Somebody's killed my kitty!" She was sobbing.

"Calm down, honey. That's terrible, but how do you know it wasn't an accident?"

"Because...well...I was looking over toward Slug's house and I saw something brown and orange, and I went out and there was Whiffy draped over the stop sign, all bloody. He's real flat, like his insides are gone. Oh God! Who'd do such a hateful thing?" Nin's words trailed off into bubbly sobs.

A chill seized Sandy, but she rebounded quickly. "I'm *so* sorry. I know how much you loved him, but, listen, Nin, call Bud Varney and report it, right now. You have a camera. Take photos from all angles. I know it's hard, but don't move the cat! Okay?"

"Okay, if I have to, but would you ask Frank to come down and take a look? Ned's already left for school. I guess he didn't notice poor Whiffy."

"Good Lord, Nin, how could Ned ride past Whiffy and not see him?" Sandy didn't think that Nin needed Frank, and she didn't want Frank to get more stressed. At the moment, he seemed to have enough on his mind.

"He was in a hurry. Besides, guys don't notice anything," she answered with a shift of tone from helplessness to authority. "Can't Frank come down?"

"Look, Frank's in the middle of something. Just call the warden, and then take the pictures. Maybe you can come up later. Okay?"

Nin reluctantly agreed then hung up.

Sandy turned to Frank, "Do you suppose our corner's jinxed?"

Frank shot her a look of astonished disbelief.

"Nin's bloody cat, Whiffy, is hanging from the stop sign," she blurted. "Last night Angus had a stroke, a few days ago Booth's truck flew into Nin's back yard. What's next?"

"About anything you can imagine. This is Venice, remember? I'm telling you, Sandy, nothing surprises me anymore."

Tuesday morning Sandy decided to walk up the hill to check on the MacTeagues. Frank was determined to finish his new P. D. James mystery. "Don't forget, honey, no good deed goes unpunished." He called after her. "You're not gonna get anything but blame from them."

Curiosity drove her to take the walk. She wanted to know if Angus was still alive. Mabel came to the door with a look of apprehension. Mabel didn't seem pleased to see her. Sandy wished she could turn and run.

"Might's well come in, but don't stay too long. He's better but he's kinda' grumpy."

Sandy was ushered into the parlor. It was only the second or third time she'd been invited into this room. Angus was propped up in a worn Naugahyde lounge chair with lumpy pillows, his bad arm resting on a hot water bottle. The room was illuminated only by daylight leaking through torn green shades and the bluish glow of the television screen. *Jeopardy* was blaring offensively. Angus waved his good hand absently and grumbled, "Sit."

The room had a sagging green flowered sofa, piles of old newspapers and magazines, a piano, its ivories yellowed like old teeth, and two upholstered chairs from the Fifties. It still smelled like the old dog they'd put down two months ago. There was a faded floral carpet on the floor and an old fashioned carpet sweeper in the corner. No books, not even *Reader's Digest* Condensed. After removing newspapers from it, Sandy sat on a sturdy footstool and scooted down in front of Angus. "How're ya doing? You had us plenty worried. Did you get checked out by Doc Dow?"

Angus eyed her suspiciously and tilted his head up to the right. Apparently he was still having trouble seeing out of one eye, and she knew that he'd never gone near the ER.

He pointed to a bottle of fat tablets on the end table. "Yup! He give me this damned blood thinner, and it makes me pee. Damned fool doctor."

"And your arm? Doing any better?"

"It'll do. Left eye drives me crazy. Can't see outa' the bottom half. Doc Dow says I can't drive. Hah! That'll be the day!"

Sandy was going to ask Angus if, before his stroke, he'd noticed Whiffy hanging on the stop sign, but just then she heard a heavy pounding on the door. Sandy excused herself and went into the kitchen where she saw Mabel greeting Mooseman. He stood heavily in the middle of the kitchen, gobs of mud dripping from his old Army boots. He was wearing jungle fatigues. *Guess Mabel isn't going to usher him into the parlor.* Sandy'd never met Mooseman formally, just had brief, roadside conversations.

He was strange looking and smelled like moss and bog water. His brown hair was scraggly, and his face smudged, but his blue eyes revealed intelligence. As she entered the kitchen, he was ranting about police cars racing up *his* road. Apparently Angus wasn't the only one asserting authority over Whiskey Road. Mabel had always befriended Moose, but, at this moment, she seemed embarrassed by him.

"Sandy, you met our neighbor George Felker?"

George walked up close to her, stared into her eyes, and then began talking as if in mid-conversation. "...goddamned sheriff's department's always on surveillance and I know why. Don't think I don't! They're tryin' to collect evidence on me. They want me gone. They're in it with the IRS. Hell, they've been tryin' to get somethin' on me ever since I moved here. I refuse to pay state or federal taxes. Man's got a constitutional right to live his life without taxes and constant surveillance. Don't you agree, Mrs.—? What's your name, anyway?"

Sandy prayed that Mabel wouldn't reveal Frank's OSI experience. That's all they'd need, Moose thinking that Frank was a government spy. "Just call me Sandy. I bet you see a lot of deer where you live."

"I'm all for deer, but I don't like those goddamned hunters. Your husband hunt, Sandy?" As he came closer, she could smell the pungent combination of wet pine, cat-piss spruce, kerosene and wood smoke.

"No! We've posted most of the hill, with permission, of course."

"Good, that's good!" Moose nodded his head, flinging drops of water onto the kitchen floor. "You can staple those signs in my woods as well. I don't countenance killin' innocent wild animals. Wild animals don't deserve to be eaten. That's why I try and scare off the hunters during huntin' season, and any other time o' year I see anyone in the woods with a rifle."

Sandy had seen him a few times, partially naked in the middle of the road, but she'd only heard about him dressed in camouflage gear, running through the woods screaming obscenities at hunters. It was only a matter of time before he got himself shot. Some folks thought that might be what he wanted. Still others, hunters mainly, thought he deserved it.

"You know, Mabel here, she's the only person in this whole town that understands me. One time I had a little fire in my house. I come down here and asked Mabel for a pail of water. She gave me *two*, and she came up and helped put out the fire. She's A-Number-One, Mabel is." Mooseman gave an overly enthusiastic nod in Mabel's direction, causing water to fly from his unruly locks.

Sandy tried to imagine how he'd looked on Wall Street. A bit better looking than average, but it was hard to tell. He had a good nose, but a scruffy beard hid his jaw line.

Sandy would hide whenever she saw yellow jeep coming down the hill. That was because twice he'd stopped her and asked odd questions such as, "Have you seen any fisher cats today?" or "Have you spied strangers on this road?" The raw electricity behind his eyes made her feel uneasy.

Moose rambled on. "I'm gonna have to build me another cabin, deeper in the woods, I guess. Gotta get away from people and traffic and noise! Wouldn't mind bein' closer to the bog, anyway. Closer to animals. Don't want no more trucks runnin' up that back road, though. I might just drop a tree right in the middle of that woods road and keep 'em out, once and for all!"

"Wouldn't you get into trouble blocking a road?" Sandy wanted to reel the words back in the minute they left her mouth.

Mooseman became more boisterous. "Guess I haven't made myself clear!" His eyes glowed as Sandy instinctively took a step back. "Let me *explain!* I don't *want* anyone in these woods! No people, no guns, no shooting, no beer cans, no litter! And *no boats!* Why, just the other day, I'm hikin' back in there to check on the grouse population, went to step over what looked like a brush pile, and there's a dang boat, right smack dab in the middle of the wilderness. Nearly broke my leg. No people, no guns, no killin'. That's what I say!"

Sandy, always the placater, quickly affirmed, "I can understand where you're coming from."

Drunk on his own words, Moose charged ahead. "Know how many deer were slaughtered last season here in Venice? Thirteen-hundred and ninety-eight, half-again the population of this town. And how many hunters got shot? Only three! People are movin' in, cuttin' trees, despoilin' the land. Bad enough old 'Clona' comes sneakin' 'round my woods in the early morning. Says she's countin' birds, but she's checkin' up on *me!*"

Just then Angus' voice boomed from the parlor, "Tell Moose I need some peace and quiet, damn it!"

Mooseman drew in, his arms folded on his chest and his head retracted into his shoulders like a startled turtle. The air went out of him. Bowing to Sandy and Mabel, he backed out of the kitchen, disappearing through the side door.

Sandy, needing to escape Angus' anger, followed him. Meekly she said, "Nice meeting you."

He stopped in the yard, now swimming in mud and ice, and smiled at her oddly. Then he stepped a few feet closer to her, his eyes shifting rapidly back and forth behind squinting lids.

"What should I call you?" Sandy was trying to figure this man out.

He tilted his head, his stringy mop of hair falling to one side, and gave her an enigmatic smile. "Mooseman, what else?"

CHAPTER 19

The weather was just plain drippy. Gullies were full, pot holes overflowed, drains clogged, and the mud was spongy with layers of ice. It all added up to a recipe for disaster. The Thoreau County road crews had gone way over budget on salt-sand, this being an extra harsh winter. Although the roads looked fairly clear, there were patches of black ice, especially where trees overhung the roads and the sun didn't reach the surface.

The Galway P.D. had dealt with numerous rear-enders, slides off curves, and vehicles stuck in snow banks. The sheriff's office had its share of calls, sometimes being asked to assist the local or state police. A Micmac Indian got sloppy drunk while playing bingo at the tribal hall on Main Street then staggered out and fell asleep behind a dumpster. Unfortunately his bed was a snow bank. He was discovered the next morning—cause of death acute alcohol poisoning resulting in hypothermia.

Countywide there'd been a crop of snowmobile accidents, nothing new in Maine. The trails stretched through Thoreau County all the way to Canada. Snowmobilers often fell victim to their own wild enthusiasm. Every year, a barbed wire fence would decapitate one or two, and several enthusiasts ended up at the bottom of ponds, trapped beneath the too thin ice.

Just then, a call came in to the dispatcher who transferred it to Sam's office. "It's the Amnesty Ambulance Service." Hazel looked upset.

Sam picked up. "Yeah, what've you got?" He listened.

"On the road to Waterville? Whereabouts? Who's jurisdiction?"

"Well, is it north or south of the mud-racing track?"

"It's not our call. The Borden Plantation is an unincorporated state township. Contact the troopers. How bad is it?"

"What's your ETA?"

"Then you'd better contact Bud Varney, too. We don't want a wreck on top of a wreck. Thanks for the info."

Frank had called Eric Eloranto about doing some work on the Zucchetti kitchen. Eric had some time between jobs and was paying them a visit to give them an estimate. The kitchen cabinets were old and ill-fitting, and Sandy wanted birch with glass doors. When the phone rang, Frank was outside showing Eric the geese. Sandy called him in, and, as she did, he had a strange premonition. Usually the sixth sense was Sandy's domain. As Frank picked up the phone, he was filled with dread.

"Frank, there's been a bad wreck on Route Twelve, just beyond the mud-racing track. Mabel called. They picked it up on the scanner."

"How bad?"

"Man versus moose, I guess. State Troopers have been dispatched, and Amnesty's there. Maybe you could help."

"Yeah, Eric's agreed to do the carpentry job and we were going to drive over to Marden's in Waterville anyway to look at salvage hardwood."

"Dat road's very narrow and curvy," Eric added. "I tell my girls to slow down dere."

"Sandy, see ya' when we see ya'. Maybe we can help with traffic control. Unfortunately, moose accidents always draw a big crowd."

By the time Frank and Eric reached the scene on a long, dark stretch of highway, they couldn't park very close because of all the gawkers. One woman was standing on the side of the road, throwing up.

"That's all we need, folks getting in the way." He moved a flare farther out from the scene. No other police had arrived except for Butch, the one dayshift Amnesty cop, who was having a hard time handling traffic around the wreck. Frank asked Eric to head beyond the wreck and slow drivers down by waving his arms. The wreck was totally blocking the southbound lane.

An old black Saab squatted in the middle of the lane, its top crunched down like an aluminum beer can. As Eric drew closer, he noticed the license plate: *CLIX*. He turned pale. "My Gott! Dat's Don's car! Dat's Don's blood! Oh my Gott!"

"Donald Wells, the photographer? Jeeze, you're right. Butch told me he's bein' transported to Townsend. Maybe it's not as bad as it looks." But Frank knew better. "You okay, Eric? You look like you're gonna pass out."

"Yah, yah, it's just..." Eric's face was white as paste.

"Listen, if you want to help, go beyond the wreck and slow traffic down. Wave your arms. Otherwise we're gonna have another wreck. By the way, how close are you to Don?"

"Best pals. He lives next property to me. His girls grew up wid my girls. Elsa's best friends with Olympia." His eyes brimmed with tears as he walked off stiffly to the other side of the wreck, still in a daze.

Frank decided he'd better stick by Eric. They were silent for a minute or two as Frank stared down at the license plate. Below the word "CLIX" it read *Vacationland*.

Eric turned. "Frank, tink about it. Don drives to the *Sentinel* office every day along dis route. If he'd been five minutes earlier or later even, he'd be okay. Tink he stands a chance? Could anybody survive dis?" He pointed to the wreck, where the front of the car was mashed nearly to the ground, creating a wedge-shaped Saab. Don's blood mingled and clotted up with the moose's, and moose parts were foliated into the crumpled wreckage. The head, hanging off the trunk by strands of cartilage, was intact. It had been a young moose, with only buds for horns, and a foot-and-a-half of tongue was dangling, touching the pavement.

Frank felt the bile rise in the back of his throat. He shook his head, at a loss for words.

"Maybe he got thrown, you tink?" Frank hadn't remembered that Eric and Don were friends and close neighbors. Poor Eric. Now Frank felt guilt on top of nausea. He and Butch moved the crowd away from the wreck then took a few more photos. Ordinarily Don would be the one clicking the shutter.

Butch sighed, "Jeeze, it's gruesome. They had a hard time getting the poor guy out. His face was all smashed. Never seen one this bad, and I been doin' this a lot o' years. Where the hell are the Staties anyway?"

"I dunno, but we've gotta keep the traffic moving. Damned gawkers everywhere."

"You know who the victim is?" Butch asked as he started to move away.

"Yeah, a hell of a nice guy—Don Wells from Venice."

"The photographer? Oh God! I know him. Didn't recognize...the...the car. I'll pray for him. He's gonna need all the prayers he can get."

Finally Frank heard the sirens, State Troopers arriving on the scene. *About damned time.* He walked over to Butch. "They'll have to measure, photograph, tape, and write it up. I gotta get out of here. You okay now?"

"I guess. Go ahead." Butch blew his nose.

Suddenly Eric was at Frank's side, his face contorted with grief. "Listen, couldn't we go to Townsend?"

"Sure."

Frank knew the dangers of this road. He thought about the possibility of another moose walking out to lick the salt off the edge of the road. Why was Don the one to collide with a moose?

The first person they met at the hospital was Chuck's son, Dr. Seth Shaw. Seth spoke first. "Hi...you're my folks' neighbor, aren't you? Frank Zuretti?" He shook hands.

"*Zucchetti,* right. Can you tell me if the moose accident victim, Don Wells, is alive?"

"Barely. I've notified his wife and advised her not to bring the kids. His brain's swelling. Doesn't look good. He's on his way up to surgery now. That's all I can tell you. Oh, is he Catholic, do you know?"

123

Eric was standing behind Frank, tears running down his cheeks. "No, he goes to the Amnesty Methodist. His wife's Greek Orthodox. Why?"

"Last rites if *he* were Catholic or Orthodox. I'll contact the hospital chaplain to meet his wife when she arrives. Sorry, I'm needed elsewhere now."

"Last rites? My god! He don't think Don'll make it, does he?"

Frank didn't know what to say. "If you believe in miracles, you'd better pray for one." Frank went to get coffee.

When he returned, he handed out steaming cups. Eric was holding Don's wife Olympia while the chaplain hovered in the background. She didn't seem to recognize Frank, but he introduced himself anyway and said he'd try to find Seth. Meanwhile Olympia and Eric sat down uncomfortably on the blue plastic and metal chairs, Eric trying to explain what happened. Olympia was choking back the grief. It suddenly occurred to Frank that Don's wife must have traveled to Waterville along the same route and seen the crushed Saab or the wrecker hauling it. *What a wrenching sight!*

The duty chaplain whispered a few words to Olympia, then disappeared through a set of double doors.

Gradually more aware than he had been, Frank looked around at the other people in the waiting room: kids with red faces, a man with a broken arm, a pregnant lady who spoke only French, and several very old, very ill looking people. Magazines littered a table: *Highlights, National Geographic, Redbook.* Would Don ever be able to pick up a magazine again, to say nothing of being able to read or comprehend it?

Seth finally came out and explained in whispered tones that Don was being worked on by a maxillary surgeon. His brain was swelling, he was in a coma, and they needed to move some facial bones that were pressing on... Frank didn't listen to the rest. All he heard at the end was that Don was in critical condition. He especially felt terrible for Don's two daughters. He'd seen them often at the Coop Market in Amnesty. What a perfect family they had been.

After about an hour, Eric told Frank he'd decided to stay at the hospital with Olympia and that he'd drive her home in her car. Frank drove home alone, passing the spot where traces of the accident still soiled the road.

CHAPTER 20

The next morning, Sandy felt just plain fed up with Venice. Not with its scenery, but with its citizens. Don's tragic accident weighed on her, and she felt as if she were drowning in the muck and mire of Venice's petty crimes, politics, madness and melodrama.

"Let's escape all this and go look at the ocean," she suggested to Frank as she came in through the back door. "By the way, Cleona called yesterday. Says she found a photo of our house that goes back to the 1880's, but that can wait."

Ordinarily, Sandy would have been anxious to see it, but not in her present mood. The whole damned town could wait. Sandy walked over to the south-facing windows and stared in the direction of the coast. It was only first-light, but she could see that the skies had cleared behind the warm front. The day would be a fine one for the seashore.

Frank put down the *Midcoast Sentinel,* with its headline *Sentinel Photographer Hit by Moose in Borden Plantation.* Next to that article, a piece encapsulating a squabble in Augusta over the "snack tax" and what constituted a "snack." Would a two-muffin pack be a snack or not? And what about beef jerky? Survival food or snack? With their constant bickering over taxation, Mainers hadn't evolved much from their English and Scots-Irish forebears. Even the Maine accent resembled that of the rustic folk of northern rural England.

"And they're still after Sam about crime in the county. If they only knew how he's busting his butt. And your idea about getting out of town? It's great!" Frank showed rare enthusiasm. "I can smell the sea air now, and let's stop off in Galway on the way back and see Sam if he's in. Maybe we can cheer him up."

"That'd be great, as long as we get home before dark. And for lunch let's go to Howard's Seafood Restaurant," Sandy suggested.

If you ironed out Maine's wrinkled coastline with all its inlets, bays and ports, it would be over twelve hundred miles long. Sandy and Frank had one favorite location: Acadia National Park. Not the expensive, touristy Deer Isle/Bar Harbor part, but the lesser-traveled Winter Harbor area. That's where Howard's restaurant was located, overlooking the ragged, rocky edges of the harbor and the handful of boats bobbing at their moorings in the bay.

Sometimes Sandy had the enthusiasm of a teenager, which worked out fine since Frank often felt like an old man. Frank would take the cynical side, saying, "You'd go anywhere, even Siberia, as long as I promised you good food." Sandy loved to grow food and prepare it, but what she enjoyed most was eating. Fortunately, her metabolism prevented her from gaining too much weight. Sandy got snarly and cantankerous when she didn't get her regular food fix.

They left at seven-thirty armed with a thermos of coffee. They journeyed through Deering and Bucksport, then on to Ellsworth where they resisted the temptation to stop at the open twenty-four hours a day L.L.Bean store. They went through Hancock and Sullivan then over the bridge to Gouldsboro. In winter these small towns looked like Currier and Ives prints, with their church spires, red barns, picturesque Victorian houses and always some remaining Christmas decorations glittering along roof edges or lining front doors that were never used. Huge round hay bales with dollops of half-melted snow on top of them dotted many of the fields, edged by dark borders of spruce and pine.

They pulled over to admire the remarkable scene at Frenchman's Bay. The brackish, steely gray water had frozen in little inlets and along the shoreline. Crusted snow draped like an ermine wrap over the north side of boulders. Five dramatic-looking black mergansers perched solemnly, like undertakers, on a dead lower limb of a bent and twisted pine. Fierce sea winds had warped and dwarfed most of the trees. Seagulls pecked away at a little section of clear beach, hoping for a snack. Above the hills to the west, a pale sliver of moon hung in the pewter-gray morning sky.

Increasingly, in ports like Winter Harbor, the wealthy summer-people moored their yachts and took their little skiffs onto shore, ate, went to the old fashioned, low priced soda shop secretly subsidized by a romantic millionaire, and walked around the quiet, quaint little village. In summer, every yard sparkled with cleomes, petunias, and hollyhocks, and window boxes overflowed with geraniums. In the fields close to the road glorious banks of lupines in blues, purples and pinks bent with the breeze. Sometimes Downeast Maine surpassed words. Even the Five & Dime was so charming, with its orange wheelbarrows against white lattice, its blue watering cans and red plastic lobsters, that it had been featured in *Smithsonian Magazine*. And always the intoxicating, briny smell of the sea.

In winter the population dropped to less than a thousand, but in summer it tripled.

"Did you notice that damn few of the farms around here look lived in? My guess is that they've become seasonal homes." Sandy sounded wistful. "Maine winters are too fierce for the weak hearted." Just then a sharp gust of wind came up, causing them to grab their hats, as if Nature were proving her point.

They drove along the winding, narrow road through Gerrishville down toward Winter Harbor. Then, according to custom, they headed out onto Schoodic Point and Acadia National Park. They continued along the sinuous one-way road that edged the sea, passing cove after cove.

"Look at that blue heron, standing on one leg, fishing at the edge of the ice!" Frank pointed. "It's caught one in its beak. Why didn't we bring our camera?"

To the east, across the choppy blue water of the inlet, lay Turtle Island, crowned with stunted pine and juniper. They got out and walked among the rocks, seaweed, and trace patches of snow. Holding her hand, Frank stopped and turned to Sandy. "Wouldn't we love to wake up every morning to the sound of the sea?"

He was surprised when she responded irritably, "Well we can't live here. Can't afford it!" With the trials of small town life still echoing in her head, Sandy was wearing her common sense cap. She plunged her hands into her pockets and looked out to sea.

Frank kicked a rock toward a tide pool its edges ringed with seaweed, black kelp shaped like lasagna noodles. "After a lot of feuding, the townies will up and leave the place to the wealthy who'll change the name of the town to Hilton Head North. I guess you're right. We could never afford it."

They continued along the beach, looking for interesting driftwood, shards of pottery, and pieces of sea glass. She placed their little treasures in the deep pockets of her jacket and looked over at Frank. He was still dreaming.

Sandy rubbed his shoulder then reached for his hand.

Frank took a deep breath. "We either dream, or go nuts." He put his hand on her cheek. "It's okay."

They drove on towards town and Howard's Restaurant. The parking lot was packed with scuffed pickup trucks and battered vans, indicating a local clientele. As they stepped inside, the smell of fried clams and chowder, hot fat, boiling lobster and cigarette smoke engulfed them. Fortunately a booth in the tiny no smoking area was available with a window overlooking the harbor. Lobster netting festooned the ceiling and an old lobster pot with a plastic lobster sat atop a videogame machine. Orange and yellow lettering reading *Leap of Death* flashed on and off as tiny digitized people leaped from flaming skyscraper windows to certain death below. "I guess if you want to see them splat, you have to put a dollar bill in the slot," Frank remarked caustically.

At the lunch counter, old fishermen sagged on wobbly stools, their denim pants tucked into orange-cuffed rubber boots. They wouldn't give a tourist the time of day, preferring their own company, retelling stories of close calls, freaks of nature pulled from the sea, and local gossip. Although the fishermen weren't all that old, years of salt and sea had weathered their faces.

"Too bad they couldn't lease a video game with a more maritime theme," Sandy quipped, removing her scarf and heavy sweater. "My God, it's hot in here!"

Just then, Gert, the waitress, well-built and pushing forty, cut short her conversation with two tired-looking fishermen at a nearby table and came over. Her red hair was pulled back into a knot of curls.

"So, what's it gonna be today, folks? Wanna hear the specials?"

Frank said, "We'll have clam chowder, lobster rolls, and we'll split an order of fries. Oh, and two coffees."

"I seen you in here before, ain't I?"

Sandy chuckled, "Two or three times a year, come hell'r high water."

"Gotcha." Gert grinned, gathered the unread menus and pirouetted toward the kitchen, her clogs clumping on linoleum.

Frank observed, "You know, Gert'd be pretty if she wore a little less makeup. Bet she's had a hard life. That's the way Jake's girlfriend Susan Johnson's going to look when she hits forty."

Sandy stared out at the fishing boats. She'd been a waitress during college, and she remembered it—mostly in her feet.

CHAPTER 21

Meals at Howard's rarely disappointed, and Sandy felt sated as they walked back to the car after leaving Gert a generous tip. They took the long way home along Route One to Galway, passing almost a dozen abandoned poultry farms.

At times Sandy felt a great sense of loss. "All that's left are a few small egg producers, and they're using Mexican labor, because the locals won't do the dirty work. I admit it...I miss my old New England, the way it was. Now most of the mills are closed, farms all but gone. You can hardly find a Holstein anymore. Everything changes; everybody sells out." They both grew silent as they wound their way down the coast.

When they reached Galway they passed two abandoned canneries, windows shattered, tin roofs rusting, rows of seagulls sat staring out to sea. "Galway must have been thriving back when the alewives and cod were running. I suppose that new Atlantis National Bank will buy up some of those abandoned canneries, bulldoze them, and turn them it into condos," Frank commented. "And people's taxes will go sky high."

Sandy looked around. "Galway isn't even the same as when we moved here. It used to be so quiet and peaceful. I'd love to have lived here a hundred years ago. Wouldn't you?"

"Of course I would. Now let's drop in on old Sam Barrows."

"Great, I'd like to see where he works. Wonder if there's been a break in the case?"

They only planned to stay a few minutes, but Sam was so delighted to see them that they decided to hang around. First he introduced them to Hazel, the dispatcher, then Barb, who, according to Sam, ran the whole department.

"Frank Zucchetti has a lot of years in law enforcement, so I might just have to deputize him, Barb."

"The sooner the better if you ask me. We need help. Anyone can see that." She smiled at Frank then turned back to Sam. "You're not the Lone Ranger, you know."

Sandy didn't know whether Sam was kidding about deputizing Frank or not, and Frank's enigmatic expression revealed nothing. Sam led them into his office where his huge map of Thoreau County had dozens of color-coded pins sticking in it. There were a lot of blue ones stuck in Venice and the Lake Mallacook area, which didn't surprise her.

Her thoughts traveled back to all the law enforcement offices she'd spent time in. Her first husband had moved from sheriff's deputy in New Hampshire to detective, then chief, in Florida. This office was the most depressing she'd ever seen. Having once been lawyers' offices it had plenty of shelves, but the light was poor, the paint peeling, and the furniture drab. Even the file cabinets were dented and gray. The only bright accents were the safety posters on one wall and a badge display.

"So, Frank, what's the status on Don Wells? Heard anything?"

"He's still listed as critical and unstable. They've induced a coma 'til the brain swelling goes down. It's gonna take a long time, if he lives, and even then, who knows?"

Sam took it in. "Hey, can Barb get you some coffee?"

"Sure," they replied in unison.

"I've got some of Darla's peanut butter brownies. Help yourself." Sam gestured for them to sit down. Barb brought in a tray with steaming mugs of coffee, milk and sugar. The office was cramped. His desk was a scarred oak monstrosity that he kept fairly well organized with three baskets. 'In' was full, 'Working' was overflowing, and 'Out' nearly empty.

"Don't mind if I do." Frank bit into a brownie and said, "Hey, these are great!" Sandy couldn't resist.

Frank filled Sam in on their adventure at the coast. "I guess you don't need that kind of trip. All you have to do is look out the window and there's the sea."

"Well, to be honest, I've never been to Winter Harbor. From what you say, it sounds worth lookin' at. I'll have to ask Darla if she's been there. I'd sure like you to meet her. She's a sweetheart. Actually, you could come over for supper tonight if I can get my paperwork done in time. I could call her and—"

"Sorry," a weary Frank interrupted. A day at the beach always tired him. "We didn't make arrangements for our neighbor to check our poultry so we need to get home. Rain check, though? We'd love to meet Darla. She and Sandy could compare notes on life with a lawman."

Sandy looked slightly miffed. "Not really. I don't want to drag Darla over that rocky road. I'd like to meet her though. I know how difficult it is to live with a person who answers to the whole community and then some." She let out a long sigh. "I'm so glad that Frank's retired."

Frank got down to the business. "Listen, Sam, as an interested party, we'd like to be of some help. I gave you a copy of the suspect list in the Moulton case, but since then, we've dropped Jane Ridley and made some other changes. Want to check 'em out?"

"Sure thing, but I wasn't just bullshitting a while ago. If you're interested, I can swear you in as one of my special detectives and pin a badge on you today. No one has to know about it, for now, and you can back me up if things get rough in Venice. You never know what's gonna break, and the only man I've got over there is Hal Hines." Sam shrugged.

"Let me think about it. I have to tell you, if I say yes, it'll be my privilege. I like the way you think, Sam. You play by the book."

"Well, I wish others did. Let me know as soon as you can. Now, the 'new' list. Have you added anyone?"

"Well, we've removed Betty Moulton, too—she has an ironclad alibi. We still have Angus and Lonnie MacTeague, Slug, Gus, and you know who I think is capable and then some? Jake. There's something fishy about those trailers out back of his store. He might be stocking drug paraphernalia or maybe a meth lab. And I've heard his girlfriend is scared to death of him."

"I've heard similar rumors. Say, why do you still have the harmless dairy farmer on the list? Isn't he an unlikely candidate, especially in view of what Chuck told us?"

"It's a long story. They had a big flap after turkey day. A lot of confusing family intrigue." Frank swallowed the last swig of cold coffee. "Angus can't talk about it sensibly or calmly, but then that's nothing new. There's a long list of topics that drive Angus over the edge, including gays. He didn't like Lester for that reason, but, hell, there are plenty of other old codgers in Venice who share those feelings."

Sam tapped a tooth with the metal button of his ballpoint pen. "Personally, I think Angus is too old and too sick to be a suspect. I interviewed him, and, in my judgment, he's a toothless old mutt."

"Maybe," Frank said.

"You know about George Felker, right?" Sandy asked.

"Felker—haven't heard the name."

"Otherwise known as Mooseman," Sandy added. "Eccentric ex-Wall Streeter, lives up past the MacTeague's in a one-room shack. I met him up close in their kitchen just the other day."

"Is he on your list?"

"No, but he hates hunters and trespassers in 'his woods,' and he's plenty wild looking. Can't tell what he'd do in a fugue state."

"So how many guns does this nutcase own?"

"Maybe none. He doesn't like guns. On the other hand, he says he loves wild animals but hates people and that they ought to be shot."

"Did he hate Lester?" Sam checked the folder.

"Not that I know of."

"According to my notes, Betty says Mooseman and Lester had a run in. Better put him on the list—with a big question mark." Sam shuffled through his notes. "The Gossams, I think they'd be at the top of your list."

"I'm under the impression they have alibis."

"As far as I'm concerned, their alibis aren't any better than your neighbor, Slug's."

"Don't forget Whiffy," Sandy interrupted.

"What's a Whiffy?" Sam looked puzzled. Venice was growing

weirder by the moment.

Frank jumped in. "Almost forgot. A strange thing happened at the bottom of the hill Monday morning early. You know Nin, that cute blonde who lives down in the house in the hole?" Sam nodded. "Well, that idiot Booth drove off the highway...hell, you know all about that and good ol' Booth running off. Just about twenty-four hours later, Nin discovers her cat's been murdered."

"Run over it on the highway?"

"No, someone slit it right down the center with a knife, slick as a whistle, gutted it and draped it over the stop sign to shock her, a real clean job. Nobody seems to know when. Could've been a warning. She reported it to Bud Varney." He looked at Sandy. "Just weird, the timing and all. Probably not connected to the rest of this mess, but who knows. Anyway, back to Angus. Bad thing happened." Frank explained about the stroke and his refusal to go to the ER.

"That's why I need to deputize you, Frank. You're plumb in the middle of a high crime area." Sam grinned. "Furthermore, I'd like to share the ME's report with you, but ethically I'm not allowed. 'Course, if you were my special deputy, I could fill you in, but can't let Sandy in on it." Sam removed some papers from a manila folder.

"Oh sure." Sandy rose. "I'll keep Barb company." Sandy knew Frank would be tempted and felt a twinge that their peace of mind was about to slip away.

Like an old racehorse at the sound of the bugle, Frank felt the adrenalin rush, the urge to right a wrong. Five minutes later, he was holding a deputy detective's badge, and Barb and Hazel had signed the papers as witnesses. "I agree. Let's keep this under wraps for the near term. I think I can do you more good that way."

"Sure thing. Hear that, ladies? Maybe you can bury the paperwork, Barb. Hazel, forget you witnessed anything."

"No sooner said than done." Hazel smiled. Sam didn't know what he'd do without his daytime dispatcher.

Sam closed the office door and shut the blinds that looked out onto the secretary's reception area then briefed Frank. "The ME begins by apologizing for not being able to do an entire workup, but the degree of decomposition made it impossible. Poor Lester had been in that water for almost six weeks. For example, my men bagged the hands, but they'd already been chewed. Pickerel probably. Anyway, white male between the ages of, hell, we know he was fifty-five, relatively good health with a slightly enlarged liver and evidence of plaque building in the arteries. Severe contusion on the forehead consistent with a fall, probably at the time of death, a minor concussion, *not* the cause of death. Doc says he probably hit his head on a sharp rock."

"Or a rock hit *him*," Frank observed.

"He had slightly abraded wrists and traces of twine indicating that his hands were tied in front of him; the M.E. can't say when. The twine had disintegrated. An abrasion on his left shoulder offered no clues. Slight traces of soil and pine needles were caught in the heel of one shoe. The other shoe was not retrieved. Could indicate the body was dragged over pine forest." Sam stopped and turned the page.

"Might point to Lester being dragged to a boat or to a place at the bog where he could be dumped." Frank studied the page Sam handed him.

"But when was he shot and precisely where? No sign at the lake house. The twine could have been tied to a heavy object to weigh the body down. If we could only find that missing shoe." Sam shook his head.

"Good thing to note though. Where that shoe is hiding could reveal a lot!"

"Let's finish up. Tox screen on blood, tissue and urine—all negative. No visible needle marks. Trace alcohol, salad, bread and melon in the stomach, no defensive wounds apparent. However, the ME calls these approximations, since so much time had passed and time of death is undetermined. Add to that the decomp and immersion factors.

"The fatal wound was a bullet in the mid-region of his back, shattering T-3 and T-4, exiting out the front about three centimeters above the navel. Probably close range, and the logical weapon would be something about the size of a 30-30 Winchester slug from a deer rifle. Because it was a through and through, no bullet has been recovered and Doc Welch found no trace elements or fragments of the bullet."

Sam looked across his desk at Frank. "That doesn't mean there isn't a bullet or a shell casing out there somewhere, but snow makes it tough to find. Hell, we don't even know where he was shot." Sam scratched his chin, then continued. "And it gets worse. Lester's pants were pulled down. The killer apparently tried to lacerate his privates, and partially succeeded, but it was a sloppy job rather than anything surgical. What the killer didn't accomplish, the pickerel did. The ME found a section of cutting consistent with a knife blade, serrated. Probably a hunter's skinning knife. Nothing much, body was in the bog too long." Sam paused, took the page that Frank handed back, tucked the report back into the jacket and laid it on his desk. "That's about it. No closer to nailing the killer than I was a week ago. Maybe Belle Whittaker in Augusta will come up with something. If only we had an eye witness."

"Got an idea," Frank offered, "but it'll mean more work for you. Of course it might be a wild goose chase."

"Go ahead. At this point, I'm willing to chase any goose."

"Well, we've got the January thaw going on up there around the lake and bog. Not as warm as here, near the ocean. I'd say it's probably up in the forties today in Venice, but it won't last long. Maybe the team should return to Lester's yard and check the mud. I'd come along, but, as we agreed, my deputy status is on the Q.T., right?"

Sam nodded and stroked the stubble on his chin. "It's worth a shot." He went over and opened the door. "Barb, get Belle Whittaker from the CIU on the line for me, please." Frank stood up.

"You know, I won't take any pay for this," Frank said.

"We'll see about that. Keep track of your mileage and expenses," Sam retorted with a grin. "Maybe you don't deserve any pay, since you refuse to wade around in the mud. Good thing I didn't call Darla and have her fix us supper, because I'm not gonna be there. Look, glad to have you on board. Call if anything occurs to you." In the front office, he shook hands with Sandy and Frank then walked them out. "And you be careful of moose, folks. We don't want another accident like Don Wells's. Keep me posted on his progress, Frank."

On the way home Sandy teased Frank about being back in the saddle.

He countered with, "Guess you're not happy unless your man's wearing a badge. Or am I wrong?"

Sandy shrugged.

CHAPTER 22

"Where were you yesterday? I called, I even came over." Rhu was beside herself, her hair disheveled, her sweater unevenly buttoned. She was standing at the front door, her doughy face staring at Frank, not giving him an opportunity to get a word in edgewise. "I need to talk to you, Frank. Where were you, for heaven's sake?"

"Out of town. Why, what's the problem?"

Rhu was blending her sentences together in a high-pitched whine. "The corner's the problem! Someone's got to do something! A truck drove right off the road and broke the guardrail. What's to prevent it happening again? And you heard about Nin's poor cat! We have a cat, you know. What's to prevent someone from killing my cat? I don't dare let Blinky out now. That corner's dangerous! Look at Angus, falling right off the road."

"I hate to tell you, Rhu, but Angus ran one wheel onto the muddy shoulder because he had a stroke. The road didn't play a part."

"Of course it did. I've asked Chuck to do something, but he won't. Angus went off the road because the town has never fixed the culvert. That culvert's on your side—you should've complained to the state. Cars could lose control and crash right into my kitchen!"

"Angus is First Selectman. I guess he could fix the ditch if he wanted to."

Sandy interrupted the volley, "Don't keep Rhu out in the mudroom. Come in, Rhu, sit down. Frank, where are your manners?" Sandy scolded in a mocking tone.

"Couldn't get the words out," he mumbled. He turned to Rhu. "Relax, Rhu. Sorry, but I can't help you. However, I do think it's wise to keep Blinky indoors. We always keep our cats in." As Rhu entered their field of vision, all three Zucchetti cats, Wolf, Panther and Tiger, took flying leaps off their respective perches and scattered.

"How about some coffee?" Sandy thought she detected the aroma of sherry and Listerine when she approached Rhu. "I've got a fresh pot."

"No, coffee'd make me jumpy. Seth prescribed some sedatives, but they don't do much good. My nerves are just in shreds over all this, but back to the subject of the corner. Sandy, can't you make Frank see that

135

something's got to be done? That poor boy Booth Gossam could have been killed."

"Hold on, Rhu. What do you mean 'poor Booth'? He was drunk and clearly at fault. And that's not all he's done in this town. I'm not shedding tears over him!" Sandy glared at Rhu, who was clinging to the arm of the chair. Everyone knew Rhu played favorites with Booth in school. On the other hand, if Rhu decided that a student was from a privileged family, life in her class could be a living hell.

"I've been thinking about Booth's home life," Rhu whined. "You ought to be more sympathetic. I don't even think Gus is his father. I had Booth in math years ago. Poor boy, tried so hard, but his parents never once came to a parent-teacher conference. But young Andy Gossam, he's a saint."

After due consideration, Frank decided to set the bait, trying to learn something that might help Sam. "So, you don't think Booth murdered Sandy's cousin?"

Rhu's jaw dropped. "He wouldn't kill anyone. You've both misjudged him, and what do you know anyway? You two haven't been here long enough."

Frank and Sandy were speechless.

Rhu continued, "Now his father, that's a different story. I've known Gus for twenty-five years, and his wife Sarah, poor thing. He's mean enough to kill, and he's rotten to her. My son Seth knows all about her trips to the ER. Townsend's his hospital, you know. My daughter-in-law's a nurse there. Lucille could tell you a thing or two."

Frank probed further, "So, Rhu, you've lived here for years. Who else do you think is capable of murdering Lester?"

"You're the ex-law man. You tell me!"

"What do you mean? How should I know?"

"Well, you're going to blame it on Betty, but I happen to know she was in the post office all that day."

Sandy couldn't keep the irritation out of her voice. "She's my cousin, Rhu, and we know about her alibi. Who *else* might have had a motive?"

"I hate to speak ill of my neighbors, but Jake's mother, Jane, despised Lester. You must've heard about the petition?" Her voice oozed venom.

"Of course, but she's got an alibi. *Plus,* she has severe arthritis."

That set her off. "Phooey! No more arthritis than this!" Rhu held up her right arm and tried in vain, or so it seemed, to bend it. "It hurts too much to bend it anymore, but I tell you, if I had to, I could shoot someone." Rhu rose from the Canadian rocker to leave. "Well, I must run. I'm expecting a phone call." No one discouraged her.

Frank and Sandy exchanged looks then said their goodbyes as Rhu rushed to get in the last word. "I *am* disappointed in you, Frank. I thought you had an *in* with the sheriff. I've seen his car over here twice. You tell him there's gonna be more trouble at this corner, mark my words, and he'd better do something about it!" She slammed the door, nearly stumbling down the front stairs in her haste to leave.

"Guess she wants to get on the suspect list," Frank chortled.

"That woman's a mess! If it weren't nine a.m., I'd suggest we have a drink. My God, she'd drive anyone to it."

Frank looked down the road to make sure Rhu was headed home. "But, for once, she didn't blame it all on Chuck. Blamed me instead," he chuckled. "What I want to know is why'd she blame Jane Ridley?"

"She merely put two and two together. Jane and Jake hated Lester, so maybe they conspired to get rid of him. Makes sense—Rhu wants to get rid of *her* enemies. Jane and Rhu have had a spat going for years. Something about the historical society. But she does think Gus is a viable suspect. Don't you?"

Frank shook his head. "He's got lots of guns, hates homosexuals. He's stupid, but cunning—angry. I like him for the murder, but we're a long way from nailing him. Need a motive. And some kind of evidence would be nice."

The next afternoon, Friday, Sam had Barb place a call to the Zucchetti home, and when Frank picked up, she put the boss on.

"Hi Frank, sorry to bother you but something's come up."

"Sure, shoot!" Frank motioned for Sandy to get him a pad and pen.

"Listen, a neighbor of yours, a Cleona Burgess, called Dispatch in hysterics. Says she was out birding, found your Mooseman, one George Felker, crawling along the Bog Road. Thinks he's been shot. Hazel dispatched an ambulance, though the directions weren't too clear."

"When did this happen?"

Sam looked at his watch. "About ten minutes ago. Problem: Hal's covering a domestic abuse case; another deputy's gone to the Moose crime scene. Got two in court and the rest in school or on time off. Wondered if you could go to Townsend Hospital, question Moose, if he's conscious. You'll have to identify yourself to hospital personnel, but maybe you can avoid the press. I need someone there and pronto."

Frank had missed seeing the ambulance, lights flashing, turning the corner onto Route Ten. "Sure, I can leave right now. Why don't I call you from the hospital?"

"I may be out of range. Leave a message at the office if you can't get me on the cell. Say, hear any gunshots this morning?"

"Sam, you're still a city boy. We hear gunshots damn near every morning here, though the target's usually coy dogs or deer, not people."

Frank filled Sandy in and asked if she wanted to go.

"No, I need to stay home and muck out the poultry houses. They're getting mighty ripe. But listen, I'll call Mabel and see if she knows anything. She talks with Moose nearly every day."

"Good. Give her a call."
"Okay. See you when you get back, hon."

As he rolled toward Waterville in the Saturn, Frank couldn't hide the excitement of working an actual case. Sure, he hadn't investigated anything for years, but he was feeling that familiar surge of adrenaline. He even played with the idea of actively participating fulltime in the Thoreau County Sheriff's Department. *Wouldn't be fair to Sandy. It's a twenty-four-seven job, and, besides, a guy can get killed in this line of work. We're finally settled. All I can do is be Sam Barrows' right hand man and help out once in a while.*

When Frank checked with the ER staff, he learned that Moose was still in an exam room. Since Frank wasn't family, they wouldn't give him any information, but they asked Frank for Moose's correct name and address. Good thing Sam had mentioned it. Frank had heard it only once before at the MacTeague's and wouldn't have remembered.

"Didn't he have a wallet?" he asked a pretty young nurse whose name tag read *Sylvia.*

"Yes, he did," she whispered in a coquettish tone, "but we need verification. Coulda' been stolen from the looks of him. Sometimes patients come in here with other people's wallets, you know."

"Felker, George Felker. Does that work for you?" Frank flashed his badge and a flirty smile at Sylvia. "Is he gonna make it? Can you at least tell me that?"

"Oh, in that case, yes, George Felker. But you need to talk with the ER doc when he comes out, sir." Nurse Sylvia stared at his badge. She was curvaceous and had enormous brown eyes, long lashes, and a tawny French-Indian complexion.

Within a few minutes, a short, East Indian physician with the name tag *Dr. Singh* emerged from the treatment bay. Frank explained his mission and showed his credentials.

In a heavy accent Doctor Singh explained, "De patient has suffered a sebeer gunshot to the left sidt of his back. He's beeng taken to recovery but he's bery fortunate. A bullet just barely knicked a wessel. If he hadn't been found vhen he vas he vouldn't have made it dees far. Loss of blood eez the big problem, BP low, dat and shock. I must go now. Excuse pleece."

As the doctor walked off, Frank reminded him. "We need the bullet, sir, as soon as you can retrieve it."

Over his shoulder, Singh said, "I am not de surgeon, but I shall relay de message. Ve are not careless about such things."

Grateful for an intelligent and efficient doctor, Frank called Sam who was back in his office. It was three o'clock. He explained the situation and promised to stay at the hospital until he knew more.

"I'm going to insist that we pay you mileage, so keep track."

"Okay. By the way, the press hasn't got wind of this, but it's just a matter of time."

They both signed off.

Frank then called Sandy. "Hey, babe, how's it goin'?"

"Fine, I guess. Mucked-out then called the MacTeague's house and got hold of Mabel. Asked her when was the last time either one of them had seen Moose. Says she saw him early this morning with a can of orange spray paint. Told her he was going out to mark trees for sugaring-off come March."

"Kind of early for that. Plenty weird..." Frank's voice trailed off into a thought.

"Anyway, I only told Mabel that Moose had an 'accident.' She sounded shook up. Said she'd tell Angus when he comes in from the woods. I'm sure she doesn't have a clue as to what happened."

"Okay," Frank sighed. "Take care, sweetie. See you when I see you."

"Don't flirt with the nurses, dear," Sandy's tone was bratty.

"Ha! Already did, but I love you most."

After hanging up, Frank to a deep breath and pondered the case. Nothing was being hunted legally during January so Moose probably wasn't out campaigning. *He wasn't hunting because that's the last thing he'd ever do. What if he found something? If he'd stumbled onto some evidence out there? Was that why he was shot? And if he got it in the back, did that suggest that he was running away from his assailant? Did he see the shooter?* Frank had to be the first to interview him, after Moose came to, *if* he came to.

Three hours later, Frank was sitting outside the recovery room nursing a poor excuse for coffee when a captivating blonde nurse came striding through the swinging doors and over to him. He recognized Lucille Shaw. He hadn't seen her since her wedding.

"Oh, Frank. I remember you. Doc Singh says you're the sheriff?"

Frank stood up. "No, I'm just *Deputy* Detective Zucchetti," he answered in a slightly smitten tone. "Why, has Mr. Felker regained consciousness?"

"He's conscious but sedated. You can have five minutes, but I don't think you'll get much information with all the meds." Her smile was enough to melt a glacier. She straightened her uniform, a size too small, and the light caught her mega-carat engagement ring.

Frank stepped quietly into the recovery room. Places like this always gave him the Willeys. His mom had been in ICU for a day after she'd had surgery for breast cancer. He'd been shot once and spent a couple of days there. It wasn't a great place to be, and he felt much more at ease around dead bodies than he did around dying ones.

"Hey, Moose, how ya' doin?"

Moose was oatmeal gray and his eyes wouldn't focus. Plastic breathing tubes were sticking up his nose, and an I.V. drip line and heart monitor wires hung all around him.

"Who the hell are you?" Moose whispered hoarsely.

"I'm your neighbor...Frank. You met my wife, Sandy, at Mabel's house. Remember? Mind if I tape this?" The last thing Frank wanted to do was remind him that he was now 'the law.'

"Oh yeah, you got a real pretty wife."

"Right! How're ya feelin'?"

"Like fog."

"Moose, would you mind if I ask you a couple of questions? Did you see the person who shot you?"

"Nah! It came out of nowhere. I was..." he paused and took a breath, drifted off a bit, then came back. "I was just walking along the woods path and suddenly it was like a truck hit me. Pow! And down I went. I wanted to get in the boat. I don't remember anything after that."

Frank noticed Nurse Shaw, leaning provocatively against the doorjamb and listening.

"Moose, listen, stay with me now. You mentioned a boat, what boat?"

"Wolf tree." Moose's eyelids closed and fluttered.

"What tree?"

"Wolf tree, you know..." Mooseman drifted off from his moorings.

"Did you see anyone when you were out in the woods?" By the look on Nurse Shaw's face, Frank figured his five minutes were running out.

"Gotta sleep now." Moose slipped away. Frank snapped off the recorder and turned to Lucille, now standing right next to him.

"Thanks for letting me in. I really appreciate it."

"Hope we see you again, Frank," she purred.

"Sure will."

Frank walked out to the reception desk. "Please let me know if there's any change," he said to Sylvia, handing her his card, which said nothing about the Sheriff's Department. He'd have to have some new ones made up. Meanwhile, he'd try to connect the dots: fog, boat, wolf tree.

CHAPTER 23

As he climbed into the car, Frank felt an electric spark of pain across his lower back. He suddenly realized how bone-weary he was, a combination of concrete floors, chrome and plastic chairs designed for a different species, and too much bad coffee. After doing some hard thinking on the way home, he'd call Sam again. "All Things Considered" was airing on Maine Public Radio with its daily mull of the world's troubles. He turned it off and listened to the tires rolling over the pavement instead, past the accident scene on Borden Plantation. He'd asked about Don at the hospital. No change. He drove past Maude's Diner, then onto Route Ten. Everything was still melting at the edges, the snow banks sagging and turning a dirty gray. He'd be glad to get home to Sandy.

Frank drove in after sundown and found a note on the fridge from Sandy, saying she was out on her daily woods walk. He was concerned that she was out alone during twilight, especially with all the deer-jacking.

Standing at the back window, staring at the woods, he decided to check in while watching for Sandy. He punched up Sam's number.

"Sam, glad I caught you. I'm finally back after five hours hangin' out at Townsend. Looks like Moose is gonna make it. The bullet nicked a vessel. Mainly, he lost a lot of blood, but they've stabilized him."

"Sorry it took so long. Were you able to get a statement?"

"Informal one. Turned on my tape recorder. Says he never saw the shooter. Came from behind. Probably knocked down by the impact before he could turn around. Not a clue as to who did it, but maybe we'll get lucky and pick up some footprints. They've retrieved the slug and it's on its way to Augusta. Oh, and Moose did say one interesting thing before he faded off into Demerol land."

"Yeah? What's that?"

"That he thought of getting in 'the boat.' He wasn't just marking trees like Mabel MacTeague thought. He's not stupid. A little crazy, certainly. We gotta' talk to him more about that boat, and he said something about a 'wolf tree.'"

"What the hell's a wolf tree?"

"I keep forgetting you're a city boy. A tree so big that it devours light, casts a shadow dark enough to kill off all the plants and saplings around it. They're fairly rare."

That would be major clue, especially if there's evidence near it."

"Want me to go over to the Lake Road location tomorrow and help out?"

"Naw, the guys are on it. Besides, you've done enough, spending half a day at the hospital. I appreciate it. Think Moose'll be up to an official interview by tomorrow?"

"Yeah! He'll still be hurting, but maybe he'll feel well enough to take his johnny off and flash the nurses. By the way, I inquired about Don Wells. No change. Still being suspended in an artificial coma."

"Thanks again. Glad you took the badge, buddy. Say, I'm gonna interview the Willard clan tomorrow morning at ten. Want to meet later, say up at the Moose shooting location? Around quarter to eleven?"

"Sounds good. See ya."

At ten the next morning Sam Barrows parked the cruiser in front of Slug's little Cape. For the first time Slug's semi wasn't parked in its usual place in front of the house. He'd moved it about two hundred yards east, down behind his sister-in-law Flo's bungalow.

An ugly brown pit bull with a long scar down its back was chained to an iron pipe in the yard. The minute it caught sight of Sam, it began to snarl and scratch at the mud and ice, straining at its chain. Undeterred, Sam knocked on the front door, which was enclosed by a little sheltering roof and side walls. The hapless dog began a series of lunges toward Sam. Finally, Bertha opened the door and yelled, "Shut up, Butchie!"

"Damn dog! That one won't last long at the rate it's goin'." Upon seeing his shield, Bertha let Sam into the living room where Slug sat watching a wrestling broadcast. Looking sullen, he shut the set off then gestured with a thumb for the sheriff to be seated. Sam chose the couch. The place smelled like tired bacon and dog dander.

"Good morning, Mr. and Mrs. Willard. I'm here to ask a few questions about Lester Moulton."

"We hardly knew him." Bertha fiddled with her blouse buttons, then stared at her cuticles. "Ain't much for goin' to church. Seen him a couple times over ta Chuck's lookin' at junk. That's 'bout all."

"Ayuh." Slug nodded in agreement.

"Well, where's your cottage at the lake, near Lester's house?"

"Nowheres near. What're you gettin' at?"

"Nothing in particular. Describe your relationship with Lester, Mr. Willard. Did you like the man?"

"Didn't know him...didn't give a shit one way or t'other."

"Any of your children have dealings with him?"

"You askin' did that *prevert* mess with my boys? Nossuh! If he had, he wouldn'a lived to tell about it."

Sam jotted down a note, then took a different tack.

"I wonder...you know anything about a dead orange cat draped over a stop sign on the corner out there?" Sam rose and walked to the picture window. He had a clear view of the sign, the road, and the side of Nin and Ned's house as he waited for one of them to reply.

Slug finally mumbled, "Didn't see nothin'. Them people let that damned cat out all hours, made the dogs bark. Just a matter of time 'fore someone killed it."

"So you're aware of whose cat it was. Did you kill it?" He stood looking down at Slug, his six feet four inches a rather demanding presence, especially with the Glock on his hip.

Slug scrunched up his face into a scowl, making wrinkles on top of his balding head. "No...and neither did my boys."

Bertha tried to break the tension, "You want a coke or somethin'?"

"No thanks, I have to be going." Sam headed toward the front hall, but turned as he approached the door. "By the way, where were you and your boys on the day after Thanksgiving?"

"We all went huntin' up to Monson near the slate quarry. Always go up there that time o' year. Got friends own a cabin. It's a family tradition."

"And where were you, Mrs. Willard?"

A look of confusion spread over her face. She thought a minute, bit her lower lip. "Well, right here. Where else would I be? I was makin' soup from left-over turkey, I'm sure."

"Did you happen to see anyone placing the cat on the sign, or hear a gunshot any time early that Sunday morning after the big party?"

"Course she didn't. Look, Sheriff!" Slug had risen from his chair and walked right up to Sam's face. Sam could smell beer on his breath. "I don't take kindly to your insinuatin' my wife needs an alibi or that she knows somethin' 'bout that cat. She's a good woman, hard-workin', and she's disabled, too."

"It's just part of my job." Then Sam stepped out the front door, into the clear, fresh, warming air. The Willards disgusted him. He'd seen the Willard type often enough in Portland. They might live in tenements rather than farm houses, but their values were similar. Any extra cash they came by went into trucks, cars, scratch cards and lottery tickets. Pets were disposable, and children were often more tormented than nurtured. Wives became servants and if they dared to rebel, they were roughed up.

Sam was eager to get into the woods where he could breathe, and to liaison with Frank at the Lake Road. He'd planned to interview the two Willard sons but decided it would be a waste of energy. They'd cover for one another anyway. The only way to get these guys was with hard evidence.

As he pulled onto the woods path leading to Hiram Bog, Sam could see Frank waving at him. He looked pleased with himself. For once the sun was shining, and the snow was melting off the tree branches and plopping

143

into the slush below. The dirt and gravel road was all mud and ice that made a sucking crunch when Sam walked in it.

After removing their gloves they shook hands.

"Guess you couldn't wait to come over here, Frank."

"Let's just say I couldn't control myself. You're gonna be mighty pleased with my find. I didn't disturb any tracks, figuring your men combed the area thoroughly and got any footprints worth getting. First, I looked over the scene where Mooseman got bushwhacked, nothin' new. Then I went way beyond the perimeter into the deep woods, following deer trails. And, Sam, I found the damned boat."

"You're shinin' me on. That's outstanding! I'm gonna have to give you a raise."

"Before you get too enthused, sorry, no shoe—unless your men found it."

"No such luck. Wonder why my regular guys couldn't find the boat. And I still haven't heard from Belle and the CIU folks. By now they should've finished taking a second look at the grounds around Lester's place. Take me to the boat. Wait, I gotta get my camera."

Sam grabbed his camera out of the trunk and locked up. The two men trudged off toward the thick grove of evergreens that bordered most of Hiram Bog, striding along like a couple of young men.

"The skiff should be transported to Augusta. I'll notify them to meet us here if they can come today. I'd carry the damned thing to Galway if I had the van instead of the cruiser. Guess we could commandeer a pickup truck from one of the locals. Now that we've found it, can't leave the thing here overnight."

"I'll wait around, help you load if you need me. It only weighs about a hundred pounds. Used to have one just like it."

"Only a hundred, huh? Piece of cake? How old did you say you were?" Sam grinned. "Let's get a look at this thing before I call the team on the cell phone. They'll send somebody right over." Pleased to have made a little progress they slogged through the slush toward the boat.

A clutch of chickadees hopped from limb to limb, chirping and buzzing, as Frank and Sam retraced Frank's footsteps from earlier in the day. The sun hung brightly in a cobalt blue sky casting splotches of whitish gold light onto the forest floor. The stand of spruce, cedar, and hackmatack was dense, and Frank took care not to let the branches snap back into Sam, following close behind. The pungent smell of stirred-up evergreens added an edge to their excitement.

"There it is, just ahead under that big wolf hemlock."

The tree had grown so large that it had deprived its neighboring competitors of light, slowly starving them out, gobbling them up. Someone had pulled the khaki brown john boat up next to the scabby trunk of the tree then turned it bottom-side up and banked it with hemlock branches. In the shadows and dappled light, it was hard to spot. A deep bed of leaf mulch covered the ground near the tree and not much moisture of any kind, not even snow, had found its way in there.

"When I was here earlier," Frank reckoned, "it would take only one person to skid this boat up under here. A rugged person, not a weakling. It rides almost friction free over these slick hemlock needles."

"Sure enough. And it's no more than a hundred yards down to the edge of the bog. Did you go down there?"

"Nope. I was anxious to get out to the road and give you the good news the minute you arrived."

Sam took a couple of snapshots with his digital camera. "Tell you what. We both got gloves on. Let's flip this puppy over and see what we can see."

The two men carefully removed the branches and scooped the needles away from the side of the boat, being careful to check for evidence.

"Okay. One, two, three, heave." The john boat flipped over with a heavy metallic thump.

"Dried blood, don't ya think?" Frank was staring at a brown stain covering about a third of the aft end.

"Boy, howdy! It'd take a mighty big fish to spill that much blood. Look how it ran down and streaked the side when the perp turned it over. Frank, I think you've found us a mighty big chunk of the crime scene." Both men felt elated, and stepped back from the boat with their arms akimbo, breathing in satisfying gulps of the piney air.

"Okay, let's have a look down here." Sam took off toward the bog.

"Hey, there's a big swath where someone dragged the boat up. Look, the pine and hemlock needles are still stirred up, and the ground must not've been completely frozen. See the indentations in the ground cover?"

They arrived at the water's edge. "Funny how some things last through all kinds of weather, especially if the prints were made during a thaw followed by a freeze," Sam said as both men examined boot indentations in the muddy bank.

"Yeah. Looks like the same person walked into the bog, then walked out, and the outbound steps are deeper and sort of elongated, skidding."

"Like he might've been tugging a boat behind him," both men said at once, their eyes riveted on the skid marks.

Sam's eyes swept the shoreline. "But what the hell was Lester doing out here?"

"Time to hypothesize," Frank mumbled. "Okay. What do we have before us, just off shore? Two Hemlock posts sticking up out of the water. Now look off to the west."

"Friends of Fowl duck boxes, right?"

"Right. And to the east?"

"Just posts. And that matches what I found in Lester's garage; i.e., unassembled duck boxes."

"Okay. Let's suppose he was planning where and how many new duck boxes to mount before the bog froze up. Maybe he was worried about migrating ducks. That would give him a good reason to be out here."

"Yup. And guess which way the current runs in the bog." Sam pointed. "From the stream at the east end down toward the lake at the west end."

"Right. And that would take the body down the deep channel of the bog toward the lake, right about where old Earl hooked the body."

"But something's missing." Sam scratched his ear, looked out across the bog, then looked up the trace left by the boat running up to the wolf tree. "The damned motor."

"You're right. The motor's missing. We know he had one. No motor with the boat, no gouge in the pine needles, no furrow in the mud. And the killer didn't come back to get it, because there's only one set of footprints in and out. *Ergo...*"

"*Ergo*, the motor's in the bog," Sam's voice had a tinge of excitement, "because our perp used it to weigh the body down. The ME's report stated that Lester's wrists had been bound with twine, twine that had probably shredded."

"Yeah, or been chewed away by a pickerel in a feeding frenzy," Frank said, a little chill running up his back. "But there's more. According to a biologist I met the other night, it takes about three weeks for a dead body in freezing water to rise up to the ice sheet. So, as time passes, Lester's body puffs up like a balloon, putting pressure on the cheap twine around his wrists. Finally, it breaks, and he floats ever so slowly westward until Earl Bagley hooks him."

"That's a plausible explanation of the delay in finding the body. If Earl hadn't gone fishing a couple of Sundays ago, by summertime what little remained of it might've turned up in Lake Mallacook, or never turned up."

"Yeah, and we wouldn't be out here up to our fannies in mud," Frank commented.

"So, suddenly you don't like police work?"

"Well, it's not as bad as Alaska in springtime. Mosquitoes the size of bats."

"Frank, try this theory. It's a murder of opportunity. Our killer is out here with a rifle, hunting. He happens on Lester, just offshore, maybe even standing up in the boat getting ready to rig up a duck box. He hates Lester, or just hates anyone out in 'his woods' during hunting season. So he plugs Lester, right there in his own boat. Which explains the blood and the knot on Lester's head. Probably hit it on the motor when he fell forward."

"I'm with you. Then our shooter comes down to check his prey. I'm guessing no one saw him because it was getting dark by that time. Days were getting mighty short. I'm gonna go with 'he hated Lester' because he pulled down his pants and gouged up the pubic area and slashed at the privates. That's consistent with a hate crime, and I'm positive it was a male. Yup! A hate crime, plain and simple."

"Aw, you really know how to tell a guy what he doesn't want to hear. If we call it a hate crime, the Fib-Eyes'll be all over this case like flies on shit, we'll never find the perp, and they'll come up with some way to take credit for another failure."

"But if we solve it, all the guys in Hallowell will love you, Sam!"

Both men felt rather ghoulish as they smiled and shook their heads at one another.

Sam went on. "So once he finished with poor old Lester, he could've walked the boat out ten or twenty feet from shore. Except for the main channel, the bog's no more than three or four feet deep. You might think it'd be easier to sink everything, body, boat and all—"

Frank interrupted. "But aluminum john boats have a habit of floating right back to the surface. Built-in air pockets. Better to hide it up under the tree."

"Anyway, our killer tied Lester's arms to the motor with available twine, loosened the lugs that held the motor to the stern of the boat, and turned the whole mess over, thus disposing of the body, but not the blood. There was already plenty of patch ice in the bog, and he figured things would just freeze up and that'd be that." Sam looked satisfied.

"Except..." Frank added.

"Except what?"

"The water was damned cold, nearly freezing. I can't see him walking out in freezing water up to his waist."

"I can see that you haven't been huntin' lately," Sam said, chuckling. "Ever hear of Briarbusters?"

"No. Heard of ballbusters though. I try to avoid them at all costs."

Sam guffawed. "Well, Briarbusters makes waterproof bib overalls, and these good ole boys just put 'em on along with waterproof knee-high hunting boots. That way they can hunt the marshes and bog edges without getting wet and sneak up better on the white-tail when he comes down to drink. See, city boys *do* know somethin'."

"Shucks, guess I'm not the outdoor type," Frank said. "So walking the boat out from the shore is a plausible theory."

"Absolutely."

"Don't we need to find the motor?"

"I'm gonna make a calculated guess that we don't need it right now to solve the case. Hate to go poking around a frozen pond with grappling hooks just to prove a theory. The bog's gonna freeze up solid again anyway, and I don't want to trouble the Staties with unnecessary work. Only got so many green stamps to spend in Augusta."

Back at the boat Sam called Barb on the cell phone who patched him through to Belle Whittaker, who'd just finished checking the shoreline around Lester's house. He gave her the news about the boat and told her how to find it. Part of him wanted to stay on the site and meet her, but his better self told him to get going.

CHAPTER 24

Hungry enough to eat raw skunk, Sam swung into the only eatery in Venice, Jake's General Store, and headed straight back to the deli counter. A small gang of regulars huddled around the lobster tank but parted to make room for the law. Sometimes when things were slow they'd bet on which lobster would be the next to make it to the bubbling pipe in the corner. For it to count, the crustacean had to touch the bubbling pipe with its primary front claw.

The only person he recognized was Petrie Potter, owner of the largest Holstein herd in Venice. He'd met him once on one of his first cases as sheriff. It didn't take a genius to find Petrie, for his boots were caked with cow manure. The smell of salami, crustaceans and manure took a little getting used to.

Anna gave him a sweet smile as she took his order.

"Hi. I'd like a big Italian sandwich on whole wheat bun, with everything but onions, and would you add a splash of hot sauce, please."

She looked at his uniform, then at his face and smiled. "You have to add the hot sauce yourself. It comes in a little packet." She pointed to a plastic basket brimming with plastic packets.

"Okay, then could you dribble some olive oil over it?"

"Sure thing," she said, smiling and batting her long lashes. "But it'll be at least ten minutes, sir."

"That's fine." He went to the front of the store and stopped at the bulletin board. There was a schedule of Weight Watchers Meetings at the Grange written on a calendar that had ended on December 31st. Several layers of tacked-up, curling cards and slips of paper advertised baby-sitting services, mongrel pups and barn kittens, a pet mongoose with cage (free!), and an endless variety of used snowmobiles and ATVs. Along the right edge of the board were business cards. He pulled out one of his with the embossed and gilded badge in the corner and tacked it up, partially covering a pink card that read *Hair-Do-U in My Home, Fri and Sat.*

Below the bulletin board he noticed a magazine rack with copies of the local shopping news, *Rolling Thunder, Uncle Henry's Swap'n Trade,* and a home-printed newsletter from Friends of Fowl, the non-profit group from

Amnesty College that looked after the needs of the migratory bird population. Sam picked up a copy and perused the front page. A solid-black outline of a duck box contained the words, "In Memoriam of our Benefactor, Lester Moulton." *I'll get that no-good bastard who did you in, Lester. I promise.*

Only a few weeks before Lester Moulton had been no more than a name, but now Sam found himself inhabiting a world of people who loved Lester—Sandy, Betty, the Friends of Fowl—and, most of all, Claire.

Sam bought the last *Midcoast Sentinel*, then headed out through the glass front door, noting that a large crack in the lower right corner had been duct-taped.

Andy Gossam was sweeping the parking lot in front of the store by the gas pumps. Jake used salt to remove the ice and sometimes the salt crusted up. Sam strode over. He was sorry, but not surprised, to see the alarm on Andy's face.

"Hi there, young man. Aren't you Andy Gossam?" He was studying Andy's black eye.

"Yes, sir." Andy stopped sweeping and leaned on the broom.

"I missed you when I was interviewing your folks. Nice to meet you." He held out his hand and Andy shook it weakly.

"Thanks."

"That's a mighty impressive shiner you got there. How'd you get it, son?"

"I...uh...fell on the ice."

"Let me guess." He was ignoring Andy's lame excuse. "You pissed off your dad, huh?"

"N...no sir!" Andy couldn't look Sam in the eye.

"Well, son, if you ever need to talk to someone, here's my card. I'm not just a lawman. Better part of my job involves helping people."

Andy took the card and jammed it into the pocket of his blue bomber jacket. Then he began sweeping vigorously. As Sam walked away, Andy responded, "Okay. Whatever. Thanks."

When Sam returned to the deli counter for his order, Anna handed him the heavy package wrapped in white meat-wrapping paper. The clot of customers had disbanded.

"Here's the hot sauce and some napkins. Need any extra stuff? We have ketchup, vinegar, mustard." There was that smile again. She was a pretty girl who would mature into a drop-dead beautiful woman.

Since no one was in sight, Sam stepped around the end of the counter. Speaking softly he said, "Anna, you don't know me. I'm Sheriff Sam Barrows." He held out his hand. She wiped hers on a kitchen towel and timidly shook hands. "I have something of a sensitive nature to ask, and, if you don't feel that you can answer, that's okay."

"I will if I can, sir." She shyly looked down at her apron.

"I expect you know Andy pretty well."

"Yeah, well, sort of, I guess."

"Can you tell me how he got his black eye?"

Anna looked around to be sure no one could hear her. She leaned toward him and whispered, "Maybe his brother Booth—he knocks him around sometimes. Andy's got a wicked bad bruise on his neck. They get into it, but please don't tell him I told you. He doesn't trust many people, but...he trusts me."

Sam thought he detected tears in Anna's eyes and decided they were a lot more than casual acquaintances or co-workers. "Not a word. This is just between us."

After Sam left, Andy walked up to the deli counter and asked Anna straight away, "What's the sheriff nosing around about?" He'd assumed a bravado that wasn't like him.

"Nothing. Like, he was investigating a huge Italian sandwich, that's what. He's a big guy! Hey, you bring your lunch today? We could eat together out in the bottle room as soon as Helen comes in to relieve me."

"Yeah, okay. I'll watch for her."

A few minutes later Anna joined him in the recycle room where they shared a bench. A dozen bins held various brands of empty beer cans and bottles, while hard liquor bottles were in the opposite corner. The heavy, sickly-sweet stench of stale beer was overpowering, but it was the only place where they had any privacy, unless someone showed up to redeem bottles or cans. That was one advantage of living in Maine. Cans and bottles could be redeemed for a nickel or more. This resulted in clean highways that were seldom littered.

"We could get drunk just breathin' in here." Andy opened his brown paper bag and took out a peanut butter and jelly sandwich.

"Yeah, but with none of the fun either."

"You drink beer?"

"Not really. Papa lets me have a little vodka in orange juice sometimes, especially on Finnish holidays. You?"

"I hate the stuff. Beer, I mean. Tastes like mouse pee."

"I've been meaning to ask, and don't get mad, Andy. Tell me how you got that black eye, and I couldn't help noticing the bruise, there." She reached over and touched his neck.

Her touch ran down his spine like a small electric shock. He held her hand, and whispered, "Anna, promise not to tell anybody?"

She blushed with embarrassment, but she could truthfully make that promise, sort of. "Hey, Andy, c'mon, I can keep a secret."

"I was stupid. It was my fault. Got between my folks last night. Pop was all over her about some dumb thing and I couldn't hack it anymore. I know it was dumb, but I squeezed in between them to keep him from hitting her. Just as she was pulling me away, he let me have it. Then he took me by the collar and shoved me into a chair. It was my fault. I shoulda' just let 'em work it out."

"*Fight* it out, you mean. Andy, it *wasn't your fault!* Sounds like your dad's a bully. Did he hurt your mom?"

"Nah, just punched her in the gut. She didn't even cry."

"Well you know you can call the...uh...ambulance, if he really hurts her." She didn't say "the law" because she didn't want him to make the connection between her and the sheriff. On impulse, she kissed him on the cheek, and he colored with embarrassment. After wiping some peanut butter from his lips, he kissed her softly on the mouth. It was brief but it took his breath away.

"Sorry," he whispered, looking down at his worn jeans.

"Don't be sorry, silly. I didn't mind." Her blue eyes were dancing. "Listen, I've got another question. You ever thought of running away? I mean, going to live someplace else? Of course, you'd want to stay in school."

"Whadd'ya mean, Anna? Run away where? If I went with an aunt or uncle, Pop'd come 'n get me so fast—"

"I've got an idea. 'Course I haven't checked with my papa, but, Jeez Andy, if things get any rougher at your house, maybe you could live in our guest cabin. Sounds crazy, but, heck, nobody's coming to visit, and it's got a wood stove, a tiny kitchen, bunk beds. It's primitive, but..."

Andy sat back and stared at her in disbelief. "You're kiddin', right? You care that much?"

She didn't know what to say, so she nodded affirmatively as she bit into her salami sandwich. Finally she said softly, in that teenage accent, "Yeaaah," turning one short word into three syllables.

He hugged her awkwardly. Suddenly, very hungry, he devoured the rest of his sandwich. As they got ready to return to work he said, "Listen, that's some offer, but ask your folks first. If it gets any worse at home, I might just take you up on it, but I gotta pay rent. If your folks say no, I'll understand."

CHAPTER 25

Sam's lower back hurt like a son-of-a-gun. He'd had a long day, one in a string of long days. Then he'd made the pain worse by helping Hal Hines lift his toolbox out of the back of his truck.

"Dumb move. I shoulda' known better," he'd said to Darla during their late supper.

After watching the eleven o'clock news on television, they decided to turn in. Darla had complained of a slight sinus headache and took some Dristan. She suggested to Sam that he might want to soak in a hot tub, then apply a hot pack to his lower back. "Don't let it get out of control, oh stubborn one. Take a pain med! What are you trying to prove, silly? You're not getting any younger, you know." She kissed him on the cheek.

He nodded agreement, though he didn't care to be reminded of his stubbornness.

As he filled the tub, he added bath salts. The label claimed they were from the Masada Desert near the Dead Sea. Darla swore by them. It read ...*relieves joint and muscle pain, eases stress.* "Can't hurt," he muttered. The crystals reminded him of the Epsom salts his aunt would put in his bath water when he was bruised and achy from a fall off his bike. *Old time bath salts were ten cents a pound. This stuff probably cost Darla twenty bucks.*

As he eased himself into the tub, he couldn't help smiling at the lion feet. Darla had painted the nails of each claw bright pink.

They really knew how to make tubs in the eighteen hundreds. Trouble is men were short back then. He began to feel his body relax. *Too many hours in that damned office chair, and miles in the cruiser. Need to walk more, and, when I feel better, I gotta get back to working out at the gym.*

He looked down at his body, his chest hair swaying slightly as he moved his hands through the water to dissolve the salts. He found the three little holes where he'd had arthroscopic knee surgery. They'd nearly disappeared. Then he bent his head down sharply, hurting his neck, and looked at the scars from two bullets, one on the shoulder, the other on his upper left arm. He was a good healer, that was for sure.

No, it wasn't old work-related injuries he was bothered by, just L-3. Ever since football at the university, linebacker, he'd had trouble. During a game against U-Conn, their biggest tight-end rocked him to the ground like a ten-ton truck. He'd been carried off the field. Two weeks and he was back playing again, but every now and then he felt a pinch, followed by pain. It usually went away on its own. This time it was really acting up, causing sciatic pain down the back of his thigh and all the way down his leg to the top of his foot. Even two of his toes felt numb. He wasn't about to reveal all this physical minutiae to Darla, who'd nag him to visit a chiropractor.

He gently let his body farther down into the tub so that his feet were sticking up into the air. As he closed his eyes and allowed his muscles to relax, his mind drifted to the current case, the most troubling of his career.

Let's see...reconstruction of the scene. This technique worked for me before. Lester is in his workshop, enjoying a quiet and peaceful afternoon. Probably playing classical music. The radio was tuned to the classical station when we checked.

Okay, he gets to wondering how many duck boxes he's gonna need, so he lays down his tools, wipes his hands on a rag, then changes. He puts on an orange jacket because he doesn't want to get shot. Yeah! Right. Poor bastard.

Sam soaped up and washed off with a sponge, then returned to his scenario. *He checks the motor and launches the john boat. Does he have an auxiliary can of gasoline with him? Maybe. Never found one at the house. None at the scene. Then he putt-putts across the lake, through the channel, and arrives at his worksite. He sees no one, but someone spies him.* Sam closed his eyes and tried to place himself in the scene.

He's in his element, a cold, gloriously clear afternoon, only a few clouds in a brilliant blue sky. He stands up in the boat and looks around, checks the poles that will hold his duck boxes, communing with nature. This is what the killer is waiting for. Maybe a crow caws a warning but Lester misses it. Then, out of nowhere, pow, a blast from a deer rifle knocks him forward, his head hits the motor, and he's down.

Lester's life doesn't flash before his eyes. It happens too fast. There's just pain, horrible mind-numbing pain, as the bullet thunders through his spinal column and out...where? If only we could recover the bullet.

Sam allowed his legs to drape over the end of the tub, as he slid down, his chin underwater. He thought about water, the water in the bog, not clean like this but filled with floating bacteria and fish shit. He imagined fishing lures hooked to lily stems, casts that fishermen couldn't retrieve, and fishing line winding among the roots of all those hibernating plants. What a jungle of dark green cords, curving, moving like letter s's through the water.

Somehow the killer slogs out to the john boat, probably wearing a smile on his face. Poor Lester lies dead, blood everywhere, his head either on the motor or maybe his entire body's in the bottom of the boat. The killer stops to think. Got to dump the body, get rid of the evidence. Maybe the heavy twine was in the boat, or he'd brought it along in his jacket pocket. None of this seems premeditated. A crime of opportunity. Overcome with rage, the killer takes out his hunting knife, pulls Lester's pants down partway, and begins slashing at Lester's privates. But something panics him, a noise, a deer stepping on a branch, or something imagined. He stops slashing and quickly ties Lester's body to the motor, then pushes the boat out into a deeper part of the bog. With some difficulty he dumps the body, the motor attached, then pulls the boat up onto shore, covers it with leaves and boughs. The killer's feeling a glow of success. For whatever reason, he hated Lester, and now Lester won't be discovered until spring. By then, no evidence. He can come back later and take care of the boat.

Gut feeling: no woman did this, not Betty, not Jane. Of course Jane could've got her worthless son to do it, though he's not rugged—crafty, maybe, but not strong. Lester weighed about one hundred and fifty pounds. Come to think of it, if Jake were high on crack, he could've done it. I can imagine the killer saying something like "Eat up, pickerel!" or "Feed the fishes, Lester." Bastard!

A chill swept over Sam's muscular frame. Goose bumps covered his inner thighs. Suddenly he was acutely aware of L-3 and 4. It felt as if a knife was jabbing him in the back, jabbing him into reality, and he realized that the tub water had cooled. Hell, it wasn't even tepid!

Jeeze, maybe I should get Belle to order a frogman team down to the bog, ice or no ice. So they're financially strapped in Augusta, so what? This is a good man who was murdered. Oughta be an all-out search!

He rose with caution, grabbed the huge bath towel, a gift from Darla with a giant red lobster emblazoned on it, and dried off. He opened the old oak medicine cabinet and plucked out the Tylenol PM. Then he went into the kitchen, flicked on the light, and grabbed a hot pack, popped it into the microwave for one minute, wrapped it in a dish towel, shut off the light, and walked quietly into the bedroom. Darla was asleep, her honey-brown hair spread like a fan across the pillow. He slipped into the king size bed beside her, placed a pillow under his knees, and the hot pack under his back.

Soon Sam's REM phase of sleep allowed him to dream deeply. Gradually he became Lester, looking with sightless eyes at the fish. The water smelled like damp gym socks. There were large and small mouth bass investigating his body. Bony little perch swam 'round and 'round, pecking at his toes. He could feel their sharp teeth. Then he noticed the beautiful pickerel with their nacreous green and purple sides, gliding through the water like graceful eels, their long, snaky bodies silvery in the diffused light of the moon. Suddenly he saw himself in Lester's body and became entwined with the tendrils of plant life as silt rose from the bog floor, darkening the water until all was green. The quiet was deafening.

Sam bolted upright in bed, his body glistening with sweat. Pain, Lester's pain! That awful, overwhelming pain of a hunter's rifle bullet was searing Sam's spinal cord. A pain both hot and icy-cold.

Sam put his hands to his forehead. He felt defeated. Sure, he had a lot of crimes to solve. He'd nearly solved the auto thefts with the help of his department, and he was making progress on the lake cabin break-ins, but the cold case involving Lester Moulton's brutal murder was his baby, his to solve. Although he was getting assistance from Frank, how much could Frank do, having been out of law enforcement for nearly a decade? Well, the guy was plenty smart, maybe he'd come through.

In the morning maybe he'd call Belle and ask her to get some frogmen out to the bog. He could make up the excuse that the ice is pretty much gone now. Use his charm. Get Belle to promise. He had to do something.

"Honey, what's wrong?" Darla snapped on the bedside lamp and rolled toward him, touching his arm. "Sam, you're dripping wet."

"Nothing, hon. Just a nightmare. Go back to sleep, sweetie, you've got to get your rest."

Darla, her face puffy with sleep, looked alarmed. Had he said Belle's name out loud? He hoped to hell he hadn't as he leaned over and kissed her.

As he drove north, Sam realized that he was spending most of his time in Venice and Amnesty, an area that he'd always expected to be relatively uneventful. He decided to postpone calling Belle. Instead, he had Barb call ahead from Galway to arrange an interview with Chuck and Rhu Shaw. Although they were certainly not potential suspects, Sam felt he needed a different perspective on Whiskey Hill folk and on Chuck and Rhu. After all, they'd been residents of Venice for almost as long as the Willards and had lived kitty- corner from them the whole time. Afterward, Sam had to check again on the crime scene where Moose had been shot, then make that half-hour drive over to Townsend Hospital in Waterville to meet and interview him. Actually, Sam was plenty curious about the eccentric hermit.

He pulled into the driveway at nine sharp, and Chuck was at the kitchen door. "Hi, Sheriff! Good to see you. Rhu's not up yet, but come on in."

Stomping his feet on the loon-decorated welcome mat, Sam stepped through the mudroom into the kitchen.

"Sit down. Kitchen's the best room in the house, if I do say so myself. Can I bribe you with a fresh-brewed cup of coffee?"

Sam smiled. It seemed as though everyone in this town knew his predilection for a strong cup of coffee. "Sure, wouldn't mind a cup, and call me Sam."

What Chuck had neglected to reveal was that he couldn't rouse Rhu from her hung-over sleep.

"Say, this is a handsome kitchen. You do all the woodworking in here?"

The long, narrow room had built-in shelves with curving end boards. A collection of old Yellowware mixing bowls lined one shelf, and, above them, a shelf of Staffordshire platters. An array of rare wooden utensils decorated the other wall. A pine plank floor showcased an array of bright blue and gray braided rugs. It was right out of *Country Living* magazine. Darla would have disliked it.

"Yeah, I enjoy working with wood. Workshop's right through there in what was once a stable." He pointed to a hand-made wooden door, rustic but finely built. "You know, old Doc Davis used this house as his office for forty years. Hundred-and-fifty years old. We even have his desk and doctor's valise."

"Well, you're taking good care of the place. The old doc would be proud."

"Say, aren't you married to Darla McClellan? I know her dad. Been out deep sea fishing with him a dozen times over the years. I've seen her but never got a chance to chat. Rough seas don't seem to bother her. And Jack—boy, he's a character."

"Say, sounds like you know everybody in the county."

"Not hardly, but I know a lot of fishermen seein' that I love to fish. I like Galway, too." He looked out the kitchen window in that direction. "Truth be told, sorta' wish we'd settled there. So is that how you met Darla?"

"Yep, on a deep sea fishing trip."

"I'll be darned. When I saw her that once she was choppin' bait and chummin' the waters. Hard to believe a crusty old salt like Jack could have such a pretty daughter."

"Yeah, and if I don't treat his only daughter right, they'll be fishing me out of Galway Bay. Speaking of fishing people out of the water, Chuck, I could use some background information on the Moulton case."

Chuck set down his coffee, leaned toward Sam and whispered, "Sure, what do you need?"

"It's your neighbors, the Willards, I'm interested in."

"Don't have much to do with any of 'em. Taught the boys in high school, of course, and Rhu teaches Becky now, I think, or was it last year? Anyway, wouldn't trust a one of 'em." Chuck traced a finger around the roses on the cotton tablecloth. "Bertha's not so bad, does the best she can. Like we discussed at Frank and Sandy's, Slug does his drug dealin' over there." Chuck rose and pointed out the kitchen window at the semi parked right by the Willard's front door. "Guess he thinks we're all stupid and don't have a clue. Hell, I coulda' kept a list of license numbers of his customers, but what's the use? Everybody around here either uses or grows."

"That so?" Chuck had Sam's full attention.

"Yeah. Remember the other day we talked about someone planting weed up in Frank's woods? I thought of something else about that. Belcher told Frank he didn't want to harvest 'til it was fully matured. Frank said, 'But what about the Air National Guard surveillance choppers that fly overhead? I'm not taking the rap for this escapade.' After that Frank sent certified letters to Belcher explaining what had taken place, cuz, like me, he didn't trust Belcher."

"I can understand that."

"My best guess, and don't quote me, is that Slug and his boys did the planting."

Sam filed it away mentally. "The Zucchettis seem like fine people."

"Frank's a good friend, and what a hard worker. I feel like I've always known him, and Sandy's a doll. You should see her out shovelin' manure for the gardens. One time I saw her drive a herd of Holsteins back up the hill, in her nightgown and slippers, no less. It was winter, mind you. She held out a couple of birch limbs to make herself look bigger and fooled the cows into thinking she was twelve feet wide. Cows are pretty dumb, you know, and, by God, she drove 'em right up the road toward the MacTeague's."

Suddenly Rhu scuffed in wearing a faded blue bathrobe, with disheveled hair, and red-rimmed eyes. Sam was surprised by her appearance. She seemed frail and far older than her husband. "Sandy made a fool of herself, that's what, out in the middle of the road with hardly anything on." Rhu poured her coffee with a shaky hand. "You get enough coffee, Sheriff? There's coffee cake left, Chuck. Why didn't you offer the man some?" Her tone was whiney.

"Because I ate it all yesterday, remember? Have you met Sam? He's asking about the Willards and such."

"Huh! The Willards, white trash throwbacks, that's what. The only one worth anything is little Becky, and she doesn't stand a chance, living with those hooligans." The movements of her doughy mouth seemed slightly out of synch with the words, like watching an old movie.

Sam wondered how anyone could be such a contrarian. "You know about the incident concerning the cat. Have you two any ideas who might've done it?"

They both answered at once, but Chuck yielded to Rhu. "Who shoots his dogs when they bark too much? Slug. And he can't abide the Forresters. Thinks they're stuck-up college people. I didn't see anything, mind you, but I know Slug's responsible."

"Have any of the Willards ever threatened you?"

"No, not directly."

"What do you mean by 'not directly'?"

"Well...they...they might've stolen things out of our garden or the barn," she said.

"What about the Forresters?"

"Little Becky tells me her parents hate the Forresters."

"Did she say why?"

"Not exactly, but they *are* from away. Flatlanders! That's plenty enough reason."

"And what about the Zucchettis? Did the Willards ever threaten them?"

She gave a non-committal shrug.

"Okay. That should do it." Sam rose to go and put on his jacket and Smoky Bear hat, but before he could get out the door, Rhu resumed her prattle. Chuck had heard it all before.

"Sheriff, you must have that guardrail repaired. Only a matter of time before someone's gonna hit what's left if it, ricochet off and land in our front dining room, or worse, fly through the gap left by Booth Gossam and crash right into the Forresters' house."

"I understand your concern, but all I can do is leave the orange warning cones and ribbons up. If I were you, I'd write to the State Director of Highway Safety in Augusta. Well, I gotta get back to work." He turned to Chuck. "Thanks for the coffee."

As he left the driveway Sam waved goodbye, muttering, "It's not my job."

He proceeded up the hill to the Mooseman crime scene. The team from Augusta had removed the boat, and no one had disturbed the crime scene tapes. He walked around the area but found no additional clues. Checking his watch, he realized that he'd better head over to Townsend Hospital.

A half hour later he was looking in on a snoring Moose, who was sharing a room with a very old man who, with his unblinking eyes and gaping jaw, looked quite dead. Nurse Sylvia came along and suggested that Sam return in about an hour if he expected to interview Moose. "By then, Mr. Felker's sleeping meds may have worn off." She smiled.

"If you don't mind my asking, is his roommate alive or dead?"

"A little of both, I'm afraid." Then, without looking at the body in the other bed, she hustled out the door and down the corridor.

Sam gazed at the probably-dead man. He'd seen "dead" many times, and this guy certainly filled the bill. He stared at Moose, whose eyes were rolling under their lids, seeing dreams.

Feeling hungry, Sam decided to check out the cafeteria or at least a snack bar. He turned the corner, went downstairs and detected the aroma of food. True, it was hospital food, but he didn't care. He'd felt cheated ever since he learned Chuck had eaten the coffee cake.

As he walked down the food aisle he noted how crowded the cafeteria was. They were still serving breakfast, but he opted for an egg salad sandwich, chocolate milk, and two molasses cookies. His aunt had convinced him, when he was an impressionable child, that molasses cookies, coffee, Jell-O, and rhubarb were good for him. Now that he was in his forties he wasn't so sure, but he ate them out of habit.

Once in the cafeteria he sat down heavily in a metal chair and glanced around. The dozens of hospital personnel in their green cotton tops reminded Sam of prisoners. Several wore bright, flowered shower caps and matching booties. *Folks don't go into the field of medicine to make a fashion statement, that's for sure.* He smiled.

Suddenly a buxom blonde plopped herself down directly across from him, dropping a plastic spoon next to her yogurt container. Her hair was swept up in a pony tail, partially hidden by her nurse's cap, and she wore two or three turquoise studs in each ear. Her name tag read *Lucille Shaw, RN,* and her smile revealed full lips and flawless teeth.

"Hi there! You must be the famous Sam Barrows. Excuse me, but is this seat taken?"

"It is now," he answered, grinning like a schoolboy. He felt about twelve years old.

"Thanks. I'm Lu Shaw. My husband's the ER Doc, Seth Shaw. I think you met him. What brings you to Townsend—Donald Wells?" Her face reflected genuine sadness as she popped the cap off of her strawberry yogurt and began taking dainty bites.

"Actually, I'm here to interview another patient, Mr. Felker, but now that you mention it, how's Don Wells doing?"

"Well, I shouldn't discuss patient status, but since it's you..."

She leaned over, revealing plump breasts, perhaps aided by a push-up bra. She hadn't bothered to button her uniform all the way. Sam thought, *Almost too perfect, perhaps.* He was having trouble remembering what they were talking about. Her complexion glowed with good health, and her dark brown eyes, flecked with green, were shadowed by long lashes. She could've been a big time beauty contest winner, and he was willing to bet she'd been a high school cheerleader.

She leaned still farther and whispered, "Don Wells is barely holding his own. Still being kept in a comatose state. We're all praying for him." She touched the small gold cross nestled in her cleavage, rubbing it between slender manicured fingers. "Sheriff, if you want to be kept posted, just call and ask for me. I'll keep you posted. After all, we're both in uniform." She grinned provocatively, then slowly licked the pink traces of yogurt off her spoon, first one side and then the other.

Sam felt that he probably had egg salad stuck in his teeth because she kept staring at his mouth. He took a swig of chocolate milk and worried about a moustache. She kept talking and he resumed listening. She used her hands a lot. *Do I detect a slight accent?* Is she Italian or maybe French-Canadian? Many of the staff members at Townsend were *Quebecois.*

"Every time I drive over to my in-laws in Venice I think about the accident. It could have been me, but I drive a big SUV so I'd have been a lot safer than Don was." She finished her yogurt and carefully wiped her mouth.

"Not necessarily. Your SUV probably has a center of gravity that could cause it to flip if you ran into a moose...or anything for that matter. I hope you always wear your seatbelt." *Boy, was that a stupid remark. She's a nurse. Of course she does.*

She reached over and patted his hand. "I appreciate your concern, Sam. Can I call you Sam? I must say, you look awesome in that uniform." Her voice was breathy and her tone overly friendly. "Love to stay and chat but I need to get back to the ward. Hope I see you again soon." *Seth must have his hands full with her.*

"See you." Sam stared at his cookies, then wrapped them in a napkin and took them with him. The cafeteria was too warm for him.

Andy was in a hurry to get to work, wanting to put in two hours restocking shelves for the weekend before customers started coming in. He grabbed a box of Cheerios and sat down at the kitchen table.

"What you doin' with them Cheerios? And don't go usin' up all the milk!"

"I didn't, Pop. There's some left."

"Don't argue with me, and get me a cup of coffee. Always in a damned rush to get outa' here." Gus sat sprawled on the couch.

Sarah walked in, wearing poofy red slippers from the Waterville Goodwill and a faded yellow bathrobe over a threadbare pink and white flannel nightgown. "There's always evaporated milk, Gus." She went to the shelf and handed him a small can.

"Goddammit, woman. Little Lord 'Font-el-roy' gets the milk and I get canned piss!" Booth, his head still bandaged from the accident at Forresters', came in just as Gus threw the can. It hit Sarah above the eye. She put her hand to her head, the blood running through her fingers and dripping down onto the dust bunnies along the edge of the kitchen floor. Sarah began sobbing.

Booth walked over and picked up the can, set it on the shelf, then headed for the television where he switched it from sports reruns to Saturday morning cartoons, turning the set up loud. He wasn't about to take sides. Andy rose and grabbed a kitchen towel and handed it to his mother. He looked pale.

Gus picked up the Cheerios box and roughly poured the rest into Andy's bowl. The little O's overflowed, rolled over the edge of the table and onto the floor. "Pick the rest up, little Andy Pansy, and eat 'em!"

"I can't eat 'em now, Pop. They're all dirty." He knelt down and stared at the dirty floor and the scattered bits of cereal. Unwilled tears spurted from his eyes.

Gus grabbed Andy's arm. Sarah cringed against the wall, and even Booth heard the bone pop as Wiley Coyote blew up the Roadrunner in the next room.

"Aieeeah! Please Poppy, don't hurt me any more." Andy was screaming in anguish and clutching his injured arm in an attempt to ease the pain, which ran clear up to his neck. "Don't hit me! I didn't do anything bad!"

"That's the whole problem, you little shit. Get on your feet like a man." As Andy staggered to his feet, Gus threw a hard jab into the boy's jaw. Andy's head snapped back, and he found himself down on the floor in a pool of sticky blood that was running out of his mouth. His teeth felt numb, like they were buzzing.

Sarah pulled herself up, staggered over to her son and knelt down.

"Always takin' his side against me." Suddenly Gus kicked her in the ribs, knocking her over, then reached down and gave her hair a hard yank, meanwhile stepping on Andy's leg. "I'm sick ta' death of the way you baby him. You'll turn him into a queer just like that Moulton guy. Then you'll get yours like Moulton got his, tippy-toein' around the edge of the bog. If you don't like it here, get the hell out, both o' ya!" His face was ablaze and spittle sprayed out of his mouth onto their faces. Gus took several deep breaths, and wiped his mouth with a hairy forearm. "I need an eye-opener," he bellowed, pulling a Bud out of the refrigerator and marching off to the living room.

Sarah, her eye still seeping and beginning to puff up, grabbed her winter coat, a set of keys and her purse. She handed Andy his bomber jacket and a dish towel to wipe his bloody face, and they left in one of the many old cars that sat in the rutted front yard.

CHAPTER 26

Andy's mother sounded shaken when she called to say that her son couldn't come in. Jake hung up then sauntered over to the deli counter. He couldn't help but notice that the two teens were getting pretty tight.

He looked Anna up and down, his face only inches from hers. "Your sweetheart Andy won't be in today. Poor kid's sick."

Anna stared at her boss, then stepped back. Ignoring the leer in Jake's eyes and the sarcasm in his voice, she demanded, "What's wrong with Andy?"

"Dunno. All his mama said was that he was sick." He shrugged and walked toward the front of the store, then said over his shoulder, "And be sure you slice up enough cheese for the noontime sandwiches."

Anna hurried to the back phone and dialed Andy. She'd memorized the number but never used it before. Gus answered. She thought about hanging up, then screwed up her courage and said, in her most grown-up tone, "Hi, this is Anna at the store. Can I please speak to Andy?"

Gus casually replied, "Well, Annie, he ain't here. His mommy's taken him to the ER in Waterville."

"Anna! My name is An-ya! So why did Mrs. Gossam take Andy to the ER?"

Gus hung up without answering. Anna hung up, turned on her heels and returned to the deli counter, but she could hardly concentrate on pizza preparation. When her half hour lunch break arrived, she called home.

"What should I do, Papa? I know something terrible's happened to Andy. I called there, but his dad wouldn't tell me anything except that Andy's mom took him to the ER. I know his dad has beaten him up again, but if I call the hospital they won't tell me anything. Could Mom maybe call and find out for me?"

Her father's concern showed in his voice. "You be patient, Anna. Your mama can't get involved. It would be unprofessional. Maybe you call the boy tonight. I'll pick you up at six and we can talk about it, *arma Anna*."

On the way home that evening, Anna explained to her father about Andy's home situation. She also revealed that his mother had been taken to the ER lots of times and for the same reason. Her blue eyes brimmed with tears and she was biting her lip.

"Honey, it's a sad truth dat in America parents don't seem always to know how to be parents. What do you want me to do? I want to help."

"Papa, I told Andy all about our family. I mentioned the guest cabin, and, uh..."

"Spit it out, little one." He was concentrating on the road because up where they lived the snow plow didn't do a very good job.

"Don't be mad at me, Papa, but I said...well...that I thought you wouldn't mind if he lived in our cabin for a while...just 'til things are better at his house. There's always a lot of drinking and violence at the Gossams'."

"And who does most of the hitting?"

"His papa, Gus. Whoever's to blame, Andy's the target—him or his Mom."

"Ya, I hear plenty stories about dis big bully Gus Gossam."

They turned onto the long driveway. Ahead of them lay the security of their all-cedar house that Eric had built under the spruce trees. Anna and her sisters always felt safe in their house, and she loved seeing their German Shepherd, Kipper, run up to the Volvo to greet them.

"And what did dis young man say about your grand plan?"

"He said he'd try it if it was okay with both you and mom, and if he could pay rent or work around the place, maybe help with chores, chop wood, you know."

Who could resist those eyes or that sweet, pleading voice? "Well, we must talk it over with your mama, girl. But if she says yes, it's okay with me."

Anna reached over and touched her father's bearded cheek. "Papa, you're so good!"

He smiled, filled with pride in his daughter.

After supper, Eric drove Anna to Townsend, hoping to see Andy. He had checked to make sure that Andy was still a patient at the hospital. They wouldn't release any information other than that Andy was resting comfortably. Eric thought *How can anyone rest in a hospital? When I was in hospital for gall stones they kept wakin' me up to see if I was sleepin'.* His wife Else worked here, but this was one of her days off. She worked four on, two off. She'd recently been promoted to nurse-supervisor on the fourth floor surgical ward.

True to her promise, Lucille Shaw tracked down Sam to tell him that Andy'd been admitted to the hospital under "suspicious circumstances." Since Moose was still asleep, Sam went directly to Andy's room only to discover that he wasn't there. Instead, Anna was curled up in the overstuffed green Naugahide chair in the corner, absorbed in reading a book. Sarah sullenly sat in a chair by the bed.

"Hi! Anna from the Venice General Store, right? And Mrs. Gossam. How are you doing?" Sam inquired as he walked over to her. He was shocked by her swollen face.

"Truth be told, not very well. I'm worried 'bout my boy."

"Are you all right, Mrs. Gossam?"

"Been better." She wouldn't look at him.

"Do you know where Andy is?"

Anna shook her head, her blue eyes bigger and bluer than usual. "They took him for more x-rays. He'll be back soon. Is Andy in trouble?"

"No, *he's* not in any trouble." Sam gave her a reassuring smile and glanced over at Sarah. "Listen, I'll be back in a bit. If he returns, tell him I need to ask him a couple of questions. And I need to speak to you privately, Mrs. Gossam, when you're up to it."

Sam needed another shot of caffeine so he went down to the first floor snack bar. He didn't like hospitals much. He'd been shot twice and had spent many days in Southern Maine Medical Center, the largest hospital in Portland. No fun at all. As he followed the green line on the floor to the vending machines and coffee shop, he wondered what made hypochondriacs tick. *Some folks'd try anything to stay in a place like this. They're sick all right.*

As he walked back to Andy's room, Sam wolfed down a cinnamon bun. It'd stuck to his fingers, so he washed his hands at the small sink. Just then, Eric walked in, followed by the shift nurse who announced that there were too many people in the room.

The two men ignored her. "Hi!" Eric said shyly. "I don't tink we've met but I'm Anna's papa. I been wanting to meet and talk wid you, Mrs. Gossam, too." Eric shook hands, but Mrs. Gossam made excuses that she needed to talk to Social Services downstairs.

"Just a moment, Mrs. Gossam." He'd followed her out into the corridor. "Have you remembered exactly where Gus and Booth were on Thanksgiving and the day after?"

"Home, I guess. I don't know. I have a lot on my mind." She winced, touching the stitches over her eye. "Andy's hurt, and I don't know what to do."

"You *guess*?"

"Oh, I don't know." She was verging on tears, so Sam veered off.

"Think about this. You could sign papers allowing your son to be safe, at least temporarily. I know you're under a lot of pressure, ma'am, but we could arrange for you *and* your son to go to safe places."

"Awright, awright. I'm goin' to the ladies room, if you don't mind." She limped off down the hall. She was switching moods at random.

Back in the room, Sam said to Eric, "I've heard a lot of favorable things about you. You're definitely one of the good guys."

"He sure is," Anna chirped from her corner chair.

Eric's face reddened, and he was at a loss for an answer.

"Your daughter here makes sandwiches for me sometimes down to the general store. Sweet girl, and polite." Anna blushed.

"Tanks. Listen, I need to tell you someting." Eric now stood inches from Sam, who was feeling somewhat crowded by European intimacy. "My Anna's good friend of Andy Gossam," he whispered. "Dat boy's a hard worker and keeps his grades up, honor roll every term. But Anna says he and his ma gets hit all de time at home, knocked around by dere papa. Dat's a bad ting!"

"Yeah, I've heard the stories. I've dropped in over there on the Bog Road, and they live poorly. I'm not surprised to learn that the wife gets in the way of Gus's fists sometimes. We can ask Children's Services to investigate, but sometimes that makes it worse for the kids. They're short-handed and it takes forever."

Eric whispered, "I had my wife call and check on it last night, and the x-rays might prove de boy's got lotsa' old injuries. Please don't involve my wife, Sheriff. She could lose her job. I jes' want to let you know dat we could let Andy live in our guest cabin. My wife has agreed. We'd keep him safe, no matter what!"

Sam put his hand on Eric's arm. "No, I won't mention her name. The resident physician has filled me in, and I've interviewed Mrs. Gossam. I'll talk with the boy when he gets back up here. Maybe the mother will sign a complaint. Andy was in x-ray again last I checked. And, thanks, Eric. If more people came forward who gave a damn about kids, we wouldn't have so much child abuse." The two men shook hands solemnly.

When Andy was wheeled back into Room 305, he found Anna, her papa, and the sheriff all waiting for him. Once the nurse got Andy settled Sam pulled up a chair next to the bed.

Anna came over, took Andy's hand in hers, and blurted out her feelings. "His daddy did this to him, and all the other broken bones and bruises and—" She burst into tears. "It's not fair!" She reached over to the bedside stand for a tissue, then rushed out of the room.

"Is this true, son? I'm here to help, if I can."

"Yeah, but my mom tries to stop him. It isn't her fault. It was all about Cheerios, stupid stuff. He hit us lots of times. He can't control his temper, especially when he's drinking. It's not his fault, not really."

"The doctor tells me you've got a dislocated shoulder, a clavicle injury, and a jaw injury. Did your dad do that?"

Andy looked down at his sheet, pulled it up as far as he could and nodded in the affirmative.

Eric, who'd been standing in the corner, moved out into the hall to console Anna and allow the sheriff to speak with the boy alone.

Sam pulled his chair closer. "Son, I know how tough this is. You're right in the middle of a nasty situation, but the x-rays don't lie. They reveal a whole catalog of injuries dating back to when you were a little kid. Broken arms, ribs, and now a fractured clavicle. Who knows how many concussions. This is why they're keeping you for observation. Are you aware of the danger you'd be in if you went home right now? I think your mom knows."

"But what *about* Ma? He'll take it out on someone, and my brothers are too big. Who's gonna protect her? He never beats my sisters, but..." Tears squirted from of Andy's eyes and ran down his cheeks. He hated crying with Anna just outside the room.

"We'll send a social worker to your home, and I'll explain the options to your mom. You know, she can always go to a safe house. But, Andy, you're a minor, and we have a legal obligation to protect you."

The nurse came back in to take Andy's vitals. Sam stepped out into the hall where Eric and Anna were waiting. "Eric, can I ask him if he wants to stay with you folks temporarily?"

"Can't I ask him? It might be easier if it came from me." Anna smiled and peeked into the room.

"We want to protect da boy. We'll do all we can." Eric hugged his daughter.

Sam noticed Sarah coming down the hallway. "Okay. Why don't you all go in?" He ushered father and daughter into the room.

He walked over to Mrs. Gossam. "I have those papers for you and Andy to sign. Then I've gotta get a hold of a judge to sign an order of protection. I think it'll all work out, for the time being anyway. The main thing is to keep you safe."

Gus Gossam, with his repeated acts of violence, moved up a notch on the suspect list.

CHAPTER 27

Early Saturday morning Cleona Burgess filled her coffee can with birdseed. As she carefully walked out back she saw a pair of nuthatches feasting on the netted sack of suet that she'd hung up. *Everything in Nature is connected,* she mused. A flock of Rufus capped sparrows pecked away excitedly at a tray of millet and sunflower seeds, while on the frozen mud below, nearly a dozen Slate juncos cleaned up the spillage like foraging mice. Cleona spied a Cooper's Hawk perched on the branch of a dead pine snag. She worried because the Cooper's was capable of eating a sparrow or two for lunch.

This backyard and the five mile radius around it, including Hiram Bog, the Rockwell place, the Back Bog Road, and the deep woods behind the MacTeagues, held everything Cleona needed. Her universe included not only small birds but loons, wood ducks, Canada Geese, stilt-legged herons, owls, wild turkey and grouse. This love of wildlife was something she had shared with Lester, and she thought with a sodden heart of her departed friend. Why couldn't they find the culprit? The violence necessary for survival in the natural world was not necessary for human beings, and it made her uneasy to think that a person capable of such violence was walking about.

Cleona had loved Saturdays for as long as she could remember. It went back to her forty-five years of teaching youngsters. She always relished Saturday, the one day of the week that was truly hers. Part of Sunday belonged to God, of course.

A spinster, she filled her free time with small pleasures. In 1975, the selectmen had appointed her Archivist of the Venice Historical Society. Her love of wildlife had led her to co-found the Friends of Fowl with Lester Moulton, and she was a lifetime member of the Audubon Society. She'd been awakened by the fussing of jays outside her bedroom window and the loud hammering of what sounded like a pileated woodpecker. "*Ceophloeus pileatus,*" she said out loud to Lester, as if he were there, next to her in the old bird watching blind on the woods path near the bog.

She'd gone over to the south window and pulled aside the muslin curtain. The late January morning glowed with golden sun spilling over the hills to the southeast, casting long, splayed shadows across the side yard.

The sky seemed made of soft, cobalt velveteen, and along its far horizons, it shimmered with a tinge of mellow violet.

Not wanting to miss another minute of such a glorious winter day, Cleona changed quickly from her night clothes into her cotton slip, house dress, long woolen sweater, canvas jacket, heavy stockings, and sturdy shoes. Her bedroom was under the upstairs eaves. Cleona had chosen the southern end because she loved the warmth of winter sunrises.

Built by her great-great grandfather, the house had originally stood in Dixville, the next town east of Venice. But after decades of boundary and tax disputes, old Jebez Burgess bought twenty-five acres on Whiskey Hill Road. He hauled the little Cape house over hill and dale, using several teams of oxen. It took him and his neighbors four hard days and three kegs of cider to accomplish the task. It was the oldest inhabited dwelling in Venice.

Neither grand nor imposing, the center chimney cape, adorned with white clapboards, stood proudly near the road, sheltered by ancient lilac bushes. The front door faced the road. Cleona always used the side entrance. Like many Maine houses, its ten-by-ten wooden sills rested atop rows of granite slabs. Beneath the house was a full cellar, complete with shelf-lined walls, root bins, and an old oil furnace. Cloudy Bell jars filled the shelves. Cleona canned much more than any single person could reasonably consume.

Her immaculate kitchen was a cheery place, albeit plain. Pine cabinets offered little shelf space, but a 1914 Hoosier cabinet had been Cleona's mother's pride. A dependable Harmony wood stove with two gas burners added in the Fifties stood near the center chimney.

Once there'd been a horse barn out back, but lightning had struck it during the Second World War. The weather vane survived, and Cleona had mounted bird feeders on it. A small shed was overflowing with wood, delivered by Angus MacTeague but stacked by Cleona herself. Although the "Great Ice Storm of 1998" had frozen her in and she'd had to ask for help, Cleona was a remarkably self-sufficient woman for her seventy-five years. Still, it was comforting to know that Angus, Mabel, and the boys lived just up the road to the north.

Finding poor George Felker face down in the woods path two days before had deepened her grief over Lester's murder. Shrouded in a heavy mood, Cleona forced herself to think of spring. Her daffodils would bloom, but first the anemones would poke their purple heads up through the snow. Then there were her dahlias. Every fall she carefully dug up thirty or so tubers and stored them in a corner of the cellar, far from the heat of the furnace. In spring she pawed over her precious treasure. Then, after mud season, when the soil was right, she planted them in rows, like students in a well ordered classroom, putting naughty bulbs in the far corners and star pupils up front. If Mooseman ever heard her talking to her tubers, he'd have understood.

Mabel MacTeague had stopped by on Friday and they'd talked

about the attack on Mooseman, how Cleona had found him shot, lying on the woods path, bleeding. Mabel offered, "Surely, it was an accident. Venice men are always shooting, and not a day goes by that I don't hear a gunshot from one direction or t'other."

Cleona had known the MacTeagues since childhood and they'd frequently visited in Angus's parents' time. Actually, old Clyde MacTeague had visited too much once he became senile. He'd wander the length of Whiskey Road, dropping in on neighbors unannounced. One morning, Cleona was getting dressed for school and went downstairs only to find Clyde seated at the pine table by the window-corner of the kitchen asking for her father, Jerome, long since dead.

By the grace of God, Clyde had rapidly declined. His wife, Margaret, followed him but six months later. Now they slept in the cemetery next to the Zucchetti property. Shortly thereafter, Angus and his bride, Mabel, had moved into the old family homestead to stay, raising six children, all of whom Cleona had taught.

Another neighbor had been Herbert Rockwell, who had a hundred-acre farm to the east behind Cleona's place. The ghost-gray barn still dominated the hillside, its roof line curved like a humpbacked whale.

Cleona walked to the front of the house to take in the view. She could clearly see the snow-covered shoulders of Mount Washington as well as Jefferson and Madison in the northward march of the Presidential Range. She looked up the road to the north, toward Mooseman's and the woods path that led down across the Bog Road to the bird-watching blind, and gazed at the dense, dark-green swath of trees that ringed the bog, recalling that she'd heard a gunshot yesterday morning while down there. Cleona hoped to sight the snowy owl that she and Lester had seen on this day exactly one year ago. She knew because she'd noted the sighting in her birding journal. *Was that the shot that hit poor George Felker?*

Determined not to live in fear of her own woods, Cleona turned away from the bright sunshine and marched resolutely back into the house. After breakfast, she'd don her boots and down-filled jacket and venture forth in search of "Snowy" and perhaps even his cousin, the "Great Gray." She might be cautious, but she certainly wasn't about to be scared off.

With the simple twist of a knob or quarter turn of a valve one can adjust an old oil furnace to do one's bidding. Once the old woman had come back from her trek to the bog and had a light lunch, she'd pulled down the bedroom shades. The furnace began to puff ever-so-slightly, building back pressure as its combustion efficiency slowly dropped.

Despite the temperature dropping into the teens, slow Johnnie MacTeague was sweating. He'd been getting a cord of maple ready for a customer, chainsawing it into eighteen inch lengths. He didn't see why folks couldn't order longer lengths and cut the wood themselves. He wiped his flannel jacket sleeve across his forehead then stretched and looked toward Cleona's house. *Wonder why Cleona's smoke looks different. Maybe better check on her.*

Cleona was an okay old gal. She'd sure been good to him while he was recuperating from his motorcycle accident. When he returned from the hospital, she'd brought up cookies and fudge. After he began to talk again, she'd read to him and made him practice words from kids' books. His memory and his faculties had got some better due to her help.

He brushed the sawdust off his flannel pants and jacket, lay down the chainsaw, took a swig of coffee from his thermos, then trudged down to Cleona's. Johnnie looked around the meadow and along the edges of the woods, wanting to tell his father about the smoke and that he was going over to Cleona's. No Angus. Johnnie looked over toward the side yard of the farmhouse, squinting against the brightness of the sun-drenched, un-melting snow. The red Ford pickup was gone, but Cleona's car, an old maroon Mercury Marquis, was sitting in her yard. He knocked on the kitchen door, then pounded. He noticed a puff of black soot slither through the partly open kitchen window. *Maybe she's out in the woods, countin' birds,* he thought, *but, Jeeze, it's awful cold to stay out all day bird watchin'.* Besides, he was pretty sure he'd seen her returning up the woods path from the bog. *Or was it yesterday?* He couldn't remember. Sometimes he couldn't even remember what was on TV the previous night.

When he didn't get a rise out of her, he sat on the step and wondered: should he walk in or go back home? His butt was getting cold so he stood up, knocked once more, then tried the unlocked door. As he entered her neat kitchen, he looked around at the smoke and touched the cold stove. *No fire there. Then how come there's smoke?* He sensed something was terribly wrong. Slowly he climbed the stairs to the bedrooms he'd helped wallpaper last year. He could remember some things.

Cleona was on top of the bedspread, covered by a quilt. Her face looked sort of rosy, but the smoke made it hard to see her clearly. Suddenly it sank in. "Jeeze, she's passed out, maybe dead. What'm I gonna do?" The sooty smoke from the backed-up heater burned his eyes and made him cough. He lifted Cleona off the bed—she weighed only a hundred pounds—and carried her downstairs. Suddenly another decision faced him. *Smoke's worse'n before. Should I take her outside?* As his coughing increased, he realized that fresh air was the answer. *But shouldn't I call the fire department first? There's the phone, but first I gotta put 'er down.*

Johnny set her in a kitchen chair, her upper body draped onto the table. He'd remembered doing this with a deer against a tree trunk. He opened the kitchen door, and carried her over his shoulder out onto the steps. Putting his bandana over his nose, he reentered the kitchen, extended the phone cord as far as he could toward the open kitchen door, and stared at the phone. He knew 911 from TV, but when he dialed it, there was a scary, squealing sound. He carefully dialed his mom and she answered on the first ring.

Twelve minutes later, the Amnesty ambulance roared up the road and veered into Cleona's driveway. The emergency team administered oxygen and placed Cleona in the ambulance just as the red pumper came up the road. Mabel had driven down and she was comforting him. Someone had wrapped him in a blanket, and he was breathing oxygen. They suggested that Mabel take him to the ER, but all he'd say was, "Just take me home, Ma."

"Johnnie, Cleona's still alive. If she makes it, you saved her life. I'm *so* proud of you." Mabel was rubbing her son's shoulder. "What in the world made you check on her anyway?"

Johnnie shrugged. "Funny smoke." He coughed.

"Think she'll make it?" Mabel asked the fireman as he slammed the ambulance door. She was beside herself with a mixture of pride in her son and fear for her old friend's safety. She knew that if Cleona didn't make it, Johnnie'd feel responsible. Whenever a barnyard cat or a bird died, he assumed partial blame.

"I gotta rest, Ma," Johnnie gasped.

Mabel put him in the car.

The firemen, wearing masks, had entered the house. There was no need for hoses since there were no flames, just lingering smoke.

A few minutes later they emerged. "Close call!" It was the deputy chief, Arnie Wallingsford. "Damndest thing! Someone blocked the air vent from the furnace to the outside and tinkered with the damper, the mixer, and the exhaust valve. All the smoke backed up, and the thermostat was set for ninety degrees. If you ask me, old Cleona's the victim of foul play. I gotta report all this to the sheriff." Arnie went over to the fire truck and got on the radio to Galway.

Sam heard the ambulance call on the cruiser radio, called Frank and asked him to go up the hill to the Burgess house ASAP. "Something bad happened to Cleona Burgess. All we know is that she's being transported to Townsend and her house is full of smoke. I need you to interview her, but first better check out the crime scene, if it is one. Your fire chief called in and said things looked suspicious."

"Okay, I'll grab my old crime kit and head up there."

"Thanks. Then could you head over to Townsend? That seems to be your destiny lately." Sam chuckled, "And do me a favor—keep track of the mileage."

Frank helped the fire department open all the windows and the cellar bulkhead. The once bright wallpaper was now dingy gray, and the oily film of smoke layered every surface. Frank hoped Cleona would make it. Just then he saw Hal Hines drive in. They taped off the area, and soon Frank was on his way to Waterville.

Two trips to the ER within a week involving Whiskey Hill residents was a pattern that Frank didn't like. *I'll bet she knows something or saw something she wasn't supposed to see. More pieces of the puzzle. Now, can we put them together?*

CHAPTER 28

Frank drove straight from the hospital to Galway. He had plenty to report about Cleona's condition, her statement, and the smoky farmhouse. Maybe he'd bring back a couple of lobsters for Sandy.

When Frank poked his head through the office doorway, Sam was poring through a mountain of paperwork while talking on the phone. Although it was Saturday evening, Barb had come in for a couple of hours. She whispered to Frank, whom she'd taken a shine to, "He'll be with you in a minute. Want some coffee? Just brewed, nice and strong."

"Sure, how can I say no?" It was a cold day and Frank's fingers still felt stiff. He was finally admitting to a touch of arthritis, and holding a warm cup would help. Frank admired Barb and knew that a busy office didn't function smoothly unless the person in charge oiled the cogs and ignored the stupid stuff. Just as Frank took his first swallow, Sam came out into the hall, smiling.

"'Bout time you showed up. What took you so long? I see Ma's coffeed you up." He playfully punched Frank in the arm, almost causing Frank to spill his coffee on his new twill slacks. That'd really annoy Sandy.

"Saturday afternoon post-game drunks drive slowly."

Okay, what'cha got? Anything that'll make my day, what's left of it." He motioned Frank into his office.

Frank produced his notebook. "Let's see, in the order of events: went to Cleona's little Cape and found it badly smoke damaged. So is she, but she'll make it. The doc isn't a hundred per cent sure she didn't suffer minor brain damage, but probably not. 'Time will tell,' the usual non-committal crap the medics dish out. And I checked the scene before the firemen muddied it up. Thermostat was set at ninety to force the furnace to work harder, air vents blocked, dampers closed, a recipe for death, so our doer had to have entered the house at some point. Not through the cellar bulkhead though; snow and ice hadn't been disturbed. Course he could've gone in through the kitchen door any time; no forced entry. We Venetians never lock our doors."

"Maybe you folks will change your ways now." Sam shoved a red pin in the wall map near the top of Whiskey Hill.

"Doubt it. Back to Cleona. Says she laid down for a nap after she walked in the bog. Meanwhile the jerk screwed with the fuel efficiency mixer valve and the damper so the house filled with smoke and carbon monoxide. Our guy either wanted to kill Cleona or render her mindless, take your pick. No usable footprints on the cellar floor, but I dusted for prints around the thermostat, vents, valves, and levers. Mostly smudges, maybe one possible readable. I brought 'em along so you can send 'em to Augusta."

"Good work. Any usable tracks in the mud or snow where the perp might've gotten out of a vehicle and headed for the steps?"

"Nope. Driveway's full of tracks. By the way, Johnnie MacTeague saved her life and risked his doin' it. You might want to send a letter of thanks or something. He's a simple, harmless guy, and he's not all there ever since he ran into a pine tree with his motorcycle."

"Any chance that 'harmless guy' rigged the furnace, then went back so he could play hero?" Sam hated to ask the question, but he'd seen worse. "Never count anyone out 'til the results are in."

"Naw. I can't make the connection. Too much like his father—just your plodding, straight-ahead farm boy. Besides, his thoughts aren't that complicated. Before the accident with the pine tree, maybe... Anyway, I took extra photos of the furnace and thermostat and talked with Wallingsford, the assistant fire chief. Says there's no doubt this was deliberate."

"Looks like Cleona must've seen something." Sam took notes. "Interesting. So what does *she* think? Or *can* she think?"

"She was somewhat sedated and on oxygen, so I didn't press her. I did ask if the furnace had been working properly, and she nodded yes. I asked, 'Do you know of anyone who'd want to see you harmed?' She shook her head no. Then she asked in a croaky voice if I thought she could go back in her house, and I told her she'd have to hire a company from Waterville or Bangor to clean up the smoke damage. She wasn't aware of it, and I'm afraid the news really upset her, her house being ruined and all. Sometimes I hate being a cop. You know the feeling, Sam. That house is her pride and joy."

"What a mess!" Sam said. "Don't suppose the old gal's insured?"

"Actually, she is. Her nephew's an Allstate agent and he's looked after her for years. Anyway, whoever did this wanted her dead and tried to make it look like an accident but was too stupid to pull it off."

"What about the nephew? Would he inherit?"

"Naw, everybody says he's a nice guy. Very responsible."

"Okay. Right now do we need to post a guard by her hospital room?"

"Absolutely. 'Course she'll have a fit. She's an independent old cuss."

"By the way, how'd you like to take home some lobsters for dinner? You can swing by the house and meet Darla before you head for Venice.

She probably thinks I've invented you. Seriously, she *does* want to meet you. Jack, her dad, had a real good morning on the water. She'll give you a couple of live ones."

Frank was impressed by the nineteenth century charm of the Barrows house. "Sam, I'm afraid Sandy'd just wanna move right in." He couldn't suppress a broad grin.

"Too bad. Not big enough for four adults, a dog, and three cats." Just then, Darla and Duchess came into the room. She was wearing tight, faded jeans and a blue-and-white reindeer sweater. "I'd like to introduce Frank Z. See, honey, he does exist. He's the deputy who specializes in the high crime area of Venice."

Darla's fresh, natural beauty blew Frank away. She seemed more than ten years younger than Sam. She was barefoot and had her toenails manicured and painted frosty pink, and her complexion was like fine porcelain.

"Hi! So good to meet you, finally." She took his hand and gave it a solid shake.

Ah, a woman of purpose and a damned pretty one at that.

They chatted at the kitchen table. Frank turned down coffee but accepted a cup of jasmine tea and a slice of bread, warm from the oven, with homemade wild strawberry jam. "Sam, how can you stay away from home so much? She's beautiful *and* she can cook." Frank turned to Darla and said, "He's a lucky guy. How'd you ever come to say yes to this old codger anyway?"

Her full lips parted in a smile. He had no idea that Darla was this good looking. "Well, you want the short version?"

Frank nodded.

"We met on Dad's lobster boat. If Sam hadn't liked the sea, I wouldn't've married him. Heck, my daddy wouldn't have let me. Jack's a seafarin' man and always has been—fourth generation! Speaking of lobsters, do me a big favor and take some home. Dad was too generous, as usual. You can carry two or three in this cooler."

Frank invited the Barrows up to Venice for an Italian meal "one of these days" and expressed his wish that Darla could meet Sandy. He was sure they'd hit it off.

Reluctantly, he headed home. On the thirty-minute drive back to Whiskey Hill, he wracked his brain trying to get the pieces to fit. Lester, Mooseman, Cleona. Were the crimes related? And how? Meanwhile, in the small world of the Styrofoam cooler resting on the floorboards sat three beady-eyed lobsters, unaware of their fate.

He thought a lot about Darla's dad and what a good reputation Jack had in the fishing community. He'd been the first man to organize the lobster fishermen into a co-op years before. *Sam must've had to pass muster with that guy.* Frank smiled at the thought of Sam on bended knee.

During the lobster feast, Sandy explored her latest theory. "Have you noticed that the phone hang-ups have stopped? And no more notes? I think Slug was sending them, and, because he's seen the sheriff's car over here a couple of times, he's decided that you're helping with the case. Makes him nervous because he wasn't hunting in Monson at all—he murdered Lester over at the bog, maybe with the help of Bobby John. Not Billy, though. He's too dumb. Slug did the cat, too, just to confuse things."

Frank mulled it over. "You mean well, but you haven't substantiated anything, except maybe about the note and calls. It's possible that the person who's been calling has no connection with Lester's murder or the attempted murder of Moose. All you've got, honey, is conjecture. Besides, we're waiting on some results from Augusta. They're slow as cold molasses, as my aunt used to say."

Just then the phone rang and Frank guessed it was Sam. He took out his notebook before answering and motioned for Sandy to get a pen.

"Hey, figured it was you. What's up? Anything from Augusta yet?" He paused. "Great. So the blood in the boat is AB negative, which matches up with Lester's. That didn't take a nuclear scientist to figure out, right?" Frank chuckled at something. "And what about the shell casing from the Moose shooting? Winchester 30-30. Well, that narrows it down to every hunter in Venice, including his sister Betty, but she's got an alibi." Frank listened for a moment and then said, "Wow, Sam, that puts more folks in the ballpark, doesn't it? Hell, let's see...Betty doesn't have an alibi then, Jake's alibi is weak, Gus could be lying, Slug might have moseyed over to the bog after dinner. We got a whole damned team of possible doers! And all alibis are off!"

Sandy was eager for Frank to get off the phone, but she whispered, "Thank him for the lobsters. They were delicious!"

Frank did just that, then hung up.

Sandy had that look that said, "Well, are you going to share or not?"

"Sandy, the stopped wristwatch would have taken up to forty-eight hours to run down. Les could've been killed *on* Thanksgiving Day, or as late as Saturday. The watch was a wind-up. Time to run down would depend on how tightly Lester wound it and when. That blows everyone's alibi, including your cousin Betty's. Blood type is Lester's, but we figured that. The shell found near Mooseman was—well, you heard."

"Great, that really narrows it down."

"Ballistics might be able to make a match if they can find the *right* rifle to compare with. Not enough evidence for a judge to issue a search warrant though."

Bright and early Monday morning, Sandy said, "Listen, we need milk. Wanna go to the store, big guy? You can eavesdrop on the locals, see what's cookin'."

"Glad to."

The store was crowded as it often was on Monday mornings. The locals wanted to catch up on their exciting weekend adventures. One would think that the January thaw would put a crimp in snowmobile activities, but not in Venice. One man described going over his back hill on his new snowmobile 'til he was down to grass, and still he kept going. "By God, what we need's a Nor'easter. Get two foot o' snow we'll have us a good time!"

Another went into detail about how he put his truck in at the bog to haul his ice house home and the back wheels started sinking in the slush. "By Jesus, had to think fast to haul that Dodge outa' there 'cuz she was sinkin' quick. Notice Earl's still got his icehouse out there. Guess he's afraid to return to the scene of the crime." The men near the lobster tank laughed.

When Frank ordered hotdogs from Phyllis, he remembered that Anna wasn't working because she and Andy were both in school. As he headed for the front of the store toward the register, he heard Eric's voice.

"Hi Frank, how ya doin'? Ya see da sheriff sometimes, yah? Would you tell him for me dat Andy's doin' great, helpin' wit chores and eatin' us outa' house and home. We really get on wid the boy. Tell him tanks!"

When Frank got home, he made a suggestion. "After lunch let's go up to Earl and Olive's. Amazingly enough, the bozos at the store made an interesting observation. They're wondering why Earl hasn't removed his fishing hut from the bog. 'Course it's nearly too late now. Unless we have a good freeze pretty soon, it'll sink."

"I'm concerned about Earl," Sandy said, reaching for her scarf. "Haven't seen him at the store or anywhere lately. Might have a cold. Anyway, good idea. Maybe he's remembered something."

CHAPTER 29

Sam hung up the phone after talking with Frank. He decided to sit very still at his desk and think things through, but reality got in the way. He stared at the "In" basket and remembered the reports he hadn't done. Spousal abuse, drunk drivers, a possible suicide attempt on the bridge, abandoned car, moose in a backyard acting peculiar, skunk in the garbage, on and on. His men wrote up decent reports, but he felt obliged to check every one. You never knew when one of these incidents was going to come back and bite you in the form of a lawsuit against the department.

Then there was the schedule for the next month. Maybe he could do that at home, but the Moulton case dominated his thoughts. It had been almost a month since the discovery of Lester's body. The powers-that-be from Augusta were now clamoring for progress reports every week. He'd gathered forensic evidence, ballistics, and crime scene evidence, yet no arrests had been made. He felt more than just a little frustrated. Felt like a headache was coming on, and he asked Barb to hold his calls for a while, but she tapped on the door and whispered, "Governor's office."

"Okay, I'll take it." He didn't have much choice.

"Hello, this is Glen McIver, the governor's chief of staff. We met at the Governor's Ball. I remember your gorgeous wife. How is she?"

"Fine, and you, sir?" He gave the obligatory responses on cue. A vague memory of Glen leering at Darla flitted past. Bless her heart, she hadn't even noticed McIver's stares.

"Listen, how's that big case coming?"

"We're hard at work on it, sir."

"Well, be great if you could tie up all the loose ends. The governor's taking a helluva lot of flack."

"We've made it our number one priority, sir. Unfortunately, we're still looking at multiple suspects for the Moulton murder. The same person may have shot Mr. Felker, but, so far, the two cases seem only indirectly connected. You may be interested to know that I've brought in a special consultant for this case."

"Good, whatever it takes. The governor would like you to hold a press conference, soon—very soon. Folks in your county are mighty scared, and you need to put their fears to rest. Think about the tourists. Trout season's coming up in April, you know."

"Yes sir, I'm aware of that. I'll have one shortly."

"Tomorrow would be best! Get on top of this, Sam. Thanks for your time, and keep us up to speed. Oh, and say hi to your pretty little wife."

"Yes, sir."

Sam hung up. His headache was now full-blown. "Barb, would you please set up a press conference for tomorrow morning early on the city hall steps? God, if this isn't one helluva Monday, I don't know what is. And bring me two aspirin, please."

"Sure thing, boss. I've been fielding queries from the press every day. They'll flip with joy."

Sam despised press conferences. Seldom did he come off looking good. He thought the least talented and laziest reporters asked the dumbest questions, and he worried that he might lose his temper. "Make it the afternoon. Tell 'em we'll hold the conference on the city hall steps at two."

"Boss, your wife could tell you that might be considered passive aggressive." Barb was shaking her head and giving him that "you're such a naughty boy" look. "Why outside?"

"Oh, I don't know. Maybe because it's twenty-two degrees with a freshening gale off the bay with flurries. At least it might dissuade the less hearty reporters from wanting to get their stories." He hoped they'd all stay in their respective bunkers. *They can make up lies there as well as anywhere else.*

"Good afternoon, ladies and gentlemen of the press. Glad you could make it on such short notice. I'll make a brief statement and then open it up for a few questions. Some time between November twenty-eighth and thirtieth, Lester Moulton was murdered. His body was discovered by a fisherman, Earl Bagley, on Sunday, January twelfth. Since that time both the Thoreau County Sheriff's Department and the CIU, headed by Lieutenant Belle Whittaker, have been working on the case. Incidentally, the Fish and Game Department, headed by Bud Varney, has been ably assisting us. We're nearer to arresting the perpetrator than we've ever been, and we're continuing to conduct interviews. We now have forensic, ballistic and crime scene evidence being processed. Some of it indicates that Mr. Moulton was probably shot in his john boat. We've been able to narrow down the crime scene to a particular section of Hiram Bog. The john boat is also being processed at the Augusta crime lab. A full investigation is in progress."

Sam continued, "The attempted murder of George Felker is not, to our knowledge, directly related to the Moulton case. We are pursuing all leads."

He could feel the tension mounting and hear the dozen or more reporters scribbling in their notebooks. Others held tape recorders, and two television cameras faced him, one from Bangor and the other from Portland.

Mikes were leaning in to catch his every word or mistake.

Q: "Do you have any other suspects, Sheriff?"

A: "Several other persons of interest."

Q: "Sir, is the shooting of George Felker tied to the Moulton murder?"

A: "I've already answered that." Sam felt sweat creeping down his ribcage.

Q: "Sheriff, there's a rumor that an elderly Venice woman was gassed while she slept and is now fighting for her life in a Waterville hospital. Do you deny these facts?"

A: "First, the facts have been distorted. An elderly Venice woman had her life threatened when her heater malfunctioned under suspicious circumstances. She's in good condition in a local hospital. We are not releasing any details or her name. I know you'll respect that."

Q: "So what you're not telling us is that a serial killer is shooting homosexuals and attempting to kill old ladies and others in the woods."

There was a slight gasp among onlookers. *This isn't going well.* Sam asked for the group to be quiet, and they simmered down.

A: Cottages are still being broken into near the lake, a man named Felker was shot at, and an older woman was placed in danger but is safe now. We don't feel that all of these crimes are related. You guys must be desperate for a story to call this the work of a serial killer."

No one laughed, and Sam felt he wasn't winning friends, but he wasn't sheriff to make friends. The wind howled around the corners of buildings, and the reporters had to yell at one another to be heard. The yelling seemed to notch up the emotions on both sides.

Q: "Have you recovered the murder weapon in the Moulton case?"

A: "We have not, but, remember, this is Maine. Maybe the weapon will be discovered come spring when the ice goes out."

Q: Sir, is it true that Felker's nickname is Mooseman? And that he draws attention to himself in the woods through bizarre behavior? In other words, was he asking for it?"

A: "No citizen *ever* asks to be shot. In my opinion, Mr. Felker has a unique personality, but, as far as we know, he's a law-abiding citizen."

The same reporter came back at Sam with another question.

Q: "Is it true, sir, that Mr. Felker, or Mooseman, if you will, (the audience laughed) was carrying a paintball gun?"

Although the reporter was almost right, Sam wouldn't give him anything.

A: "No. That's incorrect."

"One more question, folks, then I need to get back to work." Sam was weary of offering answers that would be twisted or misreported in the paper the next day.

Q: "Anne Fletcher, *Bangor Daily News.* Is George Felker gay? Maybe a gay friend of the former Mr. Moulton?"

Some of the reporters snickered and Sam was losing his patience.

179

A: "Ms. Fletcher, sexual orientation is not a common thread in these cases. To the best of my knowledge, Mr. Felker is not gay. Now, one more *relevant* question, please."

Q: Ed Phippen, *Galway Courier.* I've been interviewing people in Venice, and they're plenty worried. Can you tell us when you might make an arrest in the Moulton case?"

A: "We're making progress. New leads have just come in and these should serve to clarify several points in the investigation. My department's working round the clock and we'll keep you posted."

Another voice called out. Sam recognized it as belonging to the "sloppy copy" guy who wrote for the *High Tide Journal.* "Can you honestly tell the people of Venice that they can rest easy now, or is a killer still on the loose?"

Sam had already disappeared behind the doors to city hall. He felt engulfed in a deep sense of failure. He'd failed the victims: he'd not defended himself nor adequately protected Cleona Burgess or Moose, two eccentrics who deserved their privacy. Some days being a cop wasn't at all rewarding.

The Bagleys were pleased to have visitors. Their sons rarely came to Venice unless they wanted something. Olive had just baked banana bread and served huge pieces, along with hot chocolate topped with miniature marshmallows. The kitchen hadn't changed much in the last fifty years. The wooden cupboards had a fresh coat of butter yellow paint, but the refrigerator was ancient as was the wheezing freezer beside it. The 1912 stove was a converted wood burner, replete with warming shelf. The wallpaper had a pattern of pots, pans and roosters, a rather unfortunate combination, Sandy thought. The curtains were starched and clean, and the linoleum floor spotless. Braided rugs added a touch of color.

Once they got comfortable at the kitchen table, Frank started the conversation. "How've you folks been?"

"Fine, 'ceptin' for Olive's shoulder. And I got this stiff back most mornins', but s'pose that's to be expected at my age. Ain't complainin', mind ya'." Earl was over seventy and had worked hard all his life.

After they finished the refreshments, Earl suggested, "Let's move into the parlor. These wooden chairs are hard on my back."

"I was wondering about your fishing shack, Earl. You been over to it since the—"

Earl interrupted. "You mean since the worst day of my life? No! Keep havin' nightmares. Wakes Olive up. That pink jacket and that...that hand. God-all-mighty, wish I'd stayed home that day. What was I tryin' to prove anyway?"

"That you're an active man, Earl. Don't sell yourself short. You did everyone a favor, finding Lester. His body coulda' disappeared altogether. So you aided in a criminal investigation. Sorry about the nightmares. We've

180

all had our share of those."

Sandy added, "Earl, I hate to bring it up, but you're an astute observer, and you and Olive know this community better'n anyone. Who do you think might have reason to kill my cousin Lester?"

"Mercy me, I haven't the faintest." Olive looked flustered and acted like the question was not one that civilized folks should pursue.

Earl sat a little straighter in his chair and spoke up. "Well, I been givin' it a lot of thought, and I think the person who hated Lester most was Slug Willard. Now don't go quotin' me, but he's got a cottage over near Lester's, and I've heard him carry on 'bout how them gays was actin' in the water out by Lester's dock. I don't know as it irked him bad enough to kill him, but he has an alibi, doesn't he?"

"Not a very good one."

Sandy continued, "Did you hear that Sam Barrows made Frank a special deputy?" She glanced over at Frank, who looked uncomfortable. "So much crime in Venice they need one, right near our corner where bad things happen."

"So you're a deputy. Congratulations, I guess." Earl grimaced a little.

Frank was upset that Sandy had blown his cover, but then he figured it was probably all over town anyway, via the Hal Hines News Channel. He asked, "Did you hear about Nin finding her cat draped over the stop sign?"

Earl looked sheepish. Olive stared over at him with a question mark face. He clasped his hands together and leaned forward in the chair, his head down. "Didn't want to say nothin'," he said, staring down at the hardwood floor. Didn't tell nobody 'bout Slug, not even Olive." He looked up at his wife, now blanched white, her mouth forming a tiny o of astonishment. "Well, I just didn't want to get involved, tryin' to forget about crime and such. What happened was I was comin' home from the store early that mornin'. I went to buy some salt crystals to spread on the back sidewalk so's Olive wouldn't take another spill."

"And?" Frank was more than a little impatient.

"And I seen Slug walkin' back to his garage, with somethin' in his hand, coulda' been a knife. I waved but he didn't wave back. How'd the cat die anyway?"

"Cut. Wish you'd called the warden or me that morning, Earl. Trail's cold now, I'm afraid. It's a missed opportunity."

Earl ran his rough, wrinkled hands down his face. "Nowadays I hesitate to get involved. Tryin' to forget about that ugly mornin' on the bog. Watchin' more TV, and what do I see when I watch?" He smiled sadly at Olive, who patted his hand. "Crime, that's what, car crashes, guns blazin', folks gettin' murdered! It's wicked awful."

"Yeah, I know. But it's funny. Sandy and I watch old *Law & Order* reruns because we crave justice."

Timidly, Olive added, "I'll tell you what's my favorite, *Gunsmoke*.

Now James Arness, he's a *real* lawman."

Sandy didn't know how to respond, so she gathered her hat and mittens and looked over at Frank. He seemed back to his usual self, agreeing with Olive and snitching a hunk of banana bread off the plate on the table. "Yup! I like *Gunsmoke* myself, but my favorite is sweet Miss Kitty. Boy howdy, did she have a crush on the marshal."

Earl laughed, "Yup! But she wears too much make-up for me."

Sandy said she agreed, not bringing up the fact that Miss Kitty was the owner of a saloon and the boss of "the upstairs gals." Why spoil Earl's fantasy? Or maybe that *was* Earl's fantasy. Sandy and Frank picked up their coats and said their goodbyes.

Suddenly Olive spoke up. "Oh, I was meanin' to ask 'bout Cleona. I was so upset to hear of the trouble she had with her furnace. It's not like her. She's usually so careful."

"Still in the hospital under guard, but she'll make it, hopefully without any ill effects. Poor dear." Sandy adjusted her coat collar. "Did you see the donation jars down to the store? One's for Mooseman and the other's for Cleona."

"Neither one of 'em's done anything to anybody," Olive said. "They're just a bit...different. Oh, do take some banana bread home with you."

"No thanks," Sandy answered, committing a serious breach in country manners, but, at the moment, she felt fat.

On their way home, Sandy awaited criticism for mentioning Frank's deputy status.

"Honestly, Sandy, they didn't have to know! The fewer who know, the better."

"I thought if I told them, they might feel freer with information, and it worked, didn't it? Since they knew you were in law enforcement, what they said can be used as a statement." As they started up the hill toward the house, Sandy took a deep breath and let out a sigh. "Maybe I was wrong. Sorry." Frank put his arm around her.

No sooner had they settled into their favorite living room chairs than there was a knock on the door. It was Nin, looking fetching in a blue knit hat and scarf, her cheeks pink with the cold.

"Get in here, girl. It's cold out side." Sandy was glad to see her friend, although now wasn't the best time.

"Hi guys! How ya' doin'? Look, I've got a petition here and I need your signatures, plus the Shaws, because of your strategic location."

Frank was confused and said so. "What are you talking about, Nin?"

"Oh, sorry. Cart before the horse. It's a petition to force the Director of Safety to order the highway department to repair that guardrail and take further steps to make this intersection safe. I've called everyone concerned, but they won't do anything. I thought if enough people signed this, the Highway Department would pay attention."

Never one to discourage an act of futility, Frank shrugged and said, "Give it here, I'll sign." Then he handed it to Sandy who also signed.

"Now, will one of you come down to Rhu's and help me persuade her to sign? Chuck will sign."

"I'll come, but I don't think Chuck's at home. Wanna' come, Frank?"

"No, thanks, I'll start that soup you were talking about, Sandy. You go ahead, but don't stay all afternoon, okay?"

"Don't worry. Rhu doesn't exactly put out the welcome mat when I visit, so, Nin, what makes you think I could persuade her?"

"That's easy. Don't want to go alone." Nin looked embarrassed as she slipped back into her jacket. "Come on, it'll only take a minute."

They knocked on the Shaw's hand-carved blue kitchen door, with the Christmas wreath still hanging on it, but received no answer. They pounded harder. Nin walked around the shrubbery and peeked in the kitchen window.

She whispered, "Come here! Look! What's going on?"

Sandy peered in the window through the gap between the muslin curtains. What she saw puzzled her. Rhu had her head down on the kitchen table, her arms splayed out flat. Beside her was an empty cream sherry bottle.

"Is Rhu passed out?" Nin whispered excitedly.

"Listen, Rhu's out of it, but I don't think she's dead. Let's just leave. Chuck'll be home soon."

"Jeeze, Sandy, that's not very charitable. What if she's overdosed? Every minute counts, doesn't it?"

"Listen! I'm not being hardhearted, Nin. Rhu's got a serious problem involving prescription drugs, mixing pills with alcohol, but I know her. If we call the EMTs she'll probably sue us or at least send us the bill for the ambulance!"

Nin looked skeptical.

"I'm not kidding! Go home. I'll try to locate Chuck. There are only about three or four places where he might be. Main thing is, don't get into the middle of this. Trust me."

Nin headed down the hill and across the intersection. Sandy hurried home and asked Frank if they'd done the right thing.

"Sweetie, there's nothing for you to do. Rhu can't stand you, and she would never have forgiven you for seeing her like that. I think it's common practice with her. And her son aids and abets with those prescriptions he gives her. She also sees Dr. Dow in Amnesty and the new doctor in Deering. Gets scrips from all of 'em. Slug's not the only druggie on this corner."

"But what about Rhu? What if she's really done it this time? Overdosed, I mean."

To calm Sandy down Frank said, "I'll call the auction house. He might be over there picking up stuff he got yesterday. Then I'll call Jake's store and some other places. If I locate him, I'll tell him to go home, that we can't get a rise out of Rhu. Okay?"

"All right, but somebody's got to check on her. What if you can't get Chuck?"

"Naw, forget Chuck. I'll call Dr. Seth at the hospital. If he's not there they'll know where he is. Why not let *him* clean up the mess? After all, he helped create it."

Within thirty minutes, Seth Shaw's BMW had swerved into the Shaw driveway. Frank noticed that it was still there at 9:30 when he and Sandy turned in for the night, but Sandy was too worried to sleep.

The next morning Chuck was out freeing up ice and snow from his driveway. When he saw Frank doing the same thing, he trudged up the hill. "This January thaw didn't do us any favors. Turned snow into this icy mud. Bet some car's gonna slide down the hill this morning."

"Yeah, Nin's got a petition to the Highway Department she wants you to sign. She's really hot about the fact they haven't repaired the guardrail." Frank pointed to the house-in-the-hole. "Guess if I lived down there, I'd be anxious too."

"Hell, I'll sign it. Tell her to bring it up."

"I noticed that Seth was over last night. How's he doing?"

"Fine. Busy as a one-armed surgeon. Lots of accidents due to this black ice. Snowmobilers with cracked heads too." Chuck laughed then had a coughing fit. After he recovered, he lit up a cigarette. It started snowing big, fat flakes.

"Jesus, Chuck, I thought you were going to quit those cancer sticks."

"I did quit smokin'—inside the house. Rhu can't stand it when I light up in the kitchen. I haven't quit outside yet. But I will—someday."

Chuck was six-foot-one and carried two hundred and sixty pounds, much of it a spare truck tire around his middle. When Frank first met him, he was a good looking older man. Now his face was blotchy, his eyes a faded blue, and he was bent over. Frank worried about him but knew that there was little he could do. "Well, old man, I quit ten years ago, gave up my pipe, and started feelin' better within a few months. Now I can climb all the way to the top of the hill and not get winded."

"Well, bully for you, kid. By the way, I been wonderin'. Any news on Lester's murder? I was talkin' with Stan over at the auction Sunday. Rumor is the sheriff's been over to Gus Gossam's place twice and somehow or other the state's taken Andy away from them. He's still at Mountain Top though. Saw him last week when I dropped off papers Rhu forgot. Know anything? Gus gonna be arrested?"

Frank leaned on his shovel. "All I can tell you is the Elorantos have taken him in, kind of a foster child situation, and I'm damn glad. The Gossams' is no place for a decent kid. Wish they could get the little girls out, too. Sarah signed the papers, but she might change her mind."

"And the missus, my God, you should have seen her twenty-five years ago. She was a looker. But what about Lester's murder?"

"All I know is it's Sam's number one priority. He's had a lot on his plate what with the lake robberies and auto thefts. I figure the Mooseman's shooting might be connected to the lake cottage robberies. You heard anything?"

"I heard Moose was where he shouldn'a been and got himself shot. He's been askin' for it for a long time."

"Chuck, the Bog Road's not private property. Everybody goes there, even Cleona."

"Yeah, and look what happened to her. Ask me, a person's a damned fool to walk around over there after all that's happened." Chuck kicked a clot of snow. "Don't misread me, Frank, I like the old bird. How's she doin' anyway?"

"Better. So, let me get this straight. Why can't the citizens of Venice walk around the bog? You've got me curious." Frank stamped his cold feet.

"Because some fool is taking target practice over there. A smart man doesn't make himself a human target. And Cleona's always buttin' in where she don't belong."

"But why? Why is someone shooting people who stray over there?"

"Don't ask me. You're the big shot detective." Chuck stared up the road. The wind was bending the bare treetops. He exhaled a puff of smoke into the wind. "Jake was tellin' me he thinks you're a big time deputy now. I told him I'd know about it if you were. Made me look like a damned fool. How come you didn't let on? Is it a friggin' government secret?"

Frank felt like a small boy humiliated in front of the class. Chuck's rash judgment burned in his gut like a red hot poker. Wasn't Chuck supposed to be his friend, like a father to him? Frank wished he'd never strayed outdoors on this cold and windy morning. "Well, I haven't seen you to tell you. Yeah, I was made a special deputy, but it's not a paid position. I just help out when needed. No big deal, Chuck. Why're you so bent outa' shape? You don't confide everything to me."

Chuck looked his age and then some. His face gray, his nose beet red as he stomped out his cigarette on the ice. He wouldn't look Frank in the eye. "Maybe you're right. Gotta go in before I get frostbite. This snow's fallin' faster'n I can shovel it. See ya." He turned and began to walk away.

"Hold on a second, Chuck. *You* know something you're not telling *me?*"

"Nothin' you don't already know, Mr. Deputy." Chuck's sarcastic words hit him like bullets.

The snow began to fall heavily and the cold pellets slapped Frank's face as he watched Chuck plant his shovel in a snow bank and then disappear into the house. The snowplow, with a salt-sand spreader on the back, turned off Route Ten and ground its way up Whiskey Hill toward him, laying down a foot-high ridge of plowed-up snow across the end of his driveway.

"Aw, screw it," Frank shouted into the wind. *And it's not about me being hired, it's all about Rhu.* He tossed the snow shovel against the side of the potting shed and walked into the cellar, slamming the door behind him.

CHAPTER 30

First light arrived late on Tuesday morning due to a thick layer of dark, billowy clouds that continued to drop heavy pellets of snow. The temperature hovered at twenty degrees. Overnight more than six inches had fallen on Venice and the surrounding hill country, creating a Currier and Ives scene.

At the first sign of flakes, Sam had called Game Warden Bud Varney and suggested that they get together early next morning and make a run by the cottages around Lake Mallacook. Any new tracks would show up in the fresh snow. Sam knew that Bud would be keen for the idea, remembering how the warden had revealed his yearning to be a "real cop" that cold morning when they'd fished Lester Moulton's body out of Hiram Bog.

In the worst way Bud wanted to have a hand in nabbing those crooks who'd been ripping off the summer people. It'd prove once and for all to that city boy, Sam Barrows, that Bud Varney wasn't *just* a game warden. To tell the truth, Bud had gotten plenty miffed when Hines told him that Frank Zucchetti, that retired "suit from away," had been deputized. Why couldn't a game warden be a deputy sheriff, too?

In his dark-green, four-wheel-drive pickup with the state Fish and Game seal on the doors, Bud trolled slowly eastward along the North Lake Road. Now and then he stopped to straighten his legs, scrunch upward in the seat, lean over to the right, and aim his flashlight out the window to sweep the snow with a broad beam. He searched for any vehicle tracks or footprints into or out of the cabins.

At the driveway to the Willard place, he saw something that excited him; a set of tire tracks turned in from the road, and a three-foot wide swath exited the driveway and turned off to the east along the shoulder of the Lake Road. Bud left the motor running, the exhaust puffing blue ghosts into the morning twilight. He climbed out and investigated the tracks with his flashlight. *Pretty recent; less than an hour.* Not even a quarter of an inch of soft, new flakes had fallen into the unmistakable tread of a snowmobile. The inbound tracks, probably from a pickup with oversized, studded tires, had filled in with half an inch of new snow.

In the dim morning twilight, Bud reasoned that "person or persons" had driven in, spent time at Willard's cabin, then driven out by snowmobile. No lights shone from either the rustic cabin or the tipsy old barn-garage off to the left, where the tracks came from. He walked up the drive about a hundred paces to the garage, got up on tiptoes in his Canadian boots and peeked in the grungy side window. There was Slug's beat-up old gray Jimmy with new snow coating the hood. Empty space between the truck and the window indicated where the snowmobile had been parked. A few footprints, filling up fast with snow, were in front of the garage door where someone had gotten out of the driver's side to open it. *Hmm. Maybe he's just out snowmobilin'.*

Yearning for the warm stream of air blowing out of the heater vent, Bud climbed back into his vehicle, took off his mittens, blew on his fingers, then drove slowly eastward past several more summer homes up to the big rambling Borghese place. No tracks visible at any of them. Bud stopped and stared long and hard at the Lester Moulton house, its windows blind in the falling snow. He looked out through the pines to the lake, already re-frozen. Most of Venice's fishermen had left their sheds out on the ice, knowing that the thaw wouldn't last long enough to sink them. Bud caught a fleeting glimpse of one or two sheds, fading in and out as the sheets of falling snow thickened and then thinned. All was quiet until he heard the crack of a rifle above the whirring of the heater fan and truck engine. His heart quickened and thumped in his chest.

Bud swung open the door of the pickup and stood up, one foot on the floorboard, one on the driver's seat. Another eerie shot rang out, slightly muffled by the falling snow. *Definitely a rifle, and definitely from over near the bog. That sonofabitch ain't fishin'! He's jackin' deer!* Bud grabbed his cell phone and punched in Sam Barrows' number.

Sam had been creeping along the south shore in the Jeep Cherokee four-by, thinking defeatist thoughts. *This case is nowhere. All these cabins looted and I don't have a clue. Not one pawnbroker has called in. Why not? The scummy bastards must be hoarding the loot in a garage or storage area or maybe trucking it to Canada.* Sam's failures seemed to be piling up, like the billows of snow falling all around him. Just then, his cell phone began playing "Turkey in the Straw" from its resting place on the seat next to him. He stopped the four-by in the middle of the deserted road and picked up.

The scratchy, nasal voice came through, "Sam, we got an emergency situation here. I been up along the Lake Road checkin' cabins, and I mighta' caught Slug Willard jackin' deer. I ain't too comfortable sneakin' up on him by myself. I need back-up!"

"Sure. There's nothin' goin' on down here anyway. Glad to assist. Where do you want to rendezvous?"

"Meet me over on the Back Bog Road just east of where Old Venice is under water, down there by the thick spruce grove."

"Bud, I'm not that familiar with the area."

"Oh, yeah." Bud smiled with satisfaction at his superior knowledge.

"Okay then, drive round the east end of the lake to the *Back* Bog Road, the one that runs along the *north* side, and turn right towards the bog. You'll see my truck. Keep your cell turned on so's I can let you know if somethin' happens to change the plan."

"Got it, ten-four. Hope I can get reception out there."

Bud snapped the cell phone shut and drove east toward the Back Bog Road as fast as he dared in the now heavily falling snow which had turned to the consistency of Ivory Soap flakes. *This is the big break I been lookin' for.*

As the windshield fogged up, Bud realized he was breathing heavily. He could feel the sweat running down between his shoulder blades. Sure enough, a half-mile in on the Back Bog Road the snowmobile tracks veered off into a dense stand of Black Spruce and cedar. Bud cut the engine and checked his K-38 Special. All six rounds were loaded. He slipped it back into its holster, leaving the safety strap undone, just in case. He labored to control his breathing. Slug Willard could be a dangerous character, like a cornered wharf rat, so he'd have to take him by surprise. He waited in silence. *Where in hell's Barrows? No, wait a minute. Long as I don't hear the snowmobile start up, Slug's still in there. Maybe when Barrows gets here, we can catch him off guard. Okay, good, wait for the sheriff.*

A few minutes later, Sam's four-by-four slowed to a stop next to the Fish and Game pickup, effectively blocking the road. Bud jumped out and put his index finger to his lips, indicating the necessity for silence. Hopefully they could sneak up on Slug and catch him in the act. Sam didn't mind giving Bud the lead. After all, it was *his* territory.

Bud walked over to Sam and whispered, "Okay, Sheriff, you got your sidearm handy? Handcuffs ready?"

"'Course." Sam shook his head in amazement at the simplicity of the man, but he played along. "Brought the camera, too."

"Good. Jeeze, this all happened so fast. I oughta keep my camera in the truck at all times just for this sort of thing. Anyway, let's sneak in there, follow along to one side of the snowmobile trail and see if we can't nab the bastard. Don't think he'll hear us comin' in this weather."

The two men moved at a stalker's pace into the thick spruce grove, Bud on point, Sam trailing behind. The snow was now falling like whitewash from buckets, and the wind had picked up. Gusts, moaning and hissing through branches, whiplashed the tops of the forty and fifty foot high trees. They made their way soundlessly to a thicket and paused, peering through the branches into a small clearing. There was Slug.

A skilled hunter, Slug had dressed out the yearling in short order. He stuffed the steaming entrails, penis and musk glands into a thirty gallon plastic bag, then carefully placed the deer's liver and heart into a half gallon size Zip-Lock baggie. They'd have that tonight. Although it was a small buck, it would do. Now it was just a matter of dragging the carcass to the edge of the woods and hiding it till he went and got Bobbie John to help him haul it out. On the way home, they could dump the bags of guts at the edge of the Zookies' woods. *It's their turn anyway. It'll smell wicked ripe come the first warm spell.*

Slug let out a little chuckle. No problem with the venison spoiling in this weather. They'd hang him up in the shed out back, then Bertha'd butcher him up real good and wrap the meat. She'd learned all the different cuts working behind the meat counter at Jake's store. He smeared his gloves with new-fallen snow to cleanse them of blood and gore.

In the short time he'd spent dressing out the buck, the snow had piled up around the snowmobile but was melting off the still-warm carcass. With difficulty Slug rose to his feet, his knees stiff from being immersed in snow. The wind howled above him, although down among the spruce boughs the air was relatively still. A twig cracked somewhere in the woods, back up in the direction of the snowmobile track.

Slug grabbed the 30-30. *By God, I'm gonna get two-fers!* Off to Slug's left, branches stirred. He raised the rifle and fired—a "sound-shot." Nothing, not a rustle nor any movement from the thicket. *Woulda heard him fall or lunge if I'd a' hit 'im.* Slug stood there, stalk-still. *Shit. Musta missed!* He turned to walk out of the trees and back to the clearing, pulling his camouflage jacket around him.

Sam felt the turbulence and heard the buzz of the bullet as it whizzed within inches of his right ear and slammed into the trunk of a Black Spruce. In that strange, elongated second of the bullet's passing and the crack of Slug's rifle, the adrenalin shot through his body. Sam wasn't waiting for a second shot, as he instinctively dropped to ground and crawled over to where Bud had hunkered down behind a clump of cedar.

The next thing Slug knew, his rifle was being jerked out of his hands, his body muscled down, and his face shoved into the snow. The more he struggled to get up, the farther he sank into the cold. It felt as if someone were stepping on his back. It was Sam Barrow's size eleven boot planted firmly between Slug's shoulder blades. He felt his left arm being levered up out of the snow and heard the metallic snap of the cuff locking.

"Steven Willard, you're under arrest for assault with a deadly weapon on two law officers and for illegally taking game out of season, among other things," Bud Varney announced in a triumphant tone. "Anything you say can and will be used against you in a court of law."

"Ouch! Shit! You're breakin' my arms," Slug yowled as Sam snapped the cuff on the other wrist and yanked him up to a standing position.

"...and if you cannot afford an attorney, one will be provided for you..." Slug stood there wavering back and forth in shock, anger and humiliation. His fur-lined, ear-flap hat had fallen off, and his entire balding head had turned orange with rage.

"We'll do worse'n that, you little skunk turd." Bud plucked the hat out of the snow and stuck it on Slug's head, askew. "If I was you, I'd keep my mouth shut for once." Bud looked around the clearing. "You got anybody out here with you, Sluggo? Maybe one of them prize-winning boys of yours?"

He spat into the snow. "Ain't nobody else."

"Okay," Sam announced, taking charge and handing Bud the camera. "Here's what's gonna happen. Bud, get pictures of this mess, including that slug in the tree. Then dig it out and bag it." Sam reached into his parka and pulled out half-a-dozen small paper bags that he routinely carried and handed them to Bud. "Then take that rope over there on the snowmobile, truss up the deer and skid it out of here. We'll toss it in the back of your pickup. We can leave the snowmobile by the side of the road for now. Get somebody with a lift to take it down to the county impound lot."

"Impound? Dammit, you can't do that!" Slug yelled.

Sam didn't say anything, but Bud chimed in, "Yeah, dummy. You used it in the commission of a felony. It's goin' up fer auction. Look around. Everything you see here is now the property of the State o' Maine, includin' you, Sluggo."

"Bullshit! Screw you!" He tugged unsuccessfully on the handcuffs.

"Ayuh! And that deer's goin' to a soup kitchen in Galway or a women's shelter in Bangor."

"Bud, see if there are some more plastic garbage bags there in the stowage compartment of that snowmobile. Then put the gun and the knife in separate bags and label 'em. And see if you can find the ejected casing over there and bag that. Slug here might've put his paw print on it."

"You ain't gonna make none of this stick. It's bullshit. I'll be out tomorrow. That guy from the hardware store that shot the dumb bitch with the white mittens was found innocent. I didn't even see you guys. On NYPD Blue it's called 'trapment.'"

"Start walkin'," Sam commanded, taking Slug by the arm and propelling him up the snowmobile path.

Bud remained at the site snapping more photos. He dug the 30-30 slug out of the tree trunk, then stowed all the remaining pieces of evidence in individual paper bags.

Sam got his prisoner to the roadside and crammed him into the back seat of the Jeep behind the grill, his hands still cuffed behind him. After a few minutes, Bud roared out of the woods on the ski mobile, throwing a rooster tail of fresh snow, the deer skidding smoothly behind.

Sam was glad he hadn't brought Duchess along. She'd go nuts over the dead deer.

They hefted the carcass into the back of the truck. "Bud, you're in charge of the scene here. Stow the gun and the rest of the evidence in the back compartment of the Jeep. The tailgate's unlocked. While you're at it, get some crime scene tape out and string it from tree to tree around the area back there."

"That's a ten-four." Bud was puffed up like a grouse cock in mating season as he stowed the evidence and pulled out a roll of yellow crime scene tape. "Uh, what about the deer?"

"Whatever the usual disposition is, soup kitchen, orphanage. Keep your cell phone on and charged. Okay?"

"Roger, boss. See ya later. Ten-four."

"Right. And, Bud, great job!"

The two men waved at each other as Sam drove off. Slug craned his thick neck to see out the side window, but all he saw was the big grin on Bud's face.

As they topped Barker Hill southbound, Sam gave Hazel a call on the radio. "This is Thoreau One inbound. I'm ten-forty-six with an ETA of twenty minutes. Have Barb come up on the cell, over."

"Ten-four, Thoreau One." Hazel clicked off and a minute later "Turkey..." was playing on the cell phone.

"Whatcha got, boss?" Barb was all business.

"Slug Willard from Venice. Pull up his rap sheet and make sure we have a nice comfortable cell ready. We'll be there before nine. Might as well freshen up the coffee.

"Okay, I'm on it. See ya' in a bit." In the rearview mirror, Sam could see Slug wince at the mention of a jail cell.

As they pulled into the parking lot, a beaming deputy, Charley Henderson, came out of the back door to meet them.

"Hey, boss, that's some catch you got there. He's caused nothin' but trouble in Venice far back as I can remember."

"Want to escort Mister Willard to his new accommodations?"

"Be happy to," Charley answered. "Holding cell, Sam?"

"Yeah. That'll do for now. Soon as Barb generates the paperwork, book him."

"What charges?"

"You can start out with assault with a deadly weapon, but there's a long list. Barb'll fill you in." Charley removed Slug from the back seat and steered him through the back door and down the hallway toward the holding cell.

"Charley, how about you carry all the evidence down to Augusta in the Jeep here, then just drive it home tonight? Bring it back tomorrow morning." Sam handed him the keys.

"Sounds good. What about the official evidence tags?"

"Got so pumped, I nearly forgot. Run upstairs and ask Barb. She'll give you everything you need."

Late that afternoon Belle called from Augusta. "Hey Sammy, this is a nice 30-30 slug that Charley delivered. Looks like the one they pulled out of your Mooseman." She was in the lab, looking at the bullet. "Since this guy shot at you, let's see if Ballistics can match it to as many crimes as possible."

How could someone saying those words sound so sexy? "This shooting gives us enough probable cause to get a warrant. A thorough search might turn up more: drugs, stolen goods, the works...it's common knowledge in Venice that Slug's been dealing."

"So he's a Venice resident?"

"Sure is, lives right down the hill from my special deputy, Frank Zucchetti. Bad hombre, likes to shoot dogs just for the hell of it."

"So wouldn't it be sweet if we could tie Slug to the Moulton murder, drug dealing, *and* the cabin thefts?"

"You got that right! I've been working long hours trying to close these cases. Kinda' depressed that there hasn't been a big break in the Moulton case."

"My team'll turn his place inside out. Speaking of dogs, not Slug's of course, how's Duchess? She still stealing your socks?"

"Sure is. She's adapted pretty well to living in a little Victorian museum though. Asks for you often. Duchess is a sweetheart. Still comes to work with me."

"She still lean against your leg, begging?" Belle was looking out the window of the State Police headquarters. "Hug her for me." The sun was setting behind the western hills, casting up a pillar of yellow-white surrounded by fans of orange that faded out to violet as they spread across the wooded hilltops. The vault of the sky had turned a cloudless bruise-purple. The storm had wandered off toward Nova Scotia and the night would be bitter cold.

Sam didn't say anything.

"Sam, I gotta go now and get through all this work you sent."

They both hung up, knowing that the conversation was far from finished.

CHAPTER 31

At six forty-five the next morning, Frank answered the phone on the first ring.

"Frank, you're not gonna believe this." Sam filled him in on Slug's arrest. "And there's more…"

Frank imagined Sam's face beaming through the telephone. "Let's see. Slug confessed to all of the murders and robberies in Thoreau County? And he operates a stolen car and drug smuggling ring?"

"You sure know how to let the air out of a guy's balloon."

"Sorry, Sam, go ahead."

"Good news, buddy. Belle called me at home last night. The bullet from Slug's rifle matches the one the medics dug out of Mooseman's gut."

"Boy, she must've really taken an interest in the case to give it that much priority."

"Let's say that sometimes it helps to have a history. Anyway, that cinched Judge Roth's issuing a warrant. A search team was all over Slug's place in the wee hours. You see or hear anything?"

"Nope. Slept through it. Didn't see or hear anything." Frank walked over to the living room windows and looked down on the Willard home, its shabbiness now partially hidden by new-fallen snow.

Once Sam finished filling him in, Frank said, "Hey, that's great! Has Willard copped to the Mooseman shooting yet or lawyered up?"

"No, but I'm gonna interview him after his gourmet breakfast. See what he says when I confront him with the evidence."

"Wish I could be there, but thanks for the good news, anyway. I sort of need to stick around Venice today. Gotta' go over some stuff with Sandy."

"I shouldn't ask you for another favor, but I was going to suggest you interview MacTeague and his son, Johnnie. I need more details about precisely how Johnnie found Cleona."

"Sure, that shouldn't take too long. Maybe they'll recall something about last Saturday afternoon. They do live within sight of Cleona's place. Somebody might've seen something."

"Exactly."

"Great. I'll get back to you as soon as I talk to 'em."

"Thanks, pardner."

Frank hung up just as Sandy came in from the backyard with a basket of eight eggs. "Look, our biddies are laying again. The winter molt has ended."

"Yeah, the days are getting longer. Want me to take a half-dozen when I go up to Mabel and Angus's?"

"Why are you going up there?" Sandy realized it was childish, but she hated to be left out.

"Just hung up from a conversation with Sam. He wants me to do a follow-up with Angus and Johnnie, find out if they saw any strangers last Saturday." Frank walked over to Sandy and gave her a peck on the cheek. "Forget about giving them those eggs. This is business. You probably want to go with me, but you know how Angus likes to hurl insults to get a rise out of you and take me off the subject."

"You're right, he does, and I let him do it."

"That's why I want to go up there alone. You think Angus'll be in?"

"Maybe. I talked with Mabel yesterday. He's back working in the woods and driving all over town."

"With only one-and-a-half eyes? It's hard to separate a man from his truck." Frank shook his head. "If I ever get that way, just shoot me."

"If you ever get that way, *I'll* drive. It's so much simpler and less messy. By the way, I'm glad to see you're back to your old curmudgeonly self. So what else did Sam say?"

"You, my brilliant wife, were partially right about our distinguished neighbor, Mr. Willard." He filled Sandy in on the Slug story, the ballistics test and the matched bullet. "But not a word to anyone because Sam hasn't formally interviewed Slug yet."

"Think he'll fess up?" She finished rinsing off and putting away the eggs.

"I haven't met a bully yet who didn't crumble when faced with the facts. They're basically cowards, you know."

Sandy pulled out the Yellowware bowl, a bag of flour, and a tin of cinnamon.

"What'cha gonna bake?" Frank asked, picturing Sandy's cakes in his mind.

"We're going to celebrate my powers of astute observation with a coffee cake when you get back. But first, honey, a lot's been happening what with the Slug arrest and all. Tell me how that gets us any closer to finding my cousin's murderer."

"Maybe it doesn't. All I know is that a man who fires heedlessly at a sound in the woods is capable of firing a shot at a splash in the bog."

"I see that, but how's Sam going to prove it?"

"Through tough, old-fashioned interrogation—maybe."

Just then the phone rang.

It was Cleona.

CHAPTER 32

That same morning, Hal Hines looked around for Sam and found him leaning over Barb's desk. Hal's face reflected a degree of resentment. "Hey, what's the deal, boss? How come you didn't call me to take down Slug? How come a game warden? And I sat out back of Jake's for three long nights!" His blue eyes blazed with anger.

"Well, if you'd apprehended Slug, you coulda' brought him in, big guy," Sam quipped. "Instead, the early bird got the worm. I responded and got shot at for my trouble."

Hal's face resembled that of a boy scout whose little campfire had gone out. "Got shot at? Hey, boss, I didn't realize."

"Can we wrap up this pissin' contest and get on with the interrogation?"

"Sorry, boss. You mean I can sit in?"

"Sure. You can run the tape recorder. But listen up. Unless I look over at you, keep quiet. We'll play it by ear. Just like in Angus's kitchen. Understood?"

"Ten-four. Can I be the bad cop this time?" He had the same pitiful expression as when he'd begged his high school football coach to let him in for the last play of the game. It had turned out to be more or less the pinnacle of his life.

"Sure. By the way, I haven't had time to check the reports. What'd your stakeout yield?"

"Nothin' for sure, boss, but there's plenty of afterhours visitors to those trailers behind Jake's store. Odd thing, he's got floodlights back there, but doesn't turn 'em on 'til after midnight, when all the foot traffic stops. Couldn't make any license plates or faces."

"What's your conclusion?" Sam asked.

"Plenty goin' on. Can't tell what. Maybe the light's a signal. Light's on, don't stop. Light's off, come get your goodies."

"Okay. So far, so good. We can deal with Jake and company once we finish up this Slug business."

Sam swung open the door to the interrogation room where Slug was seated in a space not much larger than a mudroom, with a metal table under a bright light. Two metal folding chairs were placed on each side of the table. Sam and Hal entered, and the guard who'd been looking after Slug exited the room. Hal dragged a chair over against the far wall next to the tape recorder, and Sam pulled up to the table opposite Slug.

Slug looked bewildered, sitting there in his orange jump suit. The guard had removed the cuffs.

Hal tested the tape recorder: "Today is Wednesday, January twenty-three, time nine-oh-six a.m. Present are Deputy Hal Hines, Sheriff Samuel Barrows, and suspect Steven 'Slug' Willard of Venice, Maine."

"Slug, may I call you that?" Sam began.

"Why not? Everybody else does."

Sam pulled his chair closer. "Was your breakfast satisfactory? Did you get enough to eat?"

Slug leaned over the table. "Yeah, but I could use more coffee, black."

Sam pressed the intercom and asked Barb to bring in a cup of coffee.

"Did the Game Warden read you your rights at the time of your arrest, and did you understand them?

"Yeah, Bud did, and you did too. But what'm I here for anyway? All's I did was shoot a friggin' deer."

Sam leaned closer across the table. "The charges are more serious than that, Slug. For one, assault with a deadly weapon. A warrant was executed late last night, right after you called your wife, and a search of your home and property was conducted."

Hal snorted derisively. "Yeah! And wanna know what they discovered?"

Sam shot Hal a withering look to shut him up. "So, Slug, how long you been dealin' drugs outa' your truck?"

"I ain't never dealed. If you found anything, it was for my own personal use, medical use."

"Medical use?" Sam asked. "How's that?"

"'Cuz my wife has a bad back. Me too. I'm on disability, as if you didn't know. I told you that."

"Slug, we found enough marijuana in your garage to help a whole cancer ward and then some. We found, let's see, Valium, Ativan, BuSpar, Ecstasy, Oxycodone, Crystal Meth, you name it. Thought the nearest drug store was in Amnesty. Didn't know you had one in Venice. Explain that!" Sam got right in Slug's face. "I'm talking multiple counts of a class-A felony."

"Not mine!" Slug smirked. "Somebody musta' used my garage without askin'."

Hal jumped in. "Possession is nine-tenths of the law. In your case, creep, it's gonna put you away for a good, long time. We've had surveillance on you for months."

"Hal's right, Slug. We've been watching you."

Slug's belly rumbled. "Yeah, and I know who. Them damned Zookies. I mighta' known they'd be watchin'. I warned her, that know-it-all bitch!"

"Mrs. Zucchetti was way outa' line alright, 'specially for a female." Sam paused to let it sink in. "So, how'd you warn her?"

"Sent a note is all. Didn't threaten her none, but she's a damned trouble maker, that woman. Then you had to pin a badge on her worthless husband." Slug huffed and shifted in his chair. "I need a damn cigarette."

Sam was pleased with the direction of the interview. "And the phone calls, that was very clever, to wait 'til Frank was out of the house and then call her," he snickered. "You got her good with them. Nosey woman!" Sam went over to the door and opened it a crack. "Barb, bring in a pack of smokes for Mr. Willard. There're some Marlboros in the right hand drawer." Sam winked at Hal.

Hal piped up, "But boss, we don't allow smoking in here."

"Well, I think Slug's being cooperative. That'll help him at the arraignment, so I'm gonna make an exception."

Slug glared in self-righteous indignation at Hal, whom he'd never liked since the officer had stopped him once for a DWI. When handed the pack of cigarettes and matches, Slug thanked Sam and nervously lit up. The way his hand was shaking, Slug couldn't light the cigarette on the first try.

"Relax, Slug. We're just here to straighten out some things. Your cooperation is gonna help your case. I'll see to it personally."

For a moment, Slug looked thoughtful. "Listen, 'bout the deer. Go ahead and give it to an orphanage. Couldn't you look the other way on that charge?"

"Speaking of that incident, why *did* you fire at Bud and me?"

Sweat was breaking out on Slug's forehead, and the sour smell of BO filled the room. According to procedure, Barb had turned the temperature in the interview room up to eighty degrees. Slug turned to Sam. "Listen, I'm tellin' the God's honest truth. I wasn't firin' at *nobody*! Okay? So I was tryin' for another deer. Big damn deal! Heard cracklin' like a deer walkin' on branches. Maybe I was wrong to be greedy, but the first one I got was so small. I took a sound-shot, and then out of nowhere comes you two."

Barb came in, set a cold ginger ale and an open pack of Marlboros on the table then left.

Sam noticed Slug's hand still shaking. Hal saw it, too, and looked over at Sam. Slug leaned forward slightly then rocked back and forth in his chair.

"Sam, he don't look too good," Hal offered.

Sam continued, "We know you've been dealin' drugs out of the truck. We know you've been threatening your neighbors. That'd be the menacing and stalking charge. We might be able to reduce that, but only if you come clean on the rest of it. Maybe if you give us good information about your connections, we could go easy on your sons."

Slug bristled at the mention of his boys. "Come clean on what?" Slug's voice took on a whiny tone like a small child. His bald head was now wet with sweat, and he lit another cigarette from the one he was finishing. He'd gulped down the cold coffee.

"Hal, turn the damned heat down. We don't wanna' make Slug uncomfortable. He's lookin' peaked." He turned back to Slug. "For example, what percentage of the take did the druggist get? Neely, I think his name is. Five percent? Ten?"

Slug bit his cheek, then mumbled, "Ten, and the drunken bastard wanted more."

"And Jake, what was *his* cut?"

Slug squirmed. "Don't know nothin' 'bout him dealin', but just so's you know, when he's high, that guy's dangerous!"

"Is his cut more than Neely's?"

Slug stared down at the burning cigarette.

"You don't have to *say* it, Slug. Just nod yes or no."

Slug shrugged his shoulders, then nodded affirmatively.

Sam said into the recorder, "The suspect has indicated in the affirmative."

No one said anything for a few minutes, and the electric clock on the wall clicked out the seconds. It was now nine-forty. Finally Slug looked at Sam then dropped his cigarette into the empty pop can. It sizzled. He spoke, almost apologetically. "All right! It was me cut the cat and hung it over the Forresters' road sign. Guess that's what you wanted to hear. I knew she loved that sorry half-breed critter. It's just that she waves her ass, bounces her titties, and drives my son Billy crazy. Her husband's okay, but she's a cock teaser."

"Well, that certainly helps explain things. We knew that you cut the cat We have an eye witness. It's not the cat incident I'm interested in, but since you brought up your sons, Bobby John is your supplier. We've known that for months."

"How'd you...what the hell...you got it all wrong. My son's got nothin' to do with the drug thing. It's all on me!" He crossed his arms in front of his chest.

"Afraid you and your son will be doin' time on the family plan if you don't tell us more about Jake. We know about B.J.'s associations in Amnesty. You're coverin' up for folks who don't give a rat's ass about you, Slug. They're gonna hang you out to dry." Sam was bluffing, but in his experience sometimes bluffs worked pretty well, especially on bullies.

"Not Bobby John, he'd never rat out his old man. Musta' been that drunk Irishman, Neely. He can't be trusted. The snitch!"

Sam didn't know whether to take the high road or the low. If he brought up Bobby John's parentage, Slug might shut down altogether. Besides, it'd probably all come out in court anyway as part of a bleeding heart defense of Bobby John. Sam was after bigger fish. The drugs, the cat, small potatoes compared with the bog crimes. He'd have to watch himself.

"Slug, I'm gonna be honest with you. Deep down, you're a decent guy. You don't beat your kids. Now, I don't have to reveal this, but I'm going to because I think you want to do the right thing. Remember, your cooperation here could mean the difference in *years* spent behind bars at Thomaston. I can make it happen." Sam leaned forward. "Now here's what we've got: the Winchester you shot at us with—"

"I didn't shoot at you, honest!" Slug yelled. "I shot at a deer!"

"Okay, guess what. The gun you used to shoot at the 'deer' was the same gun that took out Mooseman." Sam allowed a long silence, then said, "Why'd you shoot him?"

"I...I didn't mean to hit him. I only meant to scare the bugger. He was out in *my* woods! The Bog Road's *my* territory. Shit, Willards been getting their deer outa' there for fifty, sixty years. What gives Moose, a flatlander, the right to go postin' and markin' in there? He's crazy anyway. If it wasn't me, it'd be some other hunter shootin' at him. He goes around wavin' his arms in the woods like a maniac."

"That's good, Steven, good that you cleared that up, because we've already matched the bullet from Moose to one fired from your Winchester. We knew it was either you or one of your boys. That adds to your charges, of course, but you can help yourself there, too."

Sam allowed for a two-minute pause. Slug looked down at his grease-lined nails and scratched his day's growth of beard. His eyes shifted from the floor to one of the blank, windowless walls, to Hal Hines. Finally, Slug straightened up in his chair and folded his hands together on the table, as if he were back in grammar school.

Sam knew full well that there could be no ballistics match from Slug's weapon to tie him to Lester's murder but pursued that line anyway. "So, what do you know about the murder of Lester Moulton?"

Hines leaped to his feet and got right in Slug's face. For once, his words were calm and measured. "Out with it. You'll feel better if you let it out, Steven. What about Lester?"

"Nothin'," he said, his nose running. He wiped it with his sleeve.

Sam decided to let the question sink in. "Hal, could you go find a box of Kleenex?" Hal left the room. Sam looked back at Slug and announced to the tape recorder that Hal had left the room.

"Like I said, nothin'! You're gonna pin all kinds of shit on me but not that one! I didn't like Lester, but I never killed him. Why don'tcha question Jake? He *really* hated his guts because of his whacko mom." He wiped his nose with the back of his hand. Sam could smell a faint trace of urine and wondered if Slug had wet himself.

Suddenly Barb opened the door and Stu Stammer barged in. "What the hell's been going on in here? Have they been torturing you, Slug? Punch you in the gut?"

The attorney glared at Sam, then said in an imperious tone, "Not another word, Mr. Willard. I'm here to represent my client, and he's not to say another word. Sheriff, you may be sued over this. Your interview is over."

Hal couldn't stand being quiet another minute. "Well, Stammer, you're a little late. We got a full confession out of him." Hal pointed to the tape recorder. "But you might want to rustle up a clean pair of pants for your client. That'd be helpful."

"You'll hear about this, Sheriff! You've coerced a confession, you've deprived my client of right to counsel, and you've mistreated him as well. Nothing on that tape will stand up in court."

Sam beckoned the attorney into his office while Hal took Slug back to his holding cell. Slug walked slowly, his shoulders down and his feet dragging. Hal had handcuffed Slug's hands behind his back. He seemed to have shrunk in size during the last hour.

Sam leaned down into Stammer's face, his tone of voice taking on a menacing edge. "Listen, Stammer, we didn't just fall off the turnip truck. How long you been practicing anyway? You know the law! The Game Warden read him his rights, and I did, too. Slug got his one phone call, and, funny thing, Stu, he didn't call you. A bad case of nerves can shake a lot of things loose."

"I know, his wife called me this morning early, but—"

"Last night, before she knew what hit her, we had six men searching Slug's home on a warrant. Truck and garage, including a Fed. We've got evidence up the ying-yang, and you'll get to see it, all in good time. This morning we fed Mr. Willard, gave him every damned thing he asked for, coffee, cigarettes, even some understanding. It's all on tape."

"If it's admissible," Stammer snapped.

Hal countered, "Hell, we got him dead to rights, so good luck preparing an effective defense. Slug's goin' down and he's takin' some other folks with him."

Disgusted, Stammer glared at Hal then grabbed his briefcase and left to interview his client.

Sam beamed as he handed the tape to Barb for transcription. "Take good care of this, Ma. It's golden."

Pleased with the turn of events, Hal was leaning against the door jamb when Sam took him by the arm and walked him down the hall to the men's room and motioned him inside. The door clicked shut.

"Listen, Hal, you did a good job in there."

"Thanks, boss."

"But there's a problem."

"Problem?"

"Yeah, Hal, a big one. You're a decent officer, for the most part, but I've been hearing way too much about the Hines news bulletins you been puttin' out at the Venice General Store. Any more of that shit and you'll be applying for security guard duty over at the Atlantis Bank complex. Not one word about what's gone down here this morning! This investigation is far from over. You compromise this case, and I'll rip off your badge and charge you as an accomplice after-the-fact. You got that straight?"

201

Hal had backed into a radiator and winced as it scorched the back of his pant leg. "Yes, sir. I understand completely."

After breaking Slug, Sam felt a lot better than he had the previous afternoon, and only a shadow of his headache remained.

"Barb, inform the press that I'll be making an announcement over in the city hall foyer at two this afternoon."

"Want me to write out the message and notify the press? I know what you're going to want to say, Sam."

"Notify the press, but I'm gonna wing the speech. Thanks, Ma."

Sam stood in the city hall foyer. "Good morning, folks. I wanted to update you on the recent cases involving crimes that have taken place in Venice, but no questions, please. We have arrested and arraigned the subject, Mr. Steven 'Slug' Willard of Venice. He has confessed to several crimes including animal abuse, hunting out of season, and multiple charges of assault with a deadly weapon and menacing behavior. The primary charge is his alleged shooting of Mr. George Felker. The good news is that Mr. Felker will be released from the hospital soon, and, in that regard, I hope that you'll respect his privacy. The important point I want to make is that Mr. Willard is *not* being charged with the murder of Lester Moulton. That case remains open, and I want it put out there that we won't rest until we find the perpetrator.

"But back to Mr. Willard. A further charge of attempted murder of myself and a game warden is also pending investigation." A murmur passed through the crowd. "Although it's a serious charge, unusual circumstances may apply. We'll be reviewing all the facts. Mr. Stammer will be his counsel. Finally, without the assistance of Game Warden Bud Varney, Mr. Willard would not have been apprehended." Sam looked with satisfaction at the group of reporters. "I'll keep you posted. Any further developments will be forwarded to you. Thanks, folks."

CHAPTER 33

Frank was surprised when he answered the phone and heard Cleona's voice. She was calling from her hospital room. Hesitantly, she asked for a ride home, explaining that her car was still in Venice and her nephew was out of town.

"Sure thing, Cleona," he said, still chewing on a stale brownie. "When do you want me to be there?   Okay, glad to do it. I'll see you after noon."

Sandy asked, "Why you? That's odd. I'm surprised she didn't call Mabel.   Maybe she feels she still needs protection. Want me to go with you?"

"No, hon, I'd just as soon go alone. I need her to retrace her memories of that morning, if it isn't too upsetting for her. Oh, damn, I told Sam I was going to interview Angus and Johnnie."

"Can't that wait?"

"Sure. If I don't get to it today, there's always tomorrow. Guess I oughta do the chores now and then get over to Waterville. I want to pick up the locks for Cleona's doors before I get her from the hospital. I'll grab lunch at the Dairy Queen."

"Okay. Love you, hon. Oh, and pick up some tonic water and chips, if it's convenient. We're all out."

"Ten-four, babe." He gave her a quick kiss and went out the back door. With any luck the weather would remain pleasant: partly cloudy, high of twenty-eight. He realized how he longed for signs of spring—a robin maybe.

Cleona was sitting in a wheelchair accompanied by a pretty candy striper. As soon as she was loaded into the car with her three bouquets of flowers, a half-box of chocolates, and her hospital bag, they were on their way. Cleona kept up a rapid stream of bird and weather reports, remarking on how much snow had fallen while she'd been away. She seemed perfectly normal—her chatty self—which pleased Frank.

As they turned onto Whiskey Hill Road, Frank reassured her, "I've checked your house. Steam-Kleen did a terrific job. I'm sure your insurance company'll pick up the tab."

"Well, I hope they put everything back the way it was." She shook her head. "What am I saying? I should thank the good Lord I'm still alive."

Frank didn't answer, not being a believer in divine intervention. Finally he said, "You've had lots of time to think about it, Cleona. Do you remember any voices or sounds or maybe a face from that awful day?"

"It's a funny thing. I seem to remember seeing Clyde's face. That's Angus's father, you know, and he was looking down on me, sayin', 'I'm gonna take care of you!' in a funny tone of voice." She laughed softly. "Mercy, that man's been dead for twenty some years. I musta' been out of my head."

As they pulled into Clcona's driveway, Frank gave the remark some thought. He helped her into the house then made her a cup of tea. He showed her the deadbolts he'd picked up at the hardware store in Waterville. "Mind if I install these right now? I brought my tools. Both doors, mind you, and use the locks when you're here alone."

"Well I'm never here when I'm not alone." Her cackly laugh made Frank smile. Sometimes she reminded him of his aunts.

"It's a shame. All these years I've never locked my doors except when I summered with my sister on Prince Edward Island."

"Promise me that you won't go bird watching for a while. We still haven't put Lester's killer behind bars."

She reluctantly promised, though Frank didn't put much faith in her words. She was a stubborn old coot.

Remembering to buy tonic water, Frank decided to loop back around the Bog Road then cut over to the general store. He'd do his notes from his conversation with Cleona over a g-and-t with Sandy.

The usual crowd was at the store, and Jake gave him a dirty look then scurried into the bottle recycling room. Frank grabbed two liter-size bottles of tonic water and a bag of Humpty-Dumpty chips and set them down on the counter.

"That all?" Selma the clerk asked, scrunching up her nose at the ten-dollar bill Frank handed her.

"Yup."

"Six forty-two's your change," she said automatically, laying the cash down on the counter, avoiding eye-contact. "Want a bag?"

"No thanks," he answered, picking up the bottles and walking out into the crisp air. *Screw these manner-less yokels. On second thought, maybe she's just having a bad day. How would I like to work for Jake?*

When Frank finally got home, he discovered both Sandy and the Chevy pickup gone. The note on the fridge read: "Went up to see Mabel. Have the drinks ready when I get back. I'll need one."

Sandy's probably got a dose of cabin fever. At that moment he wanted a drink, but after his stint in Thailand in the late sixties, where Chivas Regal was his constant companion between night bombing missions, Frank now made it a practice never to drink alone.

January in Maine can be rough. Though the dreary days actually grew longer, they didn't appear to, and spring weather was still four months off, usually not 'til May. Guy Swenson's wife, Loraine, had bought an impressive array of lights from a New Age catalog. The idea was to absorb the healing rays so as to drive off depression. Sandy couldn't see that it made much difference.

Sandy preferred the joy of quilting in warm colors, rich browns, reds and yellows that reminded her of high, dry desert. They provided relief from the stark white and flat gray of the world outside, with its wind whipping and sculpting the snow into waves and sinuous curves. Her second favorite thing to do was to go visiting. But whom to visit? Nin, the most preferable, was usually at the university, as she was today. Rhu with her biting sarcasm, Loraine with her depression adding to the gloom, Olive, too far up the highway. That left Mabel and Angus. She could usually tolerate Angus's mercurial temper softened by Mabel's down-home simplicity. The pair reminded her of the stock that she'd come from in New Hampshire with their crude and crusty New England charm. On this winter day Sandy was lonely enough to accept the punishment.

"Sandy, come in! We were just talkin' 'bout you." Mabel pointed to some limp saltines on a Melmac plate with a jar of goopy Cheez-whiz. "Fix you some crackers? Got plenty. Angus don't have much appetite since the...the night down to the corner." She whispered the last phrase.

"No thanks, I just popped up to look in on you. Have to get right back and fix dinner. Wanted to see how my best neighbors are doing," she lied politely.

"It's the goddamned blood thinner. Makes me feel queer...peculiar, I mean," Angus complained. "Even lost my appetite, and my mouth's always dry." He popped a peppermint into his mouth. Sandy noticed a chalky-white line around his lips and tongue.

"That's too bad, Angus. Can't you ask Doc Dow for something different?"

"Sure. He's got plenty of other stuff, but I'd hafta rob a bank. No free samples. Goddamned doctors. Stopped takin' it but Doc Dow put me back on 'em. 'Do or die,' he said."

"Want some tea, dear?" Mabel asked, heading for the microwave.

"Sure," Sandy answered. She figured she'd be able to drink it quickly since it wouldn't be all that hot.

As Mabel filled a mug with water, she glanced north, up the road toward Cleona's place. All was quiet.

"So, did you see Frank drive by? He's bringing Cleona back from the hospital today."

"No. Funny she didn't call *us*. Guess 'cuz Angus is laid up. Isn't that good, though! I'll go down later and see if she needs anything. That was awful nice of Frank."

"Oh, he's plenty nice now that he's a dep-pew-tee," Angus mumbled in a snide tone.

"Don't pay him no mind, Sandy. You and I both know Frank's a good man. Angus, you behave yourself now," Mabel scolded. Then she asked Sandy, "How's Lester's case comin'?"

"Well, they've got some new evidence, but I can't talk about it," she offered, looking across the table at Angus.

"Frank's a high falootin' detective now." Angus staggered a bit as he rose from his chair. "Better watch what we say, Mabel. Next thing ya' know he'll be haulin' us into court. Sandy, you've already blabbed to the sheriff about Lonnie. That was private!"

Angus moved threateningly toward Sandy, and she could smell whiskey mixed with the mint on his breath. He thrust a bumpy, arthritic finger at her as she reared back in the kitchen chair. "You best butt out of town affairs you don't know nawthin' about. If you'da' known who done in Lester, Frank woulda' arrested somebody by now."

Sandy felt her face burn. She'd taken verbal abuse from Angus, particularly lately, but not this time. "Angus, I'd appreciate it if you'd keep a civil tongue in your head. I came up here to see how you were—not to be insulted," she responded, summoning up her teacher's tone.

"Well who invited you? You're nothin' but a nosey old school teacher, just like that old bitch, Cleona, next door. Poor Cleona this and poor Cleona that. Got what she deserved for stickin' her nose in where it don't belong. Faggot-lovin' school-teachers is what you are." Angus stepped up to Sandy's chair, his baggy overall knees brushing against her knees. Fear gripped her throat, and her mouth went dry. She gulped some tea.

"You people from away," Angus went on, his eyes filmy. "You think you can move in here and start runnin' things. It all started with your cousin, that freakin' faggot, with his fancy degrees. Columbia! Ha! Communists, no doubt!"

"But, Angus, Lester was *from here!*" Sandy wanted to get up, to be more equal to Angus and get his attention, but he blocked her. *You pig,* she thought, *you like to pick on women, don't you? If it weren't for Mabel, I'd kick you in the balls.*

Mabel backed up against the counter, looking frantic. She'd seen her husband's rage out of control before.

"Your sicko cousin took jobs away from folks 'round here. He ruined the church, ruined Loonport, and made my son Lonnie's life a livin' hell! Then there's people like you. Frank comes along and takes a job away from somebody with a wife and kids."

Mabel risked all and took a step toward him, tugging gently on his flannel plaid shirt sleeve.

"Get away from me, woman!" Angus's arm jerked, warning her off.

"Can'tcha see we're settlin' things here?"

Sandy had no choice but to remain seated, and her hand began shaking as she set her mug down. Not wanting to show weakness, she steadied one hand with the other. The old man was twisted with rage. Many times when she was a child, Sandy had witnessed her own father so angry that he'd swung at her mother and thrown things at her. Sandy could not show fear and wanted to set Angus straight. Angus knew that Frank didn't rob anyone of a job, and he'd been asked to be a deputy, but there was no talking to Angus, whose face was now beet red.

"And checkin' up on us? You're checkin', all right! Spyin's more like it." With that he turned and headed for the milk room.

That's all he needs, another shot of whiskey, Sandy thought, feeling a mixture of relief and dread.

Sensing a big break in the case based on the interrogation of Slug, Sam had decided to drive to Venice for a no-notice interview with Jake, who now seemed a more likely suspect than ever. But on the way, he got to thinking about the attempted murder of Angus's nextdoor neighbor and the anger that seemed to float just beneath the surface when he'd interviewed the MacTeagues. Sam could write it off to coincidence, except that he didn't believe in coincidence. Whiskey Hill was sort of on the way to Jake's store, so why not pop in on the MacTeagues, no-notice? It'd only take a few minutes. Frank might've already interviewed them—or maybe not. In any case, Sam wanted to see for himself. He and Frank could compare notes later.

As he crested the hill, he noticed two red pickups and a skidder parked in the MacTeague yard. One of the trucks looked like Frank and Sandy's. Mabel's old gray Buick was parked off to one side next to her kitchen garden, now covered with snow. Back next to the barn stood a mountain of manure, steaming through holes in a black plastic covering. Around its base lay fifty old tires. Sam opened the car door and breathed in the ripe air as one of the Black Angus heifers mooed, his big, brown eyes unblinking.

Inside the kitchen, Mabel was back against the microwave, rolling her eyes and biting her fist. Sandy rose, her legs wobbly and her heart thumping. She glanced out the south window. The sheriff's car was pulling up into the yard. Before she could think of what to do, she heard a shot and the tinkle of shattering glass. *My God, is Angus firing at the sheriff's car?*

Musing over the possible joys of the rural life, Sam had just pulled into the drive and stepped out of the cruiser when a bullet from somewhere inside the glassed-in porch shattered a porch window, pinged off the bumper, and whizzed out across the south pasture.

Instinctively, Sam ducked down behind the open door of the cruiser, unsnapping the safety strap on his holster and drawing his Glock.

He chambered a round and surveyed the scene. A wild-eyed Angus peered out through the jagged pane of glass, holding what looked like a pistol. "You ain't takin' me in!"

He heard Mabel shout, "Angus, what you doin'? Shootin' out the windows?"

Sam was ready to return fire, but Angus suddenly turned away and trudged into the kitchen. Was this a hostage situation? One thing for sure, it wasn't the short interview he'd planned. And where were Sandy and Frank? And he was too far from any possible back-up.

Shouts bled out through the clapboarded walls. "You ain't gonna intimidate me no more, Miss Fancy Pants!"

"What are you doin?" Mabel screamed. "Sandy's our friend. Angus, you lost your mind?"

Sandy stood frozen, her mind turned temporarily to mush. Meanwhile Angus stepped part way toward Mabel, yelling, "Shut your damned mouth, woman. I know what I'm doin'."

Finally Sandy gathered her wits and tried to get her voice under control. "Angus, you don't want to commit a crime. I know you. You wouldn't be happy in the state pen. You're a good and decent man."

"No, I ain't. I shot your cousin, that goddamned faggot, and hauled him out into the bog. Sheriff's here to arrest me." He took a step back and pointed the gun at her chest. "Weighed him down with a friggin' boat motor, and he shoulda' stayed down 'til April or 'til the pickerel finished him off. Lester Moulton ruined my son's life, turned him into a faggot just like him, ruined my whole family. Couldn't let him get away with it." Now Angus's face had flushed to cranberry, and his hand shook violently. White droplets of foam formed at the corners of his mouth.

Sandy considered making a grab for the gun. It was a small weapon. Could she grapple the old man to the floor? He weighed twice what she did. Meanwhile, Angus kept turning from her to Mabel. Thoughts crowded her mind. *Think girl! What would Frank or Sam do?*

Suddenly the kitchen door swung open, almost coming off its hinges, and Sam filled the doorway. Angus wheeled around and fired, nicking Sam's right shoulder. Sam, thinking Angus had missed, pointed the Glock directly at him. In a deep and even voice he ordered, "Drop your weapon, Mister MacTeague. You don't want to hurt anybody. Put the gun down, then we'll talk. DROP IT NOW!"

"Shut up!" He threw an angry glance at Sam and tried to raise the pistol but couldn't. "Mind yer own business!"

Mabel had broken down and was whimpering over by the woodstove, like a scolded dog.

"I'm sick and tired of people from away coming here and messin' up my life. I wouldn't've been found out if it wasn't for Miss Smart-Ass here! I seen real jungle combat, which is more'n you can say. I killed plenty of them yellow bastards." He waved the pistol around the room wildly. "I took this Nambu away from that dirty little Jap who shot at me and missed."

Angus cackled, then raised the pistol, attempting to point it at Sam, but his arm stuck. He made an anguished cry of pain then fired. The bullet barely missed Sandy and clanged into the stove pipe. Sandy ducked down under the table as the Nambu clattered to the floor.

Sam, on the verge of pulling the trigger, stared directly into Angus's eyes, but they failed to acknowledge anything as his bulky body teetered, then tumbled forward, thumping down onto the linoleum like a sack of wet grain.

"Sam, careful! It's a trick!" Sandy said from under the table, just inches from where Angus had landed. She was too frightened to move or to grab the gun but couldn't take her eyes off the weapon. When she finally looked at Sam, she noticed his shoulder bleeding down the sleeve of his silver-tan shirt and onto his vest. Blood was dripping onto the floor like a long strand of red yarn unwinding.

"No trick!" Sam said flatly, holstering his weapon. "Looks like he's had another stroke." Sam knelt by Angus and felt his carotid, finding only a faint pulse. He looked over at Mabel, her hand still up to her mouth in stunned horror.

"Call the ambulance, NOW, Mrs. MacTeague!" She didn't budge. "On second thought, Sandy, you call!" Getting no response from her, he yelled, "Sandy, NOW!"

As Sandy hung up the phone, Frank burst through the door, took in the situation, then ran to her and wrapped his arms around her, pulling her tightly against him. She was crying softly and Frank's voice was frayed. "Jeeze, honey, are you all right? Sam, your shoulder's bleeding."

"He just winged me." Sam pressed a wad of paper napkins against the flesh wound. "Hell, didn't notice 'til just a second ago."

"I was only trying to be a good neighbor," Sandy sobbed. "Poor Angus went crazy and confessed to everything. Lucky thing Sam showed up when he did. God, Frank, Angus was going to shoot me!" Her legs felt like water, and she grabbed the back of a kitchen chair to steady herself.

Frank sat her down and shot a withering stare at Mabel, then said in a cold, measured tone. "You knew all about this, didn't you?"

Mabel had slumped down onto a chair at the far end of the table near the sink. She shrugged, staring at her husband lying on the linoleum between the table and the wood stove.

"You did," Frank went on. "You knew he'd been out hunting the day Lester was shot, and you suspected he snuck over to Cleona's and fiddled with her heater the other day, because she knew too much. You're pitiful, Mabel. You let Angus bully you into silence while he was trying to kill his neighbors. You're an accessory to murder."

Mabel commenced weeping.

Sam looked at Frank. His bleeding had slowed as he pressed a used dish towel over the wound. "Hey, buddy, it's all right now. Nobody else is going to get hurt here. Remember, when it's our loved ones, we have to pull back from the case. I'll take it from here."

"You're gonna need some help, Sam. You're wounded. Sandy, get a clean towel and tie it around that arm, not too tight."

With great difficulty, Sam removed his vest and Sandy grabbed a pair of scissors and cut off his shirtsleeve. Luckily, the bullet had missed the bone, churning up a deep, triangular divot of skin, which Sandy gently put back in place before wrapping it.

"There, Mr. Sam," she said in a soothing tone, "nearly good as new. Can't say the same for the shirt, though. How's the arm feel?"

"Burns. No big deal." Sam flexed his hand and managed to bend the arm at the elbow. "I'll get it looked at later at the ER. Seems like all the moving parts are intact, which is more than I can say for our friend Angus here. Frank, wanna do one more thing for me?"

"Sure. Name it."

"That Nambu pistol there. Bag it and tag it, would you?"

CHAPTER 34

Next morning Sam put in a few hours on reports, an obligation Barb had made obvious by piling them squarely in the center of his desk. But the first priority was to send a copy of the completed case file to Belle in Augusta so that she could put all the team's hard work into a file box marked "closed." He'd minimize references to his shoulder wound, or she might show up in Galway to see for herself. He wasn't ready to see her again. She was already on his mind enough, both dreaming and awake.

His shoulder still ached from where Angus's bullet had struck, and he was careful not to absentmindedly rub the wound and stir things up. He fully intended to take the afternoon off and fulfill a desperate need to rest and relax. He'd been neglecting Darla and planned to let her pamper him for a change.

Winter was back in full force, as if the January thaw had never happened. Actually, Sam preferred the sub-freezing weather to the drippy days they'd had, gullies full, pot holes slushy, drains and sewers clogged with dirty chunks of gray-brown ice. Everything had dripped, and the roof leaked in the back room of the office. Barb had set pails back there, and for three days it had been drip-drip-drip. Now all was quiet as Sam whipped through one report after another.

The road crews had gone way over budget on salt-sand, this being a harsh winter. Although the main roads looked fairly clear, there were still patches of black ice on curves where heavy tree lines prevented the sun from shining. The state police had covered hundreds of accidents, most alcohol or drug related. He could hear the politicians saying that anti-alcohol legislation would be "bad for tourism." Seemed to Sam that death was even worse for tourism. He shook his head as he finished up his work then dropped a fat folder onto Barb's desk. It'd be good to get home, stretch out, and watch *Law & Order* reruns.

By the next week, Sam was feeling much improved. His sutures itched—always a good sign. Darla was intent on entertaining Frank and Sandy. Duchess wagged her tail in expectation of visitors, endangering the table setting and the *hors d'oeuvres* set out on the old black trunk that served as a coffee table.

Darla and Sam didn't have company very often, but she was so relieved about Sam surviving his brush with Angus that she insisted on celebrating. She was also grateful that Sandy had tried to help Sam. Although the Zucchettis were older, Darla felt comfortable with them, especially Frank. They'd arrived on time, Sandy looking a little less "country" than usual in a wool skirt and cashmere sweater. Frank wore a plaid shirt, corduroy jacket and chinos. Sam was in his usual off-duty clothes—faded jeans and a blue shirt that matched his eyes. Darla was pleased that he looked so contented. *It's the Moulton case. He's finally put it to rest.*

Darla never ceased to be amazed by Sandy who'd brought a small basket of rhubarb and strawberry jams that she'd put up.

As she went out onto the back porch to fetch the lobsters, she realized how her life differed from Sandy's. Sandy might be a retired college lecturer, but she had a pilot's license for boats up to fifty feet, and before global positioning equipment, she'd conquered celestial and Loran navigation. While Sandy could be a stay-at-home housewife, Darla still had to work at the high school. Even as sheriff, Sam was reluctant to dip into his inheritance and didn't make enough money for them to enjoy a lot of extras. Being a guidance counselor meant bringing home problems. She tried not to bother Sam with them. He had enough on his plate, and, besides, they often disagreed on matters of juvenile behavior and discipline.

If she and Sam had daughters, she'd make sure they knew about the art of making a home, sewing, cooking, and entertaining. Well, leave that to the future. Every time she'd broached the subject of having a large family she'd gotten a vague "yes," but he refused to be pinned down. It was the Interrogator versus the Counselor, a battle she thought she could never win, especially when she was true to herself and advocated for the students.

Well, Darla thought, *let's see if I can at least be the perfect hostess.* She sat her guests in the sunny living room where she'd set out appetizers. Darla had tried to modernize the little Victorian. Last summer she'd spent hours at furniture marts, trying to find just the right item for every wall and corner of the snug house. She wanted to make 18 Dunbar Street her own, to replace the faded remnants of Sam's aunt's solitary life. Soon she was planning to re-frame all of the family photos and box up the Wallace Nutting nature scenes. She hoped that Sam would notice how she was bringing the place into the twenty-first century.

After they'd had Chardonnay and crackers with "wicked sharp" cheese and artichoke hearts, she invited them into the tiny dining room where the oak table and pressed back chairs were arranged so that everyone had a glimpse of the sea. Each guest was served a perfect, bright orange steaming lobster. "Right off daddy's boat, swimming in the Atlantic yesterday. Daddy's had such a good run of lobsterin'."

"Well," said Sandy, "the last ones you gave us were the sweetest

I've ever tasted. Hope you like my potato salad. All the vegetables are from our garden."

"Wow! You go into this organic gardening thing whole hog," Sam was in a laid back, blissful state. He took a sip of wine and continued. "Darla grows roses and had nice window boxes of geraniums, but neither of us is much of a gardener. She's more at home with the sea, but don't get her started. She's on a tirade now about farmed salmon. Thinks it's a bad idea."

Sandy flashed a smile of agreement. "Well, it is. The bacteria levels are so high that pregnant women aren't supposed to eat them at all." Darla's face reflected a strained attentiveness upon hearing the word "pregnant."

Sam quickly veered off the topic. "So when do you start preparing the soil, Sandy?"

"Last Fall," she smiled coyly. We have winter rye in, and as soon as it's four inches high, at the end of mud season, Frank'll plow it under. Then we'll start the spinach, lettuce, chard, beets and early peas. After that, it's beans, tomatoes and squashes. We save tons of money by growing our own vegetables. Even after the first snows, we dig root crops like parsnips, beets, and carrots. And our corn is so fresh we put the water on to boil, then go out to the garden and pick."

"What kind of corn do you plant?" Sam asked, feigning interest.

"Sugar and Gold. It's the sweetest." Sandy beamed, feeling in her element.

Gardening was something Sam had failed at in Portland. He'd built his ex-wife Wanda little boxes for the patio, and helped her plant tomatoes and herbs, but she'd over-watered or something and everything had turned black. "Speaking of sweet, it sure was sweet to call the governor's chief of staff and finally report that Lester Moulton's killer was identified. I hear Angus is hanging on but may not make it."

"True. The best he can hope for is a rest home. So, now what happens?" Sandy asked.

"Politically speaking, the attorney general would prefer a big, showy trial. He's up for re-election," Frank commented.

Sam looked at Frank and finished off his glass of wine. "Well, actually, Angus's stroke will save the taxpayers a lot of money, assuming he remains vegetative in a nursing home. It won't play well politically because of the sympathy angle, but somehow justice gets served, I guess. Lester was your cousin, Sandy. Do you think justice was served?"

"I'm just glad it's over. And, believe me, his sister Betty is too. She's so glad that she's turned Lester's lake house over to a Bangor realtor, and she's taken off in the truck camper for the Great Smokies and Dollywood, and then Branson, Missouri."

Sam chuckled. "That's mighty fast work for a postal employee."

Sandy nodded. "Too bad about Mabel, but she just went along, even after the shooting. And I'm pretty sure she knew about Angus's sabotaging Cleona's furnace. I guess you could call her an 'abused wife' and an 'enabler.'"

Frank jumped in. "Yeah, she just stood there with her fist in her mouth. Didn't lift a finger to help. One of those bullets came too close to you, Sandy, and another hit Sam."

"God, I almost wet my pants, I was so scared. No kidding. I had flashes of my life. Saw my college graduation, my truck when it almost went into a river, my children, my back surgery. That's *never* happened to me before. I can still feel the fear, as if it were yesterday! And I have nightmares sometimes."

"Maybe it wasn't yesterday, but it was just last week." Frank patted her arm affectionately.

Sam looked at Sandy. "Well, kid, we're all three of us combat veterans now."

Darla looked uneasy. "So, Sandy, how did you feel when Angus confessed to your cousin's murder?"

"Absolute shock! In my mind I'd had it all figured out. I was so sure Slug Willard had done it, but that he couldn't face life in prison so he wouldn't cop to the crime, even if he did cop to lesser ones. How could I have gotten it so wrong?"

Frank interrupted, "Sandy, don't feel bad. Angus had me fooled. I should've remembered how angry he was about his son Lonnie. Great kid, few times I met him. I guess Lester coached him in drama."

Sam added, "That's true, but according to Lester's friend, Clair, he actually recommended against Lonnie's going to New York. Told him to get away from small town life in Venice by joining the Navy. 'See the world, kid,' he told him."

"Then, ironically, after all the bad press of recent years, Angus decided the Navy was full of gays." Frank shook his head. "The old blowhard was his own worst enemy. He had to blame Lonnie's gayness on Lester *and* the Navy."

"This sounds textbook to me," Darla interjected. "Probably his worst fear was that it might be hereditary—that he, Angus, was a carrier of the gene, not that there is such a thing. But so much of homophobia is based on religious superstition."

Sandy said, "Yeah, in his mixed-up psyche, if it wasn't someone else's fault, it must be his own. Or maybe because he and Mabel were first cousins? That might've peaked his guilt. Who knows?" Sandy dipped lobster claw meat into the butter.

"I want to get back to Clair," Sam said. "Did I ever tell you guys that she asked me to model?"

Darla's jaw dropped. "Shut up!" she exclaimed. "You don't mean it!"

A ripple of hilarity ran through the little group.

Sam raised one eyebrow. "She's damned good with oils. I'm thinking about it." Then he broke into a big guffaw. Frank and Sandy had never seen Sam have such a good time—or be so relaxed.

Once the laughter subsided, Frank continued, "You know, Sam, in hindsight, I should have eliminated Willard as a suspect in Lester's murder." A serious look came over his face. "I guess I was too caught up in despising Slug for dealing drugs to see things clearly."

"How so?" Sam asked.

"Because of a technicality in the case. It was all the cutting and slicing. Slug Willard is fiercely proud of his skill with the skinning knife." Frank cracked a lobster claw. "If he'd shot and then cut up Lester, he'd never have left the job half done and messed up. The jacked deer, the cat— sliced up slicker'n a whistle. Only the knife work on Lester was sloppy."

"Frank, please, we're eating." Sandy looked over at Darla who rolled her eyes in agreement.

"Okay, but I'm just saying…if I'd only seen that earlier, I would've ruled out Slug and focused on Angus. He had the strongest motive. My wife put herself in harm's way and I let it happen." He played with his tiny yellow corn holders, while refusing the last of the wine.

"You may not have figured it out, buddy, but both of you had gut feelings about Angus, right? Don't beat yourself up. Hell, I liked Jake for the crime and his mama as co-conspirator. Bottom line, we solved the homicide and the attempt on Cleona's life. By the way, I'll finish that bottle of wine, Darla, if *you* don't want it."

"But what about poor Mabel?" Darla asked. "You said she was an abused wife."

"Poor Mabel, my ass!" Frank exclaimed.

Sandy reached over and put her hand on his. "Honey, she doesn't know any better. These old farm women are programmed to suffer and do what they're told by their men-folk."

"Frank, that's true," Darla interjected. "Some women don't even go into the woods because they consider it male territory. I hear it from my students."

"The total opposite of Cleona, and my cousin Betty," Sandy added.

"Well, Cleona doesn't have to worry anymore," Sam said. "Angus messed with her furnace because he thought she'd witnessed him with Lester's body at the bog. Probably thought she'd been in the bird blind the day of the murder."

"Yeah," Frank added, "when 'a man' came in, Cleona was groggy and thought it was Angus's dead father. Cleona told me later that their voices were alike. When Angus told her he'd 'take care' of her, she didn't get it. He meant take care of her *permanently*."

Darla asked, "Is she going to be okay? Is any agency helping her?"

Frank responded, "The docs are pretty sure there's no permanent damage. She remembers much more about fifty years ago than yesterday, but then she's always been that way."

Sam smiled. "That sounds like my late Aunt Nina. Her favorite topic was the Twenties. How she loved talking about her Flapper days and the big dances at the summer hotels along the coast. She was some hot chick back then. There's a photo of her over there on the sideboard." Sam raised his glass to the photo. "Let's drink to the woman who put Darla and me in this great old house."

"Here's to Aunt Nina!" A chorus of voices chimed in.

Sandy looked over at the gilt-framed photo. "I just want to say one more thing about Angus. I'm not defending him, mind you, just explaining. You see, he hated teachers, and Cleona had been one for forty years, even taught his kids. Then there's his own shame. He flunked freshman science at the university and ended up dairy farming the rest of his life, except for his Navy time, so he was twisted about education. Anyway, here's Angus with three teachers as neighbors on his road—"

"And she *does* mean *his* road," Frank interrupted. "At one town meeting he put a warrant on the ballot to change the name of Whiskey Road to MacTeague Road. Then six years ago, we arrived, and guess what's the first thing that I tell him: that Sandy's a former teacher, *and* that she's kin to Lester Moulton. He felt plagued by educators and gays. It was just too much for him!"

"I think the idea of Frank being a deputy helped drive him over the edge," Sandy added.

Sam reached for more potato salad. "God, this is good! So listen, Sandy, are you saying that he actually had a specific motive to kill you?"

"Sure, it would've made his day." Everyone laughed except Frank whose mind had wandered into a dark place at the thought of losing Sandy. He'd never plumbed the depth of Angus's rage.

Sandy noticed and changed the subject. "Will Slug take a plea?"

"Well, if he does, and we accept a lesser charge for shooting at Bud Varney and me, we can skip the trial, but it's more complicated than that. We're processing confiscated goods from his garage, the big one over by his sister-in-law's. We're hoping to add more charges, including drug trafficking."

Frank smiled, "Great! I wouldn't mind losing him as a neighbor for about twenty years. By that time I'll be too old to care."

Sam leaned back in his chair. "To hear Slug, he thinks he'll get off easy, do a deuce, then get back to dealing. He's got a surprise coming! So, I've been meaning to ask, Frank, how's the Gossam boy, Andy, the one we placed with the Elorantos?"

"Doing great! He's a good kid and a big help to the family. Saw Eric at the general store the other day and he says he's teaching Andy cabinet making. Says, 'Dat'll be real goot for him to fall back on ven he goes to college.' What a great guy Eric is. I sure couldn't take on a teenager."

"What about the budding romance between Andy and Anna?" Darla asked.

"Oh, they're cute kids, but who knows if they're still a couple," Sandy chimed in. "Crushes don't last when you're in your teens."

They finished supper then adjourned to the parlor, having fallen under the spell of good food and companionship. Sandy was reminded of how much she loved breathing in the salt air. She stopped and looked out the window at the boats bobbing on the bay. Why did they live in Venice when they could have chosen Galway? But they were about a decade too late, now that real estate prices had spiked due to the arrival of the Atlantis National Bank. There were rumors of costly condos going up on Church Street.

"Now I want you to try my French apple pie," Darla proudly announced. "Who wants vanilla ice cream on theirs? It's Ben and Jerry's."

They all said yes. The ocean on her mind, Sandy asked, "And now, what about our deep sea fishing trip, Darla? Did you get a chance to talk with your dad? Get a tentative date, maybe? I'm really excited at the prospect."

"Daddy says just name the date, and he'll work around it. Sam's all for it, aren't you, honey? I can't wait to see you, Frank, sitting at the helm, turning green."

"Sorry to disappoint you, Darla, but I happen to be an old salt. My uncle used to take me out on his trawler onto San Francisco Bay and out through the Golden Gate. I'm up to my waist in sea time."

"Lord, I hope I don't repeat what I did last time I was out on a fishing boat," Sandy moaned.

"What's that, almost fall overboard?" Darla didn't know how seaworthy Sandy was. To her she looked like a land-lubber.

"No, I caught three huge sand sharks."

"Don't worry," Sam volunteered, rescuing his wife. "Darla has a great recipe for them, too. Her dad's taught her how to cook everything that swims or crawls in the ocean. She can even make skate wings taste like sea scallops."

Darla blushed, making her round face look even prettier. "You know, we all need this vacation. Sam hasn't had a week off since he won the election. At this rate he's liable to burn out."

After they'd settled comfortably into the parlor couch and chairs, and eaten their pie *a la mode*, Darla retrieved a navigational chart of the Eastern Maine Coast from a flat cherry-wood map case. "Hey," Darla asked, spreading the chart out on the trunk, "you two ever been up to Passamaquoddy Bay, Campobello Island? We could run the Lubec Channel with the incoming tide. That's one fast ride, believe me."

"You can do that? I mean, pilot a boat that far?" Frank had a look of amazement on his face, followed by embarrassment. *Dumb thing to say. Why shouldn't she be able to do that? She's her father's daughter.*

"Sure she can. She's got the US Coast Guard seal of approval." Sam got up and squeezed Darla's shoulder and then squatted down and studied the chart, pointing to the US-Canadian border. "And if they think we're in Canada, Frank, they probably won't call us back to Galway to work a case. Whadd'ya' say, guys?"

Frank grinned. "Yeah, we could get the guy next door to watch our poultry and cats. You okay with it, Sandy?"

"You bet!" she responded. "We need to get away from Venice."

"Then you've got yourself a plan, buddy, and Darla, I'll bet your dad would love to watch Duchess, wouldn't he?" Duchess heard her name and romped over to Sam, rubbing his leg, her tail fanning the end of the chart.

"Of course. He adores dogs," Darla chuckled.

Sam handed the chart to Frank and quipped, "Just no dead bodies, that's all I ask. So, whatever happened to Earl Bagley's fish shack?"

"Bottom of the bog," Frank said.

Page Erwin is the writing duo of Carolyn Page and her husband, Ross Erwin. For nearly twenty years they have lived in central and coastal Maine where they tend their chickens and organic gardens. In a former life, Carolyn was married to a law enforcement officer and Ross is a retired Air Force navigator/bombardier who served in the Air Commandoes and at The Pentagon. Carolyn has degrees from Keene State College and advanced study at East Carolina University and Western Carolina University. Ross's are from Saint Mary's College and Central Michigan University. In their combined life experience they have raised ten children.

They have traveled extensively and lived in the South and Southwest before settling Downeast. Their hobbies include painting in watercolor and acrylics, and their walls reflect their travels, particularly in Europe. Ross spent his early years in The San Francisco Bay Area, and Carolyn grew up in small-town New Hampshire. Each of them taught for a number of years. Ross specialized in management and Bioethics while Carolyn focused upon English, literature, oral communications, art history and creative writing. They have taught Elderhostel courses from coastal Maine to Hilton Head, South Carolina.

Individually, they have read their essays on Maine Public Radio and, for a number of years, were stoneware potters. They each have two books of poetry, and their work has been widely published in literary arts journals. At present, they live in a small coastal Maine village in an 1830s farmhouse with their beloved three cats and fourteen chickens.

Printed in the United States
88450LV00004B/277-309/A

9 781591 332176